THE STORY

Fiona Perrin was a journalist and copywriter before building a career as a sales and marketing director in industry. Having always written, she completed the Curtis Brown Creative Writing course before writing *The Story After Us*. Fiona grew up in Cornwall, hung out for a long time in London and then Hertfordshire, and now writes as often as possible from her study overlooking the sea at the end of The Lizard peninsula.

THE STORY AFTER US

Fiona Perrin

First published in the United Kingdom in 2018 by Aria, an imprint of Head of Zeus Ltd

Copyright © Fiona Perrin, 2018

The moral right of Fiona Perrin to be identified as the author of this work has been asserted in accordance with the Copyright, Designs and Patents Act of 1988.

All rights reserved. No part of this publication may be reproduced, stored in a retrieval system, or transmitted, in any form or by any means, electronic, mechanical, photocopying, recording, or otherwise, without the prior permission of both the copyright owner and the above publisher of this book.

This is a work of fiction. All characters, organizations, and events portrayed in this novel are either products of the author's imagination or are used fictitiously.

9 7 5 3 1 2 4 6 8

A CIP catalogue record for this book is available from the British Library.

ISBN 9781788547338

Aria
an imprint of Head of Zeus
First Floor East
5-8 Hardwick Street
London
EC1R 4RG

About *The Story After Us*

If she tries very hard, Ami can remember when she used to
have a dynamic and exciting career and a husband who she
loved more than life itself, and who
was equally smitten with her…

Now she has two children, a terrifyingly large mortgage, and
no idea who she has become - or why she and her husband
can't even be in the same room anymore.

With life as she knew it in tatters around her, Ami is
heartbroken, and in no way pulling off 'consciously
uncoupling' like a celeb. But she's starting to wonder if she
just might come out the other side and be….happier?

For Alan, Elyse, Sienna, Tom, Laura, Soppy and Ducky –
the whole
lot of you.

Prologue

Summer 2010

'Will you, Amelia, take Lars to be your partner for life? To have and to hold until death do you part?'

I caught a wicked gleam in my nearly-husband's pale blue eyes. When we'd been writing our vows, we'd changed that line to 'to shag and to hold'. We'd practised this there and then, and had to come back to the vow-writing later. Much later.

'I will,' I said, snapping back to the present.

'Not yet,' whispered the registrar. 'There's still a bit more to go.' Lars started to laugh and there was a smattering of giggles from the small crowd in the register office in Chelsea, most loudly from Liv, my best friend and now best woman. She was going to tease me about screwing up the service until death parted us too.

'Sorry,' I whispered.

'Will you promise to talk to him, to care for him and to work towards your dreams together?' the registrar continued. 'For richer, for poorer, in sickness and in health, in good times and in bad, forsaking all others, for the rest of your lives?'

'I will,' I said, this time at the right point. 'Always.'

The registrar went on to repeat the same vows for Lars, who said in perfect English, with just a hint of his sing-song Swedish accent, 'I will. Always.'

The registrar pronounced us husband and wife and a rowdy cheer rose from our family and friends. Lars and I snogged a little more voraciously than was normal in a marriage ceremony and Liv whispered, 'Get a bloody room.'

Dad and Mum came forward and hugged us both in turn.

'Bloody great,' said Dad in my ear, his hair, despite his best efforts, standing up from his head as if he'd just had one hell of an electric shock. 'Now, marriage can be tough, but you stick together through thick and thin.'

'Absolutely lovely.' Mum wiped tears from her eyes with an actual cloth hanky.

Lars' widowed mother, Ulrika, stood beside them, as tall and thin as her son. She hugged me and said, 'I will be with you, Ami, when the winds blow warm and when they blow icily.' She had a bit of a Nordic turn of phrase sometimes.

Lars and I went to sign the register, followed by Liv, and Lars' best friend, Thorstein; he was like a Viking Ed Sheeran with a bright ginger beard and hair.

'Fuck me, imagine being married,' said Liv, who didn't do commitment. 'Seriously grown-up.' But I didn't feel grown-up, I felt full of hope about growing up and old with him.

I gripped Lars' hand as everyone threw pale pink rose

petals at us on the steps in the Kings Road. Even Liv was moved, as she fussed around straightening my white vintage baby-doll dress – chosen in homage to the sixties and seventies stars who'd married here before us. We laughed and kissed as the photographer's camera clicked.

There were thirty of us at the Bluebird for a raucous lunch, which was way swankier than anywhere any of our friends usually went, but was on my dad. Thor made a speech where the central premise was that Lars was a lucky bastard who was batting way out of his league and made everyone down shots while shouting, *'Skål'*. Liv's speech was full of stories about how Lars and I had met 'in mid-winter in the most freezing cold basement' and how we'd been keeping each other warm ever since; she finished it off with a noisy impression of her listening to us shagging through a thin wall, which made me look at my parents with horror – they were smiling though, along with everyone else.

We drank cucumber-flavoured champagne cocktails that tasted of happiness and danced like teenagers at their first disco. When night came through the windows and the house music slowed, Lars held me close, his smart navy suit now crumpled, and whispered in my ear: *'Älskling*, you and me, forever and ever.'

'Always, Lars, always.'

Part One

1

2017

Lars left me late on a Sunday afternoon in January. He threw a couple of bags into his car and drove off with a puff of smoke that could have been drawn by Walt Disney.

I stood at the top of the steps of our north London house as he disappeared around the corner of the road. I felt as if I were looking down at a sobbing thirty-seven-year-old brunette rather than that I actually *was* her. There was an overwhelming sense that, after ten years, it was Just Me Again.

But, of course, it wasn't – now I had the kids. I rushed inside and threw cold water over my face at the kitchen sink, drying myself with a tea towel before I opened the door of the playroom. Four-year-old Finn and six-year-old Tessa were sitting on the sofa, frightened by the rowing and confused by the fact that they were allowed to watch a DVD when the rule was only an hour of screen time a day and that was when I needed to moan and drink wine.

'Is everything OK, Mummy?' Finn asked, walking over to kiss me. 'Jemima's coming to my party on Saturday. She's my girlfriend and so is Tallulah. I'm going to marry both of them.'

'You can only marry one person,' scoffed his sister. 'Can't you, Mummy?'

'Well,' I said.

'Except for Henry VIII,' said Tess, whose special topic at school this term was the fat, monastery-burning Tudor. 'When he went off his wives he chopped off their heads. You could chop off Jemima's head and then marry Tallulah.'

'But Jemima's got lovely yellow hair,' said Finn, clutching me.

'You'd still have her hair if she was dead. You could keep her head in a corner.'

'That's enough, Tess.' My daughter's current favourite game was burying dolls in graves in the back garden and topping them with twigs. She also spent quite a lot of time on the floor pretending to be a corpse.

'Daddy might not be back in time for your party,' I said in a mock-cheerful voice. 'He's got to go away for work again.' In fact, Lars missing his son's birthday party had been the reason we'd had the enormous row that afternoon when he'd said he was leaving me and our marriage for good.

'Oh dear,' said Finn, who was very used to his father being away for his web business.

'Can we watch another DVD?' said Tess, who could spot a weak chink in adult armour a mile off.

I put my head into Finn's neck so that they couldn't see

14

my face. 'Yes,' I said. How would they cope if we really were getting divorced? I worried so much about the impact all our recent rows were having on them; Tess was already really macabre and splitting with her father for good could only make that worse.

I wanted to crawl under my duvet and stay there in the foetal position, but it was approaching Sunday evening. I needed to do what every other family was doing: find PE kits, pack lunches, move miserably towards Monday while still mourning Saturday.

I rang Liv. 'It's the worst row we've ever had,' I said, 'and he says he's divorcing me.' She immediately said she'd come round. Then, like a robot, I made fish fingers, gave Tess and Finn a bath, packed their school bags, put them to bed and read them *The Cat in the Hat*, making an extra effort with my snarky Cat voice.

'It's you,' I said. 'Thing One and Thing Two,' and they giggled. After that I poured myself a giant glass of red wine and waited for Liv on the sitting-room sofa, rocking back and forwards, as I relived the last few hours.

*

'That's it. We're getting divorced,' Lars shouted. It was raining outside. He stuffed paperwork – bills, bank statements – from the kitchen dresser into a bag. I wanted to pull his shirt, tug him so he couldn't move any more, but instead I just stood and cried.

The argument started because Lars claimed that I hadn't told him the right date of Finn's birthday party until it was too late to reorganise his trip to Russia.

It could, however, have been about anything – our arguments had been getting worse over the last few months, despite our going to marriage guidance counselling. They were always about one thing: how Lars spent so much time away for work and less and less time with us, his family.

I knew I'd told him about the party being on the afternoon of Finn's birthday on Saturday. And why was it my job to remind him of stuff like that anyway?

'I thought it was on the Sunday and I was going to be back for his birthday evening on Saturday. It's obviously a mix-up but it's too late now,' Lars said. 'I've got to go to Russia.'

'But we've got the Animal Man coming and we've sent out all the invitations.'

'Who's the Animal Man?'

'Who do you think he is? He's a man with animals. Guinea pigs, God knows. He's the entertainer.' I sat down at the kitchen table and put my head in my hands. Then I took a deep breath. 'Are you going to tell Finn?'

'I'll tell him the trip's been booked for weeks and at least he'll understand. Which is more than you do.'

'It's your son's fifth birthday, Lars. For once, please put your family first. Come to his birthday party.'

'I'll be there as soon as I get back from the airport. I'll still see him on his birthday.'

'The party will be over by then.'

'Ami, he'll have other birthdays, with bigger and better parties. I'll be at those instead.'

'The trouble is you know damn well you won't. You should stop pretending you'll ever change because we both know it's bullshit.'

My marriage had turned me into a person who spat out bile like rancid water from a gargoyle. Loving him so much had turned me into someone hateful.

'That's it,' he shouted. 'I've had enough. You go on and on about how bad your life is – so let's just forget it, shall we? We'll get divorced and you won't have to tell me how awful I am to this family all the time.'

We'd both used the 'D' word before in the heat of the moment, but still it seemed impossible to me that it would ever happen.

'How can it be a family when you're hardly here?' I whispered. 'Even when you're here you're somewhere else in your head.'

'I'm thinking about a future for you and the kids. But that's not good enough for you, is it?'

'What I want is for us to be *equal*. I've got a business to run too.' That Monday, I was booked to see the finance director of the tiny advertising agency I'd set up the previous year and I knew he was going to tell me that my balance sheet was looking decidedly unbalanced.

I asked, 'Lars, do you still love me?' but he didn't answer, just ran up the stairs two at a time and threw his clothes into suitcases. I thought I could cope with most things, but I didn't know whether I could face the fact that he no longer loved me.

He turned from the open wardrobe door and said very quietly, 'It's not about whether we love each other any more – that's not enough.' This was somehow worse than shouting.

'Please don't go,' I said, following him to the bedroom doorway. I hated myself for my lack of dignity in begging him to stay.

'I can't stand it – all we ever do is argue.'

'We can try...' I couldn't carry on with this half-a-marriage, but could I stand to see him finally go?

'We've tried everything.' His voice was as wintery as the day outside. 'It's time to stop trying. I'm leaving, Ami, and I'm leaving for good.'

He said it firmly, as he always did when he'd made a decision.

He carried the bags outside and into the boot of his car, light semi-frozen rain coming down on his white-blond hair so that it stuck to his face. Then he opened the car door, jumped in and drove off.

He was gone and this time it looked as if there was no going back.

*

As I sat on the sofa waiting for Liv, images rushed through

my brain the way they say they do when you are on your deathbed. The first time Lars and I ever met – me opening the door to him in a towel because he'd banged on the door of our rented flat when I was in the bath. The way my voice couldn't stop going up and down as his did then, with his strong Swedish accent. Our first date, when he'd sung Lou Reed's 'Perfect Day' to me in the same voice. Dancing in Tobago to reggae on our honeymoon. Later – when we'd bought the house we lived in now – dancing again, but around our new kitchen because we couldn't believe our luck. The sense of him – clean, loving, determined – through all those years. Watching him stride around with Tessa strapped to his chest in a sling. Conceiving Finn in a four-poster in a country-house hotel…

How had all that hope and love come to this? I hugged a cushion closer to my chest and then there was the noise of Liv arriving outside on her boneshaker of a bike.

From the window, in the yellow of the streetlight, I could see her auburn hair flying behind her and her white skin pinked with cold. I waited at the top of the steps while she locked up her bike and pulled her bag from the basket.

She climbed up, grabbed me in an enormous hug and said, 'Oh, Ami. You poor baby.'

I erupted into tears.

She shepherded me inside, took off her coat and pulled me down onto the sofa, where she held me against her scarlet jumper until I finally stopped crying.

'Thanks for that. It's really difficult getting snot out of

19

lambswool,' she said. I gave her a weak smile. 'So, is this really *it*?'

'I think so,' I said – but I didn't want to believe it and another warm tear slid down my face. I was like a thundercloud, plump with rain, which had yet to burst again, but where every so often a fat drop escaped.

Liv pulled a bottle of what looked like very expensive Châteauneuf-du-Pape from her bag. 'My landlord gave it to me. I think he wanted me to drink it with him. But this is an emergency.' Liv's landlord claimed to be a marquis, although when we'd searched online we couldn't find any mention of his title. He'd met Liv at a party, fallen in lust and rented her his basement at a rock-bottom price. He wobbled home about teatime every day from the pub, pie-eyed.

She went and got a corkscrew, emptied my glass of cheaper plonk and filled two new ones very generously. Then she sat down again and I told her, in between bouts of sobbing, what had happened.

'He thinks working so hard is the right thing to do for all of us, and I can't make him see that we need him here – *I* need him here,' I said at the end. 'He keeps going on about how broke we still are – but that's because we keep having to put money back into his business. It's a vicious circle.'

'What I do know is that it's time to stop putting up with it.'

'It couldn't have come at a worse time. I've got this really important meeting tomorrow. And Tess keeps going on

20

about dying – she's already really affected by us arguing all the time.'

She pulled me close. I quietly sobbed into her shoulder until eventually she pushed me back, thrust tissues in my face and said, 'Maybe it's for the best. He's made you so unhappy now for so long.'

'But what if I could change him back into how he was? I mean, we were so fantastic in the beginning and it just seems like life and work and kids has taken over. All I want is the old Lars back.'

'Darling, we've *so* had that conversation,' she said, but gently. 'And you know what we decide every time? There's no way that the Lars you married is coming back.'

She got up and paced up and down in front of the fireplace. Behind her was a row of silver frames showing pictures of Lars and me through the last ten years – first just the two of us, then our wedding photos surrounded by family and friends, then with Tessa and Finn.

'Look.' Liv came back and sat on the sofa and held my hands. 'This is a bloke who sometimes doesn't even turn up for bloody marriage counselling. You know what I think every time you tell me that?'

I nodded and the familiar feelings of rage started to course through my veins, followed by a crushing sadness. 'I vowed we'd stick together forever and I really wanted to make sure my children had a happy home.'

She nodded, her pale blue eyes unusually serious. 'I know, but you can't be the only one trying. He has to try too.'

I smiled weakly.

'You're going to be OK,' said Liv. 'Very OK. It's very fashionable to get divorced, you know, what with all this conscious uncoupling. Clebs do it all the time. Then they take pictures of themselves being "aren't we civilised even though we're divorced?", going out for breakfast with the kids. There's a feature I read recently: decree nisi-ly or something like that.'

I shuddered. 'There's nothing nice about this. You'd better go or you won't get up for work.' Liv quite often didn't get up for work. She was a contributing editor at a low-print-run style mag whose mission was to celebrate everything original. It was called *Pas Faux* and she'd gone to work there the previous year in an effort to save her breadline writing career before it became toast. Unfortunately, her overactive social life – mostly shagging boys who'd just passed their A levels – got in the way.

'I can stay the night?' Liv said, but I knew she hated the idea of being woken up by children in the morning.

'I'll be fine,' I said and eventually, after a little more crying and hugging, she wobbled off down the road on her bike.

I poured myself another glass of posh wine and rang my mother.

'Oh, God,' said Mum from her Gloucestershire kitchen. 'Oh, poor darling. Surely it's just an argument. He'll come back.'

'It's beyond that.'

'Do you want to come and stay? I would come to you, but, you know, your father…'

Dad suffered from a black dog that he refused to even acknowledge barked, let alone get treatment for. When he was in one of his depressions, he drank too much and stomped around the woods outside my parents' cottage, his hair white and wild in the wind, with his spaniels, Liver and Bacon, behind him.

Did it surprise me that she didn't come rushing to London to support me when I was about to become a single mother? Not really. My parents had an almost symbiotic bond – or at least, he needed her like one of those male monkeys that rely on their female partner to pick off bugs. When he was miserable – and he could get to a low mood in a moment and it could last for months – it would not occur to her to leave his side. She was there suffering alongside him, picking off the flies of his depression, as if only she could save him. Caring for me had come second ever since his low moods had become longer and more malign in my teenage years. I knew this and thought I'd come to terms with it, but it still hurt.

'Maybe don't tell him about this,' I said, not wanting to bring on another dark mood.

'I have to, but he'll be devastated. You know how much he thinks people should stay together, put the children first.'

I shouted, 'Well, he should tell Lars that, then.' I took a deep breath and a sob came out. 'I'm sorry.'

'Darling, don't worry, you're in shock,' said Mum. 'Will you be OK?'

Tessa and Finn were asleep upstairs. 'I have to be.'

Eventually I went to bed, lying just on my own side of it, rigid as a ruler, wearing two pairs of pyjamas but failing to keep out my freezing fear. I cried some more and my tears were warm.

It's not hearts that break, Lars. It's whole people, and I'm broken.

2

In the half-consciousness of troubled sleep, I dreamt that my marriage was a black amorphous beast running away from me, pausing at corners to cackle, before running on. I never caught it.

At 7 a.m., feeling as if I'd hardly slept, I showered and dressed for work as if my life were going to continue as normal.

Dad rang the house phone as I was trying to paint away the purple shadows under my eyes with thick foundation. 'Good God, girl, what a bloody mess,' he boomed down the line. 'But the important part is you're all right?'

I was so far from all right I didn't know what was left but I said, 'Of course I am, and you mustn't let it upset you.' I'd do anything to stop my father falling into one of his depressions, dragging my mother down with him.

'Upset *me*? Of course not. Just want to knock his block off. Can't stop thinking about those kiddies.'

Had he been up all night drinking whisky? His voice had a slight slur – it was either anger or alcohol.

'Now I'm going to find you a lawyer. You need to know where you stand.'

'I'm sure there's no hurry.' It seemed so official and

final. 'Are you all right, Dad, really?'

'For God's sake, girl, stop asking about me and start looking after yourself. Now, let me know how it goes.'

In the kitchen our beautiful but sulky Slovakian au pair, Luba, was giving the children breakfast in an uninterested fashion. Luba had joined our household two months back and, aside from always looking bored and cheesed off, had been dutiful, since she'd moved into the room in the loft. The kids seemed fond of her but she ignored all my overtures of friendship.

'Please can you take the children to school this morning, Luba?' I said, trying not to meet her eyes with my red ones. I knew she wouldn't think there was anything unusual about Lars not being there – he was so frequently absent.

She tossed her long, almost albino, silky hair. 'Yes.'

'Have you remembered the talk at the school tonight, and I need you to babysit for an hour?' As I'd tossed and turned in the night, I'd thought about how I was going to a talk on how to 'bring up good world citizens' at the kids' school and that I should probably take the chance to let the headteacher know what was happening. 'I'm so grateful, Luba. Thanks so much.'

'I here to help,' she said, but there was no smile on her gorgeous face.

I kissed the children and set off out into the world, all the time on the bus and Tube feeling as if I were one step from my soul.

When I entered my tiny Soho office, my only employee,

26

account executive Bridget, was seated behind *my* desk, punching away at *my* computer.

I wanted to shout, 'Would you like to suck out my red blood cells till I die? Wear my knickers? Climb in my grave?' but instead I said, 'Bridget, what're you doing at my desk?'

Bridget always got to the office at 6 a.m. to prove how efficient she was. She looked up and her round face shone with excitement. 'I thought I'd demonstrate some initiative, Amelia, by trying to win us some more business.' She moved across the room, her pink hand clutching a yellow sticky note; her white shirt was buttoned to her neck.

I wished I didn't secretly dislike Bridget – she was very useful, but because she was so overtly corporate and had no sense of humour, I had to force myself to be nice to her in the name of the sisterhood. 'We could certainly do with some new clients,' I said, and went to make myself a cup of strong coffee, breathing in its beany steam as if it would give me strength.

Then I went upstairs to meet Stephen Frost, FD of Goldwyn & Co, which co-owned Brand New, my tiny advertising agency. Last year, after seven years with Goldwyn – a massive agency – I'd persuaded my maverick boss, Marti Goldwyn, to let me set up my own sub-agency. It'd been time to prove I could do it on my own.

Marti let me take my favourite account with me – Land the Bootmaker. I'd been lucky enough a few years back, when I was just working my way up through the ranks at

Goldwyn, to be able to pitch Land some ideas on how to turn their dying boot business into something fit for the twenty-first century. I persuaded them to bring back the male brogues that had made them famous in the Second World War, call them LandGirls and market them at women, and it'd worked. Now every black-clad goth in the UK wore LandGirls.

'You'll need some bloody money coming in and Land won't stay at Goldwyn without you,' Marti said when he signed the paperwork. 'If I have to lose you, it might as well be to a business I have a part in.'

The trouble was that after the first eight months of relying on LandGirls' income while I won smaller accounts, the shoe company had gradually stopped placing advertising with us.

Stephen, round-faced with a large snub nose, was usually cheerful and optimistic with me despite being an accountant, but today he didn't smile. He waited for me to sit down opposite him, and said, 'You look tired, Ami, but that's no real surprise – you must be up all night worrying about the business.'

If only he knew that that came second to worrying about my marriage. I nodded and said, 'How bad is it?'

Stephen tapped the end of his Mont Blanc pen onto the wood of the meeting-room table. 'There's no point beating around the bush – not having any Land revenue for the last few months has had a real effect.'

'The profit and loss is basically loss?' I tried to make him smile but it was a futile attempt to head off the worst.

'It was always going to be in the first year of business, but our plan said we'd rely on their income while you won some other clients.'

'Land is concentrating on overseas expansion,' I said. 'It's all about conquering the US. There's nothing I can do to change their minds.' I'd spent quite a bit of time telling the marketing director how neglecting the UK would have a real impact on sales, but she'd just nodded and said that the 'strategy was coming from the board'. I'd then got in touch with the Land CEO to try and get a meeting but he hadn't returned my calls.

I told Stephen this and then went on, 'And I've been winning lots of others but they take time to spend – I have that mail-order firm, Think Inside the Box; a new fashion label, Boring Clothes…'

Stephen mopped his brow and said, 'That's supposed to be ironic, isn't it?'

'Yes, it is.' I smiled and rushed on. 'We've got Fat Pig too…'

'Don't tell me – exercise clothes?'

'For stick-thin women,' I agreed.

Stephen stopped smiling and took a deep breath. 'It's all very well, Ami,' he said. 'But Land owe us £50,000.'

I gasped. 'That much?'

'It's getting serious – the credit-control people aren't getting through to anyone. I'm worried.'

'Shall I go to Wakefield?' I was talking about the LandGirls factory-turned-HQ in Yorkshire. As I said it, I immediately started worrying about who was going to look after the kids while I went up north – I couldn't leave them with Luba overnight.

'I'll let you know.' Stephen shut the manila folder in front of him. 'Frankly, the best use of your time is to get out and win some more business and fast.'

'And what happens if…?'

Stephen took a breath through his over-large nostrils. 'You've got a couple of months left at best without some new work and that's assuming Land starts advertising again.'

There. He'd said it. I shivered despite the heat of the meeting room. I needed my business. I was going to be a single mother and I had no idea how I was going to pay the bills or feed the kids. Was Lars going to be OK about money? He ploughed all the profits of his business back into expansion and, after the mortgage and bills, we managed month to month as it was.

'I'm working on lots of different leads,' I said to Stephen although it wasn't true. In fact, the last few weeks with Lars had been so full of anger and arguments that I'd had trouble concentrating on work. Still, it was important that Stephen told Marti that I was working my balls off when he came back from whatever globe-trotting jaunt he was currently on.

'Look, it's all up to Marti,' Stephen said with all the resignation of a man who'd spent the last twenty years working for a brilliant, exhausting boss. 'And he's got a soft spot for you.' He said this without looking at me and I immediately started to worry. I was well aware that watercooler folklore at Goldwyn had it that I was shagging Marti – because why *else* would he have invested in my new business? – but did Stephen – sensible Stephen – believe the rumours too?

'You do know...' I said.

'Of course, I know,' said Stephen. 'He likes you because you don't report him to HR every time he says something borderline un-PC...'

He was trying to make me feel better so I smiled. Right now, all I wanted was for Marti to fly in and tell me it was all going to be OK.

'...and because you're good at your job.'

Or used to be. As I said goodbye and went down the stairs to my little basement office I wondered what the rumours would be the moment all the agency staff knew I was getting a divorce. They'd probably say it was so I had more time to get jiggy with the boss.

*

'So, you're going to be down and out as well as divorced,' said Liv, summing up the situation as only she knew how.

I'd called Liv to an emergency lunchtime summit at Ivan's – the Soho café we christened Suicide Café many years back. It was exactly halfway between our offices. The walls were nicotine-yellow; the pictures on the walls were women weeping following scenes of Cossack desecration; there were three stuffed yellow canaries in a dusty bell jar on the counter. We were very fond of the place, which never changed however much Soho gentrified.

Liv ordered me a white wine but I was crying so much again it was rapidly turning into a spritzer. I knew my face was ghostly pale against the brown curls on my head.

An aged, melancholy waiter had shuffled from the shadows and plonked mountains of risotto in front of us. There was no menu; people came to this café to drink and talk about serious subjects like how to top themselves, so the café just churned out a single cheap dish whose sole purpose was to soak up alcohol. Occasionally – just occasionally – there was also a schnitzel option.

I kept saying over and over again, 'But what am I going to do? How am I going to feed Tess and Finn?' Liv finished her own risotto so I instinctively pushed my plate in her direction and she started to eat that too. We'd established right from the start of our friendship – back on a French exchange when we were fourteen, when we'd learned to smoke Gauloises and tried to look existential – that it was her job to be the light in my life and mine to make sure she never really starved. Through the last few years I'd been grateful for Liv never being serious. Most of the mothers I knew – aside from my small group of school-gate mates – spent all their time banging on about breast pumps and Boden; the women I met through work just talked management bollocks. As Liv put it, 'When they talk about the bottom line, it isn't because you can see their knickers through their trousers.' In contrast, she could still make me laugh as if I'd just smoked an enormous bong.

'Lars is doing well though, isn't he?' Liv said. 'I mean, I have no idea what he's talking about most of the time, but isn't he trying to be the next Bill Gates?'

'He keeps going on about cashflow. And I'm really scared, Liv.'

'You need to take your mind off it. Want to come out with me tonight? I'm going to some accessories launch under the arches in London Bridge.' All the staff at *Pas Faux* relied on parties to eat because they were paid so badly. Liv always chose the ones that looked as if they might do decent canapés because she reckoned if you devoured enough they added up to the equivalent of a decent meal.

'Do I look in a fit state to go to a party?' I said. 'Anyway, I've got a thing at the school.'

'You always look very beautiful, even if you're a bit knackered,' Liv said. I knew she was just being sweet. Even though we were the same age, Liv did not have a crow's foot on her face. 'It's because you've had children,' she always said when I complained about it. 'Stitches in your whatsit and burp juice all over your clothes. Who'd want to be up the duff?'

'And I really have to get on with getting some more work.'

'Look, something will turn up,' said Liv. 'The planets will be in alignment.'

'You always think it's about Jupiter circling Uranus,' I said. Liv believed in fate because great stuff happened to her when she didn't deserve it. There were the just-out-of-adolescence boys who asked her out all the time. Or when she'd about as much chance of buying a flat in London as every other single, gainfully employed person in London – absolutely none – she bumped into a fake marquis who rented her a flat. 'Still, I could do with some of your luck.'

'It's my mission now to help you move on. I will set my mind to finding you a new man and getting you laid.'

'I don't want to go near anyone else.' I put £20 on the old Formica table and stood up. I was as closed up as a mussel that's gone bad but still finds itself floating round in a *marinière*.

'But you will soon,' said Liv and the spattering of Jackson Pollock freckles on her nose seemed to dance a little. 'It's my job to help.'

I shuddered. 'I didn't know how much of a failure I'd feel. I've let down my children.'

'No,' said Liv. 'Lars failed the children. He's the one who left. No word from him, then?'

'No, nothing,' I said.

Liv put down her fork and got to her feet and held me as I shook into her shoulder. 'Oh, poor Ami. I do love you so much, you know.'

*

That evening I sat on a pint-sized chair in a freezing classroom while the headmaster of my children's school told me lots of negative things about them in a really positive way. I'd asked to have a private word with him.

'I'm so glad you stopped by. I've been meaning to have a word about Finn eating the glue instead of using it to stick with.' Mr Carter smiled.

'I suppose it's better than sniffing it?' I said.

Mr Carter cackled for a second and then stopped. 'The latest thinking is that children need to be armed with a carrot to keep them orally distracted.'

'Finn doesn't like carrots,' I said. Mr Carter wasn't old enough to be a headteacher in my book: with his 'ironic' green corduroy jacket and gelled quiff he looked as if he should still be a student himself. He considered himself to be very progressive but he just talked a lot of crap.

'And little Tessa – so *creative*,' he said. 'Creative' was a euphemism for 'weird' but I wasn't going to argue. 'I absolutely *loved* the way she expressed her dissatisfaction with the nativity play.'

He was talking about Tessa spending most of Christmas wearing a blue tea towel on her head pinned at the back with a clothes peg and telling everyone to call her 'Mary'.

'Well, was it really fair that Jemima got picked to be Mary for the second year in a row? Tess was a bit upset about it.'

Jemima, Finn's great love, had a mother called Nadine, who was queen of the Smug Mums – or the Smugums, as my school-gate mates and I called the patronising mothers whose lives seemed to revolve around making other women feel like deficient parents. Nadine *volunteered* to go on school trips to mop up puke from a coachful of kids with rabid travel sickness and spent three weeks hand-sewing costumes for World Book Day. Jemima was therefore a slam-dunk for Mary every Christmas.

Mr Carter ignored my question, leant forward on his small chair and gave me what he thought was a sympathetic smile. 'Is everything all right on the home front?'

I tried to look anywhere but at him. Tears welled anyway and Mr Carter leapt up and grabbed a box of tissues.

'It's all quite all right; this is an open environment where everyone is encouraged to express their emotions.' God, I hated his pseudo-enlightened bollocks.

'I think my husband and I are getting a divorce,' I whispered. Just saying it out loud seemed so final, so terrible.

Mr Carter sat down on his own small chair and pushed the box of tissues at me. 'Well, you'll be pleased to know that all the teachers in the school have had training on supporting children through this. Can I call you Amelia?'

I blinked. *Really?*

'And you can call me Paul,' he said. I resolved never to call him Paul.

'We'll have to keep quite an eye on Finn and Tessa,' Mr Carter went on. 'We don't want too many repeats of the sort of episode we had last week, do we?'

Last Tuesday, I'd taken Tessa right to her coat peg and helped her unbutton her coat for school when I'd realised that while she was wearing shoes, tights and a jumper, she somehow wasn't wearing a skirt. Mr Carter and Nadine had been standing in the cloakroom when this happened.

'It was very busy that morning,' I said. 'Tessa got dressed herself and put her coat on…'

'Amelia,' Mr Carter said. 'It's exactly the way that such a traumatic time expresses itself. There is just one other thing that raises concern. Tessa does seem to be unhealthily obsessed with death. But again, this is probably the current home troubles.'

'It might be.' Tessa had always had preoccupations that seemed to go a little deeper than other kids. Between the ages of two and four she'd adored boyband One Direction so much Lars and I had taken to calling them 'One Conversation' because she'd talked about little else. Then there was the Christmas fixation with being Mary. Her refusal to wear any other pants than red until I'd simply dyed them all that colour. This interest in death could be just the latest obsession.

I really hoped it wasn't down to the atmosphere at home – new guilt washed over me and I stood up.

'Finn and Tessa will be OK, won't they? I mean, all the books say that it's better for the children if they don't have to be surrounded by all that arguing… And this isn't actually my fault…'

'No, I'm sure it isn't,' Mr Carter said and shuffled from foot to foot.

'I'm doing everything I can…'

'I'm sure you are, Amelia. Perhaps you'll sort it out.'

'I hope so, I really hope so,' I said, although at the moment I had absolutely no idea how.

*

As I sat on another small chair for the next hour with the other parents all I could think about was how I had to do everything I could to protect Tess and Finn. I vaguely heard Mr Carter instructing us all to count to ten with our children in mandarin every night and could see my gate mates, Parminder and Julia, rolling their eyes every time Nadine joined in with another Smugum remark.

'The importance of being fucking earnest,' said Parminder as we left. 'Have you ever met anyone so high on his own supply as Carter?'

Parminder was a mindfulness teacher for time-poor professionals. I'd tried one of her classes but found it was quite stressful as she barked out the breathing exercises with military precision: 'in: one, two, three, and out: one, two, three, and in: one, two, three' and so on, but apparently that was the kind of mindfulness the modern executive wanted. I'd only ever seen Parminder in exercise clothing – she shopped, cooked, worked, exercised and chilled out in stretch patterned leggings and Lycra-based tops.

'World citizen? Seriously? Toby can't even blow his own nose,' said Julia. Tall and blonde, she was in charge of something quite serious to do with our country's finances and a single mother with two boys from a man she referred to only as 'the turkey baster'. The three of us had become friends through a shared horror of all things Smugum.

'Jemima can probably already count to a hundred in mandarin,' I pointed out as we wandered towards the car park.

'You all set for Finn's party?' Parminder asked. 'Need me to do anything? I'm teaching a class so can't be there, sorry. Julia's going to drop the kids off.'

Julia looked vaguely horrified that she was being volunteered as an extra hand at the party. 'Umm… I've got a date on Saturday night,' she said. 'Thought I'd better get a hairdo and all that while the party's on if you don't mind, Ami? Luba will help, won't she? And Lars?'

'Hairdo? Is that getting your woohoo waxed?' Parminder teased.

'The hair on my head.'

'I'll be fine,' I said, trying not to think about having twenty kids running round the house high on sugar, while I reached a new low. 'Lars will get there later…' I paused as I wasn't sure I was ready to tell them my new single-mother status yet. I didn't want the pity – however well meant. And if Lars came back that meant no school-gate gossip. 'Luba will be there and maybe my mother.'

Julia looked relieved and Parminder said, 'Who's the date with, then, Jules?'

'Hopefully a banker yet not a wanker. I met him online on a site for people from the City.' I thought about a time

39

when I might have to be out there like Julia, swiping right and left, and shuddered. Neither of my friends noticed.

'You going Brazilian or Hollywood?' Parminder went on as we reached our cars.

Julia laughed. 'If you don't stop, I won't include you in my latest cake stash.' Julia stockpiled cakes in her freezer from any bake sales she came across, buying up whole tables from the WI, for example, and then bringing them along to every school event where she was required to provide something cooked in her own kitchen. She let Parminder and I join in and it was a great way of looking Smugum without actually ever turning on the oven.

'Hmm, but that's really useful currantsy,' said Parminder, getting in her car.

'Oh, your jokes, my flour,' said Julia, getting in hers.

I sniggered a little as I drove the short way home and it was only as I pulled up outside my house and saw just a light coming from Luba's room in the loft that I remembered with a thump that Lars wasn't just away on one of his trips.

This time he wasn't coming back.

<u>3</u>

'Flip it,' said one of the books I'd read on keeping your marriage together. 'When you feel that you're unable to go on, flip it and, instead, decide you can cope with anything.'

Every day I went to the office and phoned everyone I knew, looking for work. Marti was away in Australia and when he came back there was every chance he'd call me upstairs and pull the plug on Brand New.

On Wednesday I read in *Campaign* that Campury, the ancient, luxury Italian handbag brand, was looking for a new agency and cursed; it was my job to know about this stuff before it hit the press. Still, I read on. Campury had just appointed a new UK brand director by the name of Ben Jones, who was pictured looking large and scruffy for a man in the fashion industry: dirty blond hair, a strong, laughing face; even though he had a suit on, he looked as if he should have been throwing bass bins around a stage rather than working with handbags.

'Look at this,' I said to Bridget. 'I'd love to launch bags for Campury. I mean all that old school glamour but the brand's got lost. Imagine relaunching them for a younger market. Making them cool again.'

'Won't they be worried because we're so small an

agency?' Bridget asked.

'We'll pitch as part of the Goldwyn Group,' I said. 'Can you get some details, Bridget, please?'

She tapped away furiously for a few minutes.

'Ben Jones is apparently some sort of hotshot from Italy…'

'Go on.'

'Was at Pucci to start with and then he was part of the team who did the accessories launch at Gucci with the crocodiles.'

'Oh wow,' I said. No one had missed that campaign – early dawn Thai rivers, the faux-crocodile-skin belts, bags and shoes floating on reed rafts, the near-naked models cowering in fear as if they were real crocs. 'But that campaign was done by Gorgeous.' I was talking about Goldwyn's arch-rival agency. 'He'll go to them, surely.'

'Don't be defeatist,' said Bridget. 'He's lived in Italy for the last few years and is only here for the relaunch because he's got to go back for his kids. That's what it says on FashionPolice.'

'Have you got his phone number?'

'Yes. Not his mobile yet but I'm on it.'

'Give me the landline one and I'll have a go.' I picked up the phone and punched in the number.

'Ben Jones' office,' sang plum tones on the other end of the fibre-optic cable.

'Hello, this is Amelia Fitch from Goldwyn. Please would you put me through to Ben?'

'Let me see if he's available.' The posh voice sounded doubtful. I would leave a number and hope that the Goldwyn name counted enough for him to phone back.

There was a click on the line and then a male voice, with a hint of the north in it, drawled, 'Well, that was quick.'

I shook my head in confusion. 'Sorry – is that Ben Jones?'

'Yes, it is. And you're the famous Amelia – sorry, *Ami* – Fitch?'

'Well, I'm not sure about the famous bit.' Why did he sound as if he was teasing me?

'I wasn't expecting your call. I was going to ring you but thought I'd leave it a few days. And then here you are.'

'Oh! Were you going to call us – Goldwyn – in to pitch?'

'I was hoping to talk to a number of agencies…'

I raised my thumbs to Bridget. 'Well, we'd love to be part of your list. When can we meet up and get a brief?'

'You *are* very efficient,' Ben said, as if he was not surprised. I shook my head – there was something very strange about this conversation. 'Well, workwise I've got a huge amount to get my head round and we're still working on what agencies we want to include but…'

'It would be great to tell you about us.'

'I already know quite a lot about you,' he said. Was there a slight emphasis on the *you*? Was he flirting?

'It would be good to meet, I mean, and give you our credentials pitch.'

There was a big laugh from the end of the phone. 'And

very businesslike, just as I was told.'

I glared at the receiver: definitely flirting, if in a really odd way. Well, maybe he'd heard about me. I'd won a few awards; the formation of Brand New had been in the trade press.

'I hope so,' I agreed. 'Shall we make an appointment?'

'I'll put you back through to my assistant in a minute,' he said. 'But what about meeting up other than that? You and me? I know it's an unusual way to get to know each other but shall we have lunch?'

I wanted to laugh out loud at the sheer brazenness of the man. First of all, he must assume he'd had a huge load of publicity about arriving in London. Second, he was terminally unprofessional trying to mix business and pleasure – probably influenced by having lived in Italy for so long. Still, he was in charge of a huge wodge of money that needed spending with an ad agency and I wasn't going to let anything get in the way of that.

'I'm not sure we can't cover the same ground at a meeting,' I said.

'Well, at least I knew you'd be difficult to persuade to move on,' Ben said.

What *was* he talking about? He wasn't just flirty – he was deluded. Was he drunk at 11 a.m.? 'I'll make an appointment with your assistant,' I said. 'If you could put me through?'

'Well, shall I call you at some other time?'

'I'll leave my number. Thanks so much for taking my call. It'll be great to meet you.'

'OK, then.' Now he sounded confused. 'Goodbye, Ami Fitch.'

I shook my head at Bridget, said goodbye and then at the click of the phone made an appointment for a presentation the following Wednesday.

'The man is completely weird – I think he was flirting with me,' I told Bridget when I put the phone down.

'I expect you've had lots of chauvinistic men chase you?'

'The thing is, Bridget,' I said, '*never* let it cross the line between personal and professional.'

*

The week crawled on.

My mother-in-law, Ulrika, rang me from her latest trip visiting the haunts of dead authors – she was at the City Lights bookshop in San Francisco, where, with her arse-length white hair, she probably did a good impression of having hung out with Kerouac. 'Oh, Ami,' she said through the slight delay on the phone, in her light Scandi voice. 'I have been feeling blasts of ice in my soul at the news.' Lars had not just told her he was going to stay at her house in Finchley, then, he'd told her about the divorce – one more decisive move on his part. 'What can I do? Shall I come home? How are the children?'

It was hard not to notice that she volunteered to rush to my side when my own mother didn't, but I tried to push the emotion to one side. I was in bed because of the timezone.

'No, of course not, Ulrika. We'll be fine and see you in a few weeks.'

'You must do what is right, of course,' she said, as if I'd had a part in the decision-making.

'It's not me,' I said. 'You know how hard I've tried.'

'Oh, I thought so.' She said it without judgement on Lars. Ulrika was nothing if not in perpetual balance – she even wore her widowhood with stoic acceptance, her beloved husband having died of a stroke, although she'd told me once that her 'soul had died with him'. She gave out calm, measured advice from a wise perspective: what I'd grown to think of as her 'Ulrika moments'. 'Tess and Finn? How are they? I miss them so much.'

'They miss their Grandie Sweden too, but they don't really know any difference yet about what's going on,' I told her, rolling over in bed and aching for her resourceful presence. 'How's California?'

'Hot,' Ulrika said. She kept her house at a temperature of sixteen degrees in all weathers. I wore extra layers of clothing when we visited but found it hard to sit still as my fingers turned white over lunch. I'd asked Lars why, what with being Swedish and therefore up on heating and insulation, and he'd said it was her belief in consistency. 'When I complained of being cold when I was a kid, she always told me to "relax into it".'

'Who can relax into being bloody cold?' I'd asked.

Now, we discussed her return in a few weeks after a visit to the Steinbeck memorial in Monterey and I promised to look after myself for her. 'I'm here for you. We can walk this forest of confusion together,' she said, and I cried after we put the phone down. I tried to call Lars after that but his phone was switched off. I didn't even know if he was in the country.

Liv rang every day. She didn't say much about the accessories launch she'd been to – simply that she had an enormous hangover and had woken up to find carpet burns on her knees, which was annoying because she couldn't remember any of the details of the sex she'd had with her latest lover, Matthew. 'There was something I needed to tell you, though,' she said. 'I'm sure I'll remember it. But, darling, much more importantly, how are you?'

I also got a voicemail from Thor, meaning that Lars had picked up the phone to him in Seattle, where he was now trying to set himself up as a tech deal-maker, and given him the news too. 'Christ Almighty, gorgeous,' he said in his gruff message. 'I hope you are OK. Lars has told me news that is making me very sad. I hope we can change this.' I didn't ring him back because what could I say? That the woman he'd been so charming to whenever he was in the UK on one of his whirlwind trips had turned out not to be good enough for his childhood friend? That Lars hadn't been batting out of his league at all?

When Mum rang, with little hope, I asked her to come to London at the weekend and help with Finn's party, but she said she couldn't. 'Your dad needs me,' she said and went on to tell me that Dad hadn't eaten but had drunk several bottles of whisky since he'd found out about the divorce.

But I need you too, I thought. Still, I didn't blame her – instead, what I felt was weary sympathy. She'd married him when she was very young and only as they'd grown older had it become apparent that, instead of getting a husband, she'd got a patient who refused to recognise he was ill. She believed she'd signed up for 'in good times and in bad' – and if quite a lot of them ended up being bad, that, she considered, was her lot in life. After all this time, I'd stopped begging her to drag him to a doctor because she said it was hopeless.

'Just come and stay with us,' she begged.

'I can't – Finn's got twenty kids coming for a party,' I said. 'Don't worry, I'm sure Liv will help…'

'I thought Liv hated children.'

'She does,' I said, 'but all she has to do is dole out jelly.'

Liv promised to turn up, 'As long as I can have a job that doesn't involve kids.'

I cried on the way to work, ignoring anyone on the Tube who stared at me, and cried on the way home too, and somehow it was fine to sob in front of strangers. I tried very hard to appear cheerful in front of the kids and managed it mostly, despite my red eyes.

Luba said that Lars called one afternoon after the children got home from school and spoke to them each for five minutes. He sent me a terse text on Friday morning saying that he would come to 'the house' on Saturday afternoon at around 5 p.m. when his plane landed to 'see Finn and Tessa'.

This meant therefore that he was definitely not coming to Finn's birthday party, which was due to finish at 4 p.m. He hadn't changed his mind.

I typed out a response with multiple swear words in it and then deleted it. Then I typed one where I said it didn't matter, and we should sit down and work out how to stay together and that I loved him deeply, but I deleted that too. Instead I simply put:

I need to talk to you.

It took half an hour for him to reply.

We can talk on Saturday evening.

He didn't put a kiss at the end but then neither had I.

I bought a bag of balloons and spent a good hour pumping them up; made a pass the parcel where my tears made the paper soggy; made a cake that vaguely resembled a spider; and all week tried to join in with Finn's growing excitement.

When Saturday finally arrived, Nadine was the first to arrive with Jemima; she sailed up the steps in a flowing sludge-green outfit of what I was sure was ethically sourced cotton.

Finn came running out into the hallway. 'Happy Burfday to me, happy burfday to me,' he sang. 'Oh, Jemima, come and see the animals. There's no tiger, but there's a ferret.'

'Ferrets?' asked Nadine. 'Are you sure they're not

endangered?' As well as proper parenting in a conflict-free environment, Nadine strived to protect the world's species. 'Now, Jemima, have a lovely time.'

'I'm sure Jemima will be fine.'

Nadine also talked about sex as other people talked about the weather. 'It's excellent timing – a party this afternoon,' she leant forward and whispered. 'I'm right at the peak of my ovulation cycle and I need to go home and have a lovely sexy time with Freddie.'

'Have a fantastic shag, then, Nadine,' I said a little more loudly than was strictly necessary, just as two sets of other parents delivered boys called Noah and Abraham. In liberal north London, lots of parents called their children biblical names even though they were atheists or Buddhists. Nadine scuttled off down the steps while the other parents smirked and handed over presents.

'I love birthday parties when they're nothing to do with me,' said Julia as she delivered her boys, Toby and Brad, and Parminder's daughter, Priti. She went off to get whatever hair it was groomed.

I shepherded the children into the sitting room where the Animal Man had set up an entertainment post, behind which sat a series of cages containing budgies, guinea pigs, a couple of toothy ferrets and an old snowy owl with feathers missing. Small children bashed each other with plastic toys. Luba, her hair still damp and hanging to her waist, stared around her in horror while Jemima screamed over the hullabaloo that she 'just wanted her mummy'. The Animal

Man seemed to have disappeared.

'Mummy's shagging Daddy, darling,' I said under my breath then set about restoring order by bellowing, 'Everyone, please sit down.'

All the children sat down on the floor, crossed their legs and went silent. 'Now Luba's going to play Pass the Parcel with you while I go and find the Animal Man,' I told their expectant faces.

Where the hell was he? He'd arrived with his cages half an hour earlier, sporting a very seventies moustache.

'Hello,' he'd said, passing me a stinking cage. 'Right, let's get the fuckers inside.' I'd obediently started to walk towards the door – where Tessa and Finn had been jumping up and down with excitement – just as he'd added, 'No, I was talking about your kids, Mrs Fitch – they're right in the way there and we've got a good few cages to unload.'

Now, I searched until I found him in the garden, shivering behind one of the bushes and smoking a roll-up. 'Yer au pair gave it to me,' he told me.

'Can you please come inside and entertain the children?' I said. 'It's chaos in there.'

'All right, I'm sorry. It's my nerves, you see, what with the kids and everything.'

'Why are you doing this job, then?'

'Me dad died and left me this business and I thought I'd give it a go.'

'Well, you get inside and start entertaining.' I put my hands on my hips. 'It's my son's birthday and you're not going to let him down.'

It was only as he nodded in a beaten fashion that I smelt a tang in the air. 'Are you sure that's not grass?' I asked his retreating back. The entertainer was on drugs.

'What? No – it's got a terrible taste though,' said the Animal Man, starting to wobble down the garden path. 'You ought to tell that foreigner of yours to buy some proper Golden Virginia.'

But he started giggling as he went back through the kitchen. 'You know what, kids might not be such hard work today…'

I shrugged – even if he'd been having a spliff he was probably going to be more cheerful for it. Indeed, back in the sitting room the Animal Man had donned a velvet magician's hat and was rubbing his hands together in glee.

'Right, kiddies,' he roared and then giggled all over again. 'Who wants to see some animals?'

Only the animals didn't look impressed by this idea. All the children shouted, 'Meeeeee!' in return.

The doorbell rang again. I opened the door with a big fake smile and then turned it into a real one at the sight of a trembling Liv. 'Thank God it's you.'

'We'll probably need this,' said Liv, brandishing a bottle of Pol Roger. 'I nicked it from a party. How is it going?'

We went and peered through the door of the sitting room where Finn held a ferret, while the Animal Man told the children that he would have educated them all about ferrets but for some reason he couldn't remember a word of it.

'He looks like Geppetto from the old Pinocchio cartoons,' said Liv.

'I think he might be stoned. I caught him in the garden and it smelt of grass. He told me Luba gave it to him.'

'Well, it would be handy if you could score off the au pair,' Liv said. 'No sign of Lars, then?'

'No.' I bit my lip. 'No, no sign of Lars.'

For about half an hour, the Animal Man pulled it off. We sat at the back of the sitting room and took some footage of the kids with the grumpy owl rested on their arms; then the ferret preened himself while everyone had a good stroke.

As the children went to wash their hands for tea, the Animal Man started to put the ferrets and the owl back into their respective cages; if I'd looked at him I might have said he did look pale. Liv, Luba and I put all the food into the middle of a giant animal-printed tablecloth on the floor and they all dived in. I picked up the camera again.

'Do ferrets normally eat jelly?' Tessa said.

'Well, I think tame ones eat dog food or something like that, but in the wild—'

'This one quite likes jelly,' said Tessa then, quite calmly, '*and* nuggets.'

It was as I looked round to find out just what my daughter was talking about that Liv started screaming. 'Ami, there's something in the middle of the picnic… Oh, my God!' Several children started to shout.

A ferret and a couple of guinea pigs were marauding their way through the food.

'Waaaaaahhhhh,' screamed Priti. I leant forward to try and catch the ferret, which quickly slid out of my hand and raced towards the open kitchen door.

'They're escaping,' I yelled, knee deep in small children spraying splats of jelly in all directions. I tried to close the door as a guinea pig raced out too. 'Someone get the Animal Man.' I grabbed the other one by the fur at the back of its neck.

'I think he's asleep,' said Tessa, coming back into the kitchen. 'Or he might be dead. I kicked him but he didn't move.'

'Liv! Get all the kids into the playroom.'

I raced into the hallway, where the owl was flapping above my head. I turned into the sitting room only to confirm that Tessa was right and the Animal Man was well and truly passed out on the floor, yards away from a series of open cages. I threw the guinea pig into one of them and slammed the door shut.

'Oh, no.' I gave him a quick kick. He turned over and started to moan, his face behind his moustache a shade of grey that seemed only to offer the promise of certain vomit to come.

I shot back into the kitchen in time to see the second ferret escaping into the garden. I shut the outside door and flew into the playroom, where all the children were now gathered.

'The Animal Man is passed out in the sitting room,' I whispered to Liv. 'Could you please phone 999 while I try

54

and catch the owl?'

I went into the hallway to plead with the bedraggled white owl, which had taken up residency on the picture rail. 'Woo,' the owl said, its giant eyes now looking more chirpy.

I heard my mobile ringing from where I had tossed it, among coats and gloves by the door. The number was not one I recognised – probably one of the parents.

'Hello?' I said.

'Ami?' said a northern drawl.

'Speaking,' I said, and backed away from the noise of the playroom. 'Hello? I can't really hear you – it's my son's birthday party. Can I call you back?'

'This is Ben Jones,' the voice went on. 'You were so businesslike the other day, I thought I ought to be the one to make the social call.'

Oh, God. It was the flirty man from Campury.

'Ah,' I said, just as the owl started flapping noisily around the ceiling again. 'I didn't know there was going to be a social call.'

'Wasn't that the reason you were phoning the other day?' His voice took on a warmer tone.

'No,' I said. 'I was phoning about the pitch… Oh, my God!' The owl had taken a swooping dive in the narrow hallway straight at my head.

'Are you OK?'

'Yes, I'm fine.' The owl took a perch back on the rail. 'Look, can I please call you back? It's my son's birthday and… Did you get my number from your assistant?' I'd given her all my contact details when I made the appointment.

'No…' Ben started to say, then the owl let out a giant and very loud twit-t-woo. 'What the hell was that?' he said instead. 'Are you OK?'

'It's an escaped owl,' I told him with a sigh.

'A what?'

'It's a very long story,' I said.

'You'd better call me back. I wanted to know if you were free for lunch – maybe Monday?'

'No,' I said, distractedly flapping at the owl. 'Oh, my God, it's crapping on my wall!' A trickle of dirty white liquid descended down the hall paintwork. Its circular eyes widened to take up even more of its face as it did it.

The man at the end of the phone erupted. 'What a hoot.'

'Look, I don't think it's appropriate for me to talk to you like this, what with the pitch going on and everything.'

'But Liv said—'

'Liv?' I was completely confused.

'Yes, when I met her at our launch the other night. She told me all about you and how you were newly single and – listen, I don't normally do things like this, but it did sound like we had a lot in common and—'

I went ice-cold and swung in the direction of the door to the playroom. 'She did *what*? She said *what*?'

'I thought she'd told you.'

Liv came out into the hallway. 'One of the little bastards' nose is bleeding,' she said. 'What do I do?'

'Is that Liv?' Ben asked.

'Wipe up the blood, quick, before his parents arrive,' I said. I gesticulated to her that I was going to cut her throat and she looked back at me wide-eyed. 'Yes, yes, it is. Look, she should *never* have done that.'

Liv's mouth went into a grimace. 'Is that the man from the other night?' she whispered. 'I knew there was something I needed to tell you.'

I made more signs of imminent murder and she disappeared back into the kitchen.

'And then you called me straight away and I thought…' Ben went on.

'It's all a massive mistake,' I said, trying to stay calm. 'Look, I really can't talk now. I'll call you and explain later.'

'OK, goodbye.'

I clicked my phone off and threw it onto the hall table.

'He was quite good-looking if I remember rightly.' Liv reappeared with a stack of napkins.

'I'm going to kill you.' I picked up the child with the bleeding nose and carried him into the kitchen. 'Abraham, it's only a little bit of blood. We don't need to tell Mummy about it, do we?'

I mopped him as Liv told me that a paramedic was on its way but it might be some time as someone passed out and snoring wasn't an emergency. I chased the owl into the sitting room with a broom, where it sat scowling on the mantelpiece, while the Animal Man snored underneath it.

'Shit on *him*,' I told the owl, shutting the door firmly so that the chaos was hidden from view.

We gave out birthday cake to the kids and smiled while fathers and mothers collected their offspring.

'That was the best party I've ever been to,' I heard Jemima tell Nadine as they went down the path.

'Really?'

'Yes, but Mummy, what's shagging?'

Julia turned up then with new highlights and looked questioningly at me. 'I'll tell you all about it on Monday,' I said, winking. 'Your hair looks fab. Hope the date goes well.' As far as I could work out, Julia's dates always seemed to be with blokes who sounded promising but turned out to have mother issues, be scared of children or have very small penises.

I turned back to face the chaos of my household, putting a sleepy-looking Finn and his sister in front of a DVD, and then I went to find Liv.

'Now you'd better explain,' I said, 'what you're doing messing with my professional life.'

Liv sat down at the kitchen table. 'I was going to tell you, it's just that you were a bit upset this week and frankly… well, frankly… I was so drunk that I can only remember bits and pieces. It was a terrible party – really pretentious – and there was absolutely no food, just loads of free champagne. What's wrong with fashion people, by the way? Why can't they eat? They could always throw it up later.'

'Stop talking rubbish at me,' I said, violently scrubbing at the blobs of jelly that were all over the kitchen cupboards.

'What exactly did you do?'

'I was just chatting to him…'

'And you asked him if he wanted to go out with your just-getting-divorced saddo friend?'

'No, it wasn't like that. He told me he was in the same sort of industry as you, has got a couple of kids of his own, just like you, and… of course he had a massive advertising budget. I was trying to help.' Liv met my eyes.

'And that's just it, Liv. I found out about his account being up for grabs and, get this, I *rang him* on Wednesday to make an appointment.'

'You see,' said Liv. 'It's serendipity.'

'It's a massive fuck-up! We really need to win his account and it would really save my company. And when I rang him he wasn't surprised at all but he didn't say he had met you… but when I very *professionally* asked him for an appointment, he made out he was expecting me to call and now he is going to think I am some divorcee begging for a date. How much more humiliating can my life get?'

'Now, hang on,' Liv tried. 'Get some perspective, just a bit of—'

'He was flirting with me.'

'Good,' said Liv. 'What that means is he likes what I told him and he wants to meet you. It's a great situation and you're just making a big fuss about it.'

'But I'm only interested in his business, Liv. This is my actual *life* we're talking about here.'

'It's all fine. I talked to him for quite a long while if I

remember rightly – not that I remember much. I told him what you'd done with all those projects you do. Now have a drink and calm down.' Liv went to the fridge and then struggled to open the bottle of Pol Roger.

I started to giggle. 'Oh, my God,' I said, as the chuckles grew into gut-wrenching laughter and the champagne went pop. 'And there's still a passed-out man in my sitting room… ha, ha, ha…'

Liv smiled too. 'I must say the party was much more interesting than I thought it'd be.'

It was then that the doorbell rang. Behind the stained glass I could make out the tall, nervous shape of Lars shifting from foot to foot.

4

2007

Lars was hard to miss when he moved into a flat above the Bloomsbury basement Liv and I rented in our twenties. His length and colour made him stand out like a single dandelion in an acre of gravel.

'Really quite gorgeous, if you like blonds,' Liv said. She had a string of beaux at that time, all of whom she happily spent hours tying into knots of despair. I was dating a geek called Archibus from the British Museum. His fondness for ancient times extended into the bedroom where he was fond of tantric sex – I came out feeling more as if I'd had a game of Twister than got laid.

There was no real debate about whose prospect Lars was. He was blond and it'd always been the case that I liked blonds and Liv liked everyone else, and that division generally met the needs of my more promiscuous friend because there were plenty more everything elses.

'He's bloody gorgeous,' I said as we watched him come out of the door upstairs, one February Saturday, and march off into the distance. From our basement window, as we looked up at him through the railings, his legs seemed to take strides that were twice as long as anyone else's.

'I'll knock on his door later for you and ask him to come round for a drink,' said Liv.

'We don't have any drink and we can't afford any.' I was still trying to work out how the salary from my account manager job in an ad agency was supposed to feed and clothe me, let alone supplement Liv, with her series of flibbertigibbet occupations.

I groaned; my back ached from my latest sexual wrestling match with Archie and the flat was freezing. We ran out of money to top up the gas at least a week before payday every month and this was that week. Liv was wearing her outdoor coat inside and leggings under her floaty skirt. I planned to spend the afternoon in the bath to escape the cold and the urge to go round to Archie's warmer house, which would only mean bruises and aches in places that I didn't even know could be bruised and achy. The hot water came from the electricity, which wasn't yet on a pay-as-you-go meter; the heat didn't. I spent a lot of time in the bath that winter.

'I promised Nicholas I'd drop by for a shag,' Liv said, wrapping a scarf round her neck. 'He's staying at his mum's while she's away so I'll get some lunch too.'

I got in the bath. I took Jilly Cooper's *Riders* – always one of my favourite books, since at the age of fourteen it taught me much more than sex-education lessons ever had. I topped up the water with my toe every time it became lukewarm without looking up from the pages.

When there was a rather persistent knock on the door a couple of hours later, just as my bones were cooking nicely, I groaned. Liv had forgotten her keys again and she was going to want the bath to get rid of the smell of sex with Nicholas before she went out with someone called Kevin later that evening. Grumbling, I shivered out of the water and wrapped myself quickly in a threadbare towel that had once been the colour of a tangerine but was now a washed-out yellow. As I dashed across the sitting room and towards the door, the steam from my body met the frozen air and created a cartoon rainstorm behind me.

'Aaaaarrrggggghhh,' I said, pulling open the door and making to dash back to the bath.

'Hello,' said the blond from upstairs with a smile.

'Omigod.' I tried to push the door back into the space between him and me. 'I thought you were my flatmate.'

'I'm sorry,' he said but he didn't sound sorry at all. His voice from the gap between the door and the wall was sing-song and guttural. 'I am living upstairs.'

I jumped up and down to keep warm.

'Do you want me to wait till you get clothes on?' he went on.

'What do you want? The thing is, even if I get dressed I won't be warm.'

'I came to ask you. Who do we call to get heating to work? I've tried the agent but they're not open but closed. It is not so much cold as freezing cold.' He sounded out the words as if they were new to him and chuckled slightly

63

again.

'You're foreign, aren't you?'

'Yes, I'm from Sweden,' he said with slow enunciation. 'Do you know who we phone?'

'No one,' I said through the small slice of open door between us. 'There's no one to phone. And even if you do ask the agency on Monday, they don't do anything.'

'But that's outrageous,' he said, again sounding as if he'd never said this long word before.

'Yes. Look, I really have to get back in the bath.' I might turn into an ice sculpture if I stood around any longer, dripping.

'Can please I come back later? I really need to ask someone some questions about these apartments – none of my cupboards open and my socks are cold like ice in the mornings.'

'Yes,' I said, agreeing. I kept mine on my feet all night and hoped that no one would ever find out that I hadn't changed them for days.

I meant yes about the socks, but he seemed to take that as meaning he could return and went off saying he would 'be getting some food' and we could 'eat and drink lunch'. Despite his confused English, he said it as if there were absolutely no reason for me to say no and, of course, all I wanted to do was say yes. 'I will return in half an hour.'

<u>5</u>

2017

Seeing Lars knock on the door of our house was too much to bear. Usually when he got back from one of his business trips, we could hear his key being thrust in the lock before he strode in, shouting, 'I'm back. Ami, kids, I'm back.' By knocking on the door, he was clearly demonstrating that he no longer considered it home.

I pulled it open, but looked down, trying to avoid his eyes, and shouted to Finn and Tessa, who emerged from the playroom. Lars didn't move to kiss me hello.

'Daddy,' Finn cried into the embarrassed silence that followed. I stood back and let him fly by. The kids are all that is left of us, I thought.

'*Käresta*, happy birthday,' Lars said, hugging him and then Tess.

She pushed him away and glowered at her dad. 'At least you're not dead,' she said to her father.

'Tess,' I said. 'I told you we don't have to talk about being dead all the time.'

'I'm just staying with Grandie for a while.' Lars knelt

down and faced Tessa. His face was long and drawn. He was wearing the pale jeans and blue T-shirt he always wore to work at weekends. Still our eyes hadn't met.

Finn ran off down the hall to the playroom. 'Come and see my Power Rangers. The black one's head has got all blown off. We might need batteries or Sellotape.'

I watched as Lars went after him. In just a few days his presence felt alien, as if he was not supposed to be near me now. The smell of the lemon soap he always used lingered behind and I noticed it in a way I never had before he left. The first prick of tears was behind my eyeballs.

Quickly, I picked up Tess and, blinking, placed her on the shelf of my hipbone. I carried her towards the playroom door. Tess sniffed my chin. 'Daddy went to live with Grandie instead of living with us.'

'No,' I said. 'He went to *stay* with Grandie and now he's here to see you and play with you and put you to bed.' It was as if by saying it was temporary I might make it so.

I put her down inside the playroom door where Lars was sitting on the floor, talking in the mix of Swedish and English he always used with them and which now, from years of Lars, Ulrika and Thor, I could mostly understand too.

He was a little like a Power Ranger who had lost his power himself.

*

66

'He promised me he'd make it to this party but then blamed me when he screwed it up,' I whispered to Liv as I let her out of the front door extra quietly so that she didn't have to bump into Lars. Seeing him made me newly angry. 'He turns up now when it's all over and done with.'

'At least he showed up on the kid's birthday,' Liv said. 'Let me know when the paramedics have been.' She kissed me on both cheeks.

'Liv?' I called after her as she was getting on her bike.

'Yes?'

'Thank you.'

*

I shakingly poured myself another glass of champagne in the kitchen, wiped up more jelly and listened to the giggles and fake banging noises coming through the wall. Then I went and looked in on the Animal Man, who was still snoring on the rug in the sitting room. I prodded him with my foot but he just turned over with a loud sigh. He didn't appear to be dying – just in a very deep sleep. I went back into the kitchen and did more wiping.

'I'm so angry with you and so furious with myself for not being able to change this,' I told the kitchen wall, trying to stop the heat of my angry eyes turning into water.

'Talking to yourself is the first sign,' said Lars, coming into the kitchen.

'Of not having a husband around to answer you?' God,

I'd turned into a complete cow.

'Just don't start,' he said, as if a loud voice was not far from the surface. Then he took a visible deep breath. 'We'll talk once the kids are in bed. I'll have a glass of that,' he told me, gesturing at the bottle.

'Oh, will you?' I poured it anyway, thinking how inappropriate champagne was right now.

'Tessa says she's allowed ice cream instead of milk to help her tummy ache, but she's talking rubbish, isn't she?'

'Complete rubbish,' I said, pouring two cups of milk, putting them in the microwave and pressing buttons as I spoke. There was a silence while we both watched the microwave plate go round and round – it seemed as if forty seconds were forever. 'Here.' I thrust the milk at him. 'Tell them I'll come and say goodnight when they're in bed.'

*

'All right, so you've seen a lawyer?'

Did he just say that? I gasped audibly.

Lars had various bits of paperwork laid out on the kitchen table along with his open laptop. I sat paralysed at his attitude.

The kids had refused to go to sleep and bounced around until I went upstairs. I let them play for five minutes longer and fussed about cleaning their teeth so that I could avoid the administrative detail that was the end of my family.

'No, I haven't seen a lawyer,' I said as calmly as I could.

'I've been at work and looking after the kids and…' I wanted to say that I was hoping that we weren't *there* yet; I could feel all the hurt of the previous weekend as if it were new pain. 'Is it now going to be about who gets what?'

'What did you expect it to be about?' said Lars. 'Who said what to who and who shouted and who threw what and who was a—'

'Nagging machine?' I said under my breath. That was one of the kinder things he'd called me during our row on the day he'd left.

'We're way past all of that stuff now, Amelia.' He shuffled papers, moved the mouse a little bit and I put more tissues under my nose. 'We're done with talking.'

How could he sit there so intransigent, so unwilling to see any other vista than his own, like a man who buys a house in Tuscany for the view and then refuses to believe that anywhere else in the world is beautiful any more?

'Now, if we can sort out the finances and how we're going to care for the children between us, we'll save a fortune. The lawyers will just need to fill in the paperwork,' he continued, scoring a line across the title of one of the pages as if to underline how adamant he was to save money.

'And that's what's most important now, is it?'

'Yes. It is. We've decided to get a divorce.'

'*You've* decided. And thanks for telling your mother and Thor. People on entirely different continents now know I'm dumped.'

Lars ignored me. 'So, we should try very hard to make

69

sure there is as much money left as possible to ensure that we both have as good a standard of living as possible.'

'My business is really in trouble,' I told him. 'Because of my client, Land. They owe us fifty grand.'

Lars looked up sharply. 'Well, you'll have to persuade Marti to give you your old job back if the agency goes under. You need to be earning money, Amelia; the cashflows of my business aren't secure enough yet. There's my colleagues to think about.'

'Always your bloody colleagues,' I said. 'What about your family?' I thought about the evenings when he'd come home for dinner, jumping up at the sound of his phone ringing and then pacing the hallway as he had long conversations with his workmates while I sat and ate my food alone.

'I'm not going to argue with you any more,' Lars said wearily. 'It's not good for the kids to be in this environment.'

'I know,' I said in a tiny bleak voice. I'd always said – after growing up with a father with terrible mood swings – that my children would feel safe in a happy, stable home. Despite all the rowing, I'd been hoping all week that, instead of this cold conversation, he'd walk into the kitchen and say it'd all been a terrible mistake; that he wanted to come back; that he'd change and change for good and the children and I would be OK.

When had Lars become this efficient machine that could put his marriage aside, as if I were last year's fashion? I'd spent hours in the middle of so many restless nights, trying to find the point, the exact time, when his workaholic tendencies had turned into an obsession, leaving me never in vogue again.

Of course, I'd always known he was ambitious – it was something we'd shared right from the start. Then he would tell me that he wanted a brilliant career just like his dead father, a successful engineer. It was his way of honouring his dad and trying to provide some recompense for Ulrika in her grief. Now, when I'd even tried to persuade him to talk about that at marriage guidance counselling, he called it 'cod psychology' and said he was simply trying to do the best he could for our family, and why couldn't I see that?

'Money is going to be really tight,' Lars pressed on. 'We'd always planned to reinvest in my company…'

It *was* what we'd agreed in the early years, but I'd spent a lot of time in the last couple begging him to slow down on trying to expand his company and instead spend some more time with us. Now his bloody business was going to leave us broke too.

'But it's really important that the kids stay in this house,' I said. I looked around at the custard-yellow walls of the kitchen. When we'd finally moved here, we'd danced around this room, which was the same size as a whole floor in our old flat, and shouted, 'We've *always* dreamed about this.'

And Lars had taken a little while out of fitting window locks and bleeding the central heating to laugh at me and give me a hug. The kids – and Finn was just six months old at the time – had been packed off to Ulrika's for the night so that we could get on with moving. I'd dug around in a box until I'd found some sheets and pillowcases, made our double bed and we'd collapsed into it, exhausted but joyous, and celebrated in a housewarming party for two.

'I agree that it's really important to make sure the kids are as stable as possible but it's going to be tough,' Lars said and handed over a typed list of figures. Down one side were listed 'capital assets', down the other 'operational expenditure'. He pointed at various lines entitled 'council tax' and 'buildings and contents insurance'.

He really wanted to get rid of me. And as far as I could see from the spreadsheet, I needed to be earning quite a lot of money at exactly the same time as it looked as if my business was going down the drain.

'Christ,' I said. 'You're going to have to get some money back out of your company.'

'We'll have to try everything,' he said, 'but get a lawyer first. Here's the details of mine.' He handed me another piece of paper with a scan of a business card on it and stood up. I took it, feeling completely numb. Then he said, 'I assume you want to be the one who files the divorce, not me?'

'You want *me* to divorce you?' I blinked.

'We have to write down all the reasons why we can't live together. I could write down why you're impossible to live with if you like,' Lars said, and just for a second he smiled sadly.

'Oh, God.' I spluttered a huge ironic laugh that turned

very quickly to a sob.

'I thought it would give you more control,' he said and turned away.

'Did you think that it would make it hurt less?' I whispered. Ouch. A million ouches.

There was a silence during which he clicked the laptop shut and stuffed it into his briefcase. He got up, looked at me briefly and then went off down the hall. He didn't say goodbye.

It was as I laid my head to rest in my hot, heavy hands that I heard Lars shriek, *'Helvetes jävlar! För guds skull!'* and there was a lot of banging.

I sprang to my feet as I heard the furious sound of wings flapping and got to the hallway just in time to see the Animal Man, his moustache askew and his face a picture of confusion, what looked like owl shit on his head, stagger out from the sitting room and straight into Lars.

'Are you all right?' I cried. 'You seemed to faint. Have you got any idea what's happened to you? Was it that rollie you were smoking?'

Lars stood back against the wall as if he were in the presence of a rancid ghost. The Animal Man looked pallid and deranged.

'Bastard owl,' I said to the bird as it once again circled the ceiling.

Just then the pah-pah of a car ambulance screeched down the road and pulled up outside with a noisy fluster.

'Amelia, what's going on?' Lars recovered some of his

voice.

'Lars, I'd like you to meet the Animal Man.' I drew myself to my full height. 'In fact, now you can be useful... You can help in what may or may not be a minor medical emergency.' Lars looked stunned and was very quiet as I talked to the paramedics, established that the Animal Man would live and helped stack the animals back in his van. Then he climbed into his own car and followed the Animal Man as he drove off down the road.

6

2007

As the door closed I could hear the gorgeous foreigner's feet thumping up the stairs above me. Was he really going to come back? This was turning into a much better winter Saturday than I'd hoped.

I put on my dressing gown and ran around pushing the debris of my and Liv's lives under cushions. Then I hauled my still-damp body into my tightest jeans and managed to get them to do up by lying on the floor and pulling the zip up with the hook end of a wire coat hanger. I could hardly move when I'd added Liv's new black polo neck that she'd just got for her birthday and my own black boots into which I crammed my feet in two pairs of my cleanest socks. I raked through every CD we owned and tried to find something that he might possibly think was cool, settling for an ambient collection that one of Liv's DJ boyfriends had left behind. Next, I sliced open a plastic tube of old foundation with a pair of scissors so that I could get to the tiny residue that was left in the bottom and pulled it over my red face to try and tone down the effects of the bath. My hands were shrivelled like a prune. He probably won't come back, I thought as I put the copies of *Heat* to the bottom of the pile on the ring-stained coffee table and pulled one of Archie's issues of *NME* to the top.

'You're probably used to seeing girls with not many clothes on,' I told him when he did turn up exactly half an hour after he'd left, bearing a couple of cartons of leek and potato soup, a bottle of Tesco merlot and a baguette. He was wearing pale jeans, which were very clean, a puffa jacket in dark blue and a large wool scarf that packaged up his aquiline face.

He looked at me quizzically.

'What with being Swedish and all that,' I said.

He laughed – his laugh seemed to sing a little too. 'We are not spending all of the time with clothes off having sex in the snow,' he informed me, putting soup down on the bench and looking around for a saucepan as if he'd known me and my kitchen cupboards for a very long time instead of moments.

'No,' I said. 'It was just that I don't normally open the door, you know, without being dressed. But I thought you were my flatmate. She never remembers her keys.'

'She has a bicycle and red hair?'

I realised that he must have spied on us as we'd spied on him over the days since he'd arrived.

'Liv, yes. And I'm Amelia – or Ami for short.'

He looked at me solemnly and held out his hand. 'Lars.'

'From where in Sweden?' I wished my voice didn't seem

to be going up and down too as if I were taking the piss out of him.

'I was from Stockholm but I went to uni in Malmö.'

'What are you doing over here?'

'I'm setting up a business,' he said, and for some reason it didn't sound ridiculous.

'Doing what?'

'It is dotcom. I'm doing a business management course at UCL.' Lars looked around from where he was trying to get the cooker to work. 'Why it is not hot?'

I hung my head, remembering. 'We've run out of money for the gas,' I told him, embarrassed.

'What is it that you need to do?' He was brisk.

'Take some money to the corner shop and get a top-up. God, sorry, it's just it's the last week before payday and Liv doesn't really have a job and…'

He held out a tenner. I shrugged, turning pink. 'Couldn't.'

'Please,' he said. 'I really want lunch and my flatmate is in upstairs.' I blushed, because that meant he wanted to be alone with me, didn't it?

'I'll give it back to you on Friday,' I said. How humiliating. And I wanted him to think I was a competent, comprehensively together career girl.

'Go,' he said, and I pulled on my coat, scuttled round the corner and bought ten pounds of credit. When I came back Lars had already cut up the bread and found bowls, a couple of glasses and two blotchy spoons and had put them onto our old wooden tray. He smiled as I fed the meter and he flicked the cooker into life.

'Will it be warmer now?' he asked, reaching for his neck as if he could potentially loosen his scarf.

'A bit,' I said. 'But the windows leak and the door has a massive draught. I'll pay you back, by the way.'

He smiled. 'I know that. What is draught? Is important that I improve my English.'

'It's a cold wind that comes through the gaps in the doors and windows.' I gestured towards the frame of the kitchen window with its peeling paint. 'What's your flat like?'

'Pretty much same shit,' he said. 'But I'm not there. I go to classes and then I go and see other IT people.'

'Are you a geek?' I leant against the kitchen doorway. I seemed to attract them – like Archie. Liv called me the 'nerd-bird'.

'A bit probably. But I do lots of things that are not geek.'

'Like what?'

'I like music and books and funny English girls.'

I blushed and looked at the floor.

'And I like girls who open door in towels. We eat?'

We sat on the floor with our backs against the sofa and the duvet from Liv's bed over our knees and, helped by the bottle of red wine, the warmth of the soup and half an enormous baguette each, we rounded out our stomachs and knowledge of each other.

He asked me about my work and I happily tripped on about branding and how I didn't know then whether to pursue a career in the creative department or in sales.

Lars told me his dotcom idea. 'I launch a business for people's brilliant ideas. They get noticed and get funding from bigger businesses. The website will help them get what you call patents, via cheap lawyers over the Internet. I call it i-patent.com,' he finished in increasingly confident English.

'Are you going to get seed capital?' I asked and hoped like hell I'd got the terminology right.

He looked impressed. 'I have to try and meet as many backers as possible.'

Later he went and fetched his laptop so he could show me his site designs; the flat had got warmer, so we sat on top of the duvet and finished off the bottle. I tried hard to sound intelligent about his business plan and made a few suggestions for the marketing section and he smiled, nodded and took notes.

By then it was halfway through the afternoon, when any light that came through the basement windows was being rapidly eaten by the greed of the February night.

Even later still, he picked up my hand and said, 'Ami, I like you.' His grip was warm and strong.

'You might be all right too,' I said. He looked at me for a second too long and I blushed and quickly looked away. He looked and smelt very clean and male; he also smelt of ambition and, in that cold winter of my early career, that was very appealing.

Liv came back about five o'clock and seemed impressed that I'd managed to pull the new tenant from upstairs with no assistance. She didn't even mention the use of her duvet or the fact that I was wearing her new jumper.

'So, you're Swedish?' Liv said, looking at Lars. 'I do like your accent.'

'Yes, but I need to be in London to get money for my business,' Lars told her.

'Your English is very good.'

'We learn it from when we are really young in my country. Do you work in marketing like Ami?'

'No,' Liv said. 'I create and deliver the fashion of the future.'

'I will try to understand that as I become friends with you,' Lars said. 'Do you want to come to dinner with us this evening?' He hadn't actually asked me whether I was either free or willing to spend the evening with him, but I just smiled broadly.

'I've got a date,' Liv said, 'but thanks anyway.'

'And I haven't got enough money to go anywhere,' I said. I also had a tentative date with Archie but that seemed like something I used to do before I met Lars and, therefore, of little relevance. 'Until I get paid next week.'

'Well, that's what we do, then,' said Lars. 'I buy you dinner this week and you next week.'

'How do you know you'll want to go out with him next week?' Liv hissed as we both sped off into the bedroom to get tarted up.

'I just do,' I said. 'I just do.'

7

2017

On the Sunday morning after Finn's party, I woke up cold but sweating. Among all the things I could worry about, I decided to focus on the immediate – the toe-curling humiliation of trying to win the advertising account that would save my agency from a man who probably knew what I sounded like when I orgasmed, if Liv had resorted to one of her old impressions of me.

I rang her phone, imagining her rolling over in her bed and punching the 'do not accept call' button before going back to sleep. I rang again and then again, until she eventually said, 'gmmfppphh' down the line.

'I need to know everything you told Ben Jones about me,' I said.

'It's the middle of the night…'

My phone said 7.43 a.m. Clearly morning in most people's worlds when they were on a mission.

'I need to know *now*,' I said.

'Can't I at least have a coffee first?'

'No, you can't.'

'Oh, God,' Liv said. 'Well, it was one of those really pretentious parties under the arches in London Bridge, you know, fake chandeliers hung from the roof, bits of really crap modern art dotted around.'

'What kind of modern art?'

'Some bloke called Cockney, which I think is supposed to make you think of Hockney, but cool. There was one called something like "the serendipitous state of sorrow" or some other crap, which was actually an old black and white TV on its side showing a bloke masturbating. I wanted to laugh but everyone else kept walking round saying really poncey stuff about it. Matthew was with me but he got talking to a load of hipsters with beards that practically reached their navels so I was on my own.'

'When you got chatted up by Ben Jones?'

'Well, it wasn't really like that. I had about six glasses on an empty stomach. Not a canapé in sight. Anyway, he came along and was sniggering about the art too and I said something like, "If we hang around long enough do you think we'll see some serendipitous sperm?" and he laughed so we got chatting.'

'Really high-level intellectual stuff, then?'

'I can't believe you woke me up so bloody early to be all superior. I could be asleep now.'

'All right, go on.' I lay back in my own bed and listened for the sounds of the kids moving around but there silence from the landing.

'Then he said he was sorry his new company threw such

wanky parties and, once I realised who he was, I tried to get him to give me one of the bags, but he wouldn't.'

'Liv, they're like £1,500 for a tiny clutch bag.'

'I know, right? Gorgeous though, all soft calf leather, bright pop colours. Then we went and sat down, which was handy as I was about to fall down. And he started going on about how he was in London from Milan and how he didn't have any friends here any more. He was originally from the north – somewhere like Burnley or Barnsley… still probably calls a bread roll a "barm cake".'

'So, then you decided to set him up with me?'

'Well, we drank quite a bit of champagne first – actually I did. He didn't drink anything as he was driving or something like that.'

'He was as sober as a Methodist?' I groaned. That meant he'd remember all the tosh Liv told him.

'Hmmm, one whose grandma died of liver failure,' Liv said. 'So anyway, then I decided he wasn't bad-looking for an older guy – bit lived in, that's all – late thirties, early forties. Divorced, two kids. Six foot tall, dark blond hair.'

'I'm not dumb enough to go out with another blond.'

'If you're going to tell jokes this early in the morning, they need to be good ones. So anyway, I said to him: you need people to hang out with and I've got this friend who lives right near where you're staying – he's in Highgate.'

I took a deep breath while I digested being pimped in this way. 'So, what did you tell him about me?'

'Well, that's the part where it starts to get a bit hazy.'

Liv's voice was hesitant down the phone. 'But I told him about you working in branding and all that and he suddenly got really interested.'

'Bugger,' I said. 'He was probably going to ask Goldwyn to pitch, but now he's got one over on me.'

'Didn't stop you getting a meeting with him, though, did it?' Liv sounded triumphant. 'You see, really I've done you a favour.'

We talked for a little bit more as I wondered exactly what she'd told him while she had all the gusto of the truly shit-faced. Then she asked me about Lars and I told her about him telling me to get a lawyer and the phone call eventually ended when I couldn't talk for crying.

*

I slumped red-eyed in my chair at the office on Monday morning. Bridget was upstairs at a meeting and I was very glad to be alone in the tiny room. I'd dragged myself through the rest of the weekend with the kids and drunk my way through the evening, waking up in the early hours with a hangover, popping Nurofen and drinking water as the dawn light crept round the curtains.

My biggest task of the day was to call Ben and tell him all about the massive misunderstanding Liv had caused and make sure that he knew that I meant business and just business. After that I needed to do everything else possible to win some more work.

First, I'd have a coffee and clear my inbox. Let Ben have time to get in, look at his diary. Then I'd say briskly that, yes, the owl was hilarious but I wasn't in a fit state to go out with *anyone.* I intended to stay very married, if at all possible. I would still be there on Wednesday to get the brief for the pitch.

It was only a stupid phone call. When had I been terrified of making a phone call?

I picked up the receiver and then slammed it down again. Then I sat down and punched the number in before I could stop myself. 'Hello, this is Amelia Fitch for Ben Jones,' I whispered.

'I'm sorry, I didn't hear that,' said the receptionist in her modulated tones.

'Ben Jones, please.'

'Who's calling?'

'Amelia Fitch.'

'There's no need to shout.' She sniffed. 'Putting you through.'

The phone rang far too briefly. I stood up to feel more in control and switched the phone to the other ear.

'Ben Jones,' said the amused lilt from the weekend.

'Ami Fitch,' I said. 'I'm phoning about this ridiculous muddle-up. Liv had no right to tell you all about me and when I rang the other day I didn't know that she'd met you.'

'Ahh,' chuckled the voice. 'You know, when you're not shouting, your friend was quite right. Your voice *is* like a gravel pit.'

Thanks, Liv. Thanks for that one. 'I'm phoning in a professional capacity,' I said.

'Oh, really? How disappointing. Tell me, is your hair really the colour of posh chocolate?'

'It costs a lot of money,' I said with indignation, thinking about how I wouldn't be able to afford it any more. 'Look, I really want to be on the list of agencies that you might want to work with, but the personal thing is just Liv being silly.'

'You don't believe it's the next step in fate's cunning plan to get us to meet?'

'No.' I tried not to sound exasperated.

'You have to accept, Ami – and Liv said this was a little bit of an issue with you – that at some time in your life there will be some things that are beyond your control.'

I stamped my foot and made V-signs at the phone. He obviously thought the situation was hilarious. 'Well, now you come to mention it,' I said.

'Were you being sarcastic then?' Ben asked. 'It's taking me a while since I got back to England to really understand sarcasm again.'

What a bastard.

'Look,' I pleaded. 'I'm a serious person. I seem to have inadvertently become the victim of my friend being drunk. Liv should not have told you all these details about me – it was very inappropriate.'

'I haven't laughed as much in ages as when I rang you on Saturday.'

'Please. I'd like to come and see you on Wednesday to

discuss your advertising and I'd like to forget about anything between us.'

'Why?'

'I'm just not ready to go to lunch with anyone,' I said, adding to myself that even if I were, it wouldn't be with him – a bloke who clearly thought my life was one big joke purely for his benefit and who was mocking me when I felt so *distraught*. 'So, shall we stick to that appointment time on Wednesday?'

'You do like to think you are in charge, just as Liv said,' Ben went on. 'But I also know that when you forget about that you are wonderfully relaxed and just the best friend there is in the whole world.'

I groaned. It was a pretty accurate imitation of a drunk, over-affectionate Liv. 'She shouldn't have told you all that *stuff*.'

'So, yes, I will see you at 10 a.m. on Wednesday and I will expect you at 9.50 a.m. because you're always ten minutes early to everything.'

'Please stop.'

'OK, but only if you tell me what happened to the owl.'

'Eventually the paramedics came but he was fine. My husband – I mean…'

'Your nearly ex-husband?'

'Yes,' I said, 'he had to help me get the animals back in the van and off he went.'

'It was very funny.'

'Yes. As you said: a complete hoot.' My voice was thick

with sarcasm.

'Liv said you lost your sense of humour sometimes.'

'I said STOP.'

'I'll see you on Wednesday, then.'

'Look forward to it.' I could imagine him cackling to himself over in Hanover Square, sitting back in his huge important chair and thinking what a fantastic laugh it was to wind up poor divorcing, disintegrating me.

If only he weren't in charge of the only massive account in London advertising to be up for grabs at the moment.

If only my business weren't going down the drain.

If only pretty much everything really.

*

'Oh no,' Bridget said. It was later that day and she was back at her desk.

'What is it?'

Bridget went fuchsia. 'You're not going to like this…' she said and started tapping away at her laptop.

'Like *what*?'

'Land has gone bust.' She looked as if she were going to cry.

'No…' It couldn't be happening. I ran to Bridget's desk where a page from the *FT* online was kicking into life on the screen.

'Land the Bootmakers in receivership,' said the headline. I let out a caterwaul and skim-read the article. There had been huge efforts to refinance the company but the banks weren't convinced… Five hundred people were under threat of redundancy… creditors were to be contacted.

Grabbing the phone, I punched in Stephen Frost's extension number.

'Yes, I was just going to call you,' he said without saying hello.

'Does Marti know?'

'I've left a message for him for when he touches down at Heathrow,' Stephen said.

'I knew there was trouble but I didn't know it was this bad,' I said. 'I've rung the CEO but he hasn't been contactable…'

'That was because he was having his balls cut off at the top of Barclays tower.'

'I should have known.' I avoided looking at Bridget, who was pacing up and down the little office. 'I know we won't get any more work but will we get our money back?'

'Most definitely not. But I've got the team on it – they're calling the receivers now.'

'Is there anything I can do?' I was almost whispering now. I knew that Bridget would be under no illusion any more that Brand New was a going concern, but at the same time I was almost ashamed to speak out loud in front of myself: my old self, the one who was in control of stuff; who threw the dice in the right way, climbing the career ladder instead of landing on snake squares that sent me slipping right back to the bottom of the board.

'I told you – win some more business and quick. And then wait for Marti to get back.'

'Will he pull the plug?' I whispered again. Bridget was pacing so fast now that she looked like a cartoon character who'd wear a hole in the ground.

Stephen paused. 'Ami, I just don't know.'

Bridget disappeared out of the door then, iPhone in hand, probably to ring headhunters and beg them for a job somewhere where the boss hadn't lost her grip.

I let my head sink for a moment after I had put down the phone. Then I looked up and around the office with its big blow-up posters of the covers of *Campaign* and *Marketing Week* from just a year ago, triumphantly announcing the birth of my tiny agency. I had painted this little basement room in the bowels of Goldwyn myself. How magnificent my dreams had been then.

*

Bridget came back eventually, sat down at her desk and sniffed until I asked her to get on with researching Campury. 'It'll be fine,' I said as breezily as I could when all I could feel were the cold winds of failure around me. 'We'll win Campury.' Secretly, all I wanted was for Marti to come back and tell me what the options were.

It felt like several years of pain that were really only hours before the door swung open and he strode in in all his stripey-shirted glory. He had a suntan and his sixty-year-old face looked a little younger for it. I thought about all the times he'd helped me over the years.

'Afternoon,' his voice resounded around the room.

'Oh, thank God.' I stood up. I wanted to run at him, ask him to open his worldly arms, pull me into his chest. I didn't though, because he was the boss – and I could never be seen to have physical contact with Marti because agency folklore would soon have it that I was up the duff with several of his illegitimate children. No one ever let the truth stand in the way of a juicy rumour. Bridget took her phone and went out of the room, probably to tell everyone that Marti had come to see me *again*.

'Bloody shenanigans, all this LandGirls business, isn't it?' he said.

'We've been trying to call you about it.'

'I know, I know. Got the message as I was getting off the plane. But I'm here now.' Marti sat down at the little meeting table and sighed.

I tried to reassure him. 'We've got all the other clients…'

Marti looked awkward. 'It'll probably be OK,' he said. 'But you're going to have to be focused and…'

My face blushed the colour of damson jam.

Marti's over-padded face coloured too. 'Little birdie tells me that your young husband has turned out to be… well, possibly, your *first* husband… Just wanted you to know, well, that you've our full support.'

I wasn't surprised that he knew: my industry leaked like a bucket without a bottom. Someone – maybe Bridget – must have overheard me talking to Liv on the phone.

'He wants a divorce,' I said in as balanced a voice as I could manage, sitting down opposite him. 'But you know I'll always work hard.'

Marti put his large hand over mine. 'Not doubting your commitment but it is a distraction. But… anyway, got to pick yourself up, chin up and all that. You need to get on with getting some new clients.'

'I think I'm onto something. We're going to pitch for Campury.' I was desperate to impress him.

'You sure? Folks upstairs have been trying to get hold of this new brand director for a while now.'

'His name is Ben Jones and I spoke to him this morning. We go to meet him on Wednesday.'

Marti grinned and glaciers would have melted in the force of his charm. 'Now, that's more like it. Would love to get that account.'

'I know. What a challenge.'

'Listen,' Marti went on. 'I don't suppose you'd be free to talk about it some time? Plan of attack and all that? Plus, I could really do with your help with the Loosey underwear people. I need some good ideas to throw at the b'stards.'

'Now?'

'Can't do it now, girl,' said Marti. 'People like me have schedules, you know. All right for you, doing all sorts of things *on the hoof…*' He winked at me. 'No, I was thinking, you know, you might be free for supper one evening, Wednesday maybe – get someone to look after the kiddies and I could take you somewhere and we could have a bit of a natter.'

'All right, you can pick my brains for the price of a dinner.'

'I'll send my driver for you at 8. Where do you want to go?'

'The Ivy?' I said, knowing how much he liked their fish and chips and how it was stumbling distance from the club he slept at. It would also be a big treat for me.

Bridget came back into the room just as he said, 'Now, Ami, get your grey cells working. I need to be able to talk intelligently about ladies' knickers.'

I already knew that Bridget would report this to the rest of the building so that they could cackle, 'Come *on* – he already knows just how to get hers round her ankles.'

*

How can you be so small and perfect? I could see Finn through the pattern of the stained-glass windows as I ran up the steps to the front door of our house. He was sitting at the bottom of the stairs, his stubby little legs exactly the same length below the knees as the depth of the bottom step. He heard my key and started shouting, 'Mummy's home! Mummy!' As I opened the door his blue eyes shone; his cheeks were ruddy and shining with raw health.

I slammed the door shut, dropped my bag, ran to him and covered him in kisses.

After Marti had gone, I hadn't been able to escape the seeping panic that crawled around my bones. Eventually I'd locked myself in the corner cubicle of the office loo and sat down on the cold plastic lid. Should I call Lars and tell him the trouble my company was in? Would that make him come back? Once he would have been the first person I would've asked for help and he would have given it.

But then I'd remembered what he'd said on that last Sunday as he'd stalked around the kitchen. 'It's all this going on about you, you, you that has torn our marriage apart.' I couldn't call Lars. Instead I'd stayed in the loo for a while just to escape having to face anyone else from the agency who would already know that I was a borderline bankrupt.

'At school, Jemima said my party was the best ever but, Mummy, why weren't there tigers?' Finn said now.

'I think we had enough trouble with ferrets, don't you?'

'Mrs Wragley says that she saw something in her garden.' Finn was referring to my elderly neighbour. I sometimes got shopping for her since her hip operation but she always complained I'd forgotten something when she'd actually forgotten to tell me to get it.

'Whatever you do, don't tell her about the ferrets,' I said, putting my finger in front of my mouth to signify a secret.

Finn nodded gravely. 'Yes, because she said we would need to rent to kill it,' he whispered.

'We can't have that, can we?' I said. 'Where's Tess?'

'Playroom.' Finn shrugged, gesturing at the door at the back of the hall. He put his hands over his ears. I marched towards the closed door, throwing it open to discover Tess – exactly as I knew she would be – stretched out on the stained blue sofa, her eyes eating up *Sleeping Beauty*, shuddering with exquisite fear at the wicked fairy.

I punched the power button on the old white portable and Tess came back to the real world with a thud.

'Arrgah…' she wailed. 'Mummy. Ten minutes. Pleeeeease!' and I wanted to fall onto the sofa with her, hold her tight and tell her it would be all right. Instead, I had to argue about how many hours of TV-watching a day were healthy for a six-year-old.

'It's not fair. Daddy would've let me.'

'When will Daddy come back?' said Finn.

"Nikita's daddy didn't come back,' said Tess. She was talking about the father of one of her classmates who had unfortunately keeled over from a heart attack a few months ago in the North Stand at the Emirates. 'He died. But *you* said daddies don't die.'

'Nikita's father was very ill. Nikita's daddy died and it was very, very sad, but we talked about that then – and do you remember? I said to you that your daddy and your mummy were very strong and they weren't going to die. Daddy has just gone away for a little while – like he goes away all the time – and he'll be coming back to see you soon.' I dropped to my knees and looked at them both closely, drawing them to me. 'Listen to me. Tess! Listen.' The little girl's attention was already wandering. 'No one is going to die.'

'Why are you home early?' Tess changed the subject.

'Mummy's got the crying type of poorly,' said Finn. 'And she was sick in the toilet this morning. It was *real* sick. I'll show you where she did it if you like.'

'We could play being sick,' said Tess, her face lighting up. She started making retching noises and using her hands in a parody of vomit splurging from her mouth. 'Carrots come out and everything.'

'We don't play in toilets and Mummy is better now so we don't need to think about sick any more,' I said and went out to the hall to call for Luba.

Finally, there was the thud of Converse on the hall stairs and her body appeared, followed by her sleek head of hair. Even from this angle, she was spectacular-looking. 'I thought you still at work, Amelia. I put washing away upstairs,' she said.

'Please can you babysit on Wednesday?' I asked. 'I need to go to a work dinner with my boss.'

'I help yes.'

I wondered whether Luba was too sullen to be around the children, but she hadn't done anything wrong and I'd committed to a year; she probably just needed to make some more friends.

*

After the kids had gone to bed, I rang Mum. 'Oh, Ami, I feel so useless,' she said. 'I know your father can look after himself but I'd just worry so much.'

There it was again: the feeling I'd known from childhood of being the third element in a perfect balance of two. I tried hard not to mind.

Dad had a career in shipping insurance before he started writing detective novels and they moved to Gloucestershire. Out there in the country his blues could be off the paint chart. But his mood could also lift suddenly. He'd start typing again and sit down at the dinner table as if nothing had happened without ever acknowledging to Mum and me how absent he'd been to us over the previous few months. We'd learned, too, to pretend in front of him that it hadn't happened and everything went on as usual. As I grew older, I resented him for all those times when I'd climbed off the train to see my mum's exhausted face and known I was in for a holiday from uni worried about her and being suffocated by his wall of silence.

'He won't go to the doctor's,' she'd said every time I'd begged her to get help. It was only in recent years that she'd opened up at all about the tremendous toll it took on her, but when I'd got really angry, following a difficult Christmas a couple of years back, she'd shouted back, 'We know what we are dealing with here, Ami, and we don't need any help.' The 'we' was she and him.

It was the pretence that they were always happy, and had such a marriage of togetherness, that made them vocal about other marriages, especially when there were children involved. It was as if they went on the attack: they'd managed to stay together for my benefit and why couldn't others – including Lars and me – manage to do the same? My dad was the most vocal, but Mum was complicit.

Had she thought about leaving him before I surprised them by coming along when she was already forty-two? I didn't know; it was a different generation. But it was as if because they'd made one choice they were disapproving of others who made a different one. I'd grown up with the doctrine that you 'stick together' and right now I felt a failure in their eyes for not managing it.

Still, I adored my dad – when he was upbeat, he was funny, kind, generous and very old-fashioned really. He was a brilliant storyteller, a great companion and very loving to me and the kids – I knew his first urge would now be to protect us.

'He's just worried about you and the children,' Mum continued. 'He's found you a lawyer and wants to talk to you about it.'

Dad came on the phone and, after asking how the children and I were getting on, said, 'I've pulled some strings for you to see a woman called Cathy Murdoch, who's apparently quite good. I'll cover the costs of the first appointments so you don't have to worry about it. I'm going to say goodbye, darling. I need a whisky.'

I half-heartedly protested about the money and thanked him, really very grateful, before I put down the phone. Then I hugged a pillow to my knees on the sofa. How fast it was – the process of disintegrating all those years of love.

<u>8</u>

2007

At the beginning, our relationship developed far faster than Lars' English. He would pick up a phrase from a taxi driver or someone he met in class and use it obsessively until he moved on to the next one. In March, he discovered 'mate', and used it whether it was appropriate or not. In May, he found to his delight that women in English were also referred to as 'birds', and used it to tease us feminists. In August, he was always 'discombobulated' even when I knew that he was completely calm. September was all about 'doggerel', which he refused to believe was not a word in common use among the young in London at that time, having heard it on Radio 4.

On our first date, though, the evening of the day we met, the word was 'outrageous'. We went to a Spanish bistro with pavement tables round the corner from our flats and sat under the chequered canopy where outside heaters blasted down at us. As the liquid heat met the frozen February night, the air seemed to melt into droplets of rain. We ate tapas – patatas bravas, squid and tortillas - and every bite tasted new, grown-up and exotic to me. Although we were jammed in with other couples knee-to-knee round rickety tables covered in colourful oilskins, it was as if I'd stepped into a bubble, which contained just the two of us; I hoped it would never burst.

He talked about his dreams and his past. He was an only child like me; his father had died suddenly of a stroke, the previous year, he told me with tears in his eyes; he'd been an engineer, designing viaducts that crossed fjords and withstood temperatures of minus forty. He wanted to be successful in his father's memory, he said, to give his mother something to be proud of. His mother was a schoolteacher – who now, following his father's death, was withdrawn like 'bear in a cave' and he worried about her all the time.

I held his warm hand briefly but wanted to wrap my arms around him. He smiled though and went on.

He'd discovered that he was good with computers at school and taken a degree in engineering in Malmö – he told me some funny stories about sharing a flat with his great friend Thorstein, who'd gone off to the US for work now, while Lars had come to the UK. I told him about my life before him too – my marketing degree at Queen Mary's, living with Liv as I tried to get my career off the ground.

'It's outrageous how much I like you already,' Lars told me. He was still wearing the big puffa jacket and talked much too fast for his limited English. I was wrapped up in my winter coat. We drank rough Rioja tipped into cheap tumblers.

'I feel like I know you,' I said, because it was true. It wasn't very usual among the boys I knew to say out loud how they felt at all – aside from an appreciative grunt at the height of sexual excitement – so this conversation was novel.

'This boyfriend you have,' Lars said. 'Will you not have him any more?'

'He's not really my boyfriend,' I said. 'Just, you know…'

'A hook-up?' said Lars. 'I have been learning this word. He is a shag buddy? I have been learning that too.'

I blushed and looked away. I had to try to do everything I could not to get off with this man with his high cheekbones and huge hopes on our first date in case he never wanted to go out with me or talk like this to me again.

When all the other couples had gone and the waiter had slammed down our bill in a chipped white saucer, I took a biro from my bag and picked up Lars' arm. He looked at me quizzically but let me write on his wrist: 'IOU one night out'. I wondered if he could feel my pulse beating twice as fast as it should have.

'What is this IOU?' he asked and tried to keep hold of my hand.

'It says "I owe you" – it means that I promise to give you one night out in return for tonight.'

'I promise you much more than one.' Lars was fierce and my tummy did a few more gymnastics moves.

The waiter came out then and ostentatiously turned off all the heaters. Lars pulled me to my feet and, with his arm around me to protect me from the bitterness of the night, we

101

walked the short journey home.

At our house, while I needed to go down the steps into the basement, he had to go up the steps to the front door.

'Thank you for a perfect day,' I said and smiled up at him.

'I'm glad I am with you,' Lars sang in a flat parody of Lou Reed. 'Feed animals in the park.'

'I'm pretty sure it was "zoo",' I laughed and his mouth came down to meet mine until the laugh turned into a kiss that was twice as sweet and passionate as I'd hoped it might be.

'It's an outrageous kiss,' Lars whispered.

'I must go,' I said, before I let him kiss me again – at which point I knew I wouldn't stop.

'IOU one night out next Saturday?' Lars said.

'I owe you,' I said and walked towards the basement steps.

'Goodnight, perfect day Ami with the outrageous kiss.'

'Goodnight.'

9

2017

Outside the school, there was a big commotion going on. Apparently, Julia's nanny, Lila, an ebullient Aussie, had taught quite a few of the kids – including Jemima – the words and dance actions to a recent Nicki Minaj song, which involved the odd 'booty'-type reference and a lot of butt swaying.

I came out of the school to see Julia facing up to Nadine, who was talking about 'cultural appropriation'. Parminder whisperingly brought me up to speed.

'Freddie and I have worked so hard to ensure that Jemima has a well-balanced childhood, free from conflict and in harmony with all the world's races,' Nadine said.

'I'm sure there's no way she would have let them see it on purpose,' Julia said.

Nadine was obviously struggling to balance her inner calm; I'd never seen her so red in the face. 'But what if Jemima now thinks it's usual to wiggle her booty or whatever the term is?' she spluttered.

I was quite sympathetic but, given how much Nadine

lorded her Smugum-ness over us, I had to try not to giggle. She turned to me though: 'I needed to correct Jemima as to the appropriate term for making love after she visited Amelia's house; I thought that was bad enough.'

I muttered, 'Sorry, sorry,' under my breath and started for the bus stop to get to my appointment with the divorce lawyer; I could see Parminder slinking off too, making 'good luck' signs to Julia. Later that day, our group chat inbox was filled with memes of Nadine's head stuck onto Nicki Minaj's body, shaking her booty gloriously.

*

I arrived at the divorce lawyer's office near Fleet Street. She was in her early fifties, round from her knees to her generous bosom, hair pulled back from her face in a loose chignon. She was dressed in conservative lawyer kit: John Lewis maybe, or Hobbs – except that her shoes were patent leather pumps with red stacked heels. As I came through the door, she jumped to her feet – energetically for her size – and strode forward to clutch both my hands in her pink, warm ones.

'Ms Fitch? I'm Catherine but you must call me Cathy. Everyone does. Take a seat. Just here OK? Would you like tea? Or coffee? Water?' Her voice was light and cheery. Very cheery indeed.

'Water would be great.' I sat down in a winged chair and she bounced into the one behind the desk before peering at me, concerned. She poured me a glass of water and said, 'How are you feeling? Never a good time.'

Tears involuntarily came into my eyes, the way they do when someone is unexpectedly nice when you're feeling sad. She thrust a box of tissues at me. 'Best to let it all out. Then we can see what we can do to make it better. I'm here to help.'

She looked as if she mainlined Prozac for breakfast but the effect of all her smiling was that I felt compelled to try to smile back. 'Where do you want me to start?'

'We'll just take a few details first, shall we? And then we'll have a little chat.' She picked up a fountain pen and carried on looking sympathetic. In front of her was one of those yellow lined pads that only lawyers ever use.

'So, Amelia, isn't it? And Fitch? Is that your maiden name? What's your husband's?'

'Johansson. I'm not really entitled to be Mrs Johansson any more.' Even though I'd never used Lars' surname it felt sad that I was about to lose the option on the brand.

'Tell me, do you have children?'

'Two, yes.' I gave her Tessa and Finn's names and dates of birth.

'Now,' she went on, 'it's terribly vulgar but I need to ask you about money.' We rattled through various financial details: our seemingly massive mortgage, value of our house – I knew this because one two doors away had just been sold to a footballer with a yellow Ferrari – and our non-existent savings accounts, explaining about all our money going back into our nascent businesses.

I wondered whether she was married – whether she'd ever sat on this side of the table, knew what it was actually like. I tried to catch a look at her left hand but it was under the desk as she wrote with her right.

Behind her on a small corner table were a couple of framed pictures, one of which seemed to show a younger Cathy alongside a tall, thin man. 'Are you married?' I asked.

'Oh, gosh, bless you, yes, I am. To Jeremy. For the last thirty years.'

Just my luck. The happily married divorce lawyer.

'Now we'd better talk about you though? What's been going on?'

I gave her a brief history of my marriage and how Lars wanted a divorce, tears welling towards the end.

'And you don't? Poor thing.'

'Well, no, I mean, something had to change, but I never thought it would come to this, or at least I hoped it wouldn't.'

'Never a good time. Now, this is an absolutely vile thing to have to ask you.' Cathy leaned forward. 'Does this involve anyone else?'

I told her that I didn't think so, and I didn't, but the thought of Lars with another woman sent a cold shock through my capillaries.

'No other unusual sexual proclivities?' She tittered again. I opened my eyes wide and shook my head.

'So sad, these Type D divorces,' said Cathy almost

106

abstractedly.

'What do you mean?'

'Oh, it's just my theory – silly me.' She shook her head and laughed again. Was it appropriate to be quite so cheery in the face of her clients' misery? 'There are only four types of divorce really and I call them Type A, B, C and D.'

'Go on,' I said, intrigued, despite knowing that lawyers charged by periods of six minutes.

'Really? Well, Type As are classic adulterers, you know, trying to get out as fast as they can.'

'Because they're already into someone else?'

'Ha, ha, yes.' Cathy laughed at my weak joke. 'Now, we don't want to give the other side anything we don't have to, do we?' I was heartened that she actually had a tough side; I wasn't looking for a divorce shark but she did look as if she should be at home making scones. 'But Type As feel guilty so they're normally too generous.'

'Type Bs?' I asked.

'Oh, they're the wronged party and, if you don't mind me saying so, easily the most satisfying clients.' I felt inadequate but she pushed on, 'The thing is, they want to take the other party for everything they're worth. Right down to the last line on my spreadsheet.'

Good. She had a spreadsheet to match Lars'. I knew I really had to be on top of all the money stuff.

'Type C – married to a psychopath, alcoholic, drug addict, violent mad person or any combination of the above. They just want to get away but it's my moral duty to get whatever cash I can get on their behalf. This morning I had to tell a woman – of course, you don't know who – who's been married to a mad alcoholic for twenty years that he won't need any money when he's sectioned.' She shook her head.

Were lawyers allowed to be this indiscreet?

'You're a D. No single deciding motive. Just people who simply can't get on with each other. The sum of you is no longer greater than the individual elements.'

'That's exactly it.' I teared up again.

She reached out with her pudgy hand. 'You poor dear. Now, let me tell you about what could happen next if you decide to go ahead.'

'With irretrievable breakdown, there are many reasons for divorce. Desertion, adultery, separation, unreasonable behaviour are all grounds. It sounds as if in your case, we are looking at unreasonable behaviour. You or your husband will need to list several reasons as to why you can no longer live together and file the papers.' It was good that I had possession of the marital home and a job, she continued. I told her about Lars' business and how we had to get enough money out for the kids to keep their home.

'What does your husband do?' I asked.

'Oh, Jeremy's retired now but he did have a job in a distribution centre.' Cathy kept a fixed smile on her face. Her eyes flicked to the other photo, which showed the same tall thin man holding some sort of shield against a backdrop of a corporate office. 'But we really do need to talk about you, not me.' She leaned forward. 'We'll take a positive tone with the other side and hope it doesn't get ugly.' There was a spark in her eye, however, as if she would really enjoy it if it got ugly. 'We'll need him to complete an affidavit on money and you'll have to fill in some forms too. There's a court hearing where the decree nisi is published – you don't have to go usually – and then six weeks after that you get the absolute and you're no longer married.'

'It's as simple as that?' I said.

'Well, it could be.' Cathy chuckled. 'But it very rarely is.' She jumped up and clasped my hands again. 'Now, you need to look after yourself. But I'm here, ready and waiting when you are.'

I went home and rang Liv to update her. 'She's a gusher,' I said. 'Resolutely cheerful about dealing in other people's misery. And happily married.'

'Divorce lawyers shouldn't be married,' said Liv.

'Exactly. Or smile like a demented aunt who's been on the sauce. Apparently I need to write down reasons why I can't live with Lars.'

'I can think of a few, starting with he was never there. Can't you get him on desertion?'

*

I decided to take Bridget with me to the Campury meeting. My justification was giving her experience, but really I knew it was personal protection. I was determined that I would make Ben stay on a professional level.

Having pulled myself from bed that Wednesday morning, I painted my ravaged face with an extra-thick coat of make-up and climbed into a taller pair of heels than usual; I wore my most expensive Max Mara dress and jacket, a treat to myself when I'd got a bonus back in the Goldwyn days.

Bridget was waiting outside Campury House when I came round the corner from the Tube, leaning against a pillar the colour of sand. The knocker on the double oak doors gleamed with history and wealth. Bridget was clutching our portfolio and looked as if she was nearly beside herself with anticipation.

I looked at my watch. It was exactly 9.50 a.m. Damn the man.

'Hello,' I said. 'Now, Bridget, let me do the talking. You take notes. Good notes and make sure that we get all the information we need.'

'His colleague rang up last night and said she knew that you were particular about what coffee you drank and could I give her any guidance,' Bridget told me. 'It was very efficient, I thought, but, Ami, how do they know about your coffee thing?'

'I do *not* have a coffee thing,' I said. 'I like French-blend coffee – you know that, but it's not a *thing*. Now listen to me, Bridget, this is a man who I suspect likes to play mind games. However, he is also in charge of the account that will rescue Brand New, so we're going to be very professional and we're not going to let him get to us.'

Good, it was now 9.52 a.m. By the time we'd signed in at the desk it would be five to ten and I would've proved him wrong about me always being ten minutes early.

Bridget and I pushed our way into the dark-panelled lobby and told the immaculate blonde behind the sweep of oak desk why we were there. She indicated that we should wait in the deep upholstery of a couple of sofas to the left; as we sat down I could hear her picking up the phone. I looked up at what looked like a Renoir hanging from the dark panelling.

'Can't be real.' I wafted my arm at it and Bridget stared too.

'You're right, it's a fake,' came the northern voice I'd last heard on the phone, from a corridor, which led to the lift. 'But apparently the one upstairs in the boardroom is real.'

Ben sounded as if he thought that the idea of having a real old master was highly amusing. He was wearing a dark suit and a deep pink shirt. Patches of purple sat under his eyes over a fading suntan; his blond hair was a mop on his head. He was a big man – in the wrong light he could have been slightly overweight, but he was undeniably attractive.

Behind him was a polished brunette in an expensive, subtly sexy pencil skirt. Her hair swung down her back in a shining curtain of health and her cheekbones were from pure aristocratic DNA.

'Amelia.' Ben held out his hand as I rose to greet him. The hazel of his eyes was speckled with a lighter glint; the lines around them had been caused by irrepressible laughter

111

– probably at other people's expense.

I shook his enormous hand.

'This is Bridget Ashcroft.' I gestured with my left hand and realised that he was still holding firmly onto my right.

'This is Claudia Bennett.' Ben let go of my hand but carried on looking straight at me as he referred to the glossy brunette beside him.

'Hello, Claudia. Pleased to meet you.'

I bet he's trying to sleep with her. I shook hands, smiled as normally as I could and then reached behind me to gather up my briefcase and the portfolio of work.

'Shall we go straight to the conference room?' Claudia said in immaculate received pronunciation.

'Yes, let's,' I said and started to follow the little procession towards the corridor.

'Your friend was right, you know,' Ben whispered in my ear, just as I got to the lift door. 'I know it's not the done thing to say this at work, but you are very beautiful.'

I stared straight ahead of me and refused to acknowledge that he'd spoken. I was chuffed and annoyed in equal measure but I knew he'd only said it to get the upper hand.

Inside another panelled room upstairs I sat down, passed out my business card, gestured to Bridget to sit down too and zipped open the portfolio.

Ben sprawled in his chair as if it were too small for his frame. 'I think we've got some French coffee,' he said.

'That's extremely kind of you.' I tried to smile. 'But I really don't have a thing about coffee.'

112

'I love French-blend coffee too.'

I accepted a cup from Claudia and added milk. 'Shall we go through our presentation first?'

'You go ahead, Ami.' He smiled on. Claudia didn't seem to notice anything peculiar about the atmosphere, but I saw that Bridget's eyes were darting around as if she was trying to get a grip on what was happening.

I started to present the various pages of the portfolio – campaigns we'd worked on, statistics about their success. Claudia looked with interest at every page – shoe campaigns, lingerie, handbags, clothes – and asked lots of questions. Ben, however, sat smiling and looking as much at me talking as he did at the portfolio.

'Brave thing to do, set up on your own,' he said, interrupting me midflow.

'Yes, but we're still part of a much bigger group. We've access to all the Goldwyn resources but the ability to draw on all sorts of young, outside thinking.' It was my stock answer to that question.

'I like your work,' he said as if he'd seen enough now and Bridget closed the portfolio. 'You're obviously a very clever woman, Ami, but that's not surprising given the potential you showed at school and how hard you've always worked.' Damn Liv.

'I didn't know you knew each other,' Claudia said.

'We don't.' I tried very hard not to sound terse.

'I know an awful lot about Ami, though,' Ben went on.

'I admired your work with LandGirls,' Claudia said.

113

'Thank you.'

'It's a shame about that brand,' Ben said. 'Impact your agency much?'

'Well, it's not good news, of course, but we have a broad client base and—'

'And you'd like to add Campury to it?' He looked directly at me.

'We'd like that.' I stared straight back. 'Why don't you tell us what you're trying to achieve?'

As I sat back and he sat forward, I fumed like a pipe smoker spitting out new puffs of anger.

'It's probably a bigger challenge than anything you've taken on before – or than I have either,' he started. 'We will, of course, be going out for a competitive pitch with several agencies and we need to move very fast indeed if we want to get the sales growth we've projected in the UK this year. This is not a job for the faint-hearted.'

'We love a challenge,' Bridget piped up.

I tried not to glare at her.

Ben went on talking, his craggy brow pulled together in concentration. 'Campury – beautiful bags, reek of history and wealth. A bit like a Rolls-Royce in Britain. The brand has become unattainable to most people. We've got to turn it on its head and make the bags appeal to younger women – be something that they buy early in their thirties and build a collection. It's the only way we avoid a dying market.

'This can't be ordinary and it has to have a huge impact – literally reinvent the brand overnight. We've got a file of

114

demographic information and all that,' he went on. 'But that's it really – we need to double our turnover in the UK. We're prepared to throw quite a lot of money at it.'

Claudia pushed a folder full of information across the desk to Bridget.

'I'm sure we'll want to pitch if you'd like to include us.' I got ready to go. 'When do you need ideas back?'

'That's just it,' Ben said. 'We need to move fast with the campaign to get growth this summer. We need presentation of ideas back in two weeks' time.'

Two weeks. This sort of work usually needed at least six and, even then, it was an intense schedule. I was going to have to ask Luba to work some extra hours.

'I'll phone you later to see what you think,' Ben said. 'I know you like to have time to think through things and then always act decisively.'

God, he thought he was funny. But if this was what I had to put up with to get my hands on this project, then I would smile all the way through it.

*

It was back at the office, when Bridget had finally stopped asking me why Ben talked to me as if he knew me, that I really started to panic. How was I ever going to get a world-class campaign together in two weeks? I asked Bridget to go upstairs and find out what creative teams were available.

Liv rang. 'So what did you think?'

'He's a complete bastard. Thinks it's really funny to take the piss out of me in front of other people. And he's good-looking but, boy, does he know it. You must have been completely off your head when you met him.'

'Did I ever say I wasn't off my head? I freely admitted it. But I do remember thinking that he was attractive and fun and—'

'I now need to work my butt off for two weeks to pitch for an account that I will never win. I won't see the children right when they need me.'

Bridget came back as the landline phone was ringing. She mouthed across the room that Marti wanted to talk to me.

I said goodbye to Liv and picked up the receiver. 'Hello?'

'Heard he's a bit strange, this Ben Jones,' Marti said. 'Supposed to be some kind of wunderkind, however.'

'Big bloke – looks really out of place in Campury. He's certainly very sure of himself.'

'Cocky?'

'Cock, more like.'

Marti sniggered but was soon back to business. 'So you're going to pitch and you're going to try and win. This is the best chance you've got so don't bugger it up.'

*

Ben called at the end of the day when I was halfway through planning just how we were going to do all the work. Bridget had gone off to try and negotiate some media strategy time. I was busily hating Lars all over again for never having to work out how he was going to juggle time between his children and his work. How had our marriage of equals become so one-sided? How had I let his dreams become so big that even my small ones – like a happy family and my own agency – became out of reach? I had my head in my hands as the phone rang.

'It's Ben,' he said. I confirmed that we'd like to be on the pitch list. 'Good stuff. I like you, Ami.'

'I'm glad,' I said with as much enthusiasm as I could muster. 'Who else have you selected?'

He named three of London's giants. What chance did little Brand New have?

'So, I suppose now you can add "potential business conflict" to the list of reasons why you won't go out with me?'

I smiled despite myself. Maybe he was going to forget about all this silliness and get on with the job at hand?

'Yes, thanks, already thought of that one,' I said. 'And can I ask you to stop making jokes about me in front of other people?'

'Jokes? What jokes?'

'You know, dropping in those things Liv told you.'

'Did I do that? I promise you it was just teasing.'

'Well, I need to get on with working out how to come up with a killer idea.'

'So I won't ask you out again socially until after the pitch.'

I groaned down the phone. 'That's very sweet but I'm not in a position to go out with anyone. So, let's just forget the "going out socially" thing, shall we?'

'Absolutely. One of the reasons why I'm calling – to say that.'

'Thank you. I mean it.'

'And to ask you out in a business-y way.'

'To talk about the pitch?'

'Of course. We need to talk about the pitch. Lots.'

'I can't go out with you,' I said, although for a brief moment I thought about playing along if it meant getting inside information.

'You sure?'

I knew what I had to say. 'And you can't go out with me because all the other agencies would think that I had an unfair advantage. It's not professional.'

'I was never really that worried about being professional.'

'You aren't the usual…' I tried to be diplomatic and still make my voice sound the sort of smiley that potential clients with big accounts to give away deserved.

'I hate usual,' he said. 'Love people who surprise me. You surprise me.'

'Well, I won't if you keep me on the phone…'

'All right, I'll leave you alone.'

'Thank you.'

'I would say it was my pleasure but that would be a lie.'

*

When I got home that night Luba was dreamily cooking sausages and chips for the children.

'Do you think the children could have broccoli or peas or something as well?' I asked. Maybe they didn't do nutrition in Bratislava?

Luba just stared around her into space.

'Luba? Are you OK?'

'Oh, Amelia, I very OK.' I wasn't sure if I'd ever seen Luba actually smile but she did now and it reached her languid eyes and she looked even more luminous. 'Tomorrow I go out with Guy Gates.'

'The footballer from down the road?' Finn asked from the kitchen floor where he was busy smashing various Power Rangers together.

'Yes.' Luba smiled on. 'He come to door when you at school and say he will take me to football match and dinner. He say I very pretty.'

'Well, you are very pretty.' I was glad for Luba. 'I'm sure you'll have a fantastic time.'

Guy Gates seemed a bit of a jumped-up arsehole, but then what did I know? Since he'd moved in a few months back he'd just driven up and down the road in a bright yellow Ferrari, which Nadine said was a pollutant and ought to be banned. He'd also upset Mrs Wragley by getting a vulgar gold wheelie bin. Still, if it made Luba smile for once who cared?

'And you're all right about me going out tonight with my boss?'

'Oh, yes.' Luba shook the oven tray full of chips. 'I stay in and make myself more pretty for Guy Gates.' She smiled again; it was so unusual that both Finn and I carried on staring at her for several seconds.

<u>10</u>

2007

When Lars wasn't emailing potential backers for his business, he spent hours sitting on our sofa, eating inedible spaghetti, or out in the yard behind the house fixing Liv's bike. Our conversations were frenzied from the start – I needed to know absolutely everything there was to know about him as if, in knowing it all, he would belong to me completely.

It was then that I learned my first Swedish: *älskling* first – I was his honey, his darling. I also learned the popular swear words: *fy fan* – for fuck's sake – or *för fan i helvete!* – something to do with the devil in hell, for example.

Thor came to stay that winter, in London for a tech event, and I practised them on him. 'You are a potty mouth,' he said, learning an English term in exchange.

He was huge, hairy, adorable and charming. 'Good God, gorgeous,' he would say from Lars' sofa as I tiptoed past on my way to work. 'What a sight for sore eyes – that is right phrase for girls, yes?' Lars and I spent an evening getting drunk with Liv and him; we left them to it at about 1 a.m., and in the morning there were suspiciously long ginger hairs on Liv's pyjamas, clashing with her own auburn.

'He's very enthusiastic,' she reported. 'But I can't go out in public with him because our hair colours don't go together.'

Winter sprang into summer and Lars and I wandered, always hand in hand, and sat on the patchy grass of Bloomsbury's squares, talking. He talked more about his childhood – how he'd stood in awe, looking up at one of his father's bridges that seemed to float in the snowy sky as it spanned a valley. How he'd vowed then that he would make something of his life. How he'd thrown himself into studying to deal with the grief of his dad's early death.

I told him more about mine too – in London first, with parents who adored me, in our sunny house, the light weakening as my dad's short silences became longer. How Mum and I would have time together – we went to galleries, shopping, walking in the park – and how these times got fewer as Dad's illness got worse. How even then he could also be loving and inspiring, my cheerleader. Then, their move to the country and the moods getting longer, my mother effectively cut off from me because he needed her and she, in turn, could not forsake him.

We agreed that our family would never be like that. 'It needs to be perfect and complete and make the children feel as if they are always safe,' I told him fiercely.

We talked too, in my single bed in between long bouts of sex. Sometimes, afterwards, one of us would shift and let the

122

other lie on top for a while just to get some room to spread out. Then we would carry on our busy chatting.

'We live in a big house on a hill with you as my bird,' he told me one night when we were on his slightly bigger mattress upstairs. His room was completely unfurnished aside from this mattress on the floorboards, a makeshift desk from crates and an IKEA clothes rail where he hung the few clothes he owned. There was a pile of books in one corner and a pile of CDs – stuff from the early nineties mostly, Nirvana and other grunge bands.

'With wisteria growing up the windows,' I said.

'What is this? Wisteria?'

'It's a plant with fluffy flowers,' I told him. 'You'll be this hotshot tycoon and I'll be this big cheese branding person and we'll be professionally fulfilled while being admired for our artistic merit.'

'I hope we can do this.'

'We'll throw dinner parties where everyone will remark about how fabulous the food is and then we'll go out into the kitchen and laugh our heads off about how grown up it all is. And we'll spend evenings together, curled up on the sofa, after having pulled off the biggest deals in the world and the newspapers will write about how we are the most successful, glamorous couple ever... with at least seventy children, all perfectly behaved and gorgeous.'

Lars laughed in my ear. I could feel his hot breath. 'Well, two or three. They will be brilliant and beautiful, like you, *älskling*.'

I would roll the word around on my tongue when I wasn't with him. I was his *älskling*, his darling.

11

2017

I munched my way through fish pie, swilled down with champagne, as I sat side by side with Marti in the relaxed elegance of The Ivy. There was something comforting about being with someone I trusted so much and who'd always had my back. There was also something great – given my financial situation – about being out for a posh dinner.

Marti liked the contribution I was making to his forthcoming pitch on underwear branding to the snooty French.

'Absolute bloody diamond, this girl,' he told the waiter who periodically appeared and filled up my glass.

'You'll be fine if you stick to the diversity between French and English consumers,' I said, and put my knife and fork together.

'You really all right with this divorce business?' he asked, changing the subject.

'I'm still hoping it won't go ahead.' I changed it again, uncomfortable but smiling. 'How are your daughters?'

'Don't talk to me about them,' said Marti. 'Lucy has

disappeared in Brazil – her mother is thinking of hiring some sort of spook to go and search every polo farm in the place.'

I thought about the patient, careful woman who was Bonnie Goldwyn. She turned up smiling at all required company dos and was sociable and interested in the employees, but somehow always looked as if she'd rather be back in Hampshire, reading a book. She'd produced two beautiful daughters and now seemed to exist beside Marti rather than being married to him; he always talked about her affably but with a hint of fear.

'Terrified of her coming back up the duff,' Marti continued.

'She's on her gap year,' I said. 'That's what girls do – go abroad, fall in love. I'm sure she knows all about condoms.'

Marti glanced at me from underneath his bushy eyebrows. 'Johnnies?' he mock spat. 'You're talking to me about *johnnies* and my daughter in the same breath? Have you no shame?'

I laughed and we both looked at the pudding menu. 'Go on, have a crème brûlée and then so can I,' Marti said. 'And we'd better have another bottle of fizz and discuss sorting out getting some new customers.'

Ah. It wasn't Loosey underwear he wanted to talk about then. The troubles with my business were the real reason he wanted to have dinner with me. I realised that for the last half an hour I'd actually forgotten about being in so much difficulty.

'This thing with Campury sounds promising,' he went on.

'It really is a great opportunity. But we're only at the beginning.'

'Yes, don't depend on it. Everyone in town is going to want that account.'

'Yes, I know, but I've got to fill the hole of LandGirls.'

'Without another big account, I'm sorry, but Brand New just won't fly.' Marti looked away.

OK, now we were cutting to the chase. I took a deep breath and smiled on.

'I *will* get some more business,' I told him with the gusto of three glasses of champagne. 'How long have I got?'

'Couple of months.' He looked straight at me. 'Sorry.'

He paused and looked uncharacteristically uncertain for just a moment. 'The thing is, Ami, it's going to be tough to bring you back into the big agency if you can't make your own thing work.'

There it was: he'd said it. I looked my boss straight in his eyes and knew that he was telling the truth – he couldn't give me my old job. My reputation would be seriously damaged. After all the hullabaloo of the agency launch – our joint interviews in all the industry mags, the after-dinner speeches he gave where he used Brand New as a case study for how to 'teach this old dog new tricks' – he couldn't throw me another lifeline. I tried not to show any emotion. This was just another seismic shift in the Richter-scale eruptions that were rocking my life – it was surprising how quickly I was getting used to them.

'I'm sorry,' Marti went on, 'but I think I would have

trouble getting it past the rest of the board. But you *will* turn it around.'

I tried to smile. I would turn it around. I had to win Campury. It was the only account that was big enough to make a difference. 'I'll win the pitch and then you can give me *my* seat on the board.' It was an old joke between us.

'Got to wait for one of them to croak first.' Marti was clearly relieved that the difficult chat was over. 'There's old Haydon – he can't even remember which board meeting he's at; last week he was raving on about HSBC. You chosen your pudding?'

I tried to smile. 'Yes, I'll have a crème brûlée.'

'Nice to be out with a woman who actually eats,' said Marti and waved at the waiter.

In the loo twenty minutes later, I stared blearily at my reflection and prickled fresh goosebumps of fear. Then I took a deep breath and painted a new coat of lipstick onto my mouth. Holding onto the banister, I made my way up the stairs and gave Marti an affectionate smile.

'That crème brûlée was amazing,' I told him, sliding onto the bench.

'I ordered you a Grand Marnier. We'll drink that and then…'

'Then I'd better get home if I'm going to make money for you tomorrow.'

'Oh, I thought…' Marti looked down at his napkin.

'What?' I said.

'Oh, you know, I just wondered whether you'd like to

come back to my club for a nightcap.' Marti sniffed and there was something very, very unusual about the way that he rolled out the cliché.

It was one of his jokes. I smiled. 'I'd love to, but you know I can't. I'm a very respectable career woman and mother, you know.'

He looked at me and smiled again but his tone became very serious and his voice was thick. 'Do you think... do you think you could ever...?'

Please don't let this be happening. No. He just always flirted with me –as he did with lots of other women, despite having been married to Bonnie forever.

'Ha, ha,' I said and looked around for the waiter so that we could get the bill. 'Maybe we've had too much champagne.'

But then he grabbed my hand and looked me straight in the eyes. 'Always been bananas about you...'

'Oh, my God.' I started to get up from the bench, pulling my hand free from his.

'Sit down, please, sit down,' Marti said. 'Just hear me out.'

'You don't mean it, you've just had too much to drink. You know you're a married man.' I tried to be kind, to keep my tone light, and sat back down. Would I wake up in a minute from another tortured dream?

'Not *very* married, you know I'm not *very* married. Bonnie and me, you know that, complicated situation... years and years... never thought you'd be free... always that damn husband getting in the way…'

God, poor Bonnie. No wonder she would rather hang out in the country.

My rage rose on her behalf, and mine – this was Marti, who I'd always thought was out to mentor me. Very slowly I said, 'I'm really flattered, I am, but you know I'm never going to go out with anyone married. You're my boss, for God's sake… Look, you'll forget you said all this in the morning and so will I.' My voice had risen, however, in panic.

'Shush.' Marti looked at the other tables, whose occupants all studiously avoided looking around. 'No, it's not like that, you know it's not like that… I'm really, keen on you… and I just thought that maybe now, you know, what with you being on your own and everything, that you might look at me in a different way…'

'Look.' I tried to be as calm as possible. 'I've always really liked and respected you, but… there is no way I am going to become your… mistress.' I started to pull at my handbag, trying to get my credit card. What I wanted to say was, 'For God's sake, you're supposed to be my friend. Do you have any idea what I feel like right now and then you go and say this?'

'I didn't mean it like that… just thought I might look after you, you know, a bit.' All trace of the confident mogul was gone. I wanted to cry at what was happening – this man I'd always admired was reduced to saying, 'I'm lonely, Ami, just a silly old, lonely old man. I just thought…'

How could he do this? Now? With everything else going on that I had to deal with? Didn't he understand how *broken* I was?

I managed to pull a Mastercard from my bag. 'Did you really want my help with your pitch?'

Marti started grabbing at my hand again. 'Dammit, woman, you know I think you're the best brain that the bloody company has ever had. Don't start getting all insecure on me.'

I waved wildly in the direction of the waiter, who'd been pretending he wasn't listening to the minor fracas at our table; other diners had looked up though and some would undoubtedly recognise Marti. 'The bill, please.'

'Don't be ridiculous.' Marti looked woebegone. 'I've meant everything I've ever said. I also didn't mean to be… you know… disrespectful. And don't be silly about the bill – this is on me, you know that.'

I stood up and tried to smile at him and around me to indicate that everything was fine at Marti Goldwyn's table. 'Look, I think it's best if I go and we don't talk about this again. You know how much I think of you.'

'Ami, I just made a mistake. We'll forget all about it.'

'Goodbye,' I whispered, tears coming now as I sped through the restaurant, rushed along the street and waved down a black cab. As I sank down into the safety of the leather seat, I speed-dialled Liv.

She, distressingly, didn't seem to see the issue. 'Of course he was going to make a pass at you the moment you got divorced,' Liv said as if I were sixteen and terribly naive. 'He's been mad about you forever.'

'I just thought he was being charming,' I said.

'I know he's an old goat but don't let it get to you. You're going to have to get used to people propositioning you. Soon you'll be annoyed when they don't.'

'Don't be ridiculous. I keep telling you that I'm not interested in other men.'

'Well, they seem to be interested in you.'

I sobbed then, loudly, and the driver pretended that he couldn't hear me through the glass window. Liv told me to calm down, repeatedly. As the cab slid round the corner at Tufnell Park, I said over and over again, 'How can this all be happening to me, Liv? How?'

*

The next morning Marti sent me a huge bunch of cabbage roses and a note saying that he was very sorry. I immediately gave the roses to Bridget, thanking her for her support, and was relieved when I heard he'd left to go to Paris.

I tried to focus, working for as many hours a day as possible when I didn't need to sleep, take the children to school, bath them or do the basics of showering myself or eating. Lars called the kids when I was at work, according to Luba, but he didn't call me. She went out every evening, dressed up and smiling, with Guy Gates. I was glad to have the house to myself.

It was late one night – while I was bent over a spreadsheet at the kitchen table, drinking my way through a bottle of red – that the realisation came: I wasn't fighting for my marriage in the same way I was fighting to win an advertising account. I pushed the mouse away and sat back in my chair, wine glass in my hand.

'You want to save your family but you're not begging him to stay,' pointed out the devil of doubt from my left shoulder.

'But how much more humiliation can he put you through?' asked the angel of angst from my right. I thought about Marti making a pass at me, about having to explain to people I'd been dumped; how rejected I felt all the time; how he'd left me after everything we'd promised each other and been through. How he could make me feel even more humiliated if he rejected me again. 'Where's your feminist pride?'

I shook my head. In asking him to come back, I'd be saying that this lonely life with him travelling and me at home, trying to hold everything together, was acceptable to me. He'd promised so many times to change. Even in the last few months at Relate, we'd made timetables and agreements – how many days he would be away, how he'd look for someone else to take on the foreign travel, how he'd slow down the expansion into new countries to make time for our family. He'd promise sincerely and then for one or two days he'd be more than present, whistling away in the kitchen or playing with the kids before bed; then just as quickly, every time, he was gone again, responding to an 'emergency' at work but leaving behind the crisis in his marriage.

'It's worth one more try,' said the devil.

'Think about your dignity,' said the angel.

'Who cares about dignity when there are the kids to think about? And this is the man you love.'

'The man who walked out and told you to file for divorce.'

'Aarggh, shut up,' I told them both, out loud. Then, before I could reason with myself any more, and with the assistance of two large glasses of wine, I sat down again and picked up my phone, pressing Lars' name.

As it rang in a foreign ringtone, I took a deep breath. He would probably look at the screen, see it was me and press the equivalent of 'no, thanks very much'. But there was his voice with a slight delay: 'Ami? Is everything OK with the kids?' He sounded slightly sleepy.

'Yes, yes, they're fine… I just wanted to talk to you.'

'OK… is it about the divorce?'

'Isn't everything about that?' I said, then paused. 'Look, I think we need to talk now that… well, now that the dust has settled.'

'Now we've calmed down?' It was hard to read anything into his tone.

'Could we talk on FaceTime?' I asked. 'I'd like to have a proper chat.'

'OK,' he said, matter-of-factly. 'I'll call you back.'

I pressed off and then panicked about how awful I must

look with all my make-up worn off and lank hair from days of working so hard that dry shampoo was all I had energy for. But I had no time to do anything about it as the trill, trill of FaceTime on my laptop started up. I pressed *accept* and gradually an image of Lars, sitting at a desk in a beige hotel room, appeared on the screen; he looked as knackered as I felt.

'Hello,' I said, in what I hoped was a voice with a little endearment in it.

'Hello,' he said. 'So, what's up?'

'What's up is that my marriage is on the rocks,' I said, close to a whisper, 'and I can't help thinking that maybe we haven't really tried everything and… Lars, I don't want to get divorced.'

There. I'd said it. The devil of doubt had won.

Lars sighed and shook his head from the screen. 'Look—' he started.

I interrupted him. 'We said horrible things when we were really angry and I wondered… well, I keep thinking. I look at the kids and all I can think is how much better it's got to be for them to have parents who are married and I…'

'I know all that,' Lars said. 'But we're parents at war. It's been like this for years now and I can't see it getting any better. We argue all the time, make each other unhappy. We can't spend twenty-four hours together without one of us losing the plot.' His words came out slowly and his face was sad. 'That isn't good for them. This death thing with Tess might be the result of that.'

My heart swelled at the guilt. 'That's why we need to… We've got to fix this for them.' I carried on desperately. 'We could try to be more… we could try to be better…'

He shook his head. 'We've tried so much: I mean, *think* of all the talking we've done.' He meant the hours on the sofa after our rows in the old days and, more recently, the marriage guidance counselling, which became, in the impasse of our marriage, the only time we talked about our feelings any more; the rest of the time was shouting. Then I thought back to all the sessions at Relate where he just didn't turn up; when I just cried on our counsellor, Sasha, her handing me tissues. 'And,' he went on, 'you're not going to become happy suddenly. You're not going to change into someone who smiles at me when I walk through the door.'

Oh, that hurt. 'I smile when you arrive. It's the leaving I can't stand.'

'It just wears me out,' he said.

'It wears *you* out?' I said. What about me, home alone with the kids or working my arse off to try and save my company? But I'd blown it; his face curled into one I knew so well. It was a mirror back to me: he wished I could be the old laughing Ami, instead of this harridan who couldn't see his point of view and demanded so much more.

'The business means we could've had a better future together, but you just can't see that.' He was stiff and cold.

The irony was that I could see what I wanted *so* clearly – he and I walking, holding hands with nothing to hurry us away from each other; it came in that kind of picture, the

136

kind where we had *time* together as us and as a family with Tess and Finn. His future, though, now seemed to be all the stuff that went with that old dream of the wisteria house, except that we had no fluffy flowers and he wasn't actually *there*. Instead he was in a foreign hotel room while I was alone with the kids.

I stopped myself from saying that. Instead I said, 'We could try again, make some rules and stick to them...'

'Look, I'm tired and you're tired and we're not getting anywhere,' said Lars more kindly, but then, 'You told me you couldn't live like this any more, remember? You told me you'd leave if I didn't?' A flashback to an argument a few weeks ago when I'd tried to give him an ultimatum. Yes, I'd said that. Was that the moment when he'd decided he would leave me?

'But...' I said, and tears came again. I'd been as bad as he was. But I couldn't help saying, 'If you wanted to be here, you would.'

'See?' Lars said. 'Here we go again.'

'All I wanted was to have a husband who gave a fuck about me,' I said, crying now. I couldn't stop – I knew I was probably hammering the last nail into the coffin of our marriage even as I tried to bring it back to life.

'It's 1 a.m. here,' said Lars.

'And here is...?' I asked.

'I think I'm in Frankfurt,' he said and was a little bit rueful before he returned to his point. 'It's the same old argument and I'm tired... It must be midnight back there.

We need to go to bed.'

I looked straight at the screen where my husband stared back from another country and thought only about how we should be going to bed together.

'You're really, really hurting me,' I told him as the tears streaked down my face.

'Go to bed, Amelia,' he said and the screen went blank.

My shoulders shook as I got up and wobbled to bed.

Love had made us cruel in ways that shocked me, but the end of it was brutal.

When I woke up in the morning with a wine ache across my forehead, I knew I had to accept the grim realisation that it was over.

*

The next day Lars made it clear he thought it was, emailing me the 'without prejudice' spreadsheet with a note that just said: 'As discussed the other day'.

I instantly picked up the phone and made another appointment with Cathy. Then I gave up on the campaign for one evening and instead spent it scribbling the reasons why I couldn't live with him so hard that I made marks in the kitchen table. I was so angry and hurt that I couldn't cry.

'You're sure?' Cathy asked when I arrived in her office.

'Absolutely sure,' I said from the other side of the desk.

'First of all, I hope to help you keep your home. Our homes are our castles, after all.'

I wondered what her house was like, with Jeremy. 'Where do you live?'

'A little place in Bromley.' She smiled away.

'Do you think he's trying to pull a fast one?' I said, indicating the spreadsheet about our money, which was in front of her.

'It's difficult without complete financial disclosure,' Cathy said. 'We'll need to get his company accounts – *all* of them – and have a proper dig through.'

'I don't want to be unnecessarily adversarial,' I said, imagining a long drawn-out court battle over our unimpressive terraced house.

'Of course not.' Cathy winked. 'But we should never underestimate the other side. From what I can see, if you want to keep that house, you need a lump sum from your husband and to keep on working as hard as you can. That'll be the court view.'

'My largest customer went under.'

Cathy smiled sympathetically and then a gleam appeared in her eye. She was like one of those big cats on David Attenborough that loll in the sun until it's time to begin the brutal chase. 'All the more reason to get a good settlement from the other side.'

Lars was now 'the other side'. Given the way he was behaving, that felt appropriate. 'So, what happens now?'

'Have you thought of your reasons?'

'Absolutely.'

'I just *adore* an efficient client,' said Cathy, twirling her fountain pen.

'Firstly, I would like to say that he spends less than three fourteenths of his week in my and the children's company and that includes sleeping.'

'Three fourteenths?'

'I worked it out.'

'Hmm, you poor darling. However, I suggest we write that he is absent from the marital home for a significant proportion of time, leaving you lonely,' said Cathy. 'The judge might understand that better than fractions.'

'Sounds dull, though, doesn't it?' I'd spent a lot of time adding half-hours with hours to come up with a precise truth.

'What's the next one?'

'He takes no responsibility for childcare or household management.'

'How would "my husband makes no contribution to running our house and little contribution as a parent" sound?'

'It's certainly succinct.'

'And accurate?'

I was bleak. 'Well, when he's with the kids he's fantastic, but it's just less and less often so, yes, accurate.'

'Number three?'

'His career is more important than mine even though I have continually worked extremely hard for our joint benefit.'

'But you don't earn as much as him? Some women earn more, you know.' A brief cloud seemed to pass in her eyes. Was that what she'd done? Kept Jeremy from the distribution centre in a style to which he'd become accustomed?

I concentrated on the question. 'Well, no, but I did in the early days while he built his company. I supported us both and before all this I wasn't really doing badly…'

'And then it's their wives who apparently affect their manhood, emasculate them and suffer wholeheartedly as a consequence,' continued Cathy as if I hadn't spoken. Ah, all was not rosy in the little place in Bromley.

'Well, that isn't really the case in our marriage,' I said.

Cathy took a deep breath then and shook her head as if she was coming back to reality as I spoke.

I looked down at my lap. 'Number four? We're no longer lovers or even friends.'

12

2008

Lars and I were crammed into a corner of Balthazar, the teeming bistro in Soho, New York, with a silver plate of crushed ice between us, trying to decide whether meaty West Coast oysters tasted better than skinny East Coast ones.

'These take more than one gulp to get down,' I said. 'The other ones just slide.'

Lars tipped shallot vinegar onto another one; his smile was as big as mine. 'I don't need any aphrodisiacs but if this is what they taste like let's have them every day.'

Around us New Yorkers were talking a thousand to the dozen. Round tables of boisterous families jostled for attention with each other. Vast mirrors, silvered with age, hung from the walls.

'Oysters are much better with lots of chips.' I scooped several pencil-thin fries from the paper cone in front of me. Then I raised my champagne glass to him – we'd bought the cheapest bottle on the menu and it didn't come from France – and cocked my head to the side. 'Here's to you.' That morning, high up in a glass tower on Avenue of the

Americas, Lars had finally signed contracts with investors that would mean i-patent could turn from a struggling idea to a potential business – given several thousand hours of hard work from him.

I'd waited downstairs in the art deco lobby, watching striding New Yorkers go to meetings clutching coffee. I'd crossed fingers on both hands as I'd prayed that the deal would go through. I'd made Lars practise his final pitch all night in a tiny, dingy, but still barely affordable hotel room deep in the East Village, but it seemed impossible that our fortunes were really about to change.

At that time, my career was going pretty well, but Lars was still doing a bunch of part-time jobs to pay for his share of the rent while he worked on getting i-patent going. We would unravel ourselves from each other every morning in bed – by then we lived together in a shared room in another flat in our building, Liv having gone travelling – and I would put on office clothes and Lars would put on whatever logo-ed polo shirt went with the van-driving job he was currently doing. He refused to try to get anything else, saying that he needed all his mental energy to get the funding he needed.

Meanwhile, I'd just been appointed Senior Account Manager at Goldwyn. I went to meetings where I waited for colleagues and potential clients to tell me that I didn't know what I was talking about. Instead, they listened. I'd recently made it into the back pages of *Campaign* as 'one who should be watched' and the big boss, Marti, had started to take some notice of me.

'You're the clever sod, aren't you?' Marti had boomed when he'd met me in the lift. I'd blushed with pleasure and said something about not being that clever really and he'd said, as the doors had opened in the Goldwyn foyer, 'Take the praise when you get it. The right response is, "Thank you – what's the next challenge?"' I'd laughed nervously, loving every minute.

In New York, when the lift door had opened and Lars had come out, I'd been praying to every god I'd never believed in that he'd got the deal. He'd given me a small smile that had been matched by his eyes but had waited until we'd gone out through the revolving door onto the pavement before he'd let out a whoop, picked me up and whirled me round.

'Is it really real?' I'd whispered.

'For you and for me,' he'd whispered back. 'I love you, *älskling*.' It had felt like a team effort, as if every sentence of that pitch had been scribed in my brain.

We'd walked all the way downtown, twenty blocks in the odd slice of sunshine that had managed to land between the buildings into the New York street. As we'd walked he'd told me every detail of the pitch; how he was finally going to be able to buy some Apple Macs.

'This is just the beginning. I'm so happy. I couldn't have done this without you. And I'm doing this for us – we're going to have a perfect family, Ami.'

I'd clutched Lars' hand and strode along beside him in the wide New York avenue. He was wearing his one and only suit – with no tie but a blue shirt that we'd hung in the disgusting hotel shower that morning so that the creases would fall out in the steam. He looked as tall as usual but somehow bigger in all ways. We'd finally decided that we could risk spending some money on a celebration lunch.

'We'd better eat all the chips because I'm pretty sure we can't afford pudding,' I said now.

'You're very bossy,' Lars said. As his English steadily improved and the sing-song lessened to a lilt, he still experimented with words; 'bossy' had been his word of the moment for a while now, always said with a big smile.

When we'd drunk every last drop of fake champagne and eaten every chip, we went out into the dusk of Soho and started to walk again, down through Chinatown and towards the river. I'd heard that the view from the Brooklyn Bridge was the best there was of Manhattan. Eventually we could smell the Hudson. We climbed the walkway that led up to the big industrial arches across the river, dodging caricature artists and stalls selling plastic replicas of the Empire State Building.

'You must not look back,' I ordered, 'until we're at least halfway.'

'See? You're very bossy.' Lars grinned and kissed me.

Up and up we went. The steel wires of the bridge made a cage over us. Then finally, as the bridge flattened, I stopped for breath and put my hands over Lars' eyes and gently turned him. As I came round myself I gasped. Below me, crammed into what appeared to be a tiny island, were thousands of glass steeples, looking as if they were jostling

145

for every inch of space with each other. It was as if they had been dropped in, reshuffled and reshuffled again. And as I turned, there, in the speckled early evening light, was the green gleam of the Statue of Liberty.

Lars pulled me to him and with one arm tucked around each other we pointed out all the shapes from the famous skyline that we thought we recognised.

'All those dreams of all those people,' Lars said as we finally went back down.

As we walked, we talked about ours, and how they were only really just starting.

13

2017

Ben rang while I was despairing about the lack of progress on the pitch. 'Ah, Amelia,' he said. 'It's very important to feed the working brain. I know you get all stressed and busy and that's probably what keeps you so thin without exercise, which, incidentally, Liv thinks is a bit unfair because she tends to put weight on her bottom.'

Quite how shit-faced must Liv have been to tell him all this drivel? 'How's it going?' I asked.

'Manic. But as I was saying, it's very important to take regular breaks in order not to restrict the creative mind, so I wondered if you wanted lunch? Don't want to be a stalker or anything but…'

Maybe this was how single people behaved. It'd been so long; how did I know what it was like in a world where everyone swiped left and right? 'Sorry, I have a working lunch with the creative team.' This was a lie.

'You wanted to be a creative yourself originally, didn't you?'

'Yes, yes, I did,' I said. Did he know everything about

me?

'That's right. That was about the time you had a boyfriend who worked in the British Museum – let me remember, was his name really *Archibus*?'

I snorted half in amazement and half in outrage. Liv had not only told him about me, she'd given him an unadulterated biography.

I sniffed and decided to fight back – prospective client or not. 'You must have been really bored at your own work party to listen to all that crap from Liv.'

'It's true. I was really bored and then I met Liv, who tried to set me up with you, which made it much more entertaining.'

'But it was all bollocks.'

'If you'd only come for lunch with me then we could test how much of it is true.'

'Nope,' I said. 'Not doing it.'

There was a deep laugh at the end of the phone. 'Nope, not doing it,' he mimicked. 'Not never.'

'This is turning into a very childish conversation,' I said, but couldn't help smiling, 'when I have a lot to do to show you the amazing work that Goldwyn can pull off. And when you know I can't meet you socially as we have a competitive pitch on.'

'All right, I'll leave you alone,' he said. 'But amazing work, Amelia, that's exactly what we need.'

*

The trouble was, so far, it was crap. And we had just a week to go. I'd sat through a frustrating meeting that morning after Bridget triumphantly informed me that she and the creative team 'had had a breakthrough'.

'We've done an all-nighter on it.'

'You've been here *all night*?'

'Yes, all night.' Bridget was smug. 'I'll phone the boys and we'll group in five?'

The creatives – two twenty-somethings called Jake and Luis – came through the door looking grey with tiredness, their usually spiky hair flat and greasy. Jake was wearing a red T-shirt with white lettering that said, 'Fuck you. Yes I will.' I hoped they were going to present the work that I'd been struggling all week to see. My own ideas had been very lacking – it was as if I'd had some kind of creative block.

Bridget led the way to the table in the corner and we all sat down. 'It's a strategy based entirely on the latest qualitative statistics of consumer diversity among the target A purchaser group in this country,' she started.

I blinked. 'Really?'

'We're talking the renaissance of the handbag,' Bridget continued, 'as a work of art on a par with the Sistine Chapel and Michelangelo's David…'

'Shall we just let the ideas speak for themselves? I might understand a little better then.'

The two creatives shuffled.

'Luis?'

'Him,' he said, indicating Jake with a shrug of his head.

'Jake? Come on: get the boards out on the table.'

'The thing is…' Jake started.

'Yes?'

'The thing is, we're not sure that this strategy works,' he finished and refused to look at Bridget, who, turning puce, gasped and then started, her voice rising like an ill-thought crescendo.

'But, you said you wouldn't tell her. You said that you didn't think it was that bad…'

'It was six o'clock in the morning and we'd have said anything.' Luis spoke straight to me.

'And we'd had to stay all night because she wouldn't agree with any of our work…' Jake became braver. 'And so, about four in the morning, when we were just comatose, we came up with this really basic idea about works of art…'

'And she loved it,' Luis joined in.

I raised my eyes to look at Bridget, who was mouthing nothings.

'And we said we'd back her up because she was desperate… and we felt sorry for her,' Jake continued.

Bridget sank her head into her hands and clutched her temples.

'…said don't worry, she'd pull it off… she'd think of something and you'd buy it…'

'*Bridget,*' I said. Did she think I was so useless now that I would just go with a substandard idea?

'And we said we'd go along with it, if she'd just bloody leave us alone to get a couple of hours of kip.'

Bridget let out a low moan. I was angry and very sorry for her all at the same time.

'Is this true, Bridget?'

'And when we woke up just now on the sofa in the boardroom, I said to Luis, "We're not the creative brains we want to be if we let that shit go through,"' continued Jake.

'Is it true?'

'And I said, "We've got to go in there and say what we really think…"'

'So sorry, Bridget,' they chorused as a finale, 'but it was our reputation or you.'

Bridget burst into tears. 'I was just trying to push you to see how innovative we could be.'

I leant over to rub her back. I should've been more helpful, more present, more supportive; I should also have remembered what it was like to get your first big job to work on when you were in your mid-twenties and very ambitious.

'Just how crap is it?' I asked.

'It's absolutely crap.' Luis turned round an image of the Sistine Chapel roof where his rough pen had drawn handbags attached to the naked hips of cherubs.

It was truly awful. I shivered.

Jake turned round another of the statue of David with a Campury bag tucked over his shoulder. It was more than an affront to this homage to man's perfection – it was about the most basic advertising idea that was ever likely to be presented to a major European fashion company.

'You'd be laughed out of the pitch,' Jake said.

Bridget let out another moan. 'I just wanted it to be perfect. I wanted to prove myself like you did and I thought that with everything that's going on with you…'

'You mean my divorce?' I pursed my lips and Luis and Jake looked at their knees again.

'Well,' whispered Bridget, 'you know, just everything that's been going on.'

'I'm getting divorced from my husband, not my brain,' I said as calmly as I could and tried to smile.

'She going to cry too?' Luis asked Jake in a whisper.

'Not sure, mate, not sure at all.'

'It's all right,' I said, and then looked at the silent ticking of my watch showing the days falling away.

If we didn't think of something soon, I was going to face downright ritual humiliation at the hands of a man who probably knew the colour of every pair of knickers in my underwear drawer.

But much more than this, I needed this account if I was going to save my career and help my children to have a consistent roof over their heads.

'Right,' I said. Jake, Luis and Bridget waited as if I were the Dalai Lama about to dispense eternal wisdom. 'Any good ideas that Bridget threw out?' I asked the two boys.

'There was the one based on how glad the cow was to turn up as a handbag,' said Luis.

'Oh, God, no.' I put my face in my hands like Bridget.

'Or the one with the handbag in formaldehyde, very beautifully shot, suspended in time – you know, ripping off

152

Hirst…'

'Sounds better.' I saw a glimmer of light at the end of the tunnel.

'But there were problems with the copyright.' I saw the light extinguish so that I was left in claustrophobic darkness.

The two boys looked despondent. Jake asked if they could go get some kip so they could think straight again. 'We'll come up with something, Ami,' they said and shuffled off like zombies.

'You'd better go home and sleep too,' I told Bridget. I sent her off with a small stiff hug.

Please, please go, I thought. I need to be alone to scream with stress.

*

Later that day I was heading to Selfridges to research Campury's concession there and see how shoppers viewed the bags for myself, thinking it might lead to a divine moment of inspiration. I was striding down Oxford Street – still achingly cold – and glaring at all the foreign tourists. Why weren't London pavements divided into lanes, like motorways or swimming pools, so that the people with places to go, things to do, could stride purposefully in line with their stress?

My mobile rang. 'Amelia? It's Paul.'

'Paul…?'

'Paul Carter – from the school.'

'Are Tess and Finn all right?' Panic rose in me.

'Yes, absolutely fine considering the circumstances. I was just wondering whether you'd noticed anything newly odd about Tessa's behaviour at home?'

I stood with my back to the window of H&M, where plastic mannequins promised that life would always be cheap and very cheerful.

'No, well, not anything out of the ordinary, but then—'

'She's leading funeral processions in the playground, Amelia.' He said this as if my daughter had been caught selling crack with a gang of hoodie-wearing criminals.

'Oh, I see.'

'She is inveigling other children into joining in mock funerals at breaktimes,' Mr Carter whispered. 'So, you see, we need to think about an intervention here.'

Interventions were for people who drank vodka like water, had children by their brothers and went on *Jeremy Kyle*, but I said, 'Yes, I can see that that might be a little—'

'Lining children up behind her and making *the symbol of the cross*, Amelia.'

I gripped my fingers around the phone. If you weren't Tessa's teacher, I hissed to myself. 'Thank you,' I said instead. 'I appreciate the call and will certainly do everything I can to ensure that Tess realises why it's not the done thing in the playground.'

I put my fist in front of my mouth to stop the anguish of my guilt. Then I turned around and stuck my hand out for the first cab with a yellow light that would take me to look after the broken-hearted children of a broken home.

14

2009

It was midnight, dreamtime, when Lars insisted we got in his car – he'd bought an old orange Mini, the babiest car. I wanted to be warm in bed, wrapped around him, rather than being made to go out into the cold and drive. Still, he was tense with anticipation and excitement and that was hard to resist.

'Just tell me where we're going,' I grumbled as we shot in and out of the snaking London traffic. But I didn't moan too much. As i-patent.com got going, he was, more than ever, like a mountain goat that knows it's on the path to a meadow full of grass.

'Shush, bossy girl.' He grinned.

I snuggled down in the passenger seat and turned up the tinny stereo so that it played cheesy love songs even louder.

When we arrived at Primrose Hill, he awkwardly pulled a wicker hamper from the tiny boot and, ordering me to 'get going', led the way up the smooth round shape of the hill. London started to lay itself out behind us, like a carpet of Swarovski.

I huffed and puffed, wrapped up in my coat over my pyjamas. 'I really love you,' I told him, despite this, into the darkness.

'I really love you too,' he said.

At the top he cracked open champagne and carefully spread out Tupperware boxes of strawberries, chicken and bread onto an old car blanket that he laid on top of the grass.

The moon had decided to throw a single spotlight, just meant for a dancing couple. I pretended not to shiver with cold and smiled instead, even wider. Just for a moment, I dared to hope what might happen next. I'd, of course, dreamt and dreamt about the moment when we would move our story forward, just as we'd described to one another.

'I think we ought to get married, *älskling*,' he said.

'Yes, yes, yes,' I cried.

'I love you SO much,' he told me as we kissed.

He had a ring: it was a diamond that was flawless rather than huge. Each facet seemed to find a star of its own in the sky. 'It's gorgeous,' I whispered. People said hearts felt like bursting; mine felt as if it were going to sprinkle starlight when it popped.

'I chose it for the cut and colour,' he told me. 'I researched it. Lots.'

I knew that he had, because that was what he was like. I stood up on top of the hill in the middle of the freezing cold of the night and, putting my hands to my mouth to make a megaphone, started to shout: 'LONDON? Are you LISTENING? I am going to marry the MAN I LOVE!'

15

2017

'Tess, Finn,' I called, pushing open the front door. 'Darlings, Mummy's home.'

There was a clatter from the playroom and Tessa's face appeared around the door. 'Are you poorly again?'

'No, darling, I just wanted to hang out with you.'

Tessa smiled uncertainly.

'Where's Luba? And where's Finn?' I picked her up and planted kisses all over her face.

'I've buried him,' Tessa said.

'You've done what?' I put her down and strode towards the playroom door. Pushing it open, I was confronted with a vast pile of cushions – the coloured IKEA ones from the playroom sofa, the downy, decorative ones from the hall settle, the pillows from my bed and Tess and Finn's beds – rising up from the centre of the room into a rectangular mountain and, on top of that, what appeared to be the dying daffodils that this morning had been in the middle of the kitchen table, now minus their vase.

It was a macabre and naïve interpretation. It was also a

grave.

I shook with fear and gasped. 'Tess, where's Finn?'

'In the grave.' Tessa pointed to the bottom of the mountain of suffocating cushions.

'Oh, my God.' I dived towards the floor, throwing each cushion sideways, the daffodils to the left, my bed pillows to the right. 'Finn! Are you all right? Oh, Finn.'

And there, at the bottom of the pile, was Finn, eyes shut, minus the healthy red of his cheeks as I removed the big floor cushion that had been covering his face.

I screamed then, 'Oh, my God,' grabbing his head. Tears mixed with my hot breath and it was impossible to know whether Finn was sharing my air or not. I pulled him by the shoulders, limp, into my lap.

'Is he proper dead?' Tessa gasped from the doorway.

'Of course I'm not proper dead,' Finn said, opening his eyes.

My breath sounded like a steam train. 'Oh, I thought you might have suffocated,' I told him in between gasps.

'What's suffocated?' Tessa asked from behind me, and suddenly she was there, on my lap too.

I rocked to and fro, clutching the children to me. Tears rolled down my face as if they'd come from nowhere. Look at what could have happened. My heart was palpitating, my thoughts running amok: death, the incredible, unimaginable loss, the 'what if I hadn't come home?'… Where the hell was Luba? I shook my head and shouted her name, but it came out as a whispered wail, loud in intention rather than reality. I hugged the children to me ferociously. She must have gone upstairs and just left them playing.

Eventually, I began to remember that it was me who must be strong. 'Now, tell me, what's been going on?' I asked in a whisper into Tessa's hair.

'We were just playing graves,' Tessa explained with a sob that seemed to erupt somewhere deep down in the tiny volcano of her soul. 'I was pretending to bury Finn.'

Luba must have been gone for quite a while for them to build such a sophisticated pile of cushions.

'I won't be dead again,' Finn promised as the salt of his tears joined mine.

'You must never ever do that again,' I said. I pushed Tessa back and looked deep into her eyes. 'Your brother could have been seriously hurt if he'd stayed under there any longer. Do you understand?'

Tessa nodded and sobbed again. 'We were just playing.'

'I know, but, darling, you've got to stop playing at being dead. Here. In the playground – no more funerals. Look what trouble you could've got into.' I needed to have a very, very strong word with Luba. Perhaps she'd fallen asleep upstairs?

'You're going to die though,' Tessa said into my neck.

'No.' I seized her hand and looked at her. 'You have to start listening to what I'm saying. I am not going to die. Nor is Daddy. No one is dying and no one will die until they are very old and very poorly. And when they do, they will go to a beautiful place.'

'Will I see you again in heaven, Mummy?'

'Look, let's have a proper chat.' Without letting go of either of them, I pulled them onto the sofa behind me, where, with its cushions missing, the springs pressed into my bottom.

'First of all, no one is going to heaven for a very long time. Secondly, when any of us finally does go there, we'll all be together again in one place.'

'Together again with Daddy?'

I took a deep breath. 'Well, you and Finn will always be with Daddy and you will always be with me. It's just that—'

'You're not friends with Daddy now, are you?' Finn asked. 'Never mind, you will be next week.'

I hugged him closer. 'Well, Daddy and I have fallen out a little bit,' I said. Tessa looked at me, waiting to see what would happen next.

'But we're going to try to be better friends,' I continued with more certainty than I knew I had. 'It's just that Daddy and I don't think we should live together at the moment, because we argue too much.' The time had come to be truthful with them, I thought. There was clearly no going back. The books advocated sitting down together but I couldn't wait for Lars when they needed clarity.

'Like me and Paolo?' asked Tessa, talking about a classmate for whom she had a particular animosity.

'Paolo and I,' I said automatically. 'Well, a bit like that. Imagine how if you lived with Paolo, you'd argue all the time. But the thing is, just because Daddy and I aren't living in the same house any more, it doesn't mean that anything

161

nasty is going to happen. You'll see him all the time and then, maybe, he'll get his own house. And I'm still here, looking after you. The important thing is that we both love you two very much indeed and that will never change.'

'Can we go to McDonald's?' Finn asked.

'Yes,' I said and both of them looked at me with wonder and then gave me a kiss on the cheek. 'Go and put your shoes on.' Now to go and find Luba and discover just what the hell was going on.

'Luba,' I shouted, as we went into the hall. 'Luba, where are you?'

'She went out,' Tessa said.

'What do you mean, *"went out"*?'

'She went down the road to see Guy Gates.'

'He hasn't even got me a football shirt yet, the bugger,' Finn joined in. 'She said he would.'

I shook my head and tried to focus on the bigger issue. 'She went down the road to Guy Gates' house and left you here on your own?'

'It's only down the road, Mummy,' said Tessa, shrugging on her coat.

It was next door but one. 'It's only just down where?' I grabbed the hands of both children and started towards the door. I felt my blood rage hot as if it would boil from my body. She'd left the children alone to nearly die.

'But I can't go to McDonald's without wearing shoes,' Finn said as I hurried them down the cold tiles of the steps, slamming the door behind me.

'You'll get soggy socks from the person who washes the floors.' Tessa careered after me down the path. I was more than striding, I was jogging, spurred by a rage I didn't know I had in me.

'Socks don't matter for now,' I said.

'Guy Gates kisses Luba with his tongue,' Finn said in vague awe as we swung into the front garden.

'Guy and Luba sitting in a tree, K – I – S – S – I – N – G,' chanted Tess as I began to thump furiously on the blue sheen of his front door.

'Shhhh,' I told her and banged harder so that the echo of my fury resounded around the empty hallway behind the glass. I bent down and, prodding the letterbox open, started to scream out the au pair's name, louder and louder. 'Luba…' I heard my angry shriek bounce back around the hallway.

'I think Luba's been naughty,' Finn said.

Finally, the banging was joined by heavy footfalls on the stairs and, behind the glass, the thickset form of a man started shouting, 'For fuck's sake, what's the matter?'

He swung the door open, a twenty-five-year old's naked torso topped with matted, dark hair. I briefly registered that Guy Gates was wearing only a bright red towel and that he was staring in amazement at my probably equally red face, fist still poised to thump the door, the shoeless Finn beside me, with Tess behind him.

'All right, darlin'?' the footballer asked as I drew myself up to my full five feet five.

163

'No, I'm bloody not,' I started to scream. 'Just where is *my* au pair who is being paid to look after *my* children?'

'You talkin' about *my* Luba?' Guy looked quizzical.

'Where is she? Upstairs getting laid by you when she should have been looking after my children? Finn was nearly killed.'

'All right, calm down, darlin',' Guy said. 'They look perfeckly all right to me.'

What a total arsehole. I barged forward like a bailiff trying to force entry.

Guy used his bulk to block my way. 'I'll go and see if Luba wants to see you,' he said.

'She works for me, if you hadn't noticed, you ignorant tosser...' I screamed. 'I could sue her. I could get her deported. I could—'

'Luba's been very naughty,' Finn said.

'I thought you said no one was going to die and now you say that Finn was nearly killed.' Tessa burst into tears. 'That's the same as murdered.'

I squatted down beside her, cursing myself now. 'Now look what you've done,' I said to Guy, blaming him anyway.

'Luba? Darlin'? There's someone here to see you.' Guy ignored me and went back into his hallway.

She appeared slowly round the corner of the stairs, a defiant smile dancing at the corners of her mouth as she descended, languidly wrapping a long silk dressing gown around her. I mouthed words of rage like a guppy fish on amphetamines.

'Oh, hello, Ami,' she said.

I stood up and grasped Tess's head, pulling her close to my shaking body. 'What *is* going on?'

'What the fuck is going on is that she quit,' Guy said.

I mouthed more words of nothing.

Luba looked thoroughly pleased with herself. Reaching the bottom of the stairs, she grasped Guy's hairy muscle of an arm, and hung from it.

'Yep.' Guy sniffed. 'My Luba will be staying here from now on. I'll look after her.'

'Me live here?' Luba had calf eyes.

'Course you can, princess,' Guy told her in a voice thick with unrealised desire and bent his head on its short neck to kiss her.

'Luba and Guy sitting on a log, oh, my God, they done a snog,' whispered Tessa.

'For Christ's sake,' I screamed. 'I've never heard anything so ridiculous in my whole life…' Before I realised that they still had tongues locked like the antlers of stags in battle. I humphed with outrage. 'What is going on is that she is sacked! S-A-C-K-E-D with a capital S!' Their wet pink tongues caroused together as if they were simply saying, 'Up yours.'

'I will be reporting you to the police for child neglect,' I roared on. 'You will be deported and never allowed to work with children again.' I battled with myself to not wrest their heads apart as they systematically ate each other's faces. 'Just you wait.'

I scooped up Finn and marched down the path, occasionally throwing another, 'Disgusting!' over my shoulder. I heard the door slam behind me.

'Who's going to look after us now, Mummy?' Tessa asked.

'I'll sort something out,' I said. I took a deep breath. 'Now, who wants a fish burger?'

*

Seated on a pint-sized chair under the arches of McDonald's, I battled the nausea of the smell of fried food. I would phone the police as soon as we got home. I would phone the au pair agency and get her blacklisted. I would firebomb Guy Gates' house…

I rang Parminder as the children munched away. She was outraged. 'Oh, that's so awful. I know she didn't look very smiley but she always seemed to care for the kids. And Tessa! What's making her behave like this?'

It was time I started to tell people. 'It's Lars and me,' I whispered. 'We had a massive row – worse than usual – a couple of weeks ago, and he says he wants a divorce. Of course, the kids are picking up on that.'

'Poor Ami! Why didn't you tell me? I would have done everything I could to help. Are you OK? I thought you looked a bit down. What can we do? Shall I make you a casserole or a pie or something?' I almost laughed at that. I didn't need food in dishes; I needed my children healed.

'You poor thing. You should have told us. Look, we're off to Manchester to see the folks for half-term, but as soon as we get back I'll give you a break…' We talked about finding a counsellor for Tessa; Parminder recommended the NHS: 'the best people, but you have to wait'.

It was as I put the phone down to concentrate on Tess and Finn that I realised the impact of something she'd said. Half-term meant childcare all week long and I had seven days left before I was supposed to present the work that would save my agency. But even if I could find childcare, could I leave them after what had happened? I'd obviously been neglecting my children. I wanted to put my arms around them and glue them to me forever.

Around me happy families ate Happy Meals and I tried to smile on.

'I need you, Lars,' I whispered. 'Please help me.'

*

That night I called him, listening to the sound of a foreign ringtone with increasing rage, until on the fifth time of trying he answered the phone. 'Amelia? Not again. It's the middle of the night in Russia.'

'Lars, this isn't about me – it's the children.'

'Oh, my God, are they all right?'

'Well, they are now. But Luba…' Even though the kids were in bed, I kept going to check that they were breathing in the same way I did when they were babies. 'Luba… she's

167

run off with the footballer from down the road.'

'Good God, Guy Gates. Supposed to be one of the thickest players in the league.'

'She abandoned the children and they built a grave out of cushions and Finn could have suffocated and—'

'That's outrageous. Were they in real danger?'

'Well, they could've been but I came home early.'

'What happened? Are you sure they're OK?' His voice rose with the same panic I'd felt a few hours back.

'Yes, they're fine… I've rung the police but they say it's a matter for the agency as au pairs are not classified as proper childcare and, therefore, it's *our* fault—'

'Are we in trouble with the law? Did you know that about au pairs?'

'No, of course I didn't. Did you? Everyone has au pairs and they look after the kids before and after school and—'

'Christ, Amelia, what've we done?'

'We've made a decision that nearly went badly wrong,' I whispered.

'Thank God you came home in time,' he said. 'How long has this been going on for, you think? Do you think she's left them before?'

'Tess said that she had just popped out before but never for long,' I said. When I'd heard that, I'd put my head in my hands and asked Tess why she hadn't told me. She'd said she hadn't really minded because Luba had said she could watch more TV. I'd gulped down my guilt and smiled at her, making her promise that she would never hide anything like that from me again.

'I called the agency and they said they'll make sure she never works as an au pair again,' I told Lars. 'Apparently there is some sort of register. But, oh, God, Lars, it was terrible.'

'Shhh,' he said, more gently than I'd heard for a long time. 'It's over. But, God, I'm worried about the kids, Amelia.'

'And so am I.'

'They need us now. I'll try to get there as soon as I can. I was supposed to be coming home today but there's been a blizzard and there are no planes taking off at all.'

I remembered vaguely seeing something about this on Twitter and groaned.

'Lars, it's not just that. I've got a terrible problem too with this pitch – there's less than a week to go and we have no idea. If I don't win it then I'm going to have no business.'

'It's a real shame when you've worked so hard. But if it doesn't work then you can always go back to working for Marti.'

'He says I can't because he made such a big noise about what a success Brand New was going to be.' There was no point telling him about the upmarket pass Marti had made. 'I just need your help, *please*.' I tried to be calm. 'Can you come back and look after the kids for a few days – even evenings or the weekend?'

'Look, I'll call you later and see if there is any way of getting home. I'll try and get a train if there are no planes.'

'The pitch is next Thursday and it's half-term on Monday and… Do you know when your mother is coming back?'

'I think she goes to Colombia next.'

'Marquez,' I said, talking about the next author on her trip. 'Oh, God, what am I going to do?' I let out a moan as panic rose.

'I think you need to get Marti to change his mind about taking you back so that you have a job and not this kind of pressure on your business. The kids have to come first.'

'For fuck's sake, this is both of our problem, Lars. *Please…*'

Lars blew out air of exasperation. 'I know that,' he said. 'This is a real wake-up call, believe me. I can't believe it's happened. I'll call you later as soon as I know what's going on with the planes.' There was a pause when it sounded as if he was going to say something else, but then he just repeated, 'I'll call later. Try and get some rest,' and I heard the click of the phone going down.

I looked up at the ceiling towards my sleeping children and thought for a while about how I'd let them down before they'd even started in life.

16

2010

Saturday morning. Even as I woke from the restorative twelve-hour sleep that followed a week at work, I knew I was pregnant. I felt different, almost as if I were more complete.

Lars snored quietly beside me on his pillow, rhythmic intakes of breath followed by comic exhalations. I tried to count back to my last period – was it late? I'd stopped taking the pill a few months after we got married and I'd automatically started drinking very little but that was as much to do with working my arse off as with any baby that might come along. Children had been part of our plan ever since we'd frenziedly discussed what our future looked like back in Bloomsbury, but we hadn't got to the point of counting days or panicking every month yet.

At that time, Lars' business had launched in the UK, and he'd started to spend more and more time gazing at a laptop. Meanwhile, I progressed steadily, working long hours too. There were many nights when he and I managed only to eat a quick 11 p.m. takeaway before we crawled into bed. Sex was still joyous but quite often perfunctory, needing to fit around a busy diary full of ambition.

I counted back the days over Christmas and New Year and was not surprised to find that my period was a week late. I felt my boobs, which seemed somehow to have become rounder and heavier.

I was up the duff. I didn't need to wee on a stick to know that. I patted my tummy under the sheets and said very slowly in a whisper, 'Hello, you.'

*

A couple of months later, the same bed. I woke again – this time from the naps that stopped me feeling constantly as if I was about to either fall down with tiredness or vomit on the spot. I could feel Lars' hand holding my gently swelling stomach under the duvet. I didn't open my eyes but instead listened to him, talking very quietly almost to himself, almost as if he were practising speaking English: 'You're cherished,' he was saying. 'A cherished offspring. A progeny.'

'Family. Fam. We're going to be a fam,' I told him later.

'Our *familj*,' he told me, giving me another word in my growing Swedish vocabulary. 'The most important thing.'

*

Our sagging old second-hand sofa. A different day, a much

172

bigger tummy, straining under one of Lars' old shirts in the heat of the early summer. His laptop on his knees as we picked through the plan for the international expansion of i-patent.

'Shall we go for a walk?' I said. 'I think I'm going to melt.' The sash window was propped open but the air was so still it felt as if it would crush me.

'Hmmm, *älskling*?' Lars was busy inputting new figures into another column of the spreadsheet. 'No, I'm sorry, I can't. I've got to get this done.'

I remember feeling, then, the first pangs of jealousy from the sheer focus his business got, but put them aside as the irrational feelings of a pregnant woman.

I got up and slowly ambled to the corner shop by myself, where I bought two ice lollies. The first lick of mine was so sharp and cold that it ricocheted around my brain, freezing it for a little while.

*

Then the bump became a baby; the two of us became three. Those first few months I barely remember; just as a blur of extreme love for Tessa combined with a whole new understanding of exhaustion. Even when she was asleep in her cot in the silent hours of the early morning, it was time to strap myself up to the breast pump and sit in our kitchen, like a cow on a milking machine. But that meant of course that I could sometimes kick Lars in the night and beg him to feed her: 'It's your turn.' And at the weekends I would roll over, back into the depths of our bed, knowing that Lars was up; that he would be taking Tessa for a walk in the park, wrapped tight to his chest in a sling, probably still telling her that she was his progeny.

*

Tessa asleep a few months later; an evening when all I wanted was to sit in my pyjamas on the sofa with Lars and chat about a holiday. His laptop was open on his knees though.

'Should we go to New York again?' I said. 'I'm getting my energy back. We could stay in a better hotel – do lots of walking with Tessa, go to MOMA, the High Line…'

'What? Do you mind if we don't book it yet? There's a possibility that I might have to go to Germany to the focus groups for the next launch.'

'Oh… OK. You want to tell me about them?'

'Yes – it'd be great to get your input. The demographics in the UK aren't expected to be the same, you see…'

His future was part of my future – our future together. Even when we'd lain together and talked about what our world would be like, we'd always known that it would be hard work.

17

2017

The trees in next door's garden were starting to colour with blossom; from my kitchen window I watched the wind scatter petals like a carpet of pink and white on their lawn. Lars however, was still stuck behind a wall of impenetrable snow in Moscow. He'd worked out it was a fifty-hour train journey to get home and we agreed it was better for him to sit it out for a plane.

Nadine sidled up to me as I dropped off the children on Friday and hissed as if it were a subject of deep shame: 'Ami, this funeral issue… the children are obviously having some development challenges…'

I turned on her in amazement. 'I think I can deal with that, thanks, Nadine.'

'I just wanted you to know that you have our support.'

I glowered and turned on my heel, stalking to the bus stop as I muttered to myself, 'What the actual fuck? Who does she think she is?' My outrage lasted all day.

Julia called round on Saturday morning and, while the children played, I filled her in on this.

'Time to put radioactive substances in her almond-milk latte,' Julia seethed.

I also told her what had happened between Lars and me.

'I'll do anything I can to help,' she said at the end.

'Could you ask Lila to have the kids next week for a bit if Lars doesn't get back?' I asked, knowing that Julia was working.

'Fuck,' she said. 'Lila's going on holiday and they're going to a football camp all week. Look, let me think…'

'It's fine,' I said. 'I'm hoping that I can leave them with their dad. That'll make me feel better.'

'You don't want them shaking their booty anyway,' Julia said. 'Lila was mortified. Apparently, the kids clicked on her iPad while she was cooking the dinner.'

I smiled. 'Can I ask you something?'

'What?'

'Well, you manage on your own, you go on the odd date…' I knew it was a long way off but I wanted her to tell me whether it was heaven or hell out on the other side – the swipe side.

'The single mum bit is fine,' said Julia. 'I'm never going to be a Smugum and I'm lucky – I've got a good job so I can afford help. And all the rules in the house are mine. The dates – well, not so much. The point is, if I'm going to bring someone else into my life they need to be a bonus, an addition for the boys and me. And most of the ones I meet are tossers.'

I didn't know why I was asking aside from in anger at

Lars; whatever Liv said, I wasn't going out looking for a new man. 'What about your date the other day?'

'One of those people who are erudite online but mumble into their soup when you meet them,' she said dismissively. 'Also, not interested in kids – didn't say so outright but kept asking how often I had – get this – *respite* from them. The ones who like kids are hard to find.'

When she'd gone I took the kids swimming with Finn's friend, Noah. Having shivered into my costume and tipped three over-excited children into theirs, I crammed everything into a tiny locker before remembering my purse was at the bottom of my bag, which was at the back of the locker, and I needed a £1 coin to shut the bloody thing. I unpacked and repacked it all. Then I blew up armbands and stumbled down to the riotous poolside to get into the piss-filled – but still freezing – water. But I'd only just started to shout, 'Let's play sharks,' when the attendant told me that I would have to leave the pool because the ratio of supervising adults to children should have been – at the minimum – one to two.

'But I'm a single mother,' I said while the rest of the swimming-pool crowd quickly swam towards their other halves. 'There *is* only one of me.' We got dressed and went home to watch a DVD instead.

On Monday morning, I put felt tips and piles of coloured paper onto the kitchen table and begged Tessa and Finn to draw while I gave my details to a nanny agency down the phone. I had no idea how I was going to afford a properly qualified nanny but I didn't see what other choice I had. It's going to have to be someone with loads of experience and immaculate references, I thought as I shuffled money from already-stretched credit cards into our joint current account online. Both our salaries went in there, but they didn't really cover our monthly costs as it was; we relied on the odd dividend from our businesses when we could to make up the difference, but there hadn't been any of those for a while.

'The problem is it's half-term,' the agent told me. 'All our candidates are either away themselves or filling in for other families. I can send you some candidates for interview tomorrow night but they won't be able to start until Monday.' I took the bookings and checked that Tessa was drawing a picture of boats at sea rather than a graveyard.

My phone pinged with a teasing message from Ben.

Ami Fitch. I must not text Ami Fitch.

Which made me shake my head, even as I ignored it and rang Mum.

I didn't dare tell her about the suffocating incident, just that Luba hadn't worked out and had left.

'I'm so sorry, darling,' she said. 'But your father hasn't gone into his shed to write for weeks now and is hardly eating. The only thing he says is that he is going to kill Lars. Then he drinks whisky and falls asleep on the sofa. I don't know what to say… I can't leave him.'

'Can I drive them down and leave them with you for a few days?'

'The problem is he'll snap their heads off. It's even worse

178

when he's been drinking. I think seeing the children without their mother or father would make it even worse. And, Ami, I have to say, it sounds like the children really need you right now. This isn't a time to be thinking about working.'

I knew she meant well, but she twisted the piercing knife of guilt that was already stabbing me in my stomach. But she also made me furious – I was *her* child and I needed her. It brought back memories: my first big speech as a member of the debating society when I was fourteen, standing on a stage with no parent in the audience; collecting my GCSE results on my own while everyone else had a glowing mum by their side; how I'd always said 'yes' to sleepovers at friends' houses as a teenager, desperate to get away from Dad's moods and her anxiety about him.

I asked Liv to help for a couple of hours a day, so I could get to the office, but she said, 'I would, darling, but I had my appraisal and my boss said that I'm the contributing editor with the least contribution she's ever met. I have to turn up for work at 9.30 a.m. *every day*.'

I picked up the phone again and prepared to grovel to Nadine. I'll rely on outright humility. A sincere admission that I'm a bad mother while she's a good one. And then I'll beg.

But after a few rings, all I could hear was Nadine's voice informing me that she was not available and neither was Freddie. I had a tiny memory of her boasting in the playground that they were about to go to the Maldives 'as a family' to an island that had been praised for its ecological stance.

*

Lars managed to get a ticket for a plane that was leaving on Tuesday evening that would land on Wednesday, he told me down the phone, asking lots of questions about how the kids were doing. I took the children to the office with me and tried to get them to draw pictures at the meeting table while I watched Bridget sink further into despair. I called in Luis and Jake, who looked at the kids as if they were exotic zoo animals and then admitted that they had nothing.

'Ben is shagging Claudia,' Bridget said after I'd taken Finn to the loo. 'Everyone's talking about it because she's supposed to be engaged to an MP.'

I briefly wondered why polished Claudia would risk a life of home counties motherhood and apple pie for a roll around with Ben but by then Finn and Tessa were no longer able to sit still. I let them play with the vending machine in the corridor but soon there was milky brown liquid all over the floor and demented lights flashing on the front of it. I implored Bridget to think of *something* and dragged the children home.

Furious with Lars for leaving me in this situation – even though this time it wasn't, strictly speaking, his fault – I harassed Cathy Murdoch.

'Divorce is very rarely a swift business,' she told me. 'We need to press hard to get the right amount of money.

And you're going to have to let him have them for a weekend to show that we're conforming to a childcare agreement.'

'But he's never in the country for long enough,' I said with a rising sense of panic.

I got another text from Ben.

> Ami, can't wait to see the ideas (and you) on Thursday.

Couldn't he stop trying to cross a professional line for even a minute? I focused my general hatred of the entire male sex specifically on him but texted back: 'All coming together nicely', although of course, it wasn't at all.

On Tuesday evening, I interviewed three very expensive nannies. The first one lived at the other end of London and would never get to our house in time for work; the second one was morbidly obese while telling me how strict she was about the children's diets.

It was nine o'clock when the last candidate arrived. I opened the door to find the smiling face of a woman in her late twenties, mousey hair strung back in an efficient ponytail, a very sensible duffel coat done up against the cold.

Jenny lived two streets away, had seven years' experience and was looking for before-and-after-school work so she could complete her degree in child health. She was also calm and cheerful, had an up-to-date criminal records check and could start the following Monday. She would come round on Sunday to meet the children. As she left, I felt overwhelmed

181

with exhaustion but also huge relief.

The next morning I rang her references to hear her previous employers confirm that Jenny was the best nanny they'd ever had. 'I wish she'd come back and look after *me*,' said one woman in Kentish Town who sounded as if she might have started drinking even though it was 10 a.m.

I filled in all the paperwork with the agency and transferred their vast fee from the bank account. My childcare problems were over from next week but that didn't help the fact that I had less than twenty-four hours to go until I had to present a campaign to Campury.

Bridget claimed to have been working all night again but with no results and sobbed down the phone when I rang, saying that Marti had come into the room, stomped around and demanded to know where I was when my 'life was on the line'.

I tried to calm Bridget down and then my mobile rang again. I dashed into the hall to hide the noise of the children, who were playing Shopkins on the kitchen table.

Marti was obviously in the middle of a large social crowd.

'Ami? How are we doing on Campury? Assume you've got the best bloody campaign you've ever bloody delivered? You must have because I was in your office earlier and you weren't there.'

'It's all looking good,' I said and crossed my fingers behind me to justify the lie.

'I would've liked to have had a look at it today,' Marti

carried on, 'but have to go to this bloody thing at Lingfield races. Still, to all in tents with purposes… eh? Gettit, eh?'

I just about sniggered. 'Well, the presentation is tomorrow so I guess I'd better get off the phone.'

'Look,' Marti said then. 'I don't know what's going on, Amelia, but you – and I – need that handbag account. Pull it off and everything will be fine.' He left unspoken what would happen if I didn't pull it off. The phone clicked dead as he went off to do some more backslapping.

I leant against the wall and looked opposite me to where the pale stain caused by the dribble of owl shit was still evident on the paintwork.

My phone rang again.

Through my tears, I read: Lars.

'Oh, God, Lars.'

'Ami, I've landed – I was phoning to find out if everything is OK.'

'Well, of course it's not OK, Lars.'

'How are the kids?'

'They're fine. I've been at home with them.'

'I'm on my way – how's the presentation going?'

'It's in less than…' I looked down at my watch again '… twenty hours and we haven't got an idea yet and Marti is going to sack me and—'

'Wait a minute – you've still got no campaign?'

'No campaign,' I whispered, a huge lump coming in my throat from sheer panic.

'I'm going to get the Heathrow Express and then I'll

come straight there on the Tube – it'll be faster than a cab. You need to calm down and remember that you're very good at your job. I'll be there in about an hour.' It sounded as if he was already running down the long hallways of the airport.

18

2011

'But the whole point is that we have a weekend together without work,' I said. 'Please leave your phone behind.'

I wanted Finn – well, not Finn then, but to make the zygote that would eventually turn into my beautiful son. Ulrika, who'd moved from Sweden to Finchley to be nearer to us, had agreed to have Tessa for the weekend. My suitcase was packed with dresses for romantic dinners *à deux* in the country-house hotel I'd booked; I'd even spent some of the money that was now coming in from our careers on upgrading to a four-poster bed in a room that was – so the myth went – home to a ghost of a mistress of Charles II. I was vague on the history but hoped if we did see her she'd have some oranges to sell us. I planned walks by the river, papers in front of a log fire and Lars' phone was not welcome. By now, I'd become irrational enough to consider it as the third person in our relationship.

'OK,' he said, smiled and placed it back onto the kitchen counter.

'We'll make a deal where you log on once a day from the

hotel,' I said. He now had something like ten dotcom whizzes packed behind Apple Macs in a studio near Old Street roundabout. Tessa's birth had made him work even harder if that were possible – as if, if he stopped thinking about the pursuit of his dreams for too long, they would disappear.

So, we romped in the four-poster bed, looked up Nell Gwyn and spooked each other with sheets over our heads, put on our wellies and walked along the river. With a good night's sleep behind us, we talked about Tessa and how funny she was, and about how this was such a crunch time for his company.

I resolved to try harder to not mind that the dream we'd made together seemed to have become his alone.

19

2017

'Ami! Wake up.'

Don't worry, you're just having a nightmare – you're dreaming that Bridget has become your alarm clock.

Something shook my shoulder hard.

'Ami. You've got to wake up and present to Campury in less than three hours.'

Same boring old nightmare that you've been having for quite a while now. Don't worry, it'll stop soon.

I became aware that there was a very uncomfortable feeling in my cheek, as if I were lying face down on the sharp edge of a large book – or perhaps a computer keyboard.

'Ami!' My God, didn't this alarm clock even include a snooze button? I reached out an arm and tried to find something that would turn off the noise and encountered something that felt very like an Anglepoise desk lamp.

Blearily, I started to raise my head. My eyes were like sandpaper – the rough kind that rips paint from walls in one rub.

I let out a loud moan and sat bolt upright in my desk chair. 'What time is it?'

'It's eight o'clock,' said Bridget, who came into view as my aching eyes finally opened.

'I must have fallen asleep here,' I realised out loud.

'What about the campaign?' Bridget said.

My office seemed to be a sea of boards and black marker pens. Over in the corner, I could see the bodies of Luis and Jake stretched out on the carpeted floor underneath the little meeting table.

'You wake up the boys,' I told Bridget.

'But, Ami, have we got an idea?'

I thought back to the previous evening: Luis, Jake and I had been desperate through the early hours, searching every photo library we could think of for inspiration. Every so often one of us would look up from our Mac and say, 'This one?' but it was always with a doubtful tone.

We ate pizza while we carried on our search. When our bellies were full but our brains felt as if they were running on empty, we decided to try and brainstorm concepts instead, but our ideas were as bad as they'd been all week. Luis pretended to bang his head on the table in frustration.

'God, I can't wait till we get it in the bag,' said Jake with a wink.

'That's so awful.' I smiled but I was despairing inside. There was half an hour to go until the clock ticked from midnight into the day of the pitch and we were running out of steam. I couldn't blow the last opportunity I had to save the agency and provide an income for the kids and me.

'I'm going to make some coffee.' I stood up and brewed a cafetière of strong French-blended coffee – dark, slightly bitter but packed with energy. I handed out mugs. 'Let's go for the pics again. Come on, we can't give up now.'

It was the coffee that did it, of course: ten minutes later there was a sudden whisper from Luis: 'I might have it. You know, I might have it.'

Jake and I leapt behind his computer and as the image came into view I said, 'And we add the bag here…'

Then we all started to shout at once as we built on the idea. Eventually, trembling with the relief of knowing we'd finally managed to come up with something we all thought was brilliant, we set about enhancing the photo and finding more images for the campaign, until I finally passed out at my desk and the boys went to sleep on the floor.

Now, I looked up at Bridget and smiled: 'Have we got an idea? Hell, yes.'

*

It was 9.30 a.m.: the second floor of Selfridges with Bridget racing behind me. I bought a midnight-blue Reiss trouser suit to put over the top of the cheapest underwear I could buy from the Topshop concession downstairs, sticking the whole lot on my least-maxed-out credit card. I figured if I didn't save the agency then the outfit would still be good for job interviews. Then I encouraged the shop assistant to cut off all the labels that were hanging from various parts of me. Down one side of my face was still the clear imprint of the diagonal shape of the edge of a keyboard, missing only the QWERTY of the actual keys themselves.

'Paint it away,' I said to the woman behind the Mac counter, who trowelled a clear inch of foundation onto my cheeks until my skin was immovable and didn't even try and force me to buy anything.

*

'Boards? PowerPoint presentation? Handouts?' Bridget and I stalked towards the grand double old doors of the Campury HQ.

'Check,' sang Bridget. We signed our names in the leather visitors' book and the receptionist directed us to the two sofas in the corner of the ornate lobby.

My phone rang. Liv wanted to ascertain just how ready I was. 'Hair? Nails? Fantastic new outfit?'

'Well, emergency outfit. But it really doesn't matter, Liv. I just want this presentation over and done with, so that I can go home to the children and sleep.'

'Is that right?' said the laughing voice of Ben. I turned round. His face looked more tired than the last time I was there – probably all that shagging Claudia while her MP boyfriend was off voting on important national policy.

'I need to go now,' I told Liv and pressed my phone off.

I faced my tormentor and begged my poor face to find

some semblance of dignity. I just needed the strength to survive the next two hours.

'Right, shall we get going?' I asked.

'The ever-efficient Ami Fitch,' he said, leading the way to the lift.

*

'Can't wait,' said Ben when he'd seated himself at the head of the conference table in the panelled boardroom. 'You're the last to pitch, Ami.'

I had never been so simultaneously knackered and wired. I clicked the first slide into view. Then I cleared my throat and began; I could hear my voice gaining confidence as I slid into the familiar rhythms of my professional life.

'Firstly, there are few brands today with as much credibility, history, prestige and style as Campury...' Ben shifted comfortably in his chair and sat back to listen. 'So, we were thrilled to be asked to present our ideas to you.'

'Thrilled. Really?' he said.

'*Really* thrilled.' I met his desire to wind me up with pure defiance. He glared back for a second then seemed to laugh under his breath.

From then on, he let me continue. I walked the small meeting through the statistical research.

'It certainly calls for something unique. British consumers question how Campury fits into their lives: with being a modern woman today. They want to know that they can team it with jeans rather than furs, for example. Above all, this bag should be something they're more likely to buy for themselves, a symbol of independence; of a woman who stands on her own two feet and occasionally finds time from her job and her life to let them dance.'

'That's an acute analysis.' Claudia nodded to Ben and blushed when he smiled back.

'And so, today, we're going to present an idea that's very today and, at the same time, it's all the best bits of yesterday. Bridget, the first board, please.'

Bridget placed the first mocked-up artwork onto the stand. Claudia gasped: 'Oh, wow. That's *gorgeous*,' then clapped her hand over her mouth.

Ben was beside me, next to the board, examining it in detail. The image deserved it.

A girl in a Bardot bikini of red polka dots, a matching scarf tied across her blonde locks at a jaunty angle, a grin across her golden cheeks, lay on a retro-styled sunbed in the shining hot Riviera sand. In the distance were rows of pink parasols, beneath which were hundreds of pairs of sunbeds just like hers, each two occupied by a honed and toned glamorous couple. It was Club 55; it was Portofino; it was Capri.

Beside the girl was another sunlounger and instead of a perfect Adonis on it, there was a burnt-orange Campury bag sitting on its own deep-pile white towel.

Claudia stood up and walked towards the front of the room to join us. Excitement shone in her face.

I was going to show them another two ideas based around this theme – the same girl in a fabulous restaurant, with the bag opposite her on a chair; the image that Luis had finally found at around 3 a.m. that morning of Studio 54, where we'd shown her dancing, carefree, the bag positioned as the ultimate partner on the shimmering, mirrored floor.

And, when we'd finally finished, I'd been proud. I'd known that it was as good as any idea that I'd ever presented.

'Here's a test,' Ben said. 'Let's see if this says the same thing to you as a woman as it says to me. Claudia, tell me exactly what came into your head when you saw it.'

Claudia laughed and put her hands on her lovely hips. 'It quite simply says…'

'Yes?'

'It says: "Who needs a man?"'

Bridget clapped with excitement.

'Is that what you think, Ami?' said Ben.

'That's exactly what the ad is supposed to say, yes.'

'But is it what *you* think?'

There was only silence. What did he want me to say now?

'Depends on who the man is, of course,' I said and then looked away as I heard his piss-taking laugh.

'It turns the whole reverential Campury deal around, makes it about independent women who can…' Claudia said.

'Look after themselves,' said Bridget.

'Women with ambition,' said Claudia.

'Women who don't need a man to buy them handbags…'

'Women who choose Campury for themselves.'

'Do you want to look at the rest of the work?' I leapt in before this sisterhood turned into a downright coven.

'Why don't we?' said Ben and went back to sit in his chair while I put up the next boards. Bridget oozed pure pride.

After that, I tried to wrap up professionally. 'Thanks so much for taking the time to see us today. Glad to see you liked our initial thoughts.'

'We've got to really think about what we've seen in the last couple of days,' Claudia said. 'Then we'll let you know in about a week.'

'Well, we look forward to getting the call.'

There was a silence and then Ben said, 'I'd like to discuss your agency for a little longer with you, Ami. Claudia, could you take Bridget downstairs and give her a coffee?'

'I certainly can,' said Claudia and strode towards the door.

'Did you really, really like it?' I could hear Bridget gushing as they hurried towards the lift.

*

I shrugged into the silence and looked at the carpet. All the adrenaline of the presentation was gone – I was like a hot-air balloon when the fire has gone out, hissing furiously towards the ground.

There was a silence while he poured me another cup of coffee. 'It's brilliant work,' he said. 'Brilliant.'

'But?' I tried to smile.

'You know the "but". Everyone is talking about how you've lost Land the Bootmaker. Your accounts for last year show a deficit.'

'That was when we were setting up,' I said. 'No business makes a profit in the first year.'

'True,' Ben said. 'But you must understand that the safe option for Campury is to go with an agency which is financially secure.' He was direct and calm.

'Marti is my backer and he owns Goldwyn and he believes in me.'

'Word is that you and he have fallen out.'

My industry was fed on the failure of others at gossipy lunches in Soho restaurants so I didn't even bother to think about who would have told Ben this.

'That's not true,' I said, however.

'Apparently you were seen leaving The Ivy in tears after having dinner with him.' I thought back to that evening when Marti – my married boss – had made a pass at me, and my shock and desperation.

'That was just a misunderstanding.' I took a deep breath.

'What kind of misunderstanding?'

'I really don't need to tell you that.' I tried to smile. 'I can, however, ask Marti to call you and talk you through the finances of the business.' Ben sighed and played with his coffee spoon and I pressed on. 'Look, we lost Land through no fault of our own, and that was unfortunate. But I really do feel strongly that we're the agency to take Campury forward,' I said.

'Do you want to tell me what's been happening with Marti? I heard you and he go way back.'

'We do, and it's nothing.' I got to my feet.

Ben was obviously unconvinced. 'Look, why don't we have lunch and talk about the campaign some more?'

God, I was tired. All I wanted was for the hell of the last weeks – and the last twenty-four hours – to have counted for something and, instead, here was someone asking me out for lunch *again*. I heard myself saying in a high-pitched voice full of anger, 'What I don't understand is why you let me carry on with the pitch if you had no intention of giving us the account?'

'Woah, hang on there,' said Ben, coming towards me.

'I will not hang on there.' I knew my rage was inappropriate, irrational even, but I'd had enough of this man who thought he could take the piss out of me. 'I think you've made me go through this whole exercise just for your own amusement.'

'Hey!' he said, his face serious now. 'I would never do that.'

'You took the piss out of me when you knew I was going through a hard time.' I could hear my voice rising. 'You invited us to pitch for your own bloody amusement but you were never going to give us the account, were you?'

I could hear my shouts as if they were from someone else, wild with irrational anger, but I couldn't seem to stop. All the pressure of the last few months had turned into fury at this man who saw my life as his latest plaything. Even as it happened, I knew that, in professional terms, I hadn't just lost the plot, I'd lost the entire works of Shakespeare.

'Woah,' he said again, stepping back. 'I think you might need a good night's sleep.'

He'd never know how close we came to the wire – and it was all for nothing now. 'Well, the campaign took some time to get right,' I said stiffly, trying to control myself as tears welled in my eyes. 'Look, I'm sorry.'

'It's OK. It sounds like you and I have a bit of a misunderstanding going on here.' His voice was quite gentle but I made for the door. I had no option but to wipe the back of my hand across my face.

'I should never have pitched,' I said as I pulled open the door.

'Of course, you should…' his voice came after me as I started to run down the hallway. 'Stop a minute. Is there anything I can do to help?'

I just shook my head as I ran. No one could give me back the old me, where nothing like this would ever happen.

Instead of taking the lift, I dashed down the stairs and out through the oak doors without bothering to look around to see if Bridget was still there.

Ten minutes later, on the Victoria Line, all I knew was that I had blown it. Not just blown it but resolutely and absolutely buggered my career. Perhaps it would be better to call Marti and resign before he had the chance to sack me?

I stomped my way up my street then stared at the front

steps of my house. No job meant no house and more change for the children.

Lars opened the door and surprised me by smiling. He seemed to ignore the streaks of tears down my face; maybe he was just used to it. 'I hope it went well?' he said, leading the way to the kitchen. I didn't have the energy to tell him what had happened or to see the disappointment in his face when he realised quite how abjectly I'd failed. 'The children and I had a great morning. I've been showing them my websites. We went to the supermarket to buy some food.'

Tessa and Finn were sitting at the table with their faces shining with pleasure. 'Daddy didn't know what kind of things to buy but we told him,' Tessa said.

'And we're going to go and stay with him next weekend at Grandie Sweden's when she gets back so we can teach him more about how to look after us,' went on Finn.

'You are?' I tried to smile brightly although I thought that my heart might break all over again.

'Well, you don't mind, do you, Ami?' Lars asked. 'I mean, the lawyer says we need to practise the childcare arrangements. Might as well start as we mean to go on.'

20

2014

'It's so gorgeous here,' I said, leaning over the wall and gazing down at the little coloured boats bobbing on their moorings surrounded by the reflection of the harbour lights. 'I'm really glad we came.' The air seemed packed with extra ozone; the May evening was balmy.

Lars smiled back at me. 'Me too – even if it was a bit of a schlep.'

The schlep – Lars' current favourite word – had involved a couple of hours stuffing the car with all the unbelievable crap that small children needed to go away for a few days, and then six hours jostling with all the other motorway traffic until we finally swung into the little Cornish village where I'd rented a cottage for a week. Finn had slept most of the way and was now – even though it was eight at night – wide awake in his pushchair. Tessa was tugging at my hand as she wanted to carry on walking and go to the beach.

'We'll go tomorrow, darling. We can't build sandcastles in the dark.' We were on our way to the village pub where I was determined to annihilate the stress of the journey with a decent Sancerre and a plate of fish and chips. I was knackered as usual – Tessa had never been a great sleeper and when Finn arrived he just seemed to be awake when she was asleep and asleep when she was awake. Most nights in our house were a case of musical beds – as kids climbed in with us, Lars and I would escape to their small single beds instead, our feet poking out of the end of a duvet covered in cartoon characters. I was desperately hoping that – now I'd managed to get Lars to come on a whole week's holiday – he might use some of his considerable energy to give me a lie-in.

We wandered along the harbourside, past a war memorial where some local comedian had chiselled off the upward stroke of the 'G' from 'God' so it read: *'To the Glory of Cod'*. This made us both snigger and Lars held my hand briefly before we set off at a decent pace in search of the wine that would provide a fast-track to forgetting about our busy working lives in London and some much-needed romance.

*

That first morning when I came into the kitchen, refreshed from a whole ten hours' kip in a row, I smiled at the children, who were seated at the pine table eating cereal, having probably been up for a couple of hours. I was so grateful to Lars that I tried to ignore the brief stab of anger I felt when I saw he was fiddling with his laptop. He quickly shut it, saying, 'No Wi-Fi', got up, gave me a hug and poured me some coffee.

'Thanks for letting me sleep,' I said.

'We're going to the beach, we're going to the beach,' sang Tessa, her eyes bright with excitement.

'Beach, beach, beach,' her brother joined in.

I sat down next to them. 'We'll need armbands and a spade,' Tessa pointed out. She was wearing shorts and a T-shirt and under that I could see the bright dots of her new bikini.

'She had her armbands on in bed this morning,' Lars told me, 'but we took them off to have breakfast.'

'And we can have pasty for lunch,' Tess went on. 'You're allowed to eat it from the bag without a knife and fork and you don't have to have manners.'

Finn looked up with interest. 'Please, thank you,' he said.

'I'll go and see if I can find us a Sunday paper,' said Lars. 'There was a shop on the harbour that might be open.'

I smiled at him in anticipation of the week ahead but as he went out of the stable door I saw him push his phone into his pocket.

*

By midday he'd given up pretending. We were sat on towels on the beach, the kids digging beside us. Finn kept putting his red bucket on his head instead of his hat. The sun was weak but present; clouds scuttled across the sky pushed by the breeze.

Lars was still trying to get a signal. He'd been doing this most of the morning, getting up every now and again and walking off with his phone in the air as if, if it was marginally closer to a satellite, it might help him connect with the world.

'What's so urgent on a Sunday?' I said as he sighed in frustration again.

'New software release,' he muttered. 'Just want to know how it's going.'

I bit the inside of my cheek as I forced my smile wider. 'I'm sure it's all fine.'

'When you rented the cottage, didn't you check it had Wi-Fi?'

'I was a bit more worried about a high chair, frankly,' I said as calmly as I could. If it'd been so important, why couldn't he have checked? 'Can't you try the pub?'

'Good idea.' Lars jumped to his feet. 'This won't take much time. I'll be back as soon as I can.'

I made a sandcastle with the children.

*

He came back about an hour later, preceded by the smell of freshly cooked pasties and carrying four paper bags. By this time our sandcastle was a significant structure, complete with some rickety turrets and a moat. The kids were trekking back and forth from a small stream with their buckets trying to fill it up, Finn wobbling uncertainly on his tiny legs.

'Pasty,' Tessa shouted. I took a bag from Lars and pulled off a chunk of the crust so that I could try and cool it for Finn by blowing on it.

Seagulls squawked as they circled above us.

'That was a schlep,' Lars said, sitting down too. 'The only decent Wi-Fi in the village is in the other pub up on the cliff.' He pointed towards the edge of the bay where there was a white building in the distance.

'All OK?' I said, although I dreaded the answer.

'Hmmm, the guys are a bit worried about one bug they can't seem to fix,' Lars said, and shook his head from side to side. 'I'll have to check in with them again later.'

I smiled on resolutely and handed Finn the crust. It was in his hand for less than a second before a seagull swooped and, in a frenzy of flapping wings, claimed it for its own lunch.

*

That second evening Lars jumped in the car and drove up to the cliff-top pub. 'I'll be back as soon as I can,' Lars said.

The kids were exhausted and fell asleep as soon as their pyjamas were on. I smiled as I thought about the evening ahead, curled up together on the deep orange sofa in the cottage sitting room, watching a movie maybe, talking or even making love. I had a long shower, put on what I hoped was a remotely seductive pair of pyjamas and lit the log burner. I poured a glass of wine, chuckling to myself about

Finn's screaming indignation about the seagull. I would read for a while until Lars came back.

Half an hour later I put another log on the fire and put my book down to get some more wine from the fridge. An hour after that, I realised I'd drunk half the bottle and read a good hundred pages. I picked up my phone to text Lars but there was not a single bar in the top left corner. An hour after that, I poured yet more wine and tried not to let disappointment sear into my soul.

*

Lars finally returned at 11.15 p.m., when, I assumed, the pub shut and with it his Wi-Fi access. I was lying on the sofa, kept awake, despite the sea air and wine, by an anger I couldn't control.

'*älskling?* You're not in bed?' said Lars.

'No, I'm bloody not,' I said and sat up.

'They can't fix the bug.' Lars ignored my tone and sat down on the sofa, his hand to his head.

'We're supposed to be on holiday.'

'I'm going to have to go back,' he said, as if there were no other option.

'For fuck's sake – I knew it. You couldn't just come away with us for a week without panicking about bloody work.'

'Look, I know what the holiday means to you, but it's a major disaster,' Lars said coldly. 'I'm sorry, but everything

I've worked for could go down the drain.' He stood up. 'There's a train at 7 a.m. tomorrow from Redruth. I've already booked a cab to get there.'

I found a blanket and stayed where I was on the sofa; in the morning, I heard the door click as he left.

*

'Table for four?' said the waiter, who saw me struggling through the door with the pushchair. We had two large beach bags slung over its handles and Tessa was holding onto the side. The bottoms of our legs and feet were covered in sand. It was clear that the waiter expected me to be followed by a husband.

'No, just us,' I muttered. I'd thought I'd give myself a break from cooking for the kids and feed them in the pub on the way back from the beach. The waiter looked embarrassed at his gaffe and immediately made up for it by grabbing the pushchair from me and leading the way towards a corner table.

'Daddy had to go back to London because of his work,' Tessa told him.

'He must be really important, your daddy,' said the waiter, going off to get a high chair for Finn.

I took my place with our children at our table for three.

*

The week passed slowly with no adult company. Lars called and we had stiff, short conversations about the children. In the daytime, we explored other beaches, spent a day at a theme park, ate ice cream and learned to put the jam on a scone first for a proper Cornish cream tea.

It was the evenings when I let myself feel my sadness. I sat on the orange sofa and looked out at the pretty harbour lights while the children slept, and thought again and again about how lonely it could be, being with someone.

<u>21</u>

2017

The disconcerting part after the pitch was that nothing actually happened.

No Marti stalking into the office in a rage to ask me what I was doing shouting at a prospective client and breaking down in front of him. No sarcastic texts from Ben. No gossip in the hallways of the agency, as far as I was aware, about how I'd blown all my chances by being terminally unprofessional in the most important pitch of my career.

I rolled around in my bed over the next few nights, unable to bear the hot mortification that invaded my head every time I thought about what had happened; my cerebral hemispheres were now overtaken by abject humiliation.

I emailed Marti although I knew it was hopeless.

> Ben Jones might ring you. He's worried about Brand New's finances and wants some reassurance.

I also tried to manage Bridget's expectations of the outcome of the pitch, blaming the size of our little agency.

'Do you think that's what will stand in our way?' asked Bridget. 'I mean, I was there. They loved every second of what we were saying. But then when I saw you running out of the building I knew something was wrong.'

'But as I explained to you, Bridget,' I said, 'as soon as you left he said he was worried about our financial status – then I got that call saying Tessa was ill.' At this point, I crossed my fingers behind my back to protect myself from the lie.

'Claudia rang and said she and he were going away to think about it.'

'Probably taking her on a dirty weekend,' I said.

Campaign ran a story about how Campury was still trying to appoint an agency. 'We were really impressed with all the ideas,' Ben was quoted as saying. He looked scruffy but relaxed in the accompanying photograph, shot outside the Hanover Square office.

When I thought about the upcoming weekend without the kids my metaphorical umbilical cord stretched. Every night I rushed home from work but now found the children in the cheerful care of Jenny, eating plates of vegetables while they learned their times tables. I was incredibly grateful to her; still I watched the children obsessively and, with Parminder's help, set out to try and find a counsellor for Tessa.

Lars called the children nearly every night that week and as I passed the phone over one evening, he went back to the burying incident.

'It was a real shock and I can't seem to get it out of my mind,' he said. 'All that time waiting in Moscow, I was really, really worried. We could nearly have lost them.'

I gritted my teeth because it had taken an episode as traumatic as this to make him see what I'd been telling him for ages. A sense of injustice overwhelmed me but, still, I tried not to argue. 'We've just got to make sure that we don't upset them any further.'

'I know,' he said. 'I know.'

He asked whether I'd heard from Campury yet.

'No, not yet,' I said. If only he knew how drastically I'd failed.

Still, every day I got up, put on the armour of my business suit, went to the office and waited to hear that my career was over – and then came home to love my babies. I let the children come into my bed and we all snuggled down together most nights. If this was the shape of my family of the future, then it was calmer and full of love.

The children asked sometimes after Luba, who, Jenny said, emerged from the house a couple of doors up the road well after midday, looking 'polished and shiny' as she climbed into Guy's Ferrari. Jenny had supervised her collecting her few belongings.

'Luba said I could go to a bloody football match,' Finn said when he and I were having a warm evening bath together.

'You can stop swearing now she's gone,' I said. 'And *I* will take you to a football match, the moment you're old enough.'

'At least Jenny lets us eat broccoli,' Finn said. After I told him off for taking a mouthful of soapy bath water and spitting it out again all over me, he went on, 'Do you know what I like best now?'

'No, what's that, darling?'

'I like the way you're here more,' and he planted a sloppy kiss on my mouth. I *was* there more, as I waited for my future to be decided; I also vowed that, however much I needed to earn money, I would try and work as flexibly as possible in the future to be there for him and his sister.

Nadine, having found out about my divorce, kept leaving hushed messages on the answer machine recommending valerian for staying calm. 'You poor, poor thing,' she said when she saw me in the playground. 'Of course, the children will recover but it will take some time. I advocate giving them your *total* attention, Amelia, but it's difficult when you are always working. And, of course, avoiding them seeing confrontation at all costs.' I'd glued the fixed smile of fortitude on my face and then sat in my car banging my head against the steering wheel and crying tears of rage.

'Her passive aggressive is becoming proper aggressive,' Parminder said when I told her. 'How dare she?'

She told me how Tess had told Priti that they were 'going to stay with Daddy for the weekend' and how they were excited about it. Then she went on to tell me that I had to stop blaming myself – which was easier said than done – and thinking of ways to get back at Nadine.

'I just can't stand her pity,' I said. '"Staying married while Amelia doesn't" just adds to her smugness.'

'You know that Priti came home from the school trip and said that everyone else had tiny little boxes of Tupperware full of little salads and cut-up fruit and that they stacked into a bigger box,' she said in outrage. 'Apparently, a sandwich, fruit and a bag of crisps isn't good enough. I have deficient packed lunch receptacles.'

*

Cathy insisted on seeing all Lars' business accounts, took apart his spreadsheets and investment plans and informed me, over another meeting in her study, that we were very 'illiquid'. 'It means that all the money you have as a couple is tied up in the house and in working capital for Lars' business. It's not ideal at all when we need to keep you in your house.'

'What can we do?'

'I can only encourage you to spend very little and earn as much as possible while I try and reach a resolution with the other side,' she said, but crinkled her brow. 'In the meantime, shall we firm up what we're going to file as your reasons you can't live with each other?'

'What sort of thing do other people put down?' I asked.

'Someone last week wrote that his wife had seventy pairs of shoes.' Cathy chuckled to herself.

'Only seventy?'

'I don't think seventy is that many,' said Cathy. Today she was wearing patent leather pixie boots with a bright shine at the bottom of an otherwise unremarkable trouser suit. 'His point was that they had needed a bigger house to keep them all in.'

Leaning forward, I said, 'What's the worst one you've ever heard?'

'I really couldn't betray client confidence,' Cathy said, but she looked as if she was dying to.

'Oh, go on. I promise it won't go any further than these four walls. Just don't mention any names.'

'Well. It must *not* go any further, but anyway... The worst one I ever heard...' her voice sank to a whisper '... was when I was just a clerk – let's just say he was from the north, very rich, whose poor, poor wife...' her voice got louder with indignation '... wrote down that he used to get drunk and mistake the baby's cot for the toilet.'

'You mean he *pissed on his sleeping child*?'

'Shush!' But Cathy was laughing like a hyena. 'That poor woman. What an animal. I really shouldn't have told you that.'

'I promise I won't tell a soul,' I said, thinking how much this story would appeal to Liv.

*

Despite me saying I really wasn't in the mood to go anywhere, Liv was working hard on preparing me – and

212

herself – for the forthcoming weekend. She rang and told me that this was the upside of divorce: 'whole weekends without having to look after bloody kids'.

'I'm really going to miss them. It'll be so strange them not being there.'

She insisted, 'Even more reason why we have to go out on the razz.'

'Oh, I don't think… and I can't spend any money.'

'No discussion. It's free. We're going to Berkeley House. I've got us on the guest list and free dinner. I said I was going to do a review but we can think of a couple of things to write and then get shit-faced.'

'I'm not sure.'

She wasn't having any of it. 'It's the *place du jour* for *le beau monde*. The waiters' uniforms were designed by Christopher Kane.'

She went on to tell me about all the freebies she'd bagged by offering coverage in *Pas Faux*, including a facial and some samples from up-and-coming designers.

'Do you ever do any work?' I asked. 'Perhaps you should write a feature or something sometimes.'

'Too busy,' she said. 'And, so that I can join in while you hunt for a new man, I've finished with Matthew.'

'I'm not hunting for a new man, but which one was Matthew again?'

'Tall, early twenties, photographer…'

'The one with the goatee beard – in fact, generally quite goatie all round?'

'Yes, beard. He'd started to tell me he loved me while we were having sex, which was really boring of him.'

'Very dull indeed,' I said.

'And I've no time for men. My job this weekend is to make you have such a good time that you forget about the fact that you probably have no job and no husband.'

*

On Wednesday evening Mum rang.

'I've booked you and a friend – Liv, I imagine – into Champneys for the day on Sunday. Your father is paying. I told him it was just what you needed.'

'Thank you!' I knew she felt guilty about not being in London by my side, and was touched. 'How is he?'

'Miserable, just miserable,' she said. 'He refuses to eat anything other than bread and ham.'

'Is it really all about me getting divorced?'

'It doesn't really matter what starts it, does it?' My mother was bleak and unusually frank. 'But it just goes on and on.'

*

Ulrika returned from her American trip. She came to our house so that I didn't have to see how Lars had set up home with her. As she climbed out of her car, so thin and tall she looked like a stalk of wheat that would bend in the wind, she hugged me hard. She'd bought the kids a bunch of new clothes and a pair of trainers each from California, thoughtful as always given our financial situation. They gave her big kisses.

'I hear you're coming to stay with your daddy at my house,' she said.

'Yes, we're going to teach him how to look after us properly,' Tessa said.

'Doesn't he know how to do that?' she said with a broad grin. Being her, she didn't meet my eyes to laugh at her son; Ulrika wasn't going to take sides.

'And you're not allowed to tell him, Grandie,' said Finn. Tess and he shared a conspiratorial glance and I imagined they'd cooked up some great wheeze where they planned to tell their dad they went to bed at midnight every night and were allowed ice cream for breakfast.

The kids went to play and Ulrika and I sat in the kitchen. 'You are separated like the banks of the fjord, but I'm here for you, Ami,' she said, wrapping her rug-like cardigan around her.

She let me cry then for the next half an hour, without real comment aside from warm hugs and comforting words.

'It's just everything we were,' I kept saying, 'and everything I wanted us to be again.'

And all she could say, this lovely woman who'd believed in us and loved her own husband so much, was, 'I know, I know,' and, 'I wish I could fix this.'

I wanted to ask her whether she could talk to him, make

him see that his dad would not have wanted this. He'd have wanted him to have a happy family *as well as* a great career. Maybe she'd already had this talk with Lars? I knew she would have done what she thought was right.

*

Thor had been texting me quite often.

> Just checking in? You OK gorgeous? How are the kids?

And I'd reassured him. His latest text, however, told me that he was planning to visit the UK soon:

> We got to sort this thing.

I wondered how he would feel when he found out, like Ulrika, that there was nothing left to fix.

*

Friday: there was still no phone call from Campury. Bridget bit off most of her fingernails and rang Claudia, who said they were still away making a decision.

'He took her to Sorrento so that they could have time to think,' Bridget told me.

I pictured Ben throwing Claudia onto a white bed, muslin curtains blowing in the breeze behind them, where an aqua sea met an azure sky. Later, Ben would cram his big body into a Fiat 500 and she'd climb in beside him; they'd have dinner above a white beach, al fresco – probably something fishy with tomatoes. Perhaps they'd laugh as they remembered how mad old Amelia had behaved at the pitch.

This was the man who was in charge of what happened next in my life, who had seen me at my lowest professional moment, and he was away in the sunshine, shagging.

22

2015

Lars rushed round the kitchen, putting out the recycling, checking the M&S ready meals in the oven to see if they were, in fact, ready. I came down from putting the children to bed; he solicitously placed a glass of wine onto the kitchen table for me. This was one of his periods of trying – he'd committed to being more around for the kids and me; we were a few days in and, because of all the times he'd promised before and failed to deliver, I was conscious I was waiting for it to come to an end.

I sat down and tried to relax as he ran around me. Eventually, he spooned some sort of meat in a sauce onto plates – it looked nothing like the picture on the front of the packet – and sat down opposite me. We talked about the kids – a subject that shouldn't trip us up.

'Finn's fallen head over heels for Jemima at nursery,' I said. 'Keeps asking for playdates. The worst part about it is having to talk to her mother, Nadine.'

Lars smiled. 'Is she the one who's always trying to save the world?'

I nodded. 'Earnest type, always going on about dolphins and perfect parenting, which means apparently never exposing your kid to conflict. And free love. She's very out there about sex.'

'It's her husband I feel sorry for…'

'Freddie? Unfortunate beard? They keep asking us round for dinner. But it would be tofu-flavoured nut roast and we'd probably have to do a "getting to know each other" session of tai chi before we were allowed to eat. Luckily I can never say yes because you're not here.' Lars looked at me to see if I was trying to start an argument. I wasn't, it was just a statement of fact, but I tried to get the conversation back onto something fun. 'She's apparently asked one of the other mothers to a class on "how to make your orgasms multiple" with practical sessions where you get naked in an adult learning centre at Finsbury Park.'

Lars laughed and visibly relaxed. But then his phone started to ring from the kitchen counter. He looked up and stared at it. I could almost feel his stress as he tried not to jump up and answer it. 'Do you mind?' he said eventually. 'It's just…'

It's just another one of the never-ending work crises that rule our lives, I thought, but didn't say. Instead I just nodded and he leapt to his feet saying, 'Bill? Everything OK?' as he went out to stride up and down the hallway.

Can love evaporate if you don't keep a tight lid on it? Ours seemed to have been subsumed by all the big issues of growing up and being married: work, children, ambition and age. I picked up my fork and started to eat alone again.

23

2017

A vodka tonic, a bottle of champagne, absolutely no mineral water, a great dinner and a conversation where we listed every single man we'd ever slept with – or in Liv's case all those she could remember – and I felt OK for a divorced and desperate person. The dining room at Berkeley House was decorated with Summer of Love flowers and bright purple chairs. The room buzzed with the knowledge that it was the zeitgeist.

The evening hadn't started with such promise. Lars arrived to pick up the children and it seemed to me that this was the reality of divorce – weekends divided unnaturally, children wrested from the arms of their mothers into the every-other-week care of their fathers; mothers setting out to find out who they are again without the children they'd grown inside them.

Lars looked apprehensive as he stood on the doorstep. Tessa and Finn were excitable – they'd been talking about 'going to stay with Daddy' all week. I churned out instructions – bedtimes, food, where Tessa's stinky blanket was in the two sad little suitcases that sat in the hall. I kissed the children hard.

'Chilly willies, chilly willies,' sang Finn, who had a thing about the lack of heating at Ulrika's house. Lars and I talked all the while to the children so we didn't have to talk to each other.

I stood in the road and waved a mock-cheerful goodbye then went back inside and wandered around the playroom and the kitchen. I pushed back the sadness and thought about how I was going to have to get used to this.

Liv rang but managed to sound as if she wasn't phoning on purpose exactly at the point when she knew I'd be free of the kids. 'You're not even dressed yet, are you? Think what heaven it'll be to be able to get ready on your own.' I had a long bath and tried not to worry about the kids, then put on a monochrome dress I'd bought for a dinner with Lars that had never happened.

Three hours and many glasses of golden bubbles later, Liv and I decided we ought to really concentrate on the review she was supposed to be writing for *Pas Faux*. We settled for 'You'll come here' as a headline before writing about the food as if it were a passionate bout of sex. 'I delve into the warm triangle of salad, licking my lips, revelling in the rounded softness of breasts of avocado,' scribbled Liv into her notebook.

'Each mouthful caresses my taste buds, sliding into my body as if it's heading for the very centre of my desire,' I suggested.

'The hot juices spurt from my steak to the back of my throat; each chip is a cock, eager to be eaten,' Liv went on.

'That's a bit hardcore, isn't it? How about the jus wraps itself around the pulsating lamb as if they should never part?'

Liv put her notebook away, saying that was clearly enough hard work for one night. She twirled her champagne glass round and round so that the shafts of light from the chandeliers on the club roof pierced the gold of the liquid. 'Your trouble, Ami, is that you associate sex with procreation and it really has nothing to do with it.'

'Absolutely nothing at all.'

'Well, of course it does, in some circumstances. But did I tell you about the latest theory? I read about it in *Grazia*. There's ovulation man and anti-ovulation man: ones you want to have children with and ones you just want to shag for sheer pleasure. You choose the first sort when you're ovulating and the second ones when you're at infertile times of the month. Lars was your ovulation man, and now you're going to find anti-ovulation man.'

'What about you – you only shag for the three weeks of the month in which you're not ovulating?'

'God, no,' said Liv. 'You know I have injections. They take me beyond science – I never ovulate at all. Haven't for years. Anyway, let's have a dance?'

Standing up, I clung onto the back of my chair, realised I was a bit drunk and giggled. When we got to the dance floor, it was full of ultra-slim bodies making shapes. The music was eclectic in the worst sense of the word: random disco and R&B designed to find some middle ground between the twenty-somethings who made the club glamorous and the decade-older members who could afford the exorbitant membership fees.

We elbowed a little room for ourselves in the crowd and I began to move, shutting my eyes and moving into the octopus of limbs around me.

The next moment I felt the thud of a large hand smack clean into my nose. 'Aaarghhhhhh,' I screamed, more in shock than pain, and opened my eyes to see a man in his mid-twenties stop jumping up and down and, instead, peer at me with concern.

'God, I'm so sorry,' he said. 'Let me get you some ice. Got carried away there.' He led me to a chair, then disappeared in the direction of the bar.

After a few moments I looked unsteadily around for Liv but instead found myself being hit once again in the face, this time by a cloth chock-full of ice. 'Aaarghhhhhh!'

'Oh, my God, I've done it again.'

'You're trying to kill me.'

'It was an accident, I'm sorry, just got carried away dancing.'

'Arms in the air like you just don't care,' I muttered, which was what I always said to the children when trying to wrestle clothes over their heads.

I grabbed the ice from him and more delicately applied it to the centre of my nose. 'Am I bleeding?'

'I don't think so.' The man leant in closer. 'Shit, we'd

better get you into the light.' I struggled to my feet and followed him, carrying the ice, out into the brighter light of the corridor. I rested against the wall while he peered at me.

'No, no blood.' His voice sounded very well-bred. His naturally streaked hair was pulled into spikes at the top of his high forehead. His face shone with blue-blooded genes – a long nose and high cheekbones, green eyes darting around.

'Did you go to public school?' I asked.

'Yes, Harrow, why?'

'It's the way boys from public schools dance. Arms all over the place.' On sleepover nights at Liv's as a teenager, we'd been allowed to go to the local teenage dry disco, which was the favourite haunt of Hampstead's finest posh-school boys. We'd snogged a few of them, of course, but never stopped laughing at their moves.

He roared with very upper-class laughter. 'Are you taking the piss out of me?'

'It's the least I can do after you smashed me in the face.'

'Let me buy you a drink to say sorry.'

'I'll just go and check I'm all still here.' I wobbled off in the direction of the loos where I reassured myself that, in fact, though there were two of me staring back from the mirror, each version did seem to have its own nose.

I emerged to find the 'boy' lounging against the wall. 'I'm fine,' I said.

'Come with me.' He led me up some stairs into a library bar, where old leather sofas were laden with cushions the colour of overripe cherries. I sat in a high-backed chair and watched his tall body, dressed in what looked like a vintage dinner jacket and old blue jeans, go off to the bar and return with a bottle of champagne and two glasses.

'I thought I should say sorry in style.' He poured me half a glass before spilling quite a lot over the table.

'Do you think I should do that, given your track record?'

He smiled and sat down opposite me. 'At least I haven't damaged your beautiful face.'

'You might get on quite well with my friend Liv.'

'I want to get on quite well with you, but, damn.' I raised my glass to my mouth and his eyes landed on my wedding ring, which shone in the gold of my drink. 'You're married. Might have known.'

'Actually, I'm separated, but I haven't got round to taking the ring off.'

'You're lying. No one would be mad enough to let you go.'

'I'm not lying. I'm getting divorced.'

'Funny, because that's supposed to be what men always say when they're trying to get girls into bed – never heard a woman do it though.'

I wondered how we could be talking about bed and laughed.

'So, if I come home with you, there's not going to be a psychotic husband waiting in the kitchen with a shotgun?'

Now we were talking about him coming home with me. 'I think you might get on very well indeed with my friend.'

'Does that mean you don't fancy me?' He mock-hung his

head.

Half an hour and the rest of the champagne later, I was very charmed. Peter Calthorpe-Prentiss – or 'double-barrelled twat', as he swore his friends called him – worked in the City in his uncle's bank. 'Nepotism, sheer unadulterated nepotism.' He made me laugh with tales of him losing his family millions through ongoing ineptitude. He loved snowboarding and surfing.

'I bet you're an "Hon",' I teased.

'I am actually,' he admitted. 'But it doesn't pay to be posh any more, does it?'

I told him about my job and the kids – 'Blimey, two kids,' he said. 'Can't even look after myself.' – and even a little about my divorce.

'Found a new chap yet?' he asked as he ordered another bottle of champagne.

'Not looking for one.'

'May I apply for the position?' Peter picked up one of my hands and kissed it.

I laughed. 'I really ought to go and find my friend and tell her where I am. And I'm old enough to be your much older sister.'

'Don't be ridiculous. I'm thirty-seven and you can't be a day over twenty-nine.'

'That's very sweet of you but there's no way you're anywhere near thirty-seven.'

Liv appeared around the corner. 'I wondered where you'd got to,' she said, out of breath from dancing, and then took a look at the Hon Peter. 'But now I understand and forgive you.'

'Peter Calthorpe-Prentiss,' I said. 'Liv McDade.'

'Very pleased to meet you,' said Peter. The waiter delivered another glass as Liv sat down.

We all talked immense silliness as we slid through the second bottle and I bobsleighed into a state of drunkenness where little seemed to make sense or matter.

I went to the loo with Liv at one point and listened to her telling me that I was absolutely fucking nuts if I didn't go shag Peter and, later, as I tried to make sense of his laughing face, it was as if the drink, the comfort and charm of the library and the Hon Peter were all conspiring against me. I remembered that I hadn't been this drunk in a very long time and wondered why the hell not.

*

'Crouch End,' said Peter to the taxi driver and I realised he wasn't just putting me in the cab, but was climbing in alongside me, and that made very good sense indeed. As the car chugged up the hills of north London, I was voraciously snogging a manboy I'd just met in a bar, and, instead of seeming a heinous crime, it seemed exactly the right thing to be doing.

Lars wanted to divorce me. He'd stopped loving me despite everything that we'd once dreamed of together. He'd upped and left me, and hired lawyers to get rid of me. I'd snog this lovely man. He wanted me but Lars didn't.

'I never do things like this,' I said and fell against Peter as the cab crawled up Crouch Hill. He had surprisingly muscly arms that he wrapped around me and his hair gel smelt of the sea. He had another bottle of champagne with him on the seat.

'Glad you picked me to never do it with.' Peter started to burrow into my dress as he kissed me.

'Oh, my God,' I said, because there it was: the familiar old pull of desire rose from the bottom of my stomach. 'This is what I used to feel like.' I felt his strength, his hands circling my chest.

It was only when we pulled into my road that I fully realised what was happening.

'You'll have to get out here,' I told Peter, pushing him off me and banging on the cab window to attract the driver's attention. He pulled over to the kerb.

'Don't tell me you've changed your mind.'

'No. Yes. No. I don't know. I don't want the neighbours to see you,' I said. God, I wanted him but... 'I'm still married. I'm a *mother of two…*' The only thing I didn't say was: 'And I'm trying to deal with the terrible hurt of being dumped by the man I loved for so long.'

'You're a very yummy mummy,' Peter said, pulling me towards him again. 'But I'll get out here and then come and knock on the door in a minute or two.'

'No.' I was very drunk and being very drunk didn't always lead to the best decisions. My husband had been gone less than a few weeks and…

And he'd left me. He didn't want me any more.

'This isn't just any old thing, you know,' Peter said. 'When I smashed you in the face tonight, the gods were on our side.'

The cabbie sighed audibly through the glass.

'Were they?' Giggles gurgled from me at such nonsense.

'Jesus wants me for a sunbeam,' he said and then, climbing out of the cab, whispered, 'See you in a minute.'

I stumbled up the steps to my house, fumbled for a key and let myself in. There was – just for a moment – a pang of guilt, but then I said out loud, 'Fuck you, Lars,' and went to answer the door, knowing even then that what I was doing was revenge.

*

'God, you're gorgeous,' Peter told me one hundred times or more, as he undressed me in between kisses, pulling my dress awkwardly over my head, taking one step at a time, backwards up to the landing and into the spare room, where we eventually fell back onto the bed. He popped open the champagne and we swigged it straight from the bottle in between deep, soggy kisses.

He was young, strong and much more dexterous in bed than he was in life. He toured my body with the pleasure of an aficionado, and each moan from me seemed to make him happier. The drink had driven out all my inhibitions. As I undid his jeans and found his erection, I could remember very little about who I'd actually been before I experienced such sheer, friendly pleasure.

For a brief moment I remembered the smell and taste of Lars and how passionate our lovemaking had been. It seemed so long ago.

'You're so gorgeous,' Peter said, just when I thought that if he didn't put himself inside me, I would die from lust. 'Are you really sure you want to do this?'

'Of course, I am,' I said. 'Please, please get on with it…' He was very proficient at putting on a condom; I remembered the smell from so many years ago and I wondered how I'd let those raw, hopeful times go.

'Oh, my God,' he said when he finally edged his way inside me.

'Oh, my God,' I whispered in return.

There was a moment when I knew that this was it: *doing this changes everything forever*. I've slept with another man.

I breathed deeply and blocked out any bigger thought than the 'boy' above me rocking backwards and forwards breathlessly, each thrust of him coming further into me. Instinctively, I moved my hips and held him until he rested for a moment. 'Slowly,' I told him.

'Fuck me, you're sensational,' he said, covering my face in kisses from above me and then getting so carried away that he started to move again.

It wasn't the longest sex in the world. Eventually, he collapsed on top of me as I started to buck a little in turn.

I only just had time to tip him off and shut out my conscience with another swig of champagne before I passed into the dreamless vacuum of drunken sleep.

<u>24</u>

2016

I was at the launch party for Brand New in the Goldwyn boardroom. Marti made a speech that seemed to float over my head into the crowd of colleagues, journalists and clients. Liv was wearing a vintage fifties floral number; I was in a Whistles dress of cream and camel that I'd bought off The Outnet and was terrified I'd spill something over it.

Everyone congratulated me and I smiled broadly. Board directors milled around and patted Marti on his back and told me how exciting it was for the share price. I'd just finished giving an off-the-cuff interview to a reporter from the magazine for AWE – the Association of Women Entrepreneurs.

But all I could think about was Lars and the text I'd received earlier.

> So sorry, stuck in Zurich – the deal is going on and on but is really important. Very proud of you and hope it goes well.

I'd been getting a blow-dry and had to hold it together

while the hairdresser finished GHD-ing my curls into submission; but then I went outside and kicked a rubbish bin in the street in fury.

Thor texted me.

> I think they say in England, break a leg, but please don't as you have lovely legs.

Even this didn't bring a smile to my face. Ulrika messaged.

> You will be magnificent.

I read it and thought, magnificent on my own, but simply sent her kisses back.

Now, Liv appeared beside me, pushing her way through a crowd of younger women who also worked at Goldwyn. One was boasting about her long, full blonde hair and the others were feeling her head where the extensions were woven in.

'Her hair is pre-owned,' Liv hissed in my ear.

I sniggered but couldn't keep up the front I'd been pulling off in front of Liv. 'I really thought he'd make it this time. He knew how important it was to me.'

'Oh, darling, and this is your moment,' Liv said. 'I'm sure he would be here unless it was life or death.'

'It's not though, is it? It's not life and death.' It was just – in the end – his *job*. But I could feel something dying inside me.

*

The next evening, though, Lars was back, deeply sorry in the face of my cold fury. 'I will make it up to you,' he said, as he had so many times before. I let him kiss my cheek and didn't say that it was impossible for him to make up for missing the most important moment in my career to date. I was quiet instead.

He arranged a babysitter and insisted we went back to the Spanish bistro of our first date. When we arrived, he bribed the waiter to give us the table under the awning that we'd shared back then. We ate tapas and he concentrated hard on making me relay all the details of the launch. Two glasses of Rioja later, I found myself thawing. He couldn't help that his business was so demanding, could he?

He turned the conversation back to that day we met. 'Do you remember how you wrote 'IOU one night out' up my arm?'

I remembered it so clearly. I remembered the possibilities of that beginning and our naïve faith that we would achieve them all. We still could, I thought sadly. We still could.

<u>25</u>

2017

The phone rang and it was as if a brass band had been commissioned to play in my head – big baton on my eardrums, tubas in every synapse. I opened my eyes and stared at the unfamiliar sight of the ceiling in the spare room. Must have passed out in here, I thought, trying very hard as the sound of the phone ricocheted around the house to work out where and who I was.

I had to make the noise stop. It was only as I scrambled out of bed that I realised I was naked and with someone who wasn't my husband.

'Oh, what have I done?' I shrieked and the lump that was Peter beside me stirred and sat up.

'What is it?'

I grabbed my dress from the floor and, holding it in front of me, ran from the room. As I raced along the landing towards the phone in my bedroom, I had a vision of Peter above me, pushing into me.

I grabbed the phone. 'Yes?'

'Mummy?' the tentative sound of Finn's voice came

down the line. 'Why're you shouting?'

Two worlds collided as my sexual drunken animal met the purity of my mother beast. Tears welled immediately in my eyes. More pictures from last night flashed in my mind – snogging in a taxi, letting Peter come into the house, hating Lars as I did it and knowing and not caring that there was no way back. I took a deep breath. Christ, what had I done?

'Hello, darling,' I said as calmly as I could to Finn. 'How are you? Are you being good?'

'Daddy said I could ring you whenever I want. He said I could ring you now even and dialled the number but then he went back to sleep.'

'Yes, of course. I miss you and love you very much.'

'Grandie's got bent fingers,' Finn said.

'And she had a hair growing out of her chin but she let me pull it out.' Tessa came on the line.

'Are you both being good?'

'Well, Finn is being extra farty,' Tessa said.

'You're the stinker,' Finn shouted in the background and then grabbed the phone back from his sister. 'Do you want to talk to Daddy now? He's pretending to be asleep but I can jump on his head.' Before I could object, there was the sound of my son doing exactly that and Lars' muffled sleepy anger.

I have a man in my bed while I'm listening to the intimate sounds of my husband sleeping.

'They wake up so early,' Lars said.

'What're you going to do with them today?'

'We're going to the Playpit,' he said. 'Tessa says it's a

great place.' I thought of the sticky, scream-infested, fried-food-ridden hell that was the Playpit Indoor Centre, and told Lars that he'd enjoy it.

'What are you going to do?'

'Nothing much. Champneys with Liv tomorrow.'

'*Fy fan*, you can't afford to be throwing money around like that, Ami, with all this going on. Look, I'm not saying you don't deserve it, it's just—'

'My father paid for it. It's got nothing to do with you what I do.' I slammed the phone down, angry with him all over again.

The tousled but still beautiful form of the Hon Peter appeared in the doorway, wrapped in the white bedsheet from the spare room.

'Are you all right?' he asked and opened his arms to me so that the sheet fell onto the floor. He looked very young in the morning light.

After last night, there was no going back.

'I think I'm still drunk,' I said, because I couldn't say my thoughts out loud to him.

'Come back to bed.' He pulled me up and the dress I was holding to cover my nakedness dropped to the floor. He held me and breathed into my hair. I felt as if I were looking down at someone else – someone who went home with 'boys' they picked up in clubs when they were only recently separated from their husband. It didn't feel as if I was in my own body even as I stood so close to him.

'I really shouldn't have let you come home with me,' I

said. 'You know… I'm not sure I can remember much about last night.'

'We'd probably better do it again so that you can remember it properly. I'm only saying that in the interests of you not thinking you're losing your memory.' He came in to kiss me and at the same time started to lead me back to the spare room, lifting my feet onto his, so that as he walked and kissed me, I walked with him back down the landing. I didn't resist him even as my conscience started to quake somewhere deep in my soul.

'I really ought to clean my teeth,' I said just as he pushed me back down onto the bed.

*

It was later that the remorse came, heavy and unforgiving along with my hangover.

'Oh, what have you done? What have you done? Slept with someone other than Lars,' went the devil of doubt.

'But he doesn't want you,' said the angel of angst. 'You're getting divorced. You haven't done anything wrong.'

But the devil was unrelenting. I rolled round in my bed trying to escape from its accusations. 'How will you face Lars? What if your children knew what their mother had done?'

I went downstairs and took some Nurofen, then sat on the sofa with a mug of tea as I rang Liv.

'Remember what it felt like to lose your virginity? I feel like that, like everyone is going to know. Oh, Liv, what have I done?'

'You've done a perfectly normal thing and got off with someone to get over someone else,' Liv said in her perfunctory way. 'It's good for you. You haven't done anything wrong, except have some fun for once. You can't remember telling me how I wasn't going anywhere with you because you were going to go shagadelic with that boy…'

'I did not. I'm still *married*.'

'So you keep saying, but you were up for it, big time.'

'Oh, how am I going to face Lars when he brings the children back?'

'It's nothing to do with him. He got up and left you, remember? Are you going to see Peter again?'

'Well, he asked for my number but, of course, I can't. I should *never* have done it in the first place.' Despite this I told Liv how Peter had said goodbye: 'Thank you for having me,' and how I'd replied very gravely, 'Thank you for coming,' before we both collapsed in laughter. 'Listen to me. I sound like you.'

*

'You look all right considering,' Liv said when I pulled up outside her flat the following morning to collect her for our trip to Champneys. She climbed into the car wearing enormous dark glasses, which made her look not so much

Jackie O as Jackie-Oh-my-God.

'The thing is, I know that Lars walked out and everything but I feel so guilty, Liv.' I had a permanent icy feeling in my stomach, which I couldn't get rid of. How quickly Lars would think I'd moved on; how little I must care about him. Then: he doesn't give a toss if I care about him any more. Still, my cold belly would not let me forget.

'You have absolutely nothing to feel guilty about. It was just what you needed,' said Liv. 'Let's hope he's the first of many.'

*

'Do I look a bit better?' I asked in the changing room at the end of the day, when Liv and I had been plucked, scrubbed, oiled and cooked. We'd spent a good hour in the Jacuzzi and had even slowly swum a couple of lengths. The bit we'd enjoyed most, though, was having a gossip while we ate lunch in our towelling robes, toasting my dad with our water glasses. Unfortunately, I'd spent quite a bit of time while trying to relax during my massage wondering if Lars had done what I'd done and slept with someone else; it had made me squirm as I tried to stay still under the masseur's hands.

'You look gorgeous. And a little bit more relaxed. But that'll be the sex.' Liv added another couple of bottles of Champney's body lotion to her bag, along with a pair of white slippers.

'Don't forget the paper knickers,' I said. 'They're free

too.'

<u>26</u>

2016

Chickenpox. Nadine said that it was sensible to expose children deliberately to the virus, so that they had just a few spots and avoided a more serious infection later. She went in search of spotty children for Jemima to hang out with.

Frankly, that wasn't top of my list, what with my fledgling business, two kids to look after and a nearly-always-absent husband. So, the first I knew about Tessa and Finn potentially having it was when my au pair called me at work saying the kids had a fever.

'They said at school it is probably the chickenpox,' said Ingrid in her factual German way. 'There are no spots yet but Finn has a temperature and Tessa is also hot. The school says that we are not to return for one week due to the policy.'

'Oh, no. You've had it, right?' I was in the middle of forking a salad into my mouth from a plastic carton while I typed a late report for Land.

'Unfortunately, no, I have already called my mother and she says that I have not had the chickenpox,' Ingrid said. 'She is apologetic as it was a fashion to avoid the chickenpox when I was growing up.'

I groaned. 'Do you think you'll already have caught it?' I asked. The answer was probably, yes.

'My mother is saying that I should go to stay with my aunt until we are free of the contagious period,' Ingrid said. 'We are very sorry for the fashion in Germany regarding this disease but I must avoid the shingles.'

My inner stress level rose like mercury in a thermometer dropped into a hot bath; I had so much work to do in the next couple of days. I stood up and hastily unplugged my laptop. 'I'll be home as soon as I can.'

So, poor Ingrid was packed off to her aunt in south London in an Uber and the rest of that day wasn't too bad – I got the report done while the kids lay under a duvet, top and tail at both ends of the playroom sofa, happily watching back-to-back Disney.

Lars was away again – by then I'd stopped wondering where; I'd have asked Ulrika for help but she was in the Lakes on a lyrical poets' tour. I sat in the armchair in the playroom typing and monitored the kids' temperatures, which hovered around thirty-eight degrees.

It was in the middle of that night that Finn woke me in my bed; he'd trailed into the room clutching his toy dog, Barker, and was crying loudly.

'What's the matter?' I said.

'I've got a head egg,' he wailed. 'An awful head egg.'

I put out my arms and he came into them – his body felt like a mini furnace. 'Oh, poor baby.'

By the morning, three doses of Calpol later, he was less hot but covered in mini red blisters as if he were wearing a suit of irregular polka dots. Tessa, meanwhile, had just a few on her chest and happily set to treating her brother's symptoms with her plastic doctor's set until he puked all over her and the playroom carpet. Finn carried on being sick throughout the day, gushing up more food than was really possible to fit into his miniature stomach.

In the afternoon, when he finally went to sleep, I called Lars and got a UK ringtone; this was good news – it potentially meant he was on his way home.

'Ami?' He sounded as if he was walking fast.

'Lars? Where are you? The kids have got chickenpox and I need to do lots of work and Ingrid hasn't had it and—'

'I told you, I had the chance to meet some hackers who'll tell me the secrets of site security,' Lars said excitedly. I dimly remembered something about Hull?

'I'm in Hull now,' Lars confirmed. 'Just got off the train. I'll be home on Sunday probably. Are the kids OK?'

'No, they've got f-ing chickenpox,' I said. I slammed the phone down and ignored it when he tried to ring back.

By then, any determination not to mind about being left alone in my marriage had disappeared. Work, children. Work and children. The relentless repetition. And me, always waiting for Lars to be the missing piece of sky in the jigsaw of my life.

By Saturday, I'd loosely taped a pair of mittens onto Finn to stop him scratching the spots; called NHS Direct only to hear that 'unfortunately there are some cases of chickenpox that are more severe than others' and, hysterical with so little sleep, eventually pleaded with Liv to come round for an hour so I could have a bath.

'This is the best contraception I can think of,' she said in horror as she watched Finn writhe around on the sofa, bashing his head with the toy mittens and crying with the sort of sobs that ripped out my heart.

Later, when I'd finally managed to get him to sleep, Liv held me tight while I cried into her shoulder only slightly less loudly than Finn.

'This quasi-single parenthood can't go on,' Liv said. 'What are you going to do?'

'We're going to marriage guidance counselling,' I told her. 'As soon as he has time.'

'You know what? Screw Lars,' said Liv, with more force than usual. She'd adored Lars in the beginning and as he became more absent only called him 'Lars Who?' 'He should bloody make time.'

She got up, came back with mugs of tea and handed me one as she sat down. 'You need to be honest with yourself,' she said. 'Ask yourself whether you wouldn't be better off without him. I know that's not what you want to hear but I wouldn't be your friend if I didn't say it.'

Of course, I'd thought about it. In my always-present anger I sometimes thought about nothing else. The truth was, though, I still hoped that there was a route back to that incredible love from our early years and I felt fiercely that I had to do everything I could to keep our family – the fam – together, for the children – and for the dreams we'd shared.

'If I give up hoping,' I asked Liv, 'what happens then?'

She sighed. 'I can't watch you like this any more. It's killing you. You've got to make him see that he needs to look after you as well as his bloody business.'

'He thinks that looking after the future is looking after us,' I said. 'And you know, sometimes, when he's here, it's still OK – last Sunday we all had breakfast in our bed and it ended up in a tickling match.' I knew I was desperately trying to find an example of how my marriage was still functioning. 'He was home on Tuesday and we didn't argue. Sometimes, you know, when he comes home and sleeps for ages, I climb in beside him and he wraps his arms around me and, then, it's like the old Lars again.'

'Come on,' Liv said very gently. 'You can lie to me, but don't lie to yourself. What are you so afraid of? It can't be being on your own, because you've been on your own so much. You could move on, meet someone else, be happy again, like you were with Lars in the beginning.'

I wanted to tell her again how I would do everything I could to keep my family together, if it meant that we could give Tess and Finn the unfiltered, uncompromised love I'd always wanted myself from my own parents. That Lars and I had created a dream of what our lives would be and somehow, somehow, that still had to be possible.

'I can't imagine being with someone else, ever,' I said and pulled the blanket up around my neck. I gestured towards the ceiling to indicate the kids. 'And we're still a family.'

27

2017

I faced the man who was legally still my husband, knowing that I'd slept with someone else less than forty-eight hours ago. I hugged the life out of the exhausted kids, wrapping them up like babies and taking them to bed. As I came downstairs, however, there was Lars – unshaven and pale – in what had been his kitchen. He'd poured himself a glass of red wine and held one out to me.

'You can't just come and drink here now, you know,' I said. 'You should go.'

'You look different,' he said.

'I had a facial at Champneys.' I looked away from him as I took the glass.

There was a pause before he said, 'So all the papers are being sorted at your end?'

'I can't agree to anything financial until I find out if I still have a business – and we're broke, Lars, really broke already. You'll have to get some money out of your business.' I lifted my glass to my mouth and smelt the memories of Friday night. I put it on the kitchen counter.

Lars moved to the kitchen table and sat down as if I should come and sit opposite him. I stayed standing up.

'I've been thinking,' he said. 'You know the thing with the kids nearly suffocating really shook me up.'

'Me too,' I said. 'Anyway, now we know what we have to do; we've got to keep a close eye on them while all this goes on. And Jenny is great – really good for them – and I'm at home much more. How were they this weekend?'

'They were fine, but I kept watching them for signs they weren't.'

I knew what he was saying – I constantly watched for signs of trauma. Tess seemed better now she understood her living arrangements and Lars and I weren't shouting at each other all the time, but I had still got us put on a waiting list for a child counsellor.

'Didn't Ulrika think that they might need a bath even if you didn't?' I went for a simpler subject. The kids had come back smelling musty and wearing clothes splattered in food.

'Well, she did keep saying it in her way, but I never really seemed to get round to it – there wasn't *time*... what with getting up and getting them dressed and then trying to get them out of the door and then coming back and everything... and all that eating they have to do, so I told her they'd had a bath on Saturday night when she went to a poetry thing.' Lars looked wretched. 'I know all you want to say is I told you so,' he said with a half-smile. 'Yes, I admit, it isn't easy, but that's because I'm not in my own house. They're over-excited because it's all new – and the little buggers just took advantage.

'Anyway,' he said then. 'It's been making me think.'

'I'm a bit too tired for more thinking,' I said. All I wanted was for him to go so I could be alone with my guilt.

'I keep thinking about how you've said for so long that I wasn't there for you and the kids – and then what could have happened to them.'

'OK,' I said. *Now* we were going to have this conversation?

There was a silence before he said in a small bleak voice, 'I've been blind. So single-minded that I nearly let my children get into danger. All I could think about this weekend is how Finn could've been killed.'

'Yes.' The horror of that pile of cushions hit me again. 'It was my fault though – I was the one who was here and should have paid attention to the signs with Luba.'

'No. With everything going on – all the arguments, the divorce, the trouble at work – I should have been here looking after them with you. And there I was stuck in Moscow because of a stupid web conference. Anyway, I was thinking about what you said when you were drunk on FaceTime.'

I felt hot mortification again about begging him to stay with me. 'Sorry about that.'

There was another pause.

'About whether we really have tried everything, I mean.'

Hope and guilt crashed together inside me before landing with a thud of disbelief. He'd sat there with his spreadsheets and his dismissive manner; told me to get a lawyer. Now he spent a weekend alone with the kids and he wanted to try again? I gaped at him. 'You feel guilty about the kids, so you come in here and say this *now*?'

'Well, perhaps we should, you know, slow it down a bit.' He stared at the wood of the table. Then he said in a gentle tone with a hint of sing-song I hadn't heard for a very long time, 'I know everything I said and what I did and I'm sorry. We can stop all of this before it's too late. We can call it all off, give it another go. I can prove to you that I'm not the person you thought I was.'

'Seriously, Lars.' I picked up the glass of red wine and took a large gulp. I knew only that while I'd wanted to hear it, he had to mean it and, worse, I'd heard it all before in the years when he'd promised to try harder. A cold tear slid down my face. 'A few weeks ago you called me some really terrible things and said you were leaving. You can't just sit there and say you didn't mean any of it.'

And it's too late.

I've slept with someone else.

I've broken the last taboo.

I'm no longer yours.

'I've been really angry with you for so long for not seeing my point of view,' he said. 'But then, in the last few days, all I can think about is that you've been right – I've been so focused on the company that I've forgotten what really matters. You and the kids. I want to do the right thing.'

'I don't want to be the right thing!' I shouted. 'We were

in love, Lars. Really in love. You can't replace that with doing the right fucking thing.'

'I didn't mean it like that… I've never stopped loving you. I think we've stopped liking each other over the last year or so and I know that that's because you felt abandoned…'

'You're going to start telling me you're going to change again, aren't you?'

Christ, he took me for a mug. I thought of all the promises he'd made when we'd done – as he'd put it – all that *talking.* 'You promise the world and mean it for about two minutes and then you just forget we exist.' A tear hung off my cheek. I sat down at the table after all. 'You're only saying it now because you've had to look after the children all weekend and you can't cope.'

'I'm not. It's not about the kids being difficult – it's because being with them made me realise how much I miss you. Us. All of us. Together. I'm sorry for the things I said. I really am sorry.'

I raised my eyes to the ceiling. 'There is no "us" any more,' I whispered.

He tried to take my hand but I shrugged him off. 'How can you be so cold to me?'

'I'm frozen inside,' I said and my voice was cold too.

'Come on, you know we can make it.' In the moment, he looked just like Finn trying to get me to agree to buy him a treat – sweets or chocolate.

'If I compromise about everything and learn to live with

253

you around only when you want to be.' As I said them, the words were familiar to me because I'd said them – or versions of them – so often before. I'd spent many weeks now without any hope that we would get back together. In sleeping with someone else I'd effectively made it final.

'I'll be different.' I felt only exhaustion as he spoke because I'd heard it all before.

'Bollocks,' I said. 'Look, you'd better go. I don't want to be having this conversation again. It's gone too far. It's too late.'

'It's not too late,' Lars whispered. 'Nothing has changed. We can go to counselling again.'

'Everything has changed.' My voice was low and sad. I can't forgive you, now, I can't. And you would never forgive what I've done either.

'Like what?' Lars looked directly at me. 'Like what exactly?'

'You hurt me so much.' A bruise of a blush started to climb from my neck and up my chin; the more I tried to stop it, the more fierce and red it became. Still I told myself that I'd done nothing wrong.

Lars stared intensely at me and then shook his head. 'What's going on, Ami?'

'Nothing. Nothing except that I'm not just going to forget everything that's happened and let you come back into my life and hurt me all over again.' I could feel my face getting hotter and brought my glass to my mouth to cover it.

'*Fy fan…*' Lars started shaking his head. 'Fuck me. Is it

really possible?'

'What?'

'Is there…?'

'Is there what?'

'There's someone else, isn't there?' He jumped to his feet and started to pace around behind his chair.

All I had to do was deny it. 'Don't be stupid.'

'You've been seeing someone else.' Lars' voice was a whisper.

'I haven't.' I said this as decisively as I could.

His face contorted in anger. 'Who is it?'

'No one. Don't be so stupid. And stop shouting – you'll wake up the children.'

'Who is it? Tell me who it is.'

'Look.' I got up too and faced him. 'It's nothing. You'd better leave now, Lars.'

'I'm not going anywhere until you tell me what the fuck is going on.'

But you have no right to know. 'You said you didn't want me. You said it time and time again.' My chin rose. I'd as good as admitted it now.

I wanted him to hurt, I realised. I'd given my body to another man and maybe I'd got strength in return. I stared defiantly at him.

He marched around the table. 'Is it true? You're sleeping with someone else?'

I tried to shake him off. 'No, I'm not. Not sleeping with… It was just once.' Again, there was a thrill in pushing the knife of hurt further into him.

Lars took a step back from me as if I'd slapped him. 'Fuck me, no.'

'Why the fuck shouldn't I?' I whispered. 'You don't want me, so why shouldn't I?'

'I never thought that you would…' Lars' voice was quiet and he moved away from me. 'I never thought you'd do that.'

So you thought I'd always be waiting; that all you had to do was change your mind and I'd be here? 'How can you say that to me after everything that's happened?' I said. 'Everything you've done?' I fought on because if I stopped fighting I would let the guilt rush in and I knew it would never go away.

This was the real end of our marriage, after so many endings.

'Whatever's happened… however much we've fucked it up,' he said, 'you're still in my blood, Amelia.' He picked up his glass and drained it and then, in his hurry to refill it, pushed the bottle from the kitchen cabinet to the floor where it exploded with a crash. I immediately thought about the kids upstairs. 'Who is he?'

I pulled a kitchen chair in front of me. 'No one. No one,' I said. 'You'd better go.' Through the blear of my tears I tried to find the dustpan and brush in the cupboard under the sink, then gave up, simply sitting down on the kitchen floor.

'Is it someone I know?'

'No, just someone I met. It was a one-off. But there's no

reason for me to have to justify myself to you.'

'After everything we've had together? No reason to justify rushing out and screwing someone else? Christ, I can't believe it.'

'Get out, Lars.' I struggled to my feet. 'Just get out. This isn't your house any more.'

'You're not my wife any more.' He turned to the kitchen door and wiped his eyes with the back of his hand.

'No, and it was you who decided that,' I said slowly. 'Now get out.'

As he pulled open the kitchen door, there, about to reach up for the door handle, was Tessa, dragging her blanket behind her. 'I heard shouting and banging,' she said in a voice soaked in sleep.

Lars reached down for his daughter.

'Tess, it's all fine.' I went towards the door and wrestled Lars out of the way, picking Tessa up and holding her. We'd promised there would be no more of this arguing near the kids. 'Daddy was just going. Everything is all right. We broke a bottle by accident, that's all.'

Lars wiped his eyes again and pulled on his jacket. 'Goodbye, Tess,' he said and bent down to kiss his daughter on the cheek.

He didn't slam the door. Instead it closed gently on the latch behind him.

28

2016

I tried not to argue with Lars the next time he came home; bought new underwear from Agent Provocateur, put the children in bed early and cooked a recipe from a Gordon Ramsay book, which said it should take half an hour but took two.

He sat at the table and called me *älskling* and it sounded like a word from another epoch.

I smiled and tried to relax. 'I'm sorry if I've been horrible.'

Lars picked up his knife and fork. 'I'm sorry too but we need to move on.'

I looked up; I'd planned this. 'Christmas. That's a cheery subject. I was thinking that we could maybe just stay here, have your mother round for lunch, but, really, just be the four of us.'

'You don't want to go to your parents?' he said. 'It's just...'

'Well, I'm sure they'd understand that we want a bit of time on our own. I could ask them to have the kids for a couple of days and maybe the two of us…'

'I'm…' Lars paused and took a breath. 'I'm not going to have that much time off over Christmas. A couple of days but I've got a big proposal to write and it would probably be better for us to go to your mother's so that you had company.'

Hot tears rushed into my eyeballs, but I took a deep breath as I'd practised. 'I want you to have a couple of days off with us,' I said gently.

Lars put down his fork. His smile was tense. 'And I will be there, I promise,' he said. 'But it's the only time I've got and I really need these lawyers on board and I promised them a proposal.'

I thought about how Sasha, the Relate lady, advised me to deal with my husband – 'Control your anger' – and then immediately did the complete opposite. I couldn't seem to help it.

'It's fucking Christmas,' I shouted. 'A family time. And you want us safely parked at my mother's so I can't cause a fuss and you can work all you fucking want… You actually wish you weren't married to me at all, don't you?'

'Yes,' he snarled back. 'At least I wouldn't have someone asking me where I was all the time, going on and on about how bad their marriage is…' He paused then and looked exhausted. Then he said very quietly, 'This isn't right any more.'

And that was when I'd known that he was starting to think very seriously about leaving me. Still, after everything we'd shared, it seemed somehow impossible that he actually would.

29

2017

I swept up the glass from the kitchen floor and it was as if I were sweeping away my old life. I didn't cry any more. I felt only cold anger and with it came a new sense of purpose: getting divorced was the right thing to do.

In the morning, I dropped the children off with a hug. Parminder waved across the car park at me, mouthing, 'You OK?' and I smiled back: 'Yes,' feeling more determined than I had in a good few months.

At the office, I sat down in my chair and turned on my computer. The email from Ben Jones was at the top of my inbox. Finally, the day of reckoning. The subject header simply said, 'Account'. I double-clicked on it.

Ami,

I was impressed by the ideas that Brand New presented. I've conducted a review of all agency proposals and there is nothing that compares to your campaign. I would like to go back to the conversation we were having when you so unfortunately needed to leave – does 12 p.m.

today at your office suit you?

Sincerely,

Ben

As if he ever does *anything* sincerely. But I reread the email and shook my head slowly to make sure that this wasn't a dream. I beckoned to Bridget and indicated that she should come and read it from my screen, just to make sure. She strode across the office and read it over my shoulder before shouting: 'Omigod, Omigod.'

'Please ring up and say 12 p.m. is fine,' I said, standing up and then sitting down with a thud. There was a chance – a chance whose outcome was unfortunately in the hands of a man who I'd disintegrated in front of – that today might not be the day that Brand New packed up its portfolio forever. 'And ring Marti's assistant and see if he's around because we'll need him this afternoon to tell Ben that he'll back us.'

I called Liv, who sounded very smug at the other end of the phone. 'You're not going under after all.'

'What if he tells Marti I shouted at him like a lunatic?'

'Just meet him very professionally. Tell him you don't want to discuss that day. And apologise. Then get him to sign on the dotted line.'

I paused and then said, 'Liv, Lars came round last night, talking about doing the right thing for the kids and asked me to try again – and then he looked at my face and he suspected something and, well, I wanted to make him hurt so I ended

262

up telling him about Peter. He was really angry. He said I was no longer his wife.'

'I thought that was what he wanted.'

'It is. I think he was just shocked that I would actually, you know…'

'But you have and there's no point regretting it. It's done. It was fun. You're moving on. He treated you appallingly for years and he left *you*. You haven't done anything wrong. And all that about going back to him, *well*.'

'He was… he was broken, Liv.'

'Just keep remembering how many times he's broken you.'

There was a silence and then I said, 'Have you thought of being an agony aunt?'

'Yes, but how can you give original advice when everyone's problems are always the same? Now, go get that account. Be snooty, breezy and just a little bit disdainful.'

'Snooty, breezy and just a little bit disdainful.' I hung up and set to work.

Bridget hurried round setting up the projector in the big meeting room upstairs. At 11.45 a.m. I powdered my face, asked Bridget to put the coffee on and then paced up and down the boardroom.

'I'm ten minutes early. I hope you don't mind,' came Ben's sardonic voice from the doorway.

I tried to smile. He was carrying his jacket. His tousle of hair had been cut and his face was the colour of a latte although summer had yet to start in England.

263

I walked forward, a fixed smile on my face, and shook his enormous hand. Then, I gestured to a chair at the meeting table and said, 'Would you like coffee?'

'Only if it's French,' he said.

'Would that be white, black or…?' Bridget asked.

'I'll have black with milk,' he said.

'Black with milk… black with milk…' Bridget was off towards the little kitchen.

He sat down at the glass table and I sat across from him.

He smiled. 'How are you? Look, I'm sorry if I upset you…'

'You didn't. It's me who needs to apologise. I shouldn't have pushed you.' I sounded stiff and uptight, barely spitting the words out of closed lips.

'I wound you up when you were completely knackered. I'm sorry. Should we just call a truce?'

'Yes,' I said shortly. Was this another one of his games? I had to work with him, that was all – pull off the next hour without any repeat performances. 'Let's just get on with business, shall we? I apologise for my behaviour at the presentation. I was having a very bad day.'

'And I apologise for listening to your best friend and for asking you out.'

My eyes narrowed to slits.

Bridget entered the room, immune to the tension, and put a coffee cup in front of Ben. 'Black with milk is white, isn't it?' She sat down next to him at the table and got out a notepad. I rose and started to pace up and down.

'So,' I said. 'You've decided that our treatment is…'

'Absolutely revolutionary in our brand category.'

Bridget wrote that down.

'It transforms Campury in a single stroke into something that has the irony that a British woman will want…' I went on as if he hadn't said a word.

'It's fabulous,' he said. 'No one else has come up with ideas like that. You saw Claudia's face and everyone else at Campury thinks the same.'

'How is Claudia?' I couldn't help myself. Bridget flushed purple.

'Very well indeed,' Ben said and raised an eyebrow. 'Would you like me to pass on your regards?'

'Yes.'

'So, my one issue really is the stability of your agency.' He became very businesslike.

'I've asked Marti if he wouldn't mind joining us for a few minutes so that you can ask him any questions you like.'

'Excellent.'

I went for the kill. 'If that all stacks up you're giving us the account?'

Ben placed his elbows on the table in a relaxed way. 'Let's just see how it goes with Marti, shall we? Bridget, why don't you go and ask Mr Goldwyn if he's available? Not a word to anyone yet, eh?' he added as she shut the door.

There was a brief silence.

'Right,' I said.

'Right,' said Ben at exactly the same time.

I spluttered and he took the advantage: 'I think we'd better clear the air before we go any further, don't you?'

'It all seems extremely clear to me.'

'It will be extremely difficult to carry on working with you if you keep treating me like you hate me.'

'I apologised for being emotional.' I could hear the defensive note in my voice.

'Yes, but I didn't have a problem with that. I just think we got off on the wrong foot.'

'Right from the start with that ridiculous mix-up with Liv, you just wanted to laugh at me.' I felt my rage rise again. 'And I used to have *actual dignity*, you know, before all this.'

'You mean owls didn't shit on your walls before you split up with your husband?' He twinkled now and I refused to smile.

'They didn't actually. And prospective clients didn't take the piss out of me all the time either.'

'Look, I'm sorry, but I had the best of intentions. The trouble was that you were all on your high horse and that does bring out the wrong side of me... I'm sorry again if I behaved like a smart arse.'

'You are?'

He smiled on. 'I promise to take you extremely seriously.'

'Bastard,' I grunted and he chuckled. We swapped the short smile of adversaries who respect each other's fighting spirit.

Bridget came back in and, after her, in strode Marti.

'Welcome, welcome,' he boomed, shaking Ben's hand vigorously. 'Back in the UK after a spell on the continent, eh? Bet that's good news to you.'

'It certainly is when I see ideas like I have from Brand New.'

'Good old girl, Ami, isn't she?' Marti said, gesturing to me. 'Sent you the best we had.'

'She's fantastic.' Ben winked at me.

'Any other patronising remarks you two want to make about me before we start?' They both laughed.

'Now, you need some further information about us?' asked Marti. 'We'll tell you everything you need to know.'

Why didn't he just say it? That he would back me all the way? I thought about that terrible night in The Ivy, how he hadn't really done anything except berate me since then. I went cold – what if I'd got this far but Marti still intended to pull the plug?

Ben sat down and Marti creaked into the chair opposite. I sat at my boss's side and willed him to support me.

'However, as you will understand, I'm worried about Brand New being a going concern.'

'Well,' said Marti. 'Was a tough one losing LandGirls, but we'd love to add Campury to our list of accounts.'

I took a deep breath. 'I think what Ben is saying is that he wants to give us the account, but he needs to know we're financially secure.' Will you back me, Marti? Or are you going to let your bruised ego get in the way?

'Exactly that,' Ben said. 'We want the ideas and we want Ami and the team, but I need to know that we're working with a sustainable business.'

I could see a vein in Marti's head throbbing. There was no doubt about the prestige of winning Campury. He said, 'Bridget, maybe you could go and find us a copy of the accounts that show how Brand New has been performing?'

'Got them ready and waiting,' and she was off out of the door.

I took a deep breath. I needed to make this work and I had one chance. 'I just need a moment with Marti,' I told Ben.

He looked at me, surprised, but nodded. 'I need to make a call anyway.'

When he'd gone off into the hallway I rose and so did my boss. 'I need you to tell him that we're all good,' I said.

'But are we?' His voice was cold; his face showed no trace of charm.

'Of course we are.' I shook my head and realised that, not only had I bruised his ego, but, by being in front of him, I reminded him of how he'd made a huge mistake. Marti didn't really do mistakes. 'Look, I just want to forget about it, go back to being professional, go back to being friends with you.'

He shook his head slowly from side to side. 'I made a serious error of judgement,' he said.

'Come on,' I urged. 'Everyone does that, don't they? And think what we've been through together over the years. Adding Campury to the agency would top all of that.'

'It's one hell of an account,' he grunted. He looked as if he wanted to say more.

'You thought I'd never get it, though?'

'Well, you haven't been in the best state of mind lately, if you don't mind me saying so. It's not just a question of underpinning Brand New, it's a question of whether you're going to get things back on track.'

I blushed hard. He was right and it hurt. I'd been professionally absent, whether physically because of the kids, or mentally, because of Lars, in the run up to the pitch and for months before that. I'd nearly let my agency go under because I'd not kept my eye on the ball. It wasn't just that I'd hurt him, then, it was that he doubted whether I had the staying power to pull off managing such a big account.

'I'm sorry for that,' I said. 'But I promise you that I will throw absolutely everything at making this work if you make it possible. And I'm sorry I haven't been my best.'

'You've had a tough time.' But still he was right – having a tough time with Lars didn't make up for running his investment into the ground.

'I'm sorry,' I said again. 'But you can trust me. I won't screw up again.'

'One hell of a comeback, winning Campury.'

I started to hope. 'I need you to know you can rely on me.'

He smiled then – not a big smile but a small one. 'We've both gone off the boil a little bit, haven't we?'

This was probably as good a making-up as we were going

to do. 'Won't happen again.'

'We'd better get Jones back in and tell him we're on, then, hadn't we?'

Relief flooded through me. 'You won't regret it.'

'I'd bloody better not. Now we're both going to move on from all this unpleasantness and we're going to deliver the best bloody campaign we've ever done.'

I was sweating slightly as I went to the door, opened it and went along the corridor to Ben, who was looking out of the window. 'Sorry about that,' I said.

'Say some stuff that needed saying?' was all he said as he turned around.

'You could say that, but now we're all good and ready to get the paperwork done.'

Ben grinned. 'Always a good idea to stick up for yourself. You do that quite well, Ami Fitch.'

An hour later Bridget took a photograph of us signing letters where Marti promised that Goldwyn would guarantee Brand New's finances for as long as we controlled the Campury account. Marti and Ben looked pleased. I looked like a small child that had just climbed off the roller-coaster ride of her life.

*

Then Ben insisted on taking me out for 'a quick drink to tie up the details'.

'I promise this is the start of me behaving properly,' he

said. Dazed, I followed him until I found myself on a banquette in a private members' club a short walk away.

Ben ordered me a glass of very cold Sancerre. 'I know it's your favourite wine. Liv told me.' I took a huge gulp. 'Now, you're going to have to forgive me if I forget every now and again not to take the piss out of you.'

I laughed despite myself. 'Can we move on and talk about how many bags we're going to shift?'

My agency was saved. Still, I hadn't banked on how close Marti had come to losing faith in me. But, I'd pulled it off: I would have some money coming in while we worked out the divorce settlement – not much, as it would take a while for the account to start paying, but it was a start on protecting my children. I wanted to cry with relief.

Ben seemed to be trying hard. 'Here's to the future.' He held up his glass to me. I raised mine back.

'All that stuff with Marti…?'

'Just what needed saying,' I said firmly.

He nodded and changed the subject. 'Life feels a bit crazy when all the divorce stuff is going on, doesn't it?'

I raised my eyebrows, not sure where this was going, but Ben carried on. 'I got this mad adrenaline rush after I split up with my wife, worked about eighty hours a week, took the kids on all these outings – skiing, football, swimming – anywhere I could turn all the frustration into physical energy.'

'Were you gutted?'

'You know, you forget about expressions like "gutted"

when you hang around with Italian women.' He smiled. 'I was more than gutted. I was incapable of accepting it.'

'Did she walk out on you?'

'She made me do the walking,' he said. 'I kept on trying to come back. I couldn't move on. And even now, I'm pretty sure I was a very bad husband.'

'Control freak?' I raised my eyebrows at him and had another slug of wine.

He laughed. 'No, just crap at knowing how to deal with her, to calm her down, to give her what she wanted.'

'Did you help with the children?'

'Of course, I did,' he said. 'It's killing me being away from them for these few months.'

I couldn't work out whether he was a basic bloke who behaved like an egomaniacal tosser or an egomaniacal tosser who was pretending to be a basic bloke.

'Now, aren't you hungry? Feel like I should feed you meat pie and steamed pudding.'

I was ravenous. 'I know I come across as common as muck, but I'm dead sophisticated, you know, really.'

'Then how about mignon of twenty-eight-day hung Scottish heritage beast, flambéed *doucement*, escorted by a lattice sculpture – no, *installation* – of hand-turned seasonal root vegetables and served on a bed of ornamental foliage?'

'Ooh, yes, please.'

A waiter appeared at our side. 'Steak and chips twice, please,' he said and took another large gulp from his glass.

*

Later, when the kids were in bed, I called Liv and told her the whole story.

'It must be because your life was boring for so long that it has to get exciting now,' Liv said. 'But the agency is going to be OK?'

'Well, this more than fills the hole of LandGirls but we won't have any money for a while.'

'Not so bad after all, is he, Ben?'

'The man is a deranged womaniser who thinks the world is his toy set.'

After I put the phone down, I went to look over my sleeping children, cosy in the house that I was determined to keep for them. I would develop the campaign, Ben would go back to Italy, Marti and I would get back on track... and the children and I would go on in a different kind of Happy Ever After. I turned off the light and walked down the landing to bed to sleep and sleep.

Part Two

<u>30</u>

2017

Bridget was brisk with excitement as we set about making the campaign come to life. Marti was distant – our old camaraderie was gone and I knew I needed to work really hard to get his true support back.

Ben seemed to be able to conduct meetings without being offensive, busily talking about production schedules. The gossip about him and Claudia had been overshadowed by a story about an affair he was supposedly having with an account director at Gorgeous.

Now – like the proverbial buses – calls came in from other brands eager to sign up with Brand New; we were firmly back in the game. It was healing to be busy and somewhat successful again; I resolutely put Lars to the back of my mind.

It was after an exhausting week that he turned up on my doorstep at 4 a.m. on Saturday and shrieked an incoherent mixture of Swedish and English swear words up at my bedroom window. I was woken in the cradle of my bed, but struggled to work out what the noise was.

'*Fan i helvete*, Amelia,' came from somewhere below, loud but slurring; I realised a pattering of stones was raining on my window. I sat bolt upright. '*Fy fan*, open the door.' Then I heard a crash.

I leapt out of bed, pulled on my dressing gown and skidded on the floorboards over to the window. Down below, in the yellow glow of the streetlights, wobbling on the path as he bent down to try to pick up a fistful of pebbles from the gravel around the flower beds, was a very dishevelled Lars, in a shirt that had lost its crispness some hours before.

'Oh, my God.' I threw open the sash window and hissed as loudly as I dared, 'Lars, what the hell are you doing here? Go to your mother's. You'll wake up the children.'

'*För guds skull,*' Lars yelled back from where he had fallen forward onto a cactus. 'Everything I was doing, I was doing for us. That's *us*. You, me, the children…'

'Go home, mate,' came the voice of Guy Gates in the darkness from the direction of his house two doors away. 'She doesn't want you and neither do we.'

'Nanny-stealing bastard,' I shouted, forgetting to be quiet.

'Bastard,' echoed my elderly neighbour, Mrs Wragley.

Great. We're having a street party – and since when did Mrs Wragley swear?

'Thank you, Mrs Wragley,' I said into the darkness. 'Lars, I'm ringing you a taxi.'

'She don't want you, mate,' said the footballer again.

'I'm going to get you, you arsehole. You put my children in danger,' said Lars, struggling to his feet and then promptly falling into the bushes, exhaling more Swedish swear words as he did it.

'This is ridiculous,' I said out loud as I charged down the stairs towards the front door, wrenching it open to see Lars' legs sticking out from the garden onto the path.

By this time, a few more of my neighbours had thrown up their sashes to join in. I could hear their murmuring through the trees that lined the street. Gritting my teeth with humiliation, I stepped out barefoot onto the steps, shivering on the cold concrete, and made my way down until I stood over a white-faced, semi-comatose version of my husband.

'For God's sake.' I kicked him, not especially gently. 'Come on. Get up.' I reached down and tried to haul him up.

'I'm going to prove it to you, *älskling*. I'm going to be the husband you always wanted me to be.'

'Do you need a hand, love?' called Mrs Wragley. She wasn't going to be much cop when it came to raising men from the near-dead.

'I'm fine, thank you,' I called.

'I'd call the police if I was you,' shouted Guy.

'Fuck you,' I said as I managed to heave a limp Lars into a sitting position.

'And fuck you back, darlin',' shouted the footballer.

I got Lars to his feet – he seemed to have regained some control of his limbs. A slow smile of pleasure crossed his face as he looked at me. 'You see,' he slurred. 'I'm back.'

'It's just not like him, is it?' said Mrs Wragley. 'I'll pop round with a tonic tomorrow.'

277

'Better make it a vodka tonic,' I said to myself as I started to hobble with him up the steps to the door, his arm around my neck.

'You gunna get him up those steps?' called Guy.

'Take your testosterone back to bed, you tosser,' I shouted back. I pulled harder and, ultimately, managed to slam the door of the house.

When I finally got Lars into the sitting room, he lay like a great beast of uselessness on the sofa, shut his eyes and started snoring loudly almost immediately. I pulled a blanket out from under a cushion and threw it over the man I'd loved for so long. His face was the colour of ancient ash apart from the bruised purple of his closed eyes.

*

The next morning, Lars got up from the sofa at about 10 a.m. The children had woken much earlier but I'd told them that Daddy had been in the area when he'd felt ill and decided to come to the house to rest. I hated confusing them any further.

Tess and Finn hushed each other in the hallway and smiled when Lars finally stumbled into the kitchen; I was drinking coffee and we were making Easter cards.

With a sanctimonious air, I got up and thrust a packet of Nurofen and a mug of black coffee at him. He said, 'Thank you,' and sat down with a thud at the table, grey and grubby in his work clothes. I picked up my pencils again and set about colouring a carrot orange.

'Are you back to live in our house?' Finn asked.

Lars said nothing so – knowing how much the children needed clarity – I said, 'No, Daddy was just not very well so it was easier to sleep here. We're going to carry on exactly as I explained.'

'We'd like it if you'd stayed married,' said Finn almost conversationally.

I could sense Lars trying to meet my eyes but didn't look at him. How much hurt and guilt could there be in a small boy's remark?

Tess said into the silence, 'Is it the sort of time when we're allowed to watch a DVD?'

Lars gave a hollow cackle; it was the brilliant, grim insight of children who could absorb their parents' mood within seconds. 'Yes, it's exactly that sort of time. Come on. How about *The Wizard of Oz*?'

'It's for babies. The first bit's not even in colour,' Tessa said, but she and her brother stood up and went out into the hallway and Lars followed.

I started to empty the dishwasher, thrusting bowls into the cupboard. A few minutes later, Lars came back into the kitchen and stood behind me.

Without turning around, I said, 'Please, I don't want to talk about it.'

'I'm sorry for the names I called you and for whatever I did last night.'

'For causing more pain to our kids? For turning up on the doorstep three sheets to the wind? For being abusive to the neighbours? For waking up the whole street in the middle of the night?'

'Well, for the kids, yes, very sorry. I can't remember much about the rest. But mostly I know that everything that's happened is my fault. I know that you did what you did because of me. *Revenge.*'

He was talking about me shagging Peter. 'I said I don't want to talk about it.' I pulled three coffee mugs out and put them in a high cupboard. 'But it wasn't like that.'

'It keeps coming back to me – what we've got and what we're throwing away.'

I spun on my heel. 'Bit late now, don't you think?'

He looked down at his feet in yesterday's socks. 'Can't we just postpone the divorce while we do some thinking?'

'There's nothing holding it up now except you.' I stuck out my chin. 'I won the Campury account. I know where I stand.'

'Congratulations,' he said with a wan smile. 'Could you just sit down with me and talk for a bit?'

I closed my eyes. 'I don't have the strength.'

'Please.' He sat down at the table and picked up his coffee cup.

I sat down wearily. 'No shouting or name-calling.'

'I promise,' he said. 'And I'm sorry about last night – it sounds like I was an arsehole. If it helps, I feel like shit.'

'Good. And you were a complete arsehole.'

He smiled a little. 'And, well, just *sorry*. It's the children we should think about now, though. What kind of long-term damage are we doing to them?'

'*You* chose to make it this way.'

'I know, I know.' Lars reached out for my hand but I shook him off. 'What harm can it do to hold off the divorce for a couple of months? I need to show you that I can change. Dammit, Ami, this has been a real wake-up call to me, you know – all I can think about is the children.' He put his head in his hands.

'I'm not going to talk about it.' It was as if he wanted to rip my heart out of my body again, play with it like a toy and then give it to me back, its beat all broken. 'It's done. *Done.*'

Lars shook his head. 'I'm sorry for everything I've done to you. Sorry that you had to go to another man to feel loved. But I know it's all my fault. I didn't listen to you.'

The untidiness of our future; the kids shuttling between houses. 'We made this mess. And it's too late.'

'Just don't file the divorce. Please let me show you. Just give it a few months for the sake of the children. For the sake of us. It can't do any harm.'

'I don't trust you not to hurt me again.' It was more than true.

It was also true that it was nothing that I'd *said* that had made him change his mind: it was what happened to the children that had made him see that we needed him around. However, what I'd *done* – slept with someone else, looked as if I no longer wanted him – had got to him too.

But I was just about pulling my life together. 'I'm at the point of no return,' I told him.

Lars jumped up. 'I'll show you. I'll help you with the children and show you that I can be here. I was so wrong, Amelia. I thought it would be so much easier to be on my own than arguing all the time... but... now all I can think about is all of us being apart. You know I've always loved you – that never stopped.'

Finn's plaintive voice came back into my head: *We'd like it if you'd stay married*. I tried to shake it off. Then the image of him at the bottom of a pile of cushions, which was ever-present.

'Let's see if we can be friends again? Nothing more than that,' Lars pushed on. 'If we can get on and be good parents and then, if that works then maybe more. But, please, keep our fam together.'

He sounded like me a few months back, before everything that had happened.

'You can't stay here.' Christ, did I just say that?

'No, I'll stay at my mother's. But just put the divorce off.' His face seemed almost translucent. 'Think of the children. If we go through with this there'll be no going back. You have to think about this for their sake.'

I shook my head with misery. There was a pause; a very long pause. I struggled with my conscience and then struggled again. Eventually I gave a small, almost imperceptible nod, although I still couldn't quite believe I had.

'Thank you,' he said, very quietly.

'You need to go and buy flowers for Mrs Wragley and

apologise for waking her up,' I said. 'But if you see that footballer from down the road, punch him instead.'

*

'You've done *what*?' said Liv later that day.

'It's for a couple of months. Just to see. If there's anything I can do to save my marriage I have to, for the sake of the children…'

'What about the sake of *you*?'

I pushed the phone away from my ear. 'I'm not sure there is a "for the sake of me".'

All I knew was that there were three people in our family who seemed to want to make it work and just me standing in the way. And two of them were children with their futures in my hands. If there was even a small chance we could stick together, wouldn't I be crazy not to try to take it?

I went to Cathy's office on a Friday evening to explain that we were putting the divorce on hold. I still felt very uncertain about what I'd decided to do.

'Well,' she said. 'Not a Type D after all.' She was more sombre today; her bubbliness had been pricked and I wondered why.

'I still might be. I've got to think of the children.' My eyes went involuntarily to the photos on her side table; there were only her and Jeremy, no kids as part of a family holiday snap; none graduating in a mortarboard.

Cathy had followed my gaze. 'It wasn't meant to be for

283

us.'

'Was that… OK?'

'Not really.' Cathy leaned forward and her vast chest overran the edge of the desk. She looked as if she was settling in for a girlie chat; she indicated the timer clock and hit the big button on the top. Then she pointed to what was probably a drinks cabinet: 'Friday night snifter?'

'Umm, thanks, yes.'

Cathy pulled open the cabinet and made swift work of knocking up a couple of whiskies, two ice cubes each in crystal glasses.

She handed me one and sat down again on the other side of the desk. 'No, Jeremy couldn't…' Her little finger cocked and then uncocked very slightly as she held her glass so that I had to think about whether I'd actually seen her do it – perhaps I hadn't. 'Well, it wasn't meant to be. That's what we always say, but I would have liked them.'

She was married to someone who couldn't get it up. There was sharing and there was over-sharing. I wanted to ask her why she hadn't just clicked on one of the spam emails she must have had advertising Viagra, stuffed the pills down his neck one dinner time and then jumped a surprised-looking Jeremy. I tried to find something to say. 'But you and Jeremy, it's all OK apart from that? Sorry, don't mean to be nosy.'

Cathy looked as if she was going to say something positive, but then she shook her head. 'It's what people would call "rubbing along",' she said. 'Married forever.

Don't know anything different. Not like your generation – all you Type Ds that keep walking through the door, saying it's just not enough.'

'Well, why don't you…?' I started but then changed my mind. 'I mean, perhaps it *is* enough.'

'It's the way we were brought up. When we got married we really did think that once you had said, "I do," you should size up to it, realise you'd make a catastrophic mistake and get on with it.'

I could only splutter. 'Catastrophic?'

Cathy swirled the honey-coloured liquid in her glass. 'I was being silly. My marriage isn't catastrophic; in this job, you see the *real* disasters.'

Ah, the drunk who pissed on his child in the night. The poor woman she'd mentioned at our first meeting whose ex was about to be sectioned. That kind of 'real disaster'.

'Must be lovely having him at home now – you said he was retired?'

Cathy looked at me as if I'd said the moon was made of Stilton. 'Well, I suppose it is nice knowing that someone's there and he's a very kind man. But all I want to do is be left in peace to read *Vogue*'s shoe pages and, instead, I can hear him watching terrible sitcoms from his sitting room.'

His sitting room? I didn't know what it was like to be from a different generation; when 'rubbing along' was what you did. 'Jeremy must have some redeeming features?'

'He's kind, patient, sensible.' Cathy laughed ruefully as if she thought these characteristics really meant *boring*. 'I don't want you to feel sorry for me. I've been doing quite a lot of that for myself lately. Jeremy keeps hinting that he thinks it's the change but I had that a while back. He bought me an air-conditioning unit, which was sweet.'

'Does it work – the air-con unit?'

'It deals with the hot flushes but not my temper,' Cathy said.

'Wouldn't a night out help?' I felt as if I was quoting Liv.

'Perhaps it might. We could go to L'Auberge in Bromley High Street,' Cathy said. 'We haven't been in years.'

'Sounds lovely,' I said, imagining fancy-schmancy food with far too much sauce. I started to gather up my bag, wondering if I should mention also getting some magic medicine for erectile dysfunction.

'I'll suggest it to him tonight and we'll book for tomorrow,' Cathy said, sounding a lot more cheerful. Maybe if my advertising career went down the tubes I could become a marriage guidance counsellor. I got up and didn't know whether to shake hands professionally with her or give her a girlfriend-style kiss on the cheek.

Cathy solved it by giving me a big hug and saying, 'I do love our little chats, don't you?'

31

Was I doing the right thing or the wrong thing? I simply didn't know.

After the night when he'd turned up drunk, Lars was in the kitchen most nights when I got home at six.

He interrogated Jenny about children's nutrition and the eradication of nits from long hair. He listened to Finn's list of spellings and set out to make sure his son achieved ten out of ten in his test on Friday; when it was the next weekend for him to have the children, he washed and ironed their clothes – Ulrika told me that she'd watched painfully but not taken over. At our house, he played hide and seek for hours and pretended not to notice the very obvious lump behind the curtains that was Tessa until she couldn't hold in the giggles any more. He did it all as he did everything: with a commitment to succeed.

I waited for it to inevitably wear off. He would give up at the first work crisis. When a call from his office came as he was bathing the children during the first few days after his promise, I hovered outside the door ready to dash in and make sure no one drowned.

'Bill?' he said instead. 'I'm going to have to call you back – the kids are in the bath.'

287

'Take the call,' I said, striding into the steam.

'It's fine,' he said, clicking the off button. 'Now, who wants to tell me which one of these shampoos you use and how bubbly it is?'

Of course, they loved it.

At the school display of that term's handiwork, Lars amazed Mr Carter first by attending, and secondly seeming to know everything about Tessa's curriculum for the term.

'I'm so glad you could attend as a family on this occasion,' Mr Carter said. Julia overheard and rolled her eyes. Nadine was standing with some of the other Smugums in the corner, though, and nodded approvingly.

'Bastard,' I muttered as I drove home, angrily tailgating anyone who was driving at an appropriate pace in the residential area. 'Comes in and pretends to be Dad after *all this time*. Brainwashes my children. Takes them away from me for *whole weekends*. Turns up every night *at six o'clock*, when he couldn't get home at all before... bastard, bastard, bastard. And soon he'll bugger off again and we'll be back to normal except the kids will miss him even more than ever. *Bastard.*' Would he? There was a huge part of me that wanted to believe him and an equally large part that couldn't.

'Look, this has got to stop, all this temporary parenting,' I told him the following evening when the children were asleep and he was ready to go back to Ulrika's. 'It's all very well, but think of what you are doing to them. Overcompensating. Changing their routines. Making them dependent on you when you'll just go back to not being around.'

'No. I've changed my behaviour for good,' Lars said. 'I've taken on a new manager to look after most of the international travel. I *mean* all this, Ami. People do change and I'm going to be one of them.' I looked at the floor. 'I think about you in someone else's arms and…'

'I told you I'm not going to talk about it.' Within a few days of Peter, it had felt like something that had happened to someone else altogether.

'It's not just that,' he went on. 'Suddenly I could see sense – was I going to lose my family because of a little more business growth? Was I really going to be so stupid as to lose all this' – he gestured around him – 'because I couldn't see how important it was to me? Look at me. I was a mess.'

'I don't believe you,' I whispered. 'You got drunk because you felt sorry for yourself. Because you couldn't have exactly what you wanted whenever you wanted it.'

'*No.*' He tried to take my hands but I backed away. 'Look, I know there's nothing I can say. I just have to take the time to prove it to you. It's not just about the kids, either…'

I rubbed my face furiously with the sleeve of my T-shirt. 'I want you to go now.' All I could think was that he was saying this *now*, and behaving like this *now*. It made all the pain we'd gone through seem so unnecessary. Overwhelmingly, though, I didn't know whether it was too late.

'Of course, if you want me to.'

I waited until the door had slammed shut behind him before I let the tears roll like rain down a window.

*

Spring blossomed into summer in that English way that involves endless weeks of rain. Ben asked me for lunch one day promising that it wasn't 'anything more than business'.

'Don't worry, just want a bit more thinking about how we roll out in Europe,' he said as we sat down in a corner of Dean Street Townhouse.

'I'm not sure it's a good idea being female and being seen with you in public.'

He laughed. 'You going on about Claudia? You shouldn't believe gossip, Ami Fitch.'

I eyed him with mock suspicion. 'Did she help with the image change?'

Today he was wearing another suit and shirt, but this time it looked as if it might have had something to do with a tailor: the dark grey fitted over his shoulders, slimming him so that it was clear it was all muscle beneath his clothes. He'd clearly shaved.

'Scrub up all right, don't I? But, no, this isn't because of Claudia. The bosses at Campury dragged me in and told me to look like I was serious – apparently I was letting down the brand.'

'Why do you choose to look so… well, so anti everything

the fashion industry stands for?'

'I suppose because I think most of it's bollocks,' he said. 'In Italy, I could get away with it – they think the English are eccentric. But I'm not sure that me wearing the right suit is going to get more handbags sold.'

'It worked in Milan?'

'Not sure, but I was comfy.' He grinned. 'Claudia says you can still be comfy in a posh suit, so I'm giving it a try.'

'Is she going to dump her MP?'

Ben laughed. 'For me? Of course not. There's nothing going on. Now stop being so nosy, Ami, and talk to me seriously about European demand patterns.'

So, I did. He was efficient and calm as I talked statistics, demographics and tried to sell him an enhanced media strategy, which meant more money for Brand New.

But before committing to any of that, he ruined it all by saying, 'And that's quite enough of the boring – although very bright and professional – version of you,' ordered champagne 'to toast the alliance of our organisations' – a small wink in my direction – and then demanded to know what I would like to eat.

'*Extremely* bright and professional,' I said.

'Absolutely extremely,' he confirmed. 'It's just that now we've got the most important stuff out of the way, don't you think we should concentrate on complete trivia?'

'Are you ever serious?'

'I'm serious all the time. Especially now, back here without my friends and the kids. It's just nice to be able to chill out. I feel like I know you. Just a bit.'

'Well, we have…'

'Had some strange conversations?' he finished and then continued in a bad mock French accent, 'Now, would you care for *Canard à la Hoh, Heh, Hoh, Heh, Hoh* with sauce *à l'orange* and *patata dauphinoise*?'

'Not really,' I said. 'I'd like whatever is French for green salad.'

'Don't be ridiculous. Woman cannot live by lettuce alone.'

'I was just trying to look like the sort of sophisticated woman who never eats before dark,' I admitted. 'Really I'd like a truly massive plate of whatever's going.' So, we had mince and potatoes and chatted about our children as we forked it into our mouths. Around us deals were being done, and relationships forged – but it felt good to simply share stories about how funny our kids were.

He insisted we had another glass of champagne, 'Because I feel relaxed with you, Amelia,' and turned the conversation round to my divorce. 'You all right now?'

I told him that Lars was a reformed character. 'All of a sudden he's there all the time, just when I thought it was too late. We're trying to see if we can be friends.'

'Is that good or bad? You said you didn't want to get divorced.'

'I don't. Well, I didn't and then I thought it was inevitable.' He had a way of making conversation quickly intimate.

'You don't trust him to carry on like this?'

'No, I don't, but he's really trying.' I tried to shift the conversation to him. 'You seem to have a lot of fun, though, for a divorcee.'

'Lots of fun but no one to just hang out with,' he said. 'I miss my kids and my mates and it does get lonely sometimes.'

Later, when he was shaking my hand and saying he would see me at our review meeting the following Tuesday, he stopped for a minute. 'You couldn't do that, could you, Ami? Now we're over all that stuff.'

'Do what?'

'Could you just hang out with me? I don't want to be needy but sometimes you just have to say it out loud.'

'Do you think we'll know how to just hang out? What with being work-freaks and everything?' I smiled.

'I expect we could try – go to the pictures or something. Then go home and work our arses off.'

My first thought – still broke – was that going to the pictures didn't sound too expensive. And it sounded fun and I needed fun. 'All right. Nothing more than…'

'I promise you, I will never behave like that to you again.' He was sorry and sincere. 'I'm just looking for a mate. No, that came out wrong… I mean…'

We both giggled. He made more jokes. We left with plans to 'hang out'.

*

Wednesday night and Lars had the kids at Ulrika's. Ben and I met outside Muswell Hill cinema to watch a rerun of *Casablanca*. It felt like being a teenager again as we got popcorn and a bag of Revels, which, as soon as we were seated, Ben opened and threw into the box of popcorn, shaking it vigorously.

'What?' I said, looking at him with amazement. The adverts were on.

'Makes it more surprising.' He grinned. 'Do this with the kids. You never know if you're going to get a coffee cream – yuck, by the way – or, hurrah, a chocolate raisin.'

'I like the toffee ones,' I pointed out, 'and now I have to rootle round in the popcorn to get them.'

He grinned again. 'But it will feel great when you find one, Ami Fitch.'

I almost forgot who I was with as we joined the last hurrahs of those holed up in Morocco during the war. I was conscious, however, of how much of the seat he took up, so that his big shoulder was pressed against mine. Occasionally I dug into the popcorn box and found a chocolate. He found a toffee and prodded me to take it from him and I grinned back but then went back to the story. When Humphrey Bogart made the ultimate sacrifice of love on behalf of Ingrid Bergman, I felt tears slipping down my face and he wordlessly passed me a tissue and dabbed his own eyes.

Outside, in the dark of the high street, we giggled. 'Hanging out should come with a health alert,' Ben said. 'Turns you into a sniveller.'

'You old romantic,' I teased.

'And you were dry-eyed when that plane took off?'

I laughed and he indicated his car. 'Lift down the hill?'

As we drew up outside my house he said, 'The other thing that people do when they hang out is go bowling. Next week any good for you?'

I smiled. 'All right, sounds good.'

*

I'd forgotten how unbelievably crap I was at bowling though. First the staff had to go and find a size twelve in shoes for Ben; as I put mine on I tried to forget about the disgustingness of other people's feet. We were both in jeans and Ben looked much more at home in them than in his suit.

My first bowl went straight down the side chute. I turned and Ben was clearly trying not to laugh. He raised his eyebrows, picked up a heavy bowl and hit an immediate strike.

I clapped in appreciation and picked up a lighter bowl. I tried harder this time but it made it halfway down the lane and then also hit the side gulley. Ben gave up trying not to howl.

'You been bowling before, ever?' he said.

'Not so often.' I was sheepish.

'Would you think I was a tosser if I gave you some tips?'

'No, I wouldn't think you were a tosser because of *that*,' I said.

He laughed. 'So good for my ego, hanging out with you.' He then very patiently explained how to pick up the bowl, how to get some momentum in the brief run up and how to launch it so that it actually hit a skittle. Mine still didn't until the fourth go, when I managed to knock two down.

'Great,' said Ben, who by now had six strikes in a row.

'You could have told me you were a bloody bowling champion,' I grumbled, looking at our scoreboard.

'Barnsley Boys League 1996,' he admitted.

'Still got it going on.' I stepped forward with my next bowl and managed to get four. It was only on the last throw that I got a more respectable seven.

'See? You bowl me over, Ami Fitch,' said Ben.

I looked at him. 'Winning is right up your alley, isn't it?'

We took off our stinky shoes. He dropped me home. 'I reckon the next thing is an Indian in Brick Lane,' he carried on. 'We could take the creative teams?'

I smiled as I went into my house. Hanging out had a lot going for it.

*

Liv said we were going for lunch one Saturday, when I didn't have the kids, to 'discuss this whole Lars thing'. She called it an 'emergency summit' and said there was no other place to go other than the Suicide Café. When she was in that sort of mood there wasn't much point arguing with her.

The café was less gloomy than usual in the early June

sunshine. Shafts of light lit up the dust on the bell jar containing the canaries. The decrepit waiter shrugged when we came in and pointed at a table in the corner. At another table, a man with glasses that looked as if they were made from the bottom of two wine bottles was arguing loudly in Russian with a bald man. Every now and again they stopped shouting and slammed small glasses of vodka before starting all over again.

I was on my second glass of wine, having not really touched my food. I'd so far managed to avoid the Lars conversation. Liv resolutely shovelled risotto into her mouth.

'You never heard from that lovely posh guy again, then? Shame, you're looking so much better than a few months back.'

I wondered how awful I must have looked right when I was baring my everything to a bloke ten years my junior.

'Cheers for making me feel so good about that,' I said. 'But no, heard nothing and that's good; I told you, Lars and I are trying to be friends and parents.'

'You do remember how much Lars hurt you, don't you?' Liv resumed eating.

'Yes, of course.' I had a moment's respite while the bearded Russian stood up and looked as if he was going to thump the bald man, but then they both sat down again and slammed another tumbler of vodka instead. 'All that's happening is that Lars comes round some nights and reads the kids stories and then he goes home. Every so often he says we should go back to counselling or go out for dinner,

297

but I just tell him I need more time.'

'You don't want to get hurt again.'

I won't. Then I said out loud, 'Sometimes it almost seems as if he loves the challenge.'

'He always was a bit like that. You take your time.'

'It's not as if I have any space to think about it. The campaign goes live in July. Work has never been busier.'

'And you're still "hanging out" with Ben?'

'We had a curry in Brick Lane with the creative team, does that count? He needs a mate in London, that's all.'

'Hmm. So, he's not a complete arsehole after all?'

'I think he's just a guy who misses his children. He goes back to Italy most weekends to see his boys.'

Liv pondered this and then said, 'Phones you up a lot?'

'About work and whatever. He's actually all right, you know.'

'You've changed your mind about him, then?'

'He's clever and good company.'

'Doesn't Lars ask lots of questions?'

'Yes, but the truth is he's my client and on his own in London.'

Liv looked at me quizzically while I tried to avoid her eyes. 'But you don't tell Lars to stick around, get all married again?'

'No,' I said and it was true. Lars and I were civil to one another in the hours we crossed at the house; we talked about work and the children and I concentrated hard on not going near any subjects that would light the old touch papers. 'He does tell me I look great all the time.'

'Well, you do, but don't trust him, Amelia. You've been there before and he'll be all lovely and then he'll disappear.' Her voice rose. 'And you were doing so well on your own.' She signalled to the waiter for more wine but he was shuffling towards the Russians with another bottle of vodka. 'You really believe it will last?'

'I spent so long being angry with him it's hard to stop. Ben says—'

Liv visibly relaxed. 'You want to go out with Ben now, don't you?'

'No, I don't. Even if he did turn out to be all right once, well… once he'd got over himself. He's very apologetic about taking the piss out of me when we met. Which is still all your fault.'

'As is me getting you the best advertising account you could ever want.'

'Touché.' I smiled. 'Anyway, he'll be going back to Italy. And if rumours are to be believed, he's shagging practically every other woman in Soho.'

'You do know that when you talk about someone shagging someone else it's just because you actually want to shag them yourself?'

I stuck my tongue out at her.

'How long's it been now?'

'How long has what been?'

'You know. You've started to get one of those pinched expressions that old ladies have.'

'Well, unless you count the Hon Peter…'

'Few times, was it, in one night?'

'It was more the morning really,' I said, 'but if you don't count the Hon Peter, then I guess six months – and then not very often actually, at the end of my marriage.'

'Bloody hell, no wonder you're all uptight. So, the choices are getting back with Lars or going out with Ben.'

'I'm *not* going to go out with Ben.'

'Who are all these other women he's having sex with?'

'He won't admit any of it, but rumours include a woman he works with called Claudia – about twenty-five, posh, good hair.'

'Hmm.'

'And then there seems to be a whole bunch of women's names that just crop up. One girl back in Milan that he said he went to dinner with when he was over there seeing his kids a few weeks ago.'

'You think he puts it about a bit?'

'Pot, kettle, black.' I took a glug of my wine and passed the glass to Liv.

Liv ignored the dig and took a gulp. 'Does it make you a bit jealous?'

'Of course it doesn't.'

'But you like him now?'

'Well, it helped that he saved my agency.'

'No, *you* saved your agency.' Then she changed the subject. 'Is your pa any better?'

'Mum says he's started writing again. She says we need

to come and visit. It's been ages.'

'That poor woman, married to such a miserable sod.'

'He's not always miserable and when he isn't he's lovely. And you have to feel sorry for her, stuck with him in those endless downtimes.'

Liv nodded. She'd listened to me over the years, first angrily, then resignedly talking about my parents. As a teenager, she'd worked extra hard to include me in her family occasions; later, she'd wordlessly poured me a bucket of wine when I came back from visiting them.

'What will you tell him about you and Lars?'

'I don't know, Liv. I really don't.'

*

Hanging out with Ben continued, with long joking conversations, and meetings that turned into lunch. He would drop by sometimes, too, when the kids were in bed, and sit on the sofa with me, watching movies. I kept a couple of feet between us but soon relaxed. He said my house felt like being 'at home', and talked a lot about his own kids and how much he missed them. Then he leapt up to go home to call them.

The next day, the same room, but Lars playing with his children instead. And he was properly playing with them: long games building all the plastic Lego kits that Finn had got for his birthday; listening to Tessa reading, her head half engaged, the other half somewhere considering Life's Big

301

Questions. She'd stopped talking about death though and the kids both seemed to like knowing exactly what time their dad would turn up; they'd stopped asking questions about whether we were going to stay married.

Lars would come and sit at the kitchen table and talk to me and we'd laugh at what the kids had said; I felt then that it was a bit like what being married might have been like if we'd managed to make it work. Except the husband didn't normally get up and go to sleep at his mother's.

32

Sunday evening. A text from Ben.

> On my way back from Stansted – fancy hanging
> out with a cup of tea?

How lonely he must feel landing in London after leaving his kids in Italy; and after a weekend conversing only with people the size of Oompa-Loompas, I could do with some adult conversation. I was wearing a pair of Lars' pyjama trousers rolled up at the bottom, and an old festival T-shirt with *Access All Areas* emblazoned across the front, and sighed, because I'd have to get dressed. I texted him back, put my jeans and a jumper back on and painted my face with the surprising amount of make-up it took to look as if I had none on at all.

He arrived twenty minutes later, looking slightly jaded from the journey, in jeans, a white shirt and a blue jacket, which he took off and hung on the back of the kitchen chair. He thrust a bottle of limoncello at me.

'Thanks loads,' I said, putting it onto the counter with an appreciative grunt. 'Good weekend with the boys?' He sat down at the table and told me how they'd spent most of the weekend setting up an epic Scalextric track that went into every room of his apartment, while I made tea and sat down opposite him.

'Do you see your ex-wife when you go back?'

'No, not much, aside from drop-off and pick-up,' he said but smiled fondly. 'She's with someone else now.'

'And is that good?'

'Yes,' he said. 'He's a great bloke, older than her – a professor at the university, fabulous with the kids.'

'Do you hate him for being perfect?'

'Can't stand the bastard.'

I smiled. 'Do you mind me asking what went wrong with your marriage?'

Ben laughed. 'Shall I start at the very beginning?'

'It's a very good place to start.'

He told me how he'd met Patrizia shortly after he'd first moved to Italy, ten years ago, when he was twenty-eight and fighting for any kind of future in an industry that favoured camp over advertising acumen. 'I used to go back to this tiny little flat – it had a window that opened up into the roof – and I'd climb out and sit there and dream.' He was almost transported as he spoke. 'I'd look out over the city and there were all these people – dressed to the nines. It was summer when I first went and every night the whole goddamn place would go and walk around in the streets, going to the *gelateria*, zooming around on those squeaky little mopeds. I was lonely as hell. Anyway…' he smiled '… Patrizia used to come out of another flat across the street and sit on her roof terrace and there she'd be, twenty yards away, and we'd pretend, like people do in cities, that we were invisible to each other. And I would sit and stare down at the people and she would read books and smoke.'

'So, did you ask her out?'

'No way. That would have been batting out of my league. She was gorgeous.'

'How gorgeous exactly?'

'Incredibly gorgeous.'

I was glad I'd painted my face and got dressed; but then he was probably used to being with effortless Europeans who woke up looking like a magazine spread. 'Gorgeous like brunette and Italian and sultry?'

'Long dark hair, cheekbones that look like you could balance something on them. And very unattainable.'

'Unattainable like she might have been the favoured daughter of a Mafioso who would send you straight to the concrete wellies shop if he caught you messing with his girl?'

'I would have been crab food in the harbour,' he agreed. 'Except Patrizia's father is a farmer.'

'What made you talk to one another?'

'Oh, that came much later. She ignored me for a whole year – a year when for the winter she didn't come out on the roof anyway. I was miserable and totally in love with this person who'd disappeared when it got chilly. I was the original lovesick bastard in the garret. Didn't write poetry though. Or strum badly on a guitar. Or starve myself.'

'You *must* have read Jean-Paul Sartre and contemplated

methods of suicide,' I said.

'I was far too happy being miserable to die.'

'So, what happened?'

'Well, by the next summer, I felt a bit different – my job had got better by then and I'd stopped thinking that I'd never be cool enough…'

'You loved yourself by then, you mean.'

'I was Narcissus himself.' He slurped his tea. 'And I thought, go on, ask her out.'

'And she said yes.'

'No, she said no for at least another year, but then one day changed her mind. So, I thought I'd prove to her that I was different. She did this whole thing as if I was about the hundredth guy that minute to ask her out.'

I wished I were continental and snooty with epic cheekbones.

'So?'

'I borrowed a friend's car – a flash one with no roof – and I put champagne in the back in an icebox and lots of music in the stereo and I took her to Lake Como. No small journey, but I was determined.'

I sighed.

'And we talked deep stuff and walked around in the sunshine and sat down in this place straight out of Hemingway to have lunch…'

'What did you have to eat?'

'I think I had carpaccio.'

'And what did she have?'

'Again, I think she may have had the carpaccio,' he said.

'Good stuff. Do go on…'

'Any other menu details needed at this point?'

'No. Dead, raw cow, I'm there.'

'With bits of parmesan on it, of course.'

'Drizzled with olive oil?'

'Yes, and *shavings* of five-year old parmesan, a *coulis* of ancient olive oil à la Roman. Sun-dried, Sardinian raisin focaccia with it, obviously.'

'Obviously.' I smiled.

'Anyway… then we had an almighty row. And that was pretty much how it carried on. Madly in love with each other and completely outraged by each other at the same time.'

'What did you row about?'

'Absolutely everything,' he said. 'How to bring up the kids, whether we should have kids in the first place, jobs – we both had pretty demanding ones – where we should live, why I should grow up.'

'Only the fundamentals, then.'

'Yep. Only the really crucial stuff. But the trouble was, we were in love at the same time. She was passionate and very demanding – not just about me, about everything. All the things I liked about her were the same things that made it impossible for us to live together.'

'In the end, what happened?'

'In the end, she said enough. It was all too destructive, too boom and bust, too love and hate, too… well, just painful.' A small raincloud floated across his face. 'She said

307

I should go and, in a rage one night, instead of fighting her back, I did. After that she lost faith in my desire to make it work – or that's what she said. Then we tried being friends and that kind of works.'

I said bleakly, 'But that's exactly it. Lars said he wanted to divorce me and I can't believe he won't want to again.'

Ben stirred his tea. 'What happened with me is not the same as what happened with you – that's the problem with divorce war stories. What was it like for you guys in the beginning?'

I sat back and felt the prick of tears in my eyes. Then, slowly, I told Ben how Lars and I had met in what seemed someone else's story now, how sweet it had been, how full of hope, how determined we'd both been to create a beautiful future.

As I finally stopped, Ben screwed his face into a sympathetic half-smile, half-grimace.

'Change the subject?' I said, trying not to let the tears come; I'd done such a good job at managing all my emotions for the last few weeks. But I was curious about one last thing. 'Do you wish you'd stayed married?'

He considered for a moment. 'Yes, for the sake of the kids and because of the relationship we once had. But we just couldn't make it work with all the will in the world.'

'Do you want more tea?'

He shook his head and got to his feet, pulling his jacket on. 'I was just on my way home, but you know what, Oprah?' He took on the hammed-up voice of an American

TV pseudo-shrink that sounded nothing like Oprah. 'This little dig down deep in my heart has been good for my *soul*.'

I giggled and copied him, badly. 'Now you go on home to your momma, boy, and you remember what you learned today.'

He left with a quick kiss on my cheek that I found myself wishing had been longer. Was he really going straight home or was he off to see Claudia or someone else? I knew I shouldn't wonder or care, but found that I did. I grimaced to shake the thought away but dreamt that night that Ben was being pulled away from me by a woman whose cheekbones stuck out from her face like bathroom shelves.

*

Lars came round to be with the children on the night Marti held a party to celebrate the launch of the advertising campaign in early July.

'Good luck,' he said. 'You look fantastic.' I was wearing a new Cos dress – I'd learned to love The Outnet and had got quite adept at shuffling credit limits between cards. I smiled and got into my Uber.

The party was at a private members' club in one of those Mayfair streets where all the squillion quid houses were actually offices for dodgy hedge funds. The only evidence that the club was actually a club was a discreet man in a non-ironic bowler hat, standing in front of a brass plaque beside the front door; the plaque simply said No. 7.

Inside, it was all fleur-de-lys carpets and curtains. I made sure that the orange bag on my arm was hanging where all the guests could see it. My job that night was to get us an epic write-up in *Campaign*.

I could see Ben – looking remarkably smart for someone who didn't really do smart – talking away in a small group. He raised a glass of champagne to me, gave a small tilt of his head and a broad smile.

I grabbed a coupe myself from a passing waiter and was quickly cornered by a hack from one of the fashion mags, who spent twenty minutes pretending to interview me while trying to get a free bag.

'I could write about it weekly in my column,' she said desperately in the end.

'Diary of a handbag?' I raised an eyebrow and then felt sorry for her. 'Look, we don't even give them out to *Vogue* editors, except under guard for shoots.'

'Worth a go though, eh?' she said and slunk off.

For the next hour or so, Ben and I were both imprisoned at separate tables being interviewed by journalists, fêted by colleagues and shareholders, occasionally stopping mid-sentence to gesture in each other's direction about the madness around us.

I met Marti as I was coming back from the loo a little while later. He was holding a glass of wine in one hand and booming to one of the Goldwyn non-execs, Lord Haydon, about the sheer prestige of working with Campury.

'B'stards still won't give me a bag for my daughter,' he

added. 'Now here's the only woman to actually get one on account, so to speak.' He looked at the soft leather hanging from my arm.

I smiled at Marti and silently wished we could go back to the way we were before that disastrous dinner and almost losing the agency.

'Haydon, you know Ami here, don't you?' he went on now. 'Can we get you a drink?'

I shook my head. I still didn't know whether I was free from journalists' questions. Lord Haydon grasped my hand. 'In my day, girls with looks like yours pretended they didn't have brains.'

'There are still a few around who do that,' I said, spotting Liv arriving through the door, hours late and, I hoped, not three sheets to the wind. I waved and she stepped forward, dressed in cowboy boots and a floral-print seventies frock. Behind her a boy with large horn-rimmed glasses gave up the chase and sank himself into a seat near the doorway.

'Who's that?' I said, going forward to kiss her.

'I told you about him. Dominic.' Liv's breath smelt of champagne; I made a mental note to make sure she behaved. 'You look gorgeous.' We gave each other kisses where our lips actually touched each other's faces.

'You'd better come and say hello to Marti,' I said. 'And Lord Haydon of Humberside.'

'What happened to peers being attached to glamorous places?' said Liv, going forward and dimpling her cheeks at both men, so that they immediately started spluttering about getting her a drink.

'I haven't seen you for ages. Ami tells me you've got even more powerful,' Liv said to Marti.

'Hmmphh,' said Marti. 'Not like old whatsit here.'

'Old whatsit? I'll thank you to remember the name of a director of your company.'

'Ooh, I do like a fight,' said Liv.

'Shooters at dawn for you, my dear.' Haydon bowed.

'But I'd never be awake to watch it,' Liv pointed out.

'You an old friend of Ami's?'

'We met on a French exchange when we were fourteen,' Liv said. 'All we did was flirt with the boys.' She grabbed her skirts Tiller Girl style and raised her eyebrows. 'Ooh la la!'

I dragged her away. As I went I could hear Haydon saying, 'I'll say one thing for you, Goldwyn, you have the best parties… girl was flashing her knickers at me, dammit.'

I put a protective arm under Liv's elbow and hissed in her ear to 'behave'. We moved towards the more sober corner where Ben was refusing to give free handbags to two of *Elle*'s associate editors.

'It's our new corporate motto,' he told me, steering Liv towards a red velvet banquette, where she sank like a ballerina who's finally reached the last scene of *Swan Lake*. 'Just Say No.'

'People keep wanting to know what I did to deserve one,' I said.

Liv was soon joined by the boy in the horn-rimmed

spectacles and was snogging away with complete abandon. Dominic's hand was well advanced up her bare legs; her dress rucked up so that, any moment, she was in danger of flashing her pants again.

I stood in front of them trying to block them from the room and reminded myself to bollock Liv for turning up to my work party off her tits. 'I guess I'd better get her in a cab,' I said.

Ben joined me and smiled briefly. 'Or a room.' Just for a moment, I smiled back but he quickly looked away and moved towards the door where he set about getting Liv and her new man into a waiting Addy Lee.

33

Thor was 'passing through London for a meeting for one night only'. This wasn't unusual – he came every year or so – but I knew he'd added us to his route this time. He was the only person other than his mother that Lars talked to about anything emotional and he was coming to check up on us.

'Of course, he'll stay here,' I said. Lars was sitting at the kitchen table after putting the kids to bed.

'We'll try and make it as normal as possible?' Lars gestured around him.

'I don't feel up to having a whole "state of the marital nation" discussion though.'

'Shall we get Liv round?' Lars asked. 'Have a dinner like the old days?'

'Great idea,' I said. That would definitely take the pressure off. 'You can stay too...'

He looked at me with comic hope in his eyes and I had to laugh. 'On the sofa. Thor can have the spare room.' Still, it felt novel to have a little flirt with my own husband. Lars got up to leave, giving me a kiss on the cheek this time.

*

Thor was as burly and hairy as ever, and pulled me into a giant hug. He'd weathered a bit, but not much.

'You're looking great…' he said when he let me go.

'Considering what's been going on?' I smiled. We had one of those shorthand relationships where we skipped small talk.

'Going to be all good now though?' he said. Lars came through the door then, having dumped his friend's bag upstairs. Thor changed the subject, rubbing his hands together: 'So, are we going to get Liv round and get shit-faced?'

'She's on her way.' Lars smiled at him.

*

We got through a few bottles while we outdid each other with stories of being young in Bloomsbury. Thor made oblique references to the shack-ups Liv and he'd enjoyed back then; she met him flirt for flirt but made it clear that, while being exactly his age, she'd moved on to younger models. Lars joined in with the stories, laughing like a drain. He didn't mention work once, but did meet my eyes several times at particular memories. He handed out drinks and helped clear up, slipping easily back into being a host in his own house. After a while it felt like any dinner over the years when Thor was in town – as if the last few months had never happened.

'Better bloody spaghetti than that shit we used to have.'

Thor was one of those satisfying men who look as if they want to rub their bellies after you've fed them. I'd knocked up a bolognese and salad and we all waved slices of garlic bread around while we talked over each other.

It was as Thor reached for bottle number four that he started to talk about our wedding. 'Remember Ami's parents' faces when Liv made that speech?' He looked as if he was going to cry laughing at the memory.

'It was very subtle,' Liv said.

'It was SO not subtle.' Lars laughed. I watched Liv and him have their first close moment in what seemed like years.

Thor did some elegant grunting that was supposed to be Liv impersonating me.

'And this was Lars...' Liv started a loud crescendo to passionate sex with a Swedish intonation that went up and down even as it got louder.

It was impossible not to laugh. I didn't look at Lars though – it was too close to the bone to hear even an impression of the sex we used to have, but didn't any more. But it was great to be with old friends who shared our history – a history that would be broken in two if we didn't make it.

When Thor stopped chuckling he started to pour more wine. 'What about this big meeting tomorrow?' I said and cocked my head to one side.

'Oh, it's in the afternoon now,' he said airily. I raised my eyebrows, he shrugged as if to say, 'So I lied? So, what?' poured more wine into my glass and went back to telling stories.

*

Liv left about midnight and I got up to go to bed. I hugged Thor and then Lars lightly – they looked as if they were going to be at the kitchen table for a while. I locked the front door, switched off some lights and went up the stairs noticing they were now automatically talking Swedish.

It was as I climbed I heard Thor saying my name: 'Ami' a few times, a little more urgently and soberly than he'd sounded a while back. Even with a few glasses of wine in me, I slowed on the stair tread and craned my neck towards the open kitchen door.

Lars said the Swedish word for family: *familj* and children: *barn*.

I shouldn't listen to their conversation. Still, their tone made me. Thor sounded angry at Lars – it was clear that he was talking about me and then there was the word for happy: *lycklig*.

I crept back down a couple of stairs and crouched. Through the upright wooden poles of the bannister, I could see the shadow of Lars on the hall wall. He was leaning forward and talking urgently and what he said was in clear English in the middle of the Swedish: 'the right thing,' and then he repeated it with what sounded like a sad chuckle: 'the right thing'.

I slumped onto the stair and went cold. Did I hear him correctly? Did he really say that awful phrase from a few months back? Perhaps I hadn't heard right.

But Thor was now repeating my name and saying something that I understood as: 'How could you not love her?'

I sat as still as I ever had, holding my breath. I thought I might be sick while I waited for the reply.

Lars said then, 'I do love her as the mother of my children. But I just don't feel the same way any more.'

It was in another language but was as clear and painful as if it had been inscribed, already translated, on my heart with a sharp implement, letter by letter. Even in that moment, I knew it would always be there, never healing. I clutched my chest and tried hard not to gasp. My breath, when it came, was short and fast and I strained to keep quiet.

As I reeled, Thor raised his voice: something about 'beautiful' and 'impossible' and 'what you had was special'.

Lars hissed, 'It's not about that.' I heard angry: *arg* and arguments, which was the same in both languages, then *kan inte sluta* – can't stop. Then he very clearly said, 'I care deeply, but I don't love her like that any more.'

I'd thought I'd felt all the pain I could feel in the last few months, but I hadn't. Nausea rose in me, acid bile at the back of my throat. He'd said our love was dead. Gone. Never to be brought back to life.

I made no noise although everything in me wanted to scream.

Then outrage. It came fast on the heels of my hurt, racing in like Usain Bolt in the hundred metres. This was the Lars who was begging me to stay with him! The man who'd got

318

good and drunk and caused a scene; the guy who had promised to show me – and was pulling it off so far – how much the kids and I meant to him.

But it was them, not me, that was making him act as he was. They were the reason he wanted to come back.

'How long have you felt like this?' Thor asked angrily.

'I don't know, but a while,' Lars said, his voice rich with guilt. 'I was busting my gut for the business, thinking I was doing it for all of us, but, after a while, every time I came home we just argued about how I was away all the time. Ami was right, I was.'

'What do you think she's going to say, left for days and weeks at a time to bring up the kids on her own?' Thor went on, like a furious barrister, arguing my case. He was reminding Lars of times he'd flown into London and how I was always on my own and then, 'What did you fucking expect?'

Thor had always had my corner. Still, it made no difference. There was no going back: Lars had actually said out loud that he didn't love me like that any more and I'd heard him say it.

I rocked silently on the stairs.

'And somehow in the end, even though I wanted to see the kids, it was easier to stay away,' said Lars. 'I could go home and have another argument, or I could go and win some new business; for quite a while I convinced myself that that was what mattered... but in the end, I had to accept that I loved her as the mother of my children but no longer in the way we had. I didn't want to go home to her and the constant arguments. It's all my fault, I know that.'

I wanted to gasp with rage. *Now*, he admitted that most of it was down to him. But my anger couldn't compete with the overwhelming sadness I felt as he set about this slow dissection of our marriage.

'It seemed easier to divorce. Fairer on both of us. That's what I told myself. I was never going to get lovely, smiling Ami back and I didn't deserve to.'

Thor snorted. 'It's so fucked,' he said.

Then on and on like new shards of glass into the open wound that was me, Lars said again, 'I just don't feel it any more.'

Then that word again familj – family. I listened to him tell the story of the kids nearly suffocating in Swedish. Thor's expressions of indignation. Then Lars: how it had all come to make him realise he needed to change and change for good: 'ändra för gott.'

I was numb now from the plain simple truth: Lars was doing what he thought was right rather than wanting to stay with me for me. And he was pretending otherwise rather than watch his family destruct.

The slow poisoning of our marriage had no antidote.

Still I clutched at straws, desperate that he should still care; what about his anger when he'd found out about me sleeping with Peter? Didn't that show he still loved me?

No. Now he went on, talking about that, obviously well aware of his emotions. Why couldn't he have been this honest with me? I could see his shadow on the wall, slumped like a beaten man. In a low voice, he was telling Thor about me and another man. 'I was jealous, really jealous,' he said. 'But then I realised how much I must have hurt her to make her do that so soon and that it was just that – jealousy rather than anything else.'

Sober as if I hadn't drunk a drop, I knew I'd heard enough. Gradually, I got up and quietly moved again upstairs, taking care not to step where I knew the stair creaked.

I went through the motions of cleaning my teeth, pulling on a T-shirt to sleep in, crawling into bed and putting my head back onto the same pillow where I'd spent months crying.

I'd gone through the shock of Lars leaving me, then the grim acceptance that I could do nothing to stop him wanting to divorce me. But when he knew about Peter, I'd allowed myself to think that he really wanted me back too, the old me – and that had made me hope for a moment, naively, that we could go back to what we'd had.

I saw now that that was a ridiculous, romantic notion. It was born of not wanting to let go of the dreams of the early years, despite the nightmares of what came later.

He'd been trying so hard with the kids… yes, with the *kids*, and being perfectly friendly to me. Apart from the odd remark about 'going out for dinner' or 'giving me more time' and the occasional slightly forced flirtation, he hadn't tried to rebuild our relationship beyond that of parents.

Cathy and Jeremy 'rubbed along'. The fact that her and Jeremy's love had gone years ago didn't make her get up and leave. My parents stayed with one another through some false mythology they'd created even though Mum was clearly dealing with a depressive in denial.

How many other marriages were there out there, staying together for the love they once had, because the families they'd created were too precious to leave?

I guessed that Cathy and Jeremy didn't discuss it. I knew my folks didn't. I imagined the years that followed while our kids grew up: the best we could hope for was that we'd manage to get along with one another. We wouldn't discuss it either, because the moment we did it would become impossible to ignore. Even while I hated him for his dishonesty, I knew he was taking the tried and tested path of many marriages – unspokenly functioning as a family but no longer lovers.

But was I any different? Really? I'd been so hurt, so desperate to stay married, but once I'd thought he wasn't coming back I'd jumped into bed with someone else pretty fast. I'd planned a future without him. Look at how I'd closed the doors of our house and become, very quickly, my own family of three.

As the initial shock of hearing what he'd said subsided, my brain went into an overdrive of self-accusation.

Did I love Lars any more than he loved me? I didn't dream of dressing up and going out on date night with him. I didn't ask him to stick around once the kids were in bed. Or

322

long to hold him and have sex with him. There was a cautious companionship now, but the chasm between us was so wide that I hadn't wanted to try to cross it either.

All the love was gone. And I was grieving for a time that had passed: like trying to relight a candle when the wick is burnt and the wax is all splattered and done.

'You're just as false,' I told myself. 'You're doing the right fucking thing as much as he is. At least be honest with yourself.'

But was this *enough*? The price of my family staying together was that all Lars and I had was a new-style marriage of convenience? Could I live for years and years knowing that he no longer loved me and I no longer loved him?

I had a dull ache at the front of my head now and knew that I would be awake for a long time that night.

Tomorrow, though, I'd call Ulrika, the wisest person I knew.

*

I was awake early from the little sleep I'd managed. I couldn't face seeing Lars as I didn't know what I'd say, so I left a note for him asking him to drop the kids at school, kissed them and crept out into the flurry of sleepy commuters. The bus engine seemed to rhythmically echo the chant in my mind: 'the right thing to do'.

I texted Ulrika, asking if I could come round on my way home, and she replied:

It'll be lovely to see you.

Then I determinedly pushed the tiredness, hurt and anger away and got to work on thinking about Campury getting into the US.

It *was* unusual to consult a mother-in-law about whether to stay married to her son, I thought as I got on the Tube, but I needed her wisdom now – an 'Ulrika moment'.

She opened the door in a way that made it clear she knew I wasn't just dropping by for a casual chat. She kissed me, paper-cheek to mine, made me camomile tea, gave me a blanket to put over my legs on the sofa, pulled her shrug around her and waited before prompting: 'I guess you've come to talk about you and Lars.'

I blushed but nodded.

She continued, 'We haven't really had much chance to talk because I've been away and Lars has been here so much…' we both laughed at the irony of this '… but I've been so worried about you.'

'I've been OK,' I said. 'And I always knew you were there if I needed you.' The unspoken assumption was that I needed her now.

She smiled. 'But you're both trying again?'

'Yes,' I said, 'but…'

'You don't know if this is going to work?'

'Yes.' She was so understanding. 'The thing is, I'd just somehow got used to the idea that we were getting divorced and, after all the shock subsided, I was just angry, really angry with Lars. It was a really rough few months.'

'Years really?' She said it without judgement or malice – hers were observations on what humankind did to one another, gentle prods to get us less wise souls to see something from another perspective.

'Yes, years.' I took a deep breath and put my mug down. Then I told her about the previous evening: the dinner where we'd laughed together for the first time in forever and then the cold thump of hearing that he didn't have feelings like he used to have for me any more. Ulrika came and sat beside me as I cried and she held me in her long arms. Her shrug was warm.

She said nothing aside from, 'Poor Ami, so hard,' until I finally calmed down, then, 'So now it's not the grand romance it once was, and it's not the parting of the rough seas.'

'We were supposed to be trying to learn how to be friends again before we see if we could go back to being married.'

'You thought that would work?' Ulrika said. 'I mean, bring back the grand romance?'

'I think I've just not wanted to believe that it was all gone.' Her pale eyes were so like Lars'. 'I hoped, I suppose, while knowing that really we both feel the same way.'

'You didn't want to admit it to yourself...?'

'Right. And I suppose me overhearing him means I *know* and I can't ignore it any more.'

'But you're getting on?'

I nodded. 'Of course, we're not living together.'

'Hmmmm…' Ulrika pondered and prompted me at the same time.

'Do some marriages manage to keep those feelings?' I asked, thinking of the way she always talked about her husband.

'Some do,' she said. 'But all of them go through times when it's difficult and you seem to be together because of habit or the children rather than each other.'

I raised an eyebrow and she laughed. 'Even mine. Although I probably don't remember those times now as much.'

I bit my bottom lip. 'It really hurts not to be loved like you once were. But I've turned so awful, Ulrika, all I did for months was shriek at him when he was around and hate him when he wasn't. And he wanted to divorce me… and now he's with me for the wrong reasons.'

'Why are they the wrong reasons? You both care so much about being a family and for the children. Those are not the wrong reasons. Why does it have to be more than this right now? You're getting on with each other and the kids seem happy to me… that's quite a lot of progress.'

I sighed. 'Are you saying that we need to forget about the grand romance?'

'I'm just pointing out that at the moment this is maybe what it is.'

'You think the love might come back?'

'I don't know,' said Ulrika, but not unhopefully – what she meant was that she couldn't promise. 'But you're trying to do the only thing you both know how to do right now.'

'That's a good way of thinking about it,' I said. I picked up my mug but the camomile tea was tepid in the general cold of the room.

Ulrika didn't seem to notice this and carried on. 'You both need to be kind to yourself and each other; take some time; find out what happens next without pressuring yourselves.'

I hugged her again, nodding – she was right. There was no need to rush back into the solicitor's office.

Ulrika smiled. 'But how come now he lives with me he stops going away all the time?' She said it with all the affection of a mum who'd got her son back.

We chatted then about the children and how they were coping well now, before I got up to go.

'Anything I can do, I'm here,' said Ulrika, hugging me again on the doorstep.

God, I love that woman, I thought, getting on the bus. So, Lars was doing the right thing, but the right thing was an awful lot of what I'd wanted. The children were getting more stable, Tess had moved on and I was getting the slow pace I'd asked for to make up my mind. Lars and I could be in the same room for a couple of hours without sharing a cross word. We were making – as Ulrika had pointed out – progress.

'OK for now,' I said to myself.

Still, I knew that it would take a long time to get over hearing those words on the stairs: even as we stumbled forwards, there was no going back.

*

Cathy rang to tell me that she was sending me an invoice for what sounded like a huge sum. I grimaced as, with the recent money coming in from Campury, I'd had to prioritise paying Bridget and some other bills. It was going to be a while before the cold winds of poverty felt as if they'd lifted. I was going to have to get some cash from my dad.

'It sounds like a lot of money when you've changed your mind,' she said.

'I haven't yet,' I reminded her. 'It's just a decision on hold. Anyway, tell me, how was date night with Jezza?'

'Oh, you mean *Jeremy*,' she tinkled. 'It wasn't a great success.'

'Why? Food not up to it?'

'The food was fine but I'd forgotten that Jeremy slurps the garlic butter from snails. We got home and he watched TV. After that I could hear him snoring in the night; he even hisses through his teeth.'

'Why don't you put him in the spare room?'

'I did that years ago. I can hear him from down the hallway. I went downstairs and made a cup of tea.'

'I'm sorry the evening wasn't a success,' I said before saying goodbye. But she sounded so cheerful about listing Jeremy's faults today, so maybe it had served a purpose.

I had the weirdest relationship with my divorce lawyer.

*

I didn't tell Lars I'd heard him on the stairs talking to Thor. What was the point? The first evening as he went to go back to his mother's, I railed at him in my head: 'Is this enough for us?' but I said nothing out loud. Instead I thought about the children, snoring gently upstairs, relaxed by knowing that their parents weren't fighting any more and, instead, were giving them structure, routine and consistent love.

We weren't telling the truth about how we felt. The difference was that I hadn't lied about it the way I thought Lars had – pretending he wanted me as well as our family.

But what he'd actually said was he'd always love me as the mother of his children. He meant a very different love from when we'd climbed Primrose Hill and decided to spend our lives together. Now it was love between people who knew each other so well; who had a shared past – some of it good and much of it heartbreaking; but mostly two people who were mother and father to the two little people sleeping above us.

34

Ben and I were lying on the dirty grass in Soho Square. The summer had so far been the sort that promises tropical temperatures but only delivers drizzle. Today, however, a Monday, the sun had really come out. Every other inch of the square was crammed with media types trying to catch some Vitamin D in their lunch hour. We'd already eaten our Prêt sandwiches and I was wishing that I'd also ordered a raisin Danish.

'What do your mum and dad think about you and Lars?' The question came out of the blue. 'You don't talk about them much.'

'I'm off to see them this weekend. I've been worried about it to tell you the truth,' I said, sitting up and blinking in the light. I looked down at Ben and couldn't see whether his eyes were open or closed, behind his Ray-Bans. 'My father suffers from depression. Mum is being extremely nice to me from a distance – she couldn't leave him – he sank into another funk when he heard about me getting divorced.'

'They're your *parents*. They'll want whatever makes you happy.' He'd told me that his parents had both died – within a year of each other six or seven years ago.

'I know. But, of course, they have a difficult relationship

because of my dad. Somehow, though, because they've stuck together, despite it all, probably because of me, they disapprove of other people who can't make it work. Well, my dad does. Anyway, I grew up with that mentality. I'm worried they're just going to go on and on about Lars.'

'Can't he go with you?'

I shook my head. 'That'd be just like saying we'd got back together.'

There was a pause. Ben didn't say, 'Well, haven't you?' but instead said in a casual voice, 'Where do they live?'

'In the Cotswolds – Chipping Sodbury.'

He paused, then said brightly, 'Well, I need to see some people near Tetbury – old friends of mine from when I started out. I could drive you and the kids.'

'Oh, God, no. They'd never understand that we were just, you know, *friends*.'

There was another pause where I thought about how special our friendship had become to me, before he said, his eyes still inscrutable behind the sunglasses, 'Just tell them the truth – client on his way somewhere for Sunday lunch – needs a bed at theirs for the night.'

'They'd never understand.' I hugged my knees to my chest. 'They're absolutely lovely people but my father is virtually a recluse now – he's a writer – and he just shuts down for months at a time.' Talking about my parents' relationship made me feel a chill despite the sun. 'I can't stand the disappointment in their eyes.'

Ben suddenly sat up, pushed his sunglasses back onto his

head and looked at me with a hint of a smile around his mouth. 'I'm very good with parents.'

'*No.* I have to go on my own. Lars would see it all the wrong way if I took you there. He's already asking lots of questions about us hanging out.'

'Haven't you told them it's all completely innocent because, as you put it, I'm too busy shagging every other woman in London?'

I had to admit that the way he said it was a passable impression of me. I looked mock stern. 'You're actually proud of that, aren't you?'

He guffawed. 'You believe all these rumours?'

'Claudia? The one in Milan? What about Elizabeth from Gorgeous?'

'She's just a friend like you.'

'I know, but people think you're shagging her so they probably think you're shagging me.' I was indignant.

'Well, I'm not shagging either of you or anyone else. Look, what about if you went to the country and then came out for dinner with my friends and me on Saturday night? It would break it up a bit – you could leave the kids with your folks.'

'They'd still ask questions,' I said, thinking this was a fantastic idea. It would make the weekend much more bearable. 'But it would be lovely. Who are the friends?'

'One of those lovely couples who refuse to grow up,' Ben said. 'Maurice was one of my first bosses back in the day at Paul Smith when I was the intern. He made a bucket of money and married Jane – she's always covered in paint, does these portraits of famous people with surrealist bits stuck onto them. Mick Jagger with his mouth as a guitar? Camilla Parker Bowles with a riding crop for a nose?'

'Jane Feltman?' My mouth fell open; she was a controversial artist who'd been very famous a decade ago. 'Everyone's always wondering what happened to her.'

'What happened is that she married Maurice, moved to the sticks. They live in this fab house with a stream in the garden. I need to go and see them before I go back to Italy. I can ring them and see if they're around.'

'I would love to meet Jane Feltman. Does she paint now?'

'Yes, but not the same stuff she used to. Went out of fashion. Now she does these massive canvases that nobody buys, but it doesn't really matter. You know I've got to go back to Italy soon, and next week I'm off taking the boys to Greece for a fortnight. It'd be a good time to see them.'

Again, I felt a pang. How I'd miss him and our easy camaraderie. We'd have weekly teleconferences with Milan – but he was going to disappear from my immediate world.

Ben pulled his iPhone from his pocket and punched at the screen.

'Jane? It's Ben Jones.'

I could hear distant shrieks of excitement.

'Yes, I know I promised but it's been very busy.'

More shrieks.

'It's short notice but what are you and Maurice doing this weekend? It's the art festival?'

He mouthed the words, 'They're having a party,' and grinned. Then, 'I'll stay at the pub. Full? Kitchen sofa is fine. Is it OK if I bring someone on Saturday night?'

Embarrassed, I signalled he shouldn't push it. But Ben carried on, 'No. Just a friend. Very bright…' I blushed. 'And pretty…' I gave him a rude gesture with my left hand but was pleased. 'Staying with her folks down the road…'

There were more pleasantries before he prodded the bottom of the screen and looked at me from behind his sunglasses. 'All sorted,' he said. 'It'll be really good fun. I'll come and pick you up.'

'No, my parents mustn't see you,' I squeaked in panic. 'I'll drive over.'

'Don't be silly – one of those parties that are much more fun if you drink a bit. I'll get someone to sort out a taxi.'

'And book one for the way back? I won't be able to be late.'

'I'll sort it all out,' Ben said.

And that was that.

*

Julia, Parminder and I were in Highgate Woods with the kids. Julia was telling us how Nadine had a giant whiteboard on her kitchen wall with a timetable for Jemima: 'Thursday, 2 p.m., Kumon maths; 3 p.m., violin; 4 p.m. judo; 5.30 p.m. cooking lessons and so on. She talked me through it when I went to collect Toby and Brad. Talk about tiger parenting.'

'She's an animal about sex,' Parminder said.

'Shagging every minute of every day,' said Julia. 'Protecting the world's endangered species in between blow jobs.'

'And lecturing the rest of us about perfect parenting,' I said.

'I'm still apologising for the Nicki Minaj thing.' Julia started to laugh. 'But sometimes she's not so perfect though…'

Parminder and I swivelled quickly to face her. 'Do tell,' we pleaded.

'Well, she was going on about you getting divorced and then not getting divorced…' I'd thought I'd got used to being a Crouch End talking point, but still felt my blood boil.

'…and about what a perfect marriage she and Freddie have… never arguing or a cross word, peace and harmony, blah, blah, blah,' Julia said between gasps of giggles. 'And Jemima comes in and starts going on about the boys not sharing and Nadine gave her all this guff about how forgiveness was a powerful life force and Jemima said she wanted a biscuit. "And a proper biscuit with sugar in like everyone else has."' I laughed – it was a pretty good imitation of Jemima in a strop. 'And then…'

'Come on,' Parminder urged.

'So, then Nadine said no and Jemima got up and stalked to the door and slammed it behind her, shouting, "Fuck you" in a voice that was just like Freddie's.'

Julia demonstrated exactly the movement of Jemima

slamming the door while swearing like her father.

Parminder and I eventually stopped laughing. 'So, it's not all harmony round at Nadine and Fred's.'

'No,' carried on Julia. 'It was pretty clear that this was something that Jemima had seen her father do and quite often. Nadine was really embarrassed and rushed her upstairs and I left, but, I have to say, I cried with laughter as soon as I was out the door.'

I sniggered too as I got the kids onto the bus and we went back to our not-so-perfect home.

*

Lars was due to go to Amsterdam to a convention on ecommerce that weekend but, as he was leaving that evening, said that he would change his schedule to go with us to visit my folks. 'I want them to know that nothing has changed,' he said.

I shook my head, thinking again what he'd said to Thor. *Everything* had changed. 'I don't want Dad to get his hopes up, especially as he was so upset about us splitting up,' I said. 'I'll go on my own this time.'

Lars tried to come closer to me, but I indicated with a shrug that I wanted to keep my distance. *You don't have feelings like that for me any more.* However honest I was with myself and how I felt, it still hurt.

'I'd like to tell them that I'm sorry too,' he went on.

'It's not just you leaving. It's all the stuff before that. Me

336

crying down the phone.'

'But they believe in our marriage, don't they?' Lars' voice occasionally had a desperate edge now, which brought back his Swedish accent.

'Yes, probably too much,' I said. 'You know what they've always been like.'

He sat down opposite me at the table and picked up my hand. I knew it should feel like coming home after a long journey, but it didn't. I moved it but he didn't react. Instead he said, 'Guess what? I've got a new word in English.'

I smiled warily.

'It's *bogus*,' Lars said. 'Nothing we ever do again will be *bogus*.'

'Bogus is American,' I said. Did he not know that I knew he was full of shit? After what he'd told Thor, we'd never been more bogus.

'I'm going to a work party this weekend too,' I said, 'with some friends of the bloke from Campury.'

A small shadow hovered over Lars' face but he only said, 'I hope it isn't too bogus.'

35

Driving down the M4 the following Saturday morning, I was jumpy. It was July, but somehow I felt – now that the heat of the summer had arrived – as if it would soon disappear; that what was coming was an end to things. I put my foot down, swung into the outside lane and decided not to think about what that might look like.

I'd called my mother to ask if she minded looking after the kids while I went out: 'It's sort of for work.' My mother had sounded impressed that I was going to Jane Feltman's house and hadn't quibbled at all.

My parents' cottage looked as if it should collapse under the weight of the ivy that clothed it. However pretty it was, though, I never arrived without a feeling of trepidation that what I would find inside would upset and disappoint me. Now my marriage was up for discussion; I gritted my teeth.

Two springers came bounding out. 'There's Liver and Bacon,' shouted the kids, clambering out of the car.

Dad followed the dogs. He stooped now but his white shock of hair stood up at all angles. He wore wellies, green cords and a T-shirt that had faded to the colour of forget-me-nots.

'Hello, darling,' he said and kissed me. He aimed a boot

at Bacon. 'Damn mutts are all over-excited.'

'Papa,' shouted Tess and Finn, and, creaking as he knelt, he put an arm round them both.

'Who wants to give Liver and Bacon a bone?'

'Meeeeeeee.'

'Can we go to the pub with you?'

'Has Nana made chocolate cake?'

He slowly rose. 'Let's go and find out, shall we?' They ran to the red door and he picked up one of our bags and went after them.

Mum appeared. In the bright sunlight, the lines on her face had deepened and she seemed smaller than ever. 'Darlings.' She hugged all three of us.

'I bought you some Penhaligon's,' I said, handing over a parcel that made her smile, but then, typically, immediately start saying that I ought to watch money now, what with the situation. I felt the old claustrophobia that came with my parents and tried to shake it off, dragging the other bag through the door.

In the kitchen, with its bleached oak table and Aga, the kids were already sitting in the dog baskets with slices of chocolate cake.

'You can't give it to dogs,' Tess told her brother. 'It kills them, chocolate.'

'Tess, no more talking about dying,' I said. Then I drank a cup of coffee and survived the first hour of interrogation.

'Agency is doing really well... no need to worry any more. Lars is seeing lots of the children... no, not travelling so much but he's away this weekend in Holland, sends his love... Liv is fine, she has a new boyfriend...' and on and on.

Then Dad got up to take the dogs and children out into the fields.

'No digging holes in the garden this time,' Mum said, shuffling them out. 'I've never seen such big holes after you were both here at Christmas.' That'd been when Tess was in her period of digging fake graves. When they'd gone, Mum gestured to the cafetière and I nodded. With another cup of coffee poured for each of us, she sat down and peered at me.

I waited.

'So, what's really going on with Lars?'

'We're taking it slow. Getting on with each other... trying to be friends again.'

Mum looked hopeful. As a child, I'd tried so hard to please them; later I knew that this was a subconscious acknowledgement that something in our household was wrong and an impulse to make it better if I could. She went on, 'But it sounds like he's changed for good, so what's the problem? Surely you should let him move back in – stop all this uncertainty.'

'We need more time and we're getting on well.'

'But you still love him?'

Love meant so many different things, I thought, but answered, 'Yes, he's the father of my children.'

'Well, we think you should call off the whole silly business,' Mum said.

I nodded slowly. *Just get through it.* 'You mean Dad does.' I felt some of my old frustration with her: can't you stand up for yourself? Why are all your opinions really his?

'*We* do. Is there someone else?'

'Of course not.'

'Well, I've had my say,' Mum said, as if this was what she'd agreed would happen on behalf of Dad. 'You have to think of the children.'

'They're doing much better, Mum. We've stuck to the same routine for weeks now and that's helped. Mostly they just can't be around us arguing any more.' I picked up my coffee and told her a really long story about Tess's history homework. Then how Finn was doing at football. Lastly, I extolled the attributes of Jenny, until she could only say, 'Well, she does sound a lot better than the last one.'

At that I leapt to my feet and said, 'Let me help with dinner.'

Later, I left her shuffling different dishes between Aga drawers, while I bathed the children in the bathroom that had been mine on my visits. I thought about how I'd hidden in there one particularly difficult Christmas in my twenties, pretending to be taking long baths with a book, just to escape from downstairs.

'I love you so much,' I told my own children in recompense.

They peered back at me from within huge towels like luxurious elves. 'We love you too, Mummy.'

There'd be fun too, though, in this house: another

Christmas when my dad was really getting into playing charades but picking the most obscure books so that when he finally told us what we were supposed to be guessing, Lars, Mum and I rolled around on the floor laughing. Or Mum stirring gravy while she drank a sherry, telling the kids about Christmas when she was a girl. Or back in the old house where I grew up in London, Dad letting me ride him down the hallway like a horse. Or taking me to the pub with him, with all the same sense of occasion Finn and Tess enjoyed.

I steered the kids towards my old bedroom at the back of the house, tucked blankets around them and put my bag in the spare room. Then I went downstairs where Dad was slicing runner beans and talking to Mum. They fell silent as I walked into the room – in much the same way as they always had when I was a child.

'You sure you don't mind looking after them while I go to this party?' I said to make the awkward moment go away.

'We love looking after them,' said Mum. 'And it will be good for you to go to a party like that. Imagine, Jane Feltman! You'll have to tell us what her house is like. How did you meet them again?'

'Oh, I'm just going with my new client,' I said, as if this were the sort of thing that happened every week. 'They're old friends of his and he's visiting before he goes back to Italy.'

'Poor Jane – it's so confusing having people from the Mediterranean to stay: all that sleeping in the middle of the day and smoking everywhere,' Mum said.

'Ben is English, Ma,' I said.

'Probably still got some foreign habits,' Dad said. 'He after you, then, this Italian?'

I tried hard not to blush. 'Dad, don't be silly.'

'He does know you're married, eh?' Dad was trying to sound as if he was teasing but there was an undertone that made me immediately suggest that I 'ought to be getting in the shower', although I knew the taxi wasn't coming for another hour.

'Divorce doesn't do anyone any favours,' went on Dad, as if that was the only subject on offer. 'Look at those two kiddies: they don't want all this modern thing of being shuffled from one home to another, not knowing where they're going to sleep tonight.'

'But it's not like that…' I began. 'They're fine and Lars is trying really hard and we're really putting the kids first.'

He didn't seem to listen. 'Could kill him for making you miserable.' A black shadow crossed his face. 'Just would've thought it's got to be better to have two parents living under the same roof.'

I bit my tongue and escaped from the room, spending a good fifteen minutes rinsing off the day, ten painting my face into what I hoped was a healthy glow and another five trying to make my hair look frizz-free.

I looked at my reflection in the silver-specked mirror and told myself it was to give me confidence at the party that I'd made so much effort.

Dad looked up approvingly as I came back into the

kitchen wearing a pale yellow fifties-style dress that I'd bought a good ten years back and found in the back of my cupboard; it was like having something new. 'Your mother used to have a dress exactly the same,' he said.

A grey car pulled into the drive and I took a door key, promised not to be late and climbed into the back, making chit-chat with the driver as we sped down the country roads.

'Going to be a big old do you're going to,' he said. 'My wife does baking and they've ordered five massive apple pies, two peach tarts and a chocolate cake.'

'Is it all local people?'

'No. Place turns into a circus this weekend every year. Jane organises what she calls an art festival, but really it's just a few loony bits of art in the village hall and then her excuse for a big piss up.'

I smiled in the back seat while he went on. 'I'm not moaning, mind. They need loads of taxis for all the drunks going back to the B&Bs and hotels. Got my son out in the other car and my brother-in-law in his 'cos I'm the only taxi in the village. The wife's taking the calls – but don't you worry, I'm bringing you back at midnight. The woman who booked me gave me a big tip too.'

I smiled at Claudia's efficiency, hoping she was happy, back in the arms of her young MP and over her crush on Ben.

We eventually passed through iron gates and started to climb a gentle hill. I could see a converted barn – only with one giant wall replaced with glass – from which thousands of lights cascaded like a waterfall in the dusk.

'Wow,' I said and, through the open windows of the taxi, I heard the babble of people, spilling out of the doorway across the drive.

I climbed out and was glad I hadn't brought a jacket. It was still around twenty degrees as the yellow ball of the sun started to turn gold. To one side of the giant sheet of glass was another pale stone barn, to the other, meadow poured down a hill.

'Good luck,' shouted the cabbie and sped off to collect another member of the circus.

I pushed my way through what looked like a group of artists – the women with long, centre-parted hair, the men with beards – who were crowding the doorway. 'Maurice's parties are so decadent,' one of them was telling another as they swigged glasses of bubbles. The living room stretched the length of the barn: there were huge abstract canvases on the double-height wall; a massive scarlet sofa on the floorboards. A creeper climbed up one wall and came to rest on a balustrade that stretched around the upper floor on two sides.

I'd been imagining this party a little bit like an art opening – warm wine in paper cups, everyone quoting *The Guardian*. Instead there was a very Eurotrash group to my left; one gorgeous statuesque blonde wearing what I thought was Valentino and drinking Moët straight from the bottle. A group of teens was raucously trying to dance in a corner.

But there was no Ben and I didn't know where to start to

find him – or my hosts. A waiter appeared from the crowd and offered me a tray of drinks that didn't seem to have a soft option on it. I grasped a glass of champagne and looked around with embarrassment. 'Do you know where I can find Jane?' I asked the waiter.

'Are you looking for me?' I turned. Jane had wild white-blonde hair sticking out at angles from her pixie-shaped face, a gold smock and colt-like legs in faded blue jeans. She walked towards me with her arms outstretched, looking exactly as I remembered her from all the fuss in the papers.

'Darling,' she shouted, as if she'd known me forever. 'I'm so glad to see you.'

She'd clearly got me muddled up with someone else. 'I'm Amelia Fitch, Ami,' I said as Jane hugged me in a waft of Chanel No5. 'I really hope you don't mind me coming – Ben invited me.'

'I thought you must be her,' shouted back Jane. 'Ben's been here all afternoon, going on about you. Now what's this bollocks about you being just friends?' By this time, I was being led by the elbow as Jane pushed her way through the throng to a door that led, via a packed kitchen, out onto a huge stone terrace that perched on the top of a tumbling valley.

'It's so beautiful,' I said.

'It is, isn't it?' Jane didn't bother not to look smug. She carried on steering me through the crowd until she came to a fat, short man holding a giant cigar and a group of guests in stitches. His red face shone with good living; his shirt, pulled tightly over his belly, came from the wardrobe of an unashamed bon viveur.

'Maurice, this is the gorgeous woman that Ben's been talking about all afternoon.' Jane handed me over to her husband. He stopped talking mid-sentence but then immediately started asking me questions in an East End brogue about whether I'd got a drink, travelled here easily and why I wasn't staying with them, as there was plenty of room.

'Thanks so much for having me,' I said. 'Do you know where Ben is?'

'I'm here.' Ben appeared from behind Maurice. 'I heard what Jane said. You do look gorgeous but I promise you I haven't been going on about you all afternoon.'

Ben was holding a glass of champagne and wearing very old jeans and a faded red T-shirt with a CND symbol on the front. His big arms stretched the fabric; his feet – like many of those in the group – were bare. There was a grass stain on his left big toe.

'You can run around in the grass too, later,' he told me. 'I've had such a great day hanging out here. I haven't been to this party in ten years but it's just the same.'

He'd lost some weight, I thought as he kissed me on the cheek – there was just muscle under the old T-shirt and he smelled of barbeque. I wrinkled my nose slightly and he laughed. 'They're spit-roasting a pig down there.' He pointed towards one side of the house. 'I got the job of sorting it out. I did have a shower though.'

He looked at me more closely. 'Love that dress. Is it tough at the folks' place?'

I grimaced. 'They just keep going on and on about Lars.'

'At least you can forget about it tonight.' Ben took my hand. He was warm, as if the sun had supplemented his own body heat. 'Let's get you another drink and some of my fantastic pig. They've been breeding her just for the party and everyone is going on about how fantastic Henrietta tastes.'

She did taste really good, I agreed half an hour later, replete on a massive pork and apple sauce roll and with another two glasses of champagne inside me. By this time, I was enmeshed in the group on the terrace where Maurice held the stage with outrageous story after story about his days in fashion houses.

'You've never seen so much coke... She had to be sobered up with ten cups of coffee and a cold shower before she could go on the catwalk... He just never got round to designing a collection so we had to cut up the curtains in the studio the night before, pin them on the models and say we were going with a chintz theme. Got better reviews than the real collections...' He probably wasn't letting the truth get in the way of a good story, but he was such a fantastic raconteur nobody minded.

After a while a ten-piece funk band started playing soulful tunes that ramped up to very seventies disco; the crowd spilled out from the house and the packed terrace began to move. The Valentino-clad beauty danced barefoot on a bench.

Ben pulled me into the middle of the crowd and we started to dance about two feet from each other. He wasn't exactly Mick Jagger but he was on the beat and obviously enjoying himself. Occasionally someone came over and he'd shout, 'Hello,' and kiss cheeks, but mostly he seemed to love every minute of whooping along to the horns with me. I found myself grinning widely as I danced; I felt free.

We had more drinks when the band had a break. Jane walked around the terrace shouting at people to 'bloody eat the pudding I've bloody cooked for you,' and Ben sniggered when I told him all the desserts had been provided by the cabbie's wife.

'What lovely people,' I said.

'Amazing. It was Maurice who said I should go to Milan all those years back.'

The band launched into another set and the party got wilder. At around ten the sun disappeared over the horizon and lights lit up the gold of the barn walls. Stars started to appear in a sky the colour of purple ink. I danced and it was as if I were shaking off my cares and worries forever. Maurice threw me enthusiastically around the terrace but when he looked as if he was about to have a coronary, Ben appeared again at my elbow.

'You want to go and look at the river?' he shouted. 'I need to cool down.'

36

As we slipped down the terrace steps into the long slope of the wild grass, I pulled off my sandals and felt the cold springiness underfoot. Eventually the noise of the band died to just the beat and we walked side by side, Ben carrying a bottle of champagne in his hand, first with the lights of the house to guide us and after that with just the stars and the big round moon.

'How far does their land go on?' I asked after we'd walked for five minutes.

'There's a little river – more of a stream – and a wood at the bottom.'

I relaxed. There was an hour and a half until I turned into Cinderella and went back to my folks and the children.

A cow moo-ed vehemently from the other side of the valley as we came to a copse of trees and there, in front of us, was the gurgle of the stream, sliding gently downwards and making a natural break.

'Sit for a bit?' Ben gestured with the champagne bottle. He disappeared for a moment behind a tree and came back out with an old picnic blanket and what looked like an oil lamp.

'Where did you get those?'

'Jane and Maurice keep them in an old box for when they come here. They reminded me this afternoon.'

Such matchmakers. I teased him. 'They thought you might pull at the party and come down here with someone?'

'No. I was talking about how beautiful it was here and, well…' He went silent for a minute. 'They think I'm keen on you. Anyway, come and sit down and we'll have a drink.' He pulled out a match and lit the lamp, which fluttered into life and smelt of the past.

I felt a big stab of disappointment but went and sat on the rug. He didn't say he *wasn't* keen on me. Taking a swig of the champagne, I said, 'Here's to friendship, eh?'

There was a pause. I seemed to move slowly towards him, without even knowing why, so I shuffled my arse back on the rug again.

'It's a beautiful place,' Ben said.

There was another pause and I wondered if it felt as long for him as it did for me.

Nothing was going to happen. It mustn't.

I gabbled on. 'You should have brought someone else down here with you.'

But then he simply said, 'For fuck's sake, Ami, stop it.'

I couldn't look at him. Did he really just call it? Say it out loud? There was another silence. It was the kind of silence that could have been a million years, covering a couple of formations of new planets, at least one ice age, a range of continental displacements and the extinction of entire animal species.

Or it could have been less than a second.

'Hey,' he said next.

And then he moved his hand over mine.

I took a breath at his touch and we both heard it.

'Look,' I said, looking straight ahead into the darkness rather than at him – but I didn't move my hand. 'There's no point. I have to think of the kids and… you're moving back home. We have to work together.'

'Any other big old reasons you want to list?' He said it with a sad smile.

I looked at him and stuck out my bottom lip.

He stuck his out back at me and it was impossible not to laugh.

I wanted to forget about being half married and forget about him leaving.

I wanted him to kiss me and I knew he mustn't.

'The thing is…' he went on very seriously now, and he looked not at me but down at the blanket. 'I think it would be wrong not to tell you before I go how much I like you, Ami.'

Was this really happening? Had I let myself think or hope it might? Of course I had. But it had been really hard work pretending to myself I hadn't.

He didn't seem to even be breathing but his hand was big and warm. Mine was shaking.

'I… I… like you too,' I whispered. 'We're good at being friends…'

'But we could have been more and we both know that.' He looked straight at me now in the darkness. 'Let's not pretend any more.'

I nodded slowly. I would never know what it might have been like to be more than friends and that hurt more than it should have.

'I just want you to know how much I would have loved that,' he went on very gently.

'I wouldn't have wanted to be another one of your…'

'You wouldn't have been. It would have been different with you,' he said with the same brutal honesty.

'What about Claudia?' Every time he'd left me to go home, I'd imagined he'd been going to her even though he'd said he was going home. I'd just poured myself another glass of wine and convinced myself I didn't care.

Ben burst out laughing and just for a moment all the tension disappeared. 'Oh, yes, Claudia. Well, the last thing she said to me was how stupid I was not to be with you.'

I sniffed but with some satisfaction. 'Really? So you haven't been…?'

'There's been hardly anyone – a one-off with Elizabeth…' I knew this was his ex-lover and now-friend but I still bristled; she was a fairly spectacular blonde. 'Ami, if you just knew how hard it's been not to try to kiss you, all those nights when I took you home or was sitting with you.'

'Well, why didn't you?' I still didn't move my hand, but I did know that if he'd tried to jump me before now – despite wanting him to quite a lot – I would've pushed him off me and told myself I was shocked.

'Because I promised you I wouldn't? Because of all the

reasons you've just said? Because you were so vulnerable and so brave and you haven't quite split up with your husband and…'

I thought for a few moments about how Lars was pretending that he still had feelings for me, still believed in us – and all that shit about *bogus*. I knew I should get up and go back to the party but, maybe because of that, I didn't. Instead I said, 'But I…'

'And because I couldn't risk falling in love with you.' Ben half-whispered this as if to himself.

Oh, no, but *oh, yes*. I felt myself move closer to him and rest my chin on his big shoulder. He smelt of dancing now as well as the barbeque and his big hand gripped mine tighter. 'I couldn't stand lying to you any more.' He smiled the big sad grin again.

'If only it wasn't so complicated.' I wanted him very badly to forget about all the reasons why it was complicated.

Ben's face flickered in the light of the lamp. 'So, I just wanted to tell you, that's all. I know I shouldn't but I'm going back to Italy and… I promise I will never mention it again. It's been a very special time for me, Ami, hanging out with you.'

'And for me.' It felt as if he was going to leave a hole that no one would be able to fill.

'Look, I shouldn't have said any of this and I've tried very, very hard to leave you alone. You just are bloody gorgeous.'

I smiled and bit my lip. Our eyes met and I felt as if I

might just fall into him.

Instead Ben took a deep breath. 'I wouldn't have said anything if I hadn't been drinking and it's so…'

'Romantic?'

'Yes, but we can make it unromantic. Let's just lie down for a while here, look at the stars in a really unromantic way and then go back to the party.'

Bugger. That wasn't what he was supposed to say next. I unplugged my hand from his, edged my arse down the blanket and lay down aching with disappointment. The stars looked as if they might tumble from the sky and land around us.

I felt Ben lie down too and he passed me the bottle of champagne and our hands touched again. I could feel his shoulder occasionally rub against mine.

'I must not seduce Ami Fitch. I must not seduce Ami Fitch,' Ben muttered to himself.

All I could think about was rolling over and demanding he pull me into his arms and seduce me very thoroughly indeed.

He had to kiss me. He had to.

There was a silence.

'I've got an idea,' I heard myself say.

'Go on, then.'

'We could just have one kiss to see what it's like. No harm done. One kiss can't really hurt.' Did I really know what I was doing? Probably.

'That's a really, really bad idea,' he told me in the

darkness. 'I want you far too much.'

I took another involuntary breath of excitement. I should really go back to the party. What harm could one kiss do? And I very badly wanted to kiss him. I rolled over slightly and he rolled too so that we were facing each other.

'One kiss,' I said, hardly breathing.

'Stupid idea.' He shook his head but seemed to come a little bit closer.

'We would just know what it was like and then we wouldn't go round wondering all the time.' Please just bloody kiss me.

'Do you go round wondering all the time?'

I'd been wondering quite a bit over the last few weeks but pushing the thoughts away as fast as they came.

'I spend pretty much every waking hour wondering what it's like to kiss you,' he told me then and I melted like ice cream left out in the sun. He came closer still until I could feel the warmth of his breath.

'Listen, Ami, the thing is… I know I shouldn't do this…' and then his lips came down on mine and he was pulling me into his arms roughly.

'Just one kiss,' I managed but I was kissing him hard back, trying to be as close to him as I could. My back curved up to meet him as he pulled me closer and kissed me as if he were never going to stop. I didn't know if I ever wanted him to.

'My God,' he said eventually into my neck. 'I wanted you so much, but I didn't know whether you were going to go back to Lars and… I wanted you to trust me. I upset you in the beginning and then I really started to care about not hurting you. I promise never to hurt you and I promise to…'

'Oh, kiss me again,' I pleaded and he did and that was when it seemed as if the washing machine in my stomach would never ever finish the spin cycle.

37

The next morning, I came into my parents' kitchen to find Tessa, Finn and Dad sitting at the table while Mum fussed around, feeding everyone eggs and bacon.

'Hello, darling,' she said to me, then turned to Dad. 'Another egg, William?'

'I always say one egg is an *oeuf*.' He winked at me as he repeated the childhood joke.

I grinned and remembered how I'd run to climb into the midnight taxi, shouting thanks to Jane and Maurice, Ben still holding my hand and kissing me very firmly goodbye. He'd promised to come to see me that evening when I returned to London.

'I am fucking nuts about you, woman,' he'd said gruffly as he'd finally shut the taxi door.

So, Ben was going back to Italy rightly, for his kids – I could get on a plane every second weekend and go and see him if I could get the cash together. We'd walk around Milan together hand in hand, eat pizza in tiny corner restaurants and then rush back to his apartment – I imagined it being all shiny polished minimalism – and tumble into bed where he would make love to me over and over again. My tummy flipped with the memory of those kisses last night, the groans from both of us as our bodies came together through our clothes, desperate to be closer still. And he'd told me how much he wanted me, how beautiful I was… And that sweet midnight hour of kisses had gone like seconds.

He'd come and see me that evening and we'd decide that, though whole countries separated us physically, nothing could really come between us. He would need to come to the UK for work and I could visit him. Would that be enough? I convinced myself it was.

I didn't let myself think about Lars except to remember what he'd told Thor. I'd hardly slept – instead I'd allowed myself to dream of a sort of future with Ben. I bit my lips and remembered how he'd kissed them and all I could think about was how he was going to kiss them again.

So, I hugged my children and beamed at Mum and Dad.

'We're going to clean out the pond with Papa,' Tessa said. 'And then we're going to the pub.'

Finn told his granddad about the wonders of Jemima. 'She's got yellow hair like Nana had in the olden days,' he said.

We sat and drank coffee; I told my parents the less salacious bits of my evening and Dad told me precisely why the UK's modern artistic output was beneath contempt.

It was all quintessentially English.

*

The phone rang. Mum darted towards the dresser and threw

papers around until she found the receiver and then immediately coloured.

'Well, hello, Lars,' she said, looking at me. 'How lovely to hear from you.'

It was like a wrecking ball coming into my conscience. Smash. Smash again.

Dad met my eyes and then picked up the colour supplement.

'Yes, the children and Ami, all here, all very well, having a lovely weekend, thank you,' Mum went on.

'Is that Daddy?' said Tess from the dog basket.

Dad sat up. 'I've a mind to have a word with him.'

Oh, good God. 'Dad, please, I'd rather you didn't.'

'Now, Coco.' He was on his feet and his face had taken on the familiar darkness of anger. 'Give me that telephone.'

'Dad!'

But it was too late. Mum sighed and said, 'Lars, William wants a word while you're on the phone. I know you rang to talk to the children, but he wants to talk first.'

Dad grabbed the receiver from her and slammed out of the kitchen door where his raised voice could be heard demanding, 'So isn't it about time you told me what's going on?' before a further crash of the door that led to the dining room. The children looked worried and looked at Mum and I for reassurance. The old guilt came flying back.

Mum leapt in. 'Tess and Finn, you'd better get your wellies on if we're going to do the pond.' As they went from the room, her face was haggard. 'Now Papa may not feel like

360

it, but we'll do it together.'

When we were alone in the kitchen I put my face in my hands as Mum said, 'You can't stop him. He has to have his say.'

In fact, Dad's say did not last long. He was back inside the kitchen within three or four minutes, a frown set in his forehead, his hands ruffling his hair. He threw the phone back onto the dresser.

'Says he's been spending quite a bit of time with the kiddies.'

'I told you – he's got so much better,' I said, colouring again.

'Says he wants to come back but you won't let him,' Dad went on. That felt very unfair: Lars knew that he was with me because of our family but he'd either not told Dad that or Dad had chosen not to listen.

'It's not that simple,' I said as calmly as I could. 'We've agreed that we can't just get back together without making sure we get it right and—'

'You're choosing to live without the father of your children. You're ruining the lives of these kiddies. I'm not sure there is anything more to say.' With one final glance at me, Dad quietly turned on his heel and went out of the back door.

*

Later I couldn't remember how I got through that terrible

Sunday lunch when Dad refused to sit down at the table, disappearing with his dogs instead. The children were miserable because they'd been promised a trip to the pub. Mum busied herself with ensuring we ate as much as possible but said very little. As soon as I could, I stuffed the children's clothes into their bags and Mum raised only a small wave at the door before rushing back to do what she could to save Dad from himself.

Up the motorway, I played I Spy and Farmer Went to Market out loud while inside I wrestled with myself. Eventually I put on a CD of *James and the Giant Peach* and Tessa and Finn listened in silence.

I thought of my father, about to tumble back down into depths only he knew; rationally I knew it wasn't my fault, but I couldn't ignore it when Mum was so overwrought.

Being with them had brought it all back – how I'd spent all my life trying to have a family that wasn't like the one I grew up in. But mostly how I'd vowed that my children would always feel protected, wanted and included; that they'd never creep around worried about upsetting someone.

I pictured the children smiling up at Lars as he sat on the floor of the playroom. How he'd spent months and months now trying to prove he could be the father to them I'd asked for.

That thought again: it was only me standing in the way of us all coming together. I looked at the kids and the thought of making their lives difficult again ripped me apart.

I'd acted as if I were a free woman. Kissing a man who…

well, a man I needed to forget about.

I'd never wanted to get divorced – I'd been so certain of that. Lars was the father of my children.

My husband. For richer, for poorer, in sickness and in health, in good times and in bad.

Forsaking all others.

*

Back in Crouch End I made the children ravioli, stirring the saucepan furiously. I put plates down onto the table and then into the dishwasher ten minutes later.

When Tessa and Finn went to bed I paced up and down the hallway until at last, there he was – the shape of Ben behind the stained glass of the door.

I walked bleakly towards it and opened it. He carried a huge bunch of pale pink roses, fat with summer, and his smile was so big the rest of his face seemed to disappear under it.

I burst into tears.

'My God, what is it?' Ben threw the roses onto the hall table and pulled me into his arms.

'It's my dad,' I sobbed into his big shoulder. 'Lars rang up and Dad grabbed the phone and Lars told him he was doing everything he could to get us all back together. Dad hit the roof – told me I was ruining the children's lives. Oh, Ben, it was awful.'

Ben took my hand and pulled me into the sitting room.

He sat down heavily on the sofa and dragged me down next to him.

'And maybe he's right. What am I doing? Kissing you. Pretending that I'm not married any more. That there might be a chance for you and me…'

Ben's face was stricken. 'I should never have said anything.'

'But I…'

'Yes, and me too,' he said. 'But I was wrong… I should've left you alone.'

'It's the children.' My tears were streaming now. 'And the idea of our family. When I look at them all playing together now, those three sets of bright eyes staring up at me… how can I do that to them?' Sitting beside him, I wanted to say the complete opposite of what was coming out of my mouth.

'Maybe you can't. Look, Ami, I… I was wrong to go near you and I'm sorry, really sorry.'

'You think I should go back to Lars too?'

Ben seemed to be staring somewhere beyond himself as he said very quietly, 'If there is remotely the chance that you can make the relationship with the father of your children work, then you should give it every possible go.'

And there was a chance. There was still – despite everything – a chance.

He stood up and went towards the mantelpiece, picking up a frame with a picture of Lars, me and the children, which had been taken shortly after Finn was born.

'I should never have…' Ben shook his head at the photograph and replaced it onto the mantelpiece.

'But I… I really am crazy about you.' I needed him to know that. Less than twelve hours ago I'd been fantasising – I saw it so clearly now – about managing to be with him.

Ben pulled me to my feet and held my arms to my side. 'Shush. Look, Ami, we've got to forget about last night. I shouldn't be here now. Your husband is doing everything he possibly can to show you that he can be a better man…'

I felt compelled to tell him the truth. 'But he doesn't want *me* any more – he's just had a massive wake-up call about losing his family. There was a big episode with the kids – the au pair left them alone and Finn could have suffocated – and it's only since then, he's been trying everything to be a better dad.'

'OK,' said Ben cautiously.

I rushed on with the injustice of it all. 'His best mate was here and I heard him talking. He said he didn't love me in the same way any more…' It was still difficult to say it out loud, but I pressed on. 'He said it was about doing the right thing.'

'Christ, poor you.' Ben held me and the size and smell of him made the tears start all over again. But he went on, 'You're not ready to move on either. This isn't just because of your father. You've always said you didn't want to get divorced; that the kids came first.'

'I could've been… I could've been with you…'

'Divorce isn't pretty, Ami – you know that. It creates complications – massive complications.' He grabbed my hands though while he said it. I could feel his pulse, beating like a mad metronome. 'If you can stay married, if there's a chance… I can't come in the way of that.'

He was right and I hated him for it. It was like Humphrey Bogart being noble in *Casablanca* all over again. He stepped towards the door. 'I'm so sorry. Last night was wrong. But now I'm going to leave you alone.'

'But, it was…' I rushed towards him.

'Don't say it,' he said then, putting his finger gently in front of my lips. 'There's no point, Ami, no point at all. I'm trying hard to do the decent thing here. And, well, we both know, even if we were together – God, that would be so great – I'm in one country and you're in another. We wouldn't be a proper family. I would've bust a gut to make it work but…'

I'd pictured the every-other-weekend but I hadn't pictured the everyday, home on my own, missing him. How cruel to put plane-rides between us.

'I have to let you go to make up your mind.' He said it through determined lips and looked at the floor.

'You really think I should go back to him?'

'Come on. The last thing I'm going to tell you to do is go back to another man. You're in no fit state to decide what you want to do. But you need to look after yourself for me.' He moved towards the door. 'It's probably best if I go and…'

'But…' I started.

He came forward and put his finger over my mouth again.

'Don't.'

'But…' I tried again.

'No.'

And then he replaced his finger with a single kiss.

'Goodbye.'

'Goodbye,' I said and he walked out of the door into his future while I was left with mine.

<u>Part Three</u>

'Isn't this wonderful, *älskling*?' Lars beamed as we hung over the balcony and watched the true blue of the sea clash with the false hue of the swimming pool.

Tessa joined us. She seemed skinnier, bonier, older lately. 'There are four swimming pools,' she told us. 'I'm going to swim in them all every day.'

'I'm not going in any of them,' Finn said, coming out too. 'The water will make you ill. They told us that on the bus.'

'They only mean the tap water, not the swimming pool water,' Lars said and we shared a laugh.

We'd told the kids that we were going on holiday all together because Daddy and I were friends again.

'Are you going to live here now?' Tessa had asked Lars.

In the moment when he'd been trying to frame an answer, Finn had piped up, 'Sometimes you didn't really live here before because you were in other countries.' Lars and I had both given a nervous chuckle before our son had added, 'So it's good now really.'

I'd looked at Lars and raised my eyebrow. 'Well, the point is that Daddy is here all the time now and we both love you very much,' I'd said, 'and we thought we could have a great holiday all together.' The kids had gone on to talk about how you got 'free shampoo and lots of creams' in hotel rooms. They hadn't asked any more questions.

Now, as we went back into our small suite, Lars said, 'Fabulous hotel for the money.'

Yes, but not very authentic, was my immediate thought, and then I told myself off for being negative. I'd committed in our weekly counselling session, now that we were going on a family reunion holiday to Greece, to try hard to be more positive.

'How can we make a future together if you won't forgive the past?' Lars had asked during last Wednesday's session and Sasha, our Relate counsellor, obviously impressed by the new, improved Lars, had nodded her agreement and asked me to concentrate on 'looking forward'. I was trying very hard to do that. I didn't mention Lars' conversation with Thor, for example, even to the counsellor, instead concentrating on what was most beneficial for the children: structure, routine and parents who didn't argue. This holiday was the next step forward.

But the weeks since Ben had gone seemed like decades. I almost looked forward to the bus ride to Finsbury Park so that I could wallow in my misery and relive our kissing on the carpet of flowers under the stars. I got on the Tube and told myself to pull myself together – that it had been an aberration, a momentary lapse. But at work I missed him too, for not being part of my daily world any more – the phone calls about work, his teasing; and I missed hanging out with him. We had weekly teleconferences but these were formal team sessions, focused on the campaign and its results and, aside from cheerfully saying hello, there was never a moment of intimacy.

I stopped myself ringing him by sitting on my hands; wrote emails but managed to never press send.

If only I hadn't kissed him, I thought, and then, thank God I did. Was it better to have loved and lost? I couldn't say I was really sure about that.

But on days like today, with my children and their devoted dad next to me, as we settled down at our family hotel, I knew it was crazy not to thank the lucky stars that would undoubtedly twinkle above me tonight.

Tessa struggled into her swimming costume while I got all the bottles of shampoo and body lotion out of Finn's bag and put them back on the bathroom shelf. Lars unpacked his clothes into the wardrobe we'd share in one of the bedrooms. He winked at me as he flung a T-shirt down on one of the pillows of the twin beds that could be pushed together to create one giant one, but he didn't suggest closing the gap yet. However, knowing that we would sleep together again on this holiday if things went well, I tried to remember what it felt like to wrap myself around Lars' hard body. It would feel familiar and it should feel right.

'What a lovely family,' the receptionist had exclaimed as we'd checked in and there we were, two generations, balanced by gender, everything that the modern family should aspire to be. 'You're going to have such a wonderful holiday.'

It was all down to me. I blew up Finn's armbands and smiled back at the man who'd so recently nearly been my ex-husband.

*

That first night, Lars crawled into his bed and reached a hand out across the gap. 'There's no pressure,' he whispered. 'Let's take our time.'

I whispered, 'Thank you.'

He said, 'It's lovely being here with you all though – goodnight.'

I held his hand for a while and eventually felt it go limp in mine, still warm and now rhythmically moving as he fell quickly into deep sleep. I let myself fall asleep too.

In the morning, I opened my eyes to see a tray beside my bed wafting hot coffee and pastries and a note in his scrawl with the extra Scandinavian loops.

> *We thought you might want a lie-in – see you*
> *at the pool, love Lars, Tessa and Finn*

It was later that day when Lars, seemingly out to prove that he could put no foot wrong, had taken the kids to play mini golf on the other side of the complex, and I was lying on a sunbed by the pool, that Liv rang.

'Liv? It's lovely to hear your voice.'

'Aren't you having a fabulous time?'

'Of course I am. Absolutely brilliant. Fab weather, the hotel is fine, the children are in heaven. Lars is being lovely – he's taken them to play mini golf.'

'How horrendous,' said Liv. 'Is it really sexy being back together again?'

'We haven't got to the sex bit yet. I'm kind of working up to it. Probably tonight. We've got a dinner on our own in the beach restaurant. Lars has booked a babysitter.'

'Probably a good idea to get completely pissed and just get on with it. Before you know it, it will be just like normal,' said Liv.

'Liv…'

'Yes?'

'It's lovely to hear your voice.' It was. I wanted her to tell me something frivolous. 'What've you been doing?'

'Well,' said Liv, sounding evasive. 'You only went yesterday, so not much.'

'Liv?' She was hiding something. 'What did you do last night?'

'I looked after one of our mutual interests,' she said.

'What do you mean, "mutual interests"?'

'Umm, well it's quite a long story but…'

'I've got nothing better to do than listen,' I said, lying back and taking a slurp of my Diet Coke.

'Look,' Liv began. 'I don't suppose you'll mind…'

'If you've interfered in my life again the way you did by telling Ben all that codswallop about me…' I started.

'Aren't you glad I did now? I saved your agency and gave

you a new man to go all gooey about.'

'I'm not gooey about him,' I said. 'And I could've won the account without you.'

'Whatever,' said Liv. 'But it's nothing like that.'

'What is it, then?'

'Well, I was out last night at a bar,' Liv said.

'No, really, not you…'

'Are you going to be quiet and let me tell you what happened? So, there I was, and who should walk in looking very posh?'

'Not the Hon Peter?' I nearly squealed. It was hard to remember that night a few months back without a small, fond smile.

'He nearly tripped over my foot, so I said, "You owe me an apology." He looked absolutely petrified; it was obvious that he couldn't really place me.'

'He really is the most enormous player, isn't he?'

'I said, "Don't worry, you haven't slept with me," – are you sure you're OK with this?'

'Of course, tell me what happened.' This was a very Liv story. I rolled over on my sunbed.

'And so, I said he'd shagged you, taken your number and never called. And he said was he apologising for being shit in bed or was it for not calling? Promise you won't mind? It was quite funny.'

'He was a complete charmer,' I said.

'And then he said he remembered us all having a drink together at Berkeley Street.'

Suddenly I saw how this story was going to end. Tears of laughter started streaming down my face. 'So, he's in your bed now, then?' I snorted. 'Go on, I bet you got off with him.'

'Well, I did a bit,' said Liv. 'And, yes, he is here, still asleep – you don't mind, do you?'

'Of course not, I think it's hilarious.'

'Well, I thought you were back being all married on your middle-class holiday and… well, we'd had a few drinks. I didn't mean to sleep with him but he was so persuasive. I tell you something else – he's got stamina.'

'I'm not sure I need to know the details,' I said, 'but, yes, he did like to keep going.'

Liv's voice dropped to a whisper. 'He's in my bed and his cock is erect all over again. It's turned the sheets into a tent.'

I spied the kids coming back with Lars.

'Oh, my God. You cheer me up. I've got to go. I'll speak to you in a few days.' I put the phone down, picturing Liv realising that she'd just met someone who was, if possible, even more commitment-phobic than she was.

*

I decided to drink for England, Europe and the world that evening. Tess and Finn were tucked up in bed; I watched their faces move very quickly from alert to asleep. In the sitting room of the suite was an old Greek lady who took our mobile phone numbers and waited impatiently for us to go down to the restaurant and leave her in peace with the TV.

The palm-fringed restaurant was packed with couples scoffing freedom from their offspring along with their food. Women flush with tans and alcohol were chatting with husbands who were looking lovingly back as if suddenly remembering why they were married. The air was thick with the sound of cicadas and whispered nothings.

'What would you like to drink?' Lars asked as I studied my menu. 'Cosmopolitan?'

'Of course I am,' I said and he laughed. When it arrived, I gulped it quickly; it was strong.

'So,' I said.

'So.' Lars smiled.

'What shall we have to eat?' We discussed the various options before ordering; I refrained from making any menu jokes but still thought about Ben.

'Aren't we having a lovely holiday?' Lars said.

I downed the rest of my drink. 'Gorgeous.' I just needed to relax. I felt nervous, but after everything that had gone on between us, that was quite expected.

'You look great with your tan,' Lars went on. 'I'm not being bogus.'

But you are, you're pretending to still love me. I pushed the thought away and said, 'You're looking pretty fit too. Shall we have champagne?'

'Why not? We need to celebrate the future after all.'

We watched as the waiter popped a bottle of house bubbly and filled our glasses to the brim.

'To us,' Lars said, raising his to me in a toast.

'To us,' I agreed and then swallowed the glassful as if I were a student in a boat race.

'Going a bit, aren't you?'

'Fill it up again.' I smiled at him.

He poured me another, saying, 'What happens when we get back?'

'What do you mean, what happens?'

'Well, I'll pack up my stuff from Mum's and move back in, shall I?'

'Well, yes,' I said but immediately felt claustrophobic.

'I mean, we're back together for good, aren't we? And it seems silly me living in another house. Of course, we're going to have to explain it to the children very carefully. But don't you think we need to put these last few months behind us?'

'We have, haven't we?' I drank half of the next glass of pop and smiled on.

'I'll just get my stuff organised and then I'll move back.' There was a pause while the waiter delivered prosciutto-wrapped asparagus to both of us.

'Great,' I said, picking up my knife and fork.

'Ami, I need to know this is what you want.'

I'd thought I'd been saying all the right things. 'Look, do we have to have this conversation now?' I didn't want to talk; I wanted to make it all go away. One sure route to doing that was to get pissed with Lars, get sleeping with one another over and done with, and wake up tomorrow with my

377

future a done deal.

'Well, yes, yes, we do,' said Lars and I sat back with a chill. 'Now, I need you to believe me, Amelia. It's been too discombobulating.' He smiled at me. 'Nothing bogus.'

'Stop saying that!' I couldn't help myself. 'Everything is bogus.'

Lars jumped as my voice rose. 'Shush,' he hissed, looking around him. 'What do you mean?'

My sadness felt as if it would crush me. 'We both know that…' I took a deep breath. If we were going to have this conversation – and I still didn't know where it would end up – then I had to be honest. 'Look… I heard you talking to Thor.'

Lars looked confused and I rushed on. 'You were speaking Swedish… I was going to bed… but…' Lars coloured and looked down. 'You were saying you were staying because it was the right thing to do, because of the kids… it wasn't because of you and me.'

'Oh, Ami, it was just me trying to explain what had been going on. I didn't mean it like that.' His voice was quiet and entreating. He put down his knife and fork.

I smiled very sadly. 'Lars, I heard you say that you only loved me as the mother of your children.'

His face screwed in pain. 'Oh, that was the drink talking…'

I couldn't stand more lies: 'Be honest: it's not because of me any more.'

Lars brought his hand to his eye. 'I don't think that's—'

'The thing is, though,' I carried on, relief rushing through me now that I was no longer pretending that everything was OK. He deserved me to be honest too. 'It's not just you. I spent so long trying to get you to stay with me because I thought it was the right thing to do too.'

'The kids could've died,' Lars said and I quickly held his wrist.

'Look at me,' I said. 'They didn't die. It was terrible but it happened at a time when we were both feeling really awful and guilty and showed us that we need to look after them more, make it better, and we've done that – given them certainty and structure.' I paused. 'This has to be about me and you too.'

After everything we'd shared, were we going to be one of those couples that rubbed along? Or that lived with a giant unspoken lie at the heart of their relationship like my folks? The feelings I had for Ben made me realise – even if I'd probably always known it – that that wasn't going to be enough for me; I suspected it wouldn't be enough for Lars either, despite whatever he told himself. There was 'for the sake of the kids' but there also had to be a 'for the sake of me', however selfish that sounded.

He nodded slowly and I let his arm go. I started to eat, remembering we were in a restaurant with other couples.

'I've changed,' Lars said. 'You have to believe that now.'

'I do,' I said and I meant it. He'd already told me there was a short trip to China coming up, but he'd done it in a way that allowed Jenny and I to plan ahead.

Now, I sliced through the ham and the asparagus stalk. 'We're both here now, doing this, because we're clinging onto some hope that we can get back some version of what we had, but it's not realistic.'

Lars' face was bleak but still he tried. 'But, now we've learned how to be mates again, it might work...'

'You mean that love we had at the beginning will come back?' Tears were rolling down my face now as if from nowhere.

'Is everything OK?' The waiter came by as Lars passed me his napkin. As I dabbed my eyes, I could see other couples stare and then look happily back at each other; they were glad this scene wasn't starring their marriages.

Lars flushed red. 'Yes, absolutely fine. Please take the plates and hold our main courses.'

'Certainly, sir.' The waiter scooted off and I started to apologise.

'Look,' Lars went on, ignoring the answer to my question. 'I know we've got a way to go. I know we need to stick with the counselling. We need to spend more time together. We need to make more progress.'

Progress. That was the word Ulrika had said. In managing to get structure into the kids' lives and get on with one another – from some sort of distance – we'd made progress.

'Maybe there's another way to think about it,' I said slowly.

'I don't see what. From what you're saying, we've fucked

it up despite all the trying.'

'But we haven't! In the last few months we've managed to get on, make the kids more stable and let them have a much better relationship with you.' I drank more champagne and tried to breathe more slowly as my tears dried up. 'So, we've made progress, compared to when we were at each other's throats.'

'I suppose so,' Lars said. 'How do you say that in English: "small relief"?'

I smiled hollowly. 'But maybe, maybe we're not supposed to take it any further.'

'You mean get divorced after all?' Lars said this in a low whisper.

'The kids have a routine. You could move back in with us and they'll get used to that – but if this is how we feel about each other isn't that the worst thing we could possibly do? What if we screw it up for them and make it worse?'

'You think that's what would happen?'

'I don't know, but given our track record there's a good chance. You've only got to look at Tess now to know that she's settled and... you know what? I think what she needs more than ever is certainty. Her parents in her life but with an absolute commitment she's going to be loved and that everything is consistent. Finn too, of course, but it's got to her more.'

The waiter was trying to catch our eye. Lars said, 'Shall we go for a walk after our food and talk some more, then?'

We quickly made our way through the rest of our dinner.

I felt shell-shocked, jolted, but with a new clarity. If Lars moved back in, we couldn't promise that our explosive arguments wouldn't reignite. That had to be worse for the kids than the situation now.

After signing the bill, we walked with other couples along the artificial boulevard that ran across the top of the beach; most of them held hands, but we didn't. The sea had never been darker. It merged with a sky that seemed to have been wiped clean of stars by an over-efficient housekeeper.

It was when we finally got to the end of the wooden promenade that Lars turned to me and pointed to a small bench. It was positioned for people to gaze out to sea with some privacy – couples, I thought.

I sat down and Lars sat heavily beside me. 'So, what you're saying is that it's not enough for you?'

'Be honest. It's not enough for you either,' I said.

Lars held my hand and I squeezed it. 'I'm so sorry.' His eyes glistened with tears in the darkness.

'And I'm so sorry too.'

How well I know you. How well you know me. I pulled him towards me and we gently rocked together.

'I'm sorry I ruined our marriage,' Lars whispered in my ear. It wasn't just him though, and we both knew that. 'I told myself all the time that all the hard work was for you and the kids…'

'I know,' I said. 'It doesn't matter now.'

He shrugged me off, got up and paced around the wooden slats of the deck. I could hear the sea whooshing in and out, back and forth in the distance.

'And you changed,' he said but with no anger now. 'You didn't need me any more because I was never there when you needed me in the first place.'

My sobs came in rolling waves from my lower stomach. I stood up too and held out my arms. 'I'm sorry, so sorry,' I said and he came into them and held me again.

'Do you remember...?' I wanted to say as I shuddered into his shoulder. 'Do you remember?'

We carried on clinging to each other for a while longer until we were both still and then, silently, we got up and started to walk back, this time arm in arm. We talked about how to make it work for the kids.

'They've got a routine now that we should stick to as much as possible. You come round when you can and put them to bed and have them every other weekend.'

'If I get a place of my own I'll have them one or two nights a week?' Lars said.

'OK.'

'I'm going to have to ask for the investors to buy some more of my shares,' said Lars. 'Then with everything you've managed to pull off, we'll bust a gut to keep the house. We're not going to have much money though. I'll rent as cheap a flat as I can find but with a spare room for them so they feel it's theirs.'

'Do you think the kids will understand?'

'We'll tell them at some point on this holiday, shall we? Give them a few days to make the next step while we're together…' Then he stopped and looked at me. 'You don't want me to go home, do you?'

'No, I think we can handle being with each other for a fortnight? And if you left that would make Tess and Finn think we can't get on with one another after all.'

Lars smiled. 'Of course, you're absolutely right.'

'And we've spent any money we had on this break,' I went on. 'I really want them to have a brilliant time.'

We got back to the hotel room and paid the Greek lady, who went off smiling; then we went and looked at the twin beds of our sleeping children.

'A new kind of fam,' I said.

Lars smiled. 'But still a fam.'

I went into the bathroom to get changed into pyjamas. I sat for a moment on the loo lid while I cleaned my teeth.

I ached with sadness but I also felt calm and a sense of liberation. We hadn't managed to keep our marriage, but we'd managed to protect our children from more change.

The right thing to do, after all, was create this new kind of fam.

<u>39</u>

The first morning back in the office, I walked in to find Bridget seated behind my desk again.

'Good morning, Bridget,' I said. 'Any chance you can shift your butt back to your own desk?'

Bridget jumped up. 'I've been holding the fort,' she said, scurrying over to her side of the office.

I took off my jacket and swung it onto the back of the chair. My arms were the colour of honey. 'I'm sure you've been exemplary, but now I'm back,' I said. 'Oooh.' I picked up a stiff piece of ivory card from the pile of mail in from of me. 'OOOOOOH. Oh, Bridget, why didn't you tell me? I've been waiting for one of these for my entire career.'

You are invited to the
2017 International Luxury Goods Awards
Rome,
November 4th 2017,
8 p.m.,
where you have been nominated in the category
'Best Print Campaign for a European Brand'
for the Campury 'Who needs a man?' campaign.

'Isn't it amazing?' Bridget said. 'A Lux! It only arrived this morning. I've already rung and said we'd definitely be there.'

Wow, oh, wow. I hugged her and then sprinted out of the door and into the lift, bursting through the door of Marti's office and shouting about the Lux.

'Good God, girl, these are the best gongs in the industry,' he said. 'Every worthwhile client in the western world will be there. At least you look all right in a posh frock.'

*

Liv was still in bed at 11 a.m. when I rang to tell her that we were going to Rome. She didn't say she was still in bed but it was pretty obvious from her muffled, breathless voice that she had been mid roll-around with someone – probably Peter.

'I thought, we might as well make a weekend of it,' I said to her. 'Marti's so chuffed with me, he says I can bring anyone I want to; Lars has committed to having the kids for the weekend – he's being great – and I can get my dress paid for on expenses.'

'Can I get a Campury bag?'

'Don't push your luck,' I said. 'You've got enough freebies. And we'll stay in a great hotel, all paid for by the company.'

'And can I *really* come with you?'

'My plus one. Bridget and Marti will fly in for the event

itself,' I said. 'He's invited a couple of the board members. You'll probably have to sit next to one of them, but that's the only crap bit about it. Now what's been happening? Still shagging Peter?'

'Hmm, yes,' said Liv shiftily and changed the subject. 'How's Lars?' I'd rung her from holiday to tell her about what had happened.

'It's weird. We have a strange new hope: I think we're going to manage to be quite good friends after the last few months. Like I said, we went on to have quite a good holiday – just hanging out with the kids and getting on with each other.'

'Are they OK?'

'We sat and talked to them for quite a while halfway through the holiday. Tess wanted to know if she now got two of everything – "Two beds!" she kept shouting. "And two birthdays." They both said how much they liked seeing their dad regularly when they knew it was happening – "Daddy's house every week after football" – that kind of thing. Damn, all I know is that they'd have been more unhappy if I'd carried on pretending.'

We'd come home and Lars had gone to Ulrika's and said he'd ring the kids from China, I went on. Tessa had said she wanted to go with him, which, instead of being heartbreaking, was heart-warming.

'Awwww,' said Liv in the kind of voice that meant she'd lost interest completely.

There was a pause. I turned the Lux invitation over again

in my hand.

'Ami?' asked Liv.

'Yes?'

'This thing in Rome you're forcing me to go to?'

'I'm so sorry to put you through such hardship.'

'Isn't there a little bit of a chance that Ben will be there?'

'Ben who?' I asked down the phone. I shook my head to make the thought of him go away.

'Don't pretend with me.'

'I was just feeling happy and you go and make me all miserable again.'

'Is it such a fabulous idea to go and see him right when you're all so happy?'

'Oh, don't worry,' I said. 'I'm fine now about all that. Ben was right. I wasn't ready to go out with anyone else. So, I'm going to steer clear of all men and that's him included.'

'Yes, but wouldn't it be much easier to steer clear of him if you didn't get on a plane and go to Rome and be at the same dinner as him?'

'Oh, Liv. It'll be fine. I'm not sure he'll come and even if he does then we're two grown-ups who know it's impossible to be together. So now we'll be friends. Colleagues and friends. Anyway, it's all a good couple of months away. Now I'd really better get back to work.'

'You're only making me ring off because I'm talking to you about something you don't feel comfortable talking about.'

'Liv?'

'Yes?'

'There really are some people in the world who actually have to do something in exchange for money.'

'Big kiss to you, wage slave.'

'And one back to you, lazy old tart.'

*

I was resolute when I rang my parents: I was going to tell them what we'd decided, and I would not allow them to make me feel guilty. I knew that what I was saying could throw Dad into one of his funks and my mother would suffer; I wanted to protect her but also knew that that wasn't my responsibility.

Dad answered the phone rather than Mum, which was unusual and a very good sign. 'How was the holiday?' he asked in an upbeat voice.

'It was good, thanks.'

'I expect the kids thought it was marvellous,' he carried on. 'We loved their postcard.' He was certainly in a much better mood than before we'd left; I hoped I wasn't going to destroy that.

'I need to tell you something, Dad.' I spoke fast, without pause. 'Lars and I have decided we *are* going to get divorced. We're going to build on the progress we've made with the kids and he'll be very much part of their lives, but we're going to get divorced.'

There was a pause before Dad said, 'Well, I'm glad

you've made a decision.'

'OK.' I waited.

'I've really been thinking since I last saw you, Amelia,' he carried on. 'You've been so worried, the weight of the world on your shoulders for the last few years. Lars let you down and I know he's been trying hard again lately but I... well, your mother and I've been talking and we'd rather see you happy than settle for something second best.'

'Really?' I said, flabbergasted. 'But you've always said —'

'It was your mother,' Dad interrupted. 'She made me see that it's probably the right thing, if that's what you chose to do. That children should grow up with two happy parents if at all possible.'

It was the closest to an admission that that hadn't been true throughout my childhood that I'd ever heard him say. It was also the closest I was going to get to an apology for that awful Sunday. I gulped back a lump in my throat – I knew how difficult it must be for this proud man to admit his failings.

I explained the practicalities of what Lars and I had decided – how he'd get a flat and get some money out of his company and how that and the Campury account would really help.

'That sounds well thought through,' Dad said. 'Your mother said the kids will be fine – and it certainly sounds from what you're telling me that that's true,' he continued, almost as if he'd been practising this speech. 'We want you to be happy, darling.'

'Thank you,' I said, feeling the ever-present guilt at letting them down lift. 'It means a lot to have your support.'

'Always on your side,' my dad humphed. 'And I'll pick up the lawyer's bills, like I said. Now, you'd better speak to your mother.'

Mum and I discussed the holiday for a while before I told her; she didn't sound surprised, but echoed what my dad had said. 'We'll do everything we can to help,' she said.

'Mum?'

'Yes, darling?'

'What did you say to make Dad see my side?'

'We've had a few chats, that's all,' she said. 'After that Sunday when he was so awful, it's taken a while to get him back to normal but he also agreed that if it happens again, he'll go to the doctor's.'

'That's amazing,' I said, knowing how hard it must have been for her to even bring up the subject with him. 'What made you…?'

'What made me do something I should have done years ago?' she said with some force and a new, very direct tone.

'Well, yes.'

'I think it was seeing you so unhappy and not being able to help,' she said. 'I wanted to come to London but instead I had to stay with your father because he refuses to believe he's ill. I was so worried about you.' She was still talking in an unusually frank way.

'It was fine,' I said. 'I understood.'

'But you shouldn't have to understand!' Mum was angry now. 'And then when we did see you, that awful row, and we didn't listen to your point of view... but really, I knew that if you'd wanted to go back to Lars, you'd have done it by then. We were trying to make you stay in a marriage that made you unhappy and I couldn't force that on anyone.'

Wow. Mum had had some sort of epiphany. It was as if she'd found her old spark again and wasn't going to let it go out.

'And the kids were fine,' she went on. 'Anyone could see that. Tessa was in a better frame of mind than she had been at Christmas when you and Lars were still together.'

'Thank you,' I said. It meant a great deal for her to tell me we'd done a good job despite it all.

'And plenty of kids grow up to be fine,' Mum went on as if, now she was allowed to speak her own mind, she wasn't going to stop. 'And William was ridiculous, stomping around and making all that fuss. Anyway, after you'd gone that Sunday I really lost it with him...'

So, when I'd been driving up the M4 desperately worried about her dealing with another of his moods, she'd in fact been having a big row with Dad.

'...and told him he'd got to get his act together and support his own daughter. And that you were old enough to know what you were doing.'

'You didn't need to do that for me,' I said.

'It wasn't just for you,' she said in a voice that meant it was also for her own benefit. 'I couldn't, just couldn't go through another few months of misery and I told him that.'

She and Dad had really had a heart-to-heart. 'Anyway, after that we had a few more talks, and he's finally admitted that he might have a problem and that talking to someone might help.'

My proud dad. I knew this had taken him enormous courage.

'So, if he gets into another bad place, we're going to go to the doctor's,' she said emphatically.

'That's so great,' I said. 'But he sounds OK at the moment?'

'Funnily enough, it's as if a switch has been flipped. He's been writing and being his old self.'

'So good to hear,' I said. 'I'm really pleased.'

Mum changed the subject. 'Now, tell me, is there any progress at all with Liv's love life? It really is time she at least thought about settling down.'

*

'I wanted to say something,' Cathy said, now we were back in her office, resurrecting the old divorce paperwork. I knew we were moving from lawyer to friends again, as she tapped the top of her clock.

I hoped she wasn't going to tell me that she was dumping Jezza: I didn't want to be responsible for raising the divorce rate for retiring couples in Bromley. Instead she said, 'I wanted to tell you that I think you're an inspiration.'

'What? I thought divorces like mine were boring.'

Cathy had the grace to colour slightly. 'Ha, ha, no, no. But you walked through the door and I thought, Poor dear. And you were so hurt. And now look at you a few months later: you've been the one making the decisions about what you want.'

'Wow,' I said. 'Thank you.' I didn't know if it was a speech she rolled out to all her clients, but I figured I'd take the compliment. 'And for all the help you've given me – for making sure I got it all right.'

Cathy came round the desk and hugged me to her ample proportions: 'Type D's *can* be satisfying after all. Now, shall we have a snifter?'

*

Here we were then, the kids and me: a new kind of fam. Lars and I agreed he'd come round to put the kids to bed a couple of times a week and would have them every other weekend and every Wednesday night to start with. We also agreed that we would do everything we could to stick to that routine and, if we changed it, we'd sit down and talk to the children.

He rented a flat with an extra bedroom down the road in Crouch Hill and they excitedly helped him buy a new TV and a sofa over their first weekend there; he took his books, his clothes and some pictures from our house, but said he was completely capable of a trip to IKEA to equip the rest of the place. I had a look round the first time I dropped off Tess and Finn and it was like the flats we'd had in the early years – makeshift and empty with nothing really coordinating; we both laughed about that without the conversation turning too sad.

We also documented some rules for the future with Sasha – these included the childcare arrangements and an agreement about introducing any new partners we might have to the kids.

That was a difficult conversation: despite how I'd felt – still felt – about Ben, it hurt to think of Lars looking at someone else in the same way he'd once looked at me. But much more than that, even the *idea* of another woman in my children's lives made me want to stand up and shout, 'Get away from my babies.'

'I haven't really thought about other women,' Lars said. This was a little dig at my one-night shack-up with what he called through his teeth 'that other man'; but it was also a lie. He was human and even if he hadn't jumped into bed with anyone so far, he would have thought about it and would want to. But it was no longer anything to do with me unless it affected the children, so I just raised one eyebrow at him and tried to be businesslike.

'I wouldn't feel comfortable with anyone who tried to be too *motherly* with them.'

'Of course not. They've only got one mum. I feel the same: any man needs to be kind and loving to my children, but I don't want anyone trying to take over my role,' Lars said.

We agreed some wording and Sasha wrote it down.

'Six months' relationship before either of us introduces the kids to anyone else?' I asked. 'So we know it's serious?' I didn't want a procession of women coming in and out of their lives.

Lars nodded. 'Sounds fair. But we should also agree that before the children meet someone who is more than a friend, we let the other person know and potentially meet up first.'

Sasha nodded approvingly and wrote that down. 'I'm so glad you two are getting somewhere,' she said as we left.

It was as if all the reasons for being angry and hurt had gone, leaving an understanding that we'd had some very special years, but they were over. I was heading for a new future; for the first time it felt exciting rather than terrifying.

*

The weeks sped by. Tess and Finn settled into the routine. They went up a year at school and, Paul Carter assured me, 'were getting on quite nicely, Amelia'. They went to clubs – football, street dance, swimming.

Parminder was almost militant in her support. She arranged that she and I would spend time with the children 'doing normal things – like gossiping and drinking wine while the kids play. It's good for their health and ours.'

Julia was the only surprise. She popped round one Saturday morning and kept suggesting the children went out into the garden; it was clear she wanted a private chat.

When they'd gone she sat down at the table and grasped her coffee. 'So, all good with you and Lars now, then?'

I filled her in on our new arrangements. 'The divorce will come through in six weeks or so, I hope.'

'I'm not sure if congratulations is the right thing to say,' Julia said, 'but it does sound like you've done really well. I wanted to ask you something, now that it's all settled.' She looked uncharacteristically uncomfortable.

'Oh?'

'You know how hard it is to meet single men who like children…'

'Well, from what you've told me, yes.' I laughed. She was going to ask me to go and hang around in bars in the City with her and pick up blokes; I'd have to tell her that wasn't my scene.

But instead she said, 'And Lars being free, now…' I tried not to gasp as she carried on: 'And I wondered whether you'd mind if I… well, I asked Lars out.'

Good God. It must be *really* hard to find a child-friendly man if the moment a local dad became single he became a target.

'I, I… well, of course, it's completely up to him,' I spluttered eventually. I tried to imagine Lars' reaction: Julia was certainly ambitious, tall, blonde and attractive but he'd never seemed to like her above anyone else.

Julia had the grace to colour. 'But I wouldn't do it if you minded…' she said.

'I just think it might be a bit weird for the kids? What

with being so close and in the same class?' I said, still horrified.

'Yes, I thought about that, but, of course, there's no assumption we'd actually get on or he'd say yes in the first place and they wouldn't know about it to start with and...' My outrage was subsiding and I felt sorry for her instead. I hadn't known how desperate she was for a new relationship.

However, I did need to put the kids first. I decided to be assertive. 'Julia, it's good of you to ask me, but, really... well, my view is that you should probably wait for a while. As you know, Tess in particular has had a rough time coming to terms with our situation and she's still quite fragile...'

'Of course, of course.' She looked really embarrassed. 'I should have thought and—'

'It's fine,' I said, trying to move the conversation on. 'Now, did I tell you about how Parminder says Nadine is going to start a playground campaign for everyone to grow their pubic hair in protest against the patriarchy?'

We laughed as we returned to familiar ground, but I knew our friendship would probably never be the same again.

Ulrika reacted as I knew she would, with stoic calm. 'That was what was right then, and this is what's right now,' she said over a cup of camomile tea.

I sat shivering on her sofa wondering if it would be rude to put my coat back on. 'Please promise me you'll always be my mother-in-law,' I begged.

'Ha! We need new terms for the way relationships are changing today,' she marvelled. 'I will always be your *extra mother.*'

And Ben. Ben was back in Milan and, now that the campaign was in full swing and delivering sales, I heard from him less. When we did speak – at the start of a review call, for example – he would ask me how I was and I would say 'Fine,' knowing that colleagues could hear, but listened to every enunciation of every syllable he said to see if I could find any hidden meaning in it.

There was a day when he seemed to put some extra endearment into: 'How are you, Ami Fitch?' but I knew I could've imagined it.

I dreamt of him often, waking feeling as if I could taste his kisses, smell him and feel his big arms wrapped around me. Several times during that end of summer and into autumn I picked up my phone and nearly pressed his name but managed to stop myself – it was the thought of the kids, his and mine, and how they would always come first.

*

Liv was trying very hard not to fall in love with Peter. One Saturday, as the weekend in Rome approached, we met at the Suicide Café. I'd been to the hairdresser's and was enjoying the smooth swish of newly chocolate curls around my shoulders, while Liv tried to get the melancholy waiter to bring us some wine.

'So, this morning Peter said to me, "You don't fancy a deep and meaningful relationship, do you?"' she said, looking distressed. 'I said, "If I ever did, darling-face, it would be with you," and tried to laugh it off.'

'And this is so bad because...?'

'Then he said it was the first time he'd ever said anything like that to anyone and it was mean of me to laugh.'

'Well, it was a bit mean,' I said as the waiter finally got to our table and deposited two glasses of Sauvignon Blanc onto the Formica. 'You do really like him – why don't you just admit it?'

'Good God,' said Liv, but she paused for a moment as if it were occurring to her that it might be a possibility. 'Then he said, "You're something entirely different and I kind of like it."'

'Oooh,' I said. 'Practically a declaration of love.'

Liv pushed her risotto away so I knew that this was affecting her badly. 'People are always telling me that one day I'll meet a man and want to settle down. But the older I get, and the more I know of monogamy, I think it's society that's got it wrong, not me. I don't want the same person in my bed every night forever. People keep going on about my biological clock and I think I just talk too much to hear it ticking. I explained all that to Peter.'

'What did he say?'

'That I was a refreshing kind of bird. And then we made bacon sandwiches.'

'Really romantic,' I said.

Liv laughed and changed the subject to Rome. 'Who else is going to the dinner? Did Marti hear from Ben?'

Whenever I heard his name, I felt a warm shock. And despite everything, I had hoped that he would turn up, because just to see him would be amazing. But he'd sent his apologies to Marti's invitation, because he was going to be in New York; he'd asked to hold the place for a European colleague of his I'd never met. When Marti told me, I convinced myself it really was the best thing.

'Even if there was something between us, he still lives in another country with his children while I'm here with mine. And I'm really getting my act together on my own with the kids,' I explained to Liv, with a feeling of pride.

'To you.' Liv clinked her glass against mine.

'And to you, being all moony about my ex-shag.'

'It was sweet of you to share your leftovers with me.' Liv had a decidedly soft look in her eyes.

*

'Hallelujah, we can have dough balls,' said Tessa. It was Saturday lunchtime in late October and we were in the Pizza Express in Muswell Hill: a canteen for yummy mummies, nannies and kids. 'We need to remember to say grace.'

My daughter was currently Born Again. Her favourite activity was watching fundamentalist Christian ministers from the American mid-West on YouTube on my iPad, despite my efforts to stop her. She'd also taken to playing a tambourine.

It had started when she'd been taken by Mr Carter on a

school outing to St Albans cathedral a couple of weeks back. There was a happy-clappy choir that had performed for the children, which had all seemed innocent enough until, a few days later, I'd found Tessa on the playroom sofa, reading my very old copy of the Bible, turning its wafer-thin pages slowly as she pretended to be able to understand the tiny print.

'Umm, are you interested in that, darling?' I'd said, surprised. Lars and I had always been quite fundamentalist non-believers.

'I would like to know more about Jesus and accept Him into my heart,' Tessa had said. I'd nodded slowly and she'd explained about how the minister at St Albans had told her that Jesus was for everyone. Then she'd started singing 'Kumbaya my Lord'.

I'd reminded her that there were many religions and she could choose one if she wanted to when she was older, and she'd said, 'I know that.' Later that evening I'd gone onto Amazon and ordered a picture-rich book about the religions of the world.

Lars had told me she'd asked to be taken to church one Sunday when she was with him; they'd gone to the one at the top of Crouch Hill and joined in the hymns. Afterwards, however, Tessa had asked to go to one with more guitars, singing and shouting. 'You know, the sort where people get saved and cry,' she'd said. 'They shout hallelujah a lot.' We'd decided to try and find a child-friendly Sunday school for her if it carried on.

Of course, her having a new obsession had made me worried, but we'd finally seen the child counsellor who'd assured me that Tessa was a highly intelligent child and her preoccupation with things was a sign of a curious mind.

I'd asked whether she thought my daughter had been affected by her parents' marital breakdown and the counsellor had nodded and said, 'It will impact all children one way or another, but, from what Tessa has told me, she sees quite a lot of her father now, and she seems happy that you and he are friends again. You've done quite a good job in the circumstances.' It had been like being given a gold star for divorce; it had also been an enormous relief.

Now we looked at the menu. As usual, Finn wanted margherita; Tessa wanted pepperoni and dough balls. I ordered a large glass of wine and sat back, while they coloured in their sheets with the crayons the waitress had automatically plonked on the table.

Both looked up, though, when they saw their father arrive.

As Lars wound his way through the tables, my first thought was that he looked well; there was a little more fat on him.

Lars smiled broadly at us and the children started waving. He kissed them both with gusto and I stood up. We awkwardly circled for a bit before he settled for a kiss on my cheek. He still smelt of lemon soap.

'How's it going, gang?' he said.

'We waited for you to order,' I said. 'What do you want

to drink?'

'Beer, please.' Lars took off his puffa jacket and hung it on the back of the wooden chair, then sat down at the table. He picked up Finn's crayons and said, 'Bet I can do this faster than you.'

'Gambling is a sin, Daddy,' Tessa said and he caught my eye as we both tried not to laugh.

*

Lars and I chatted about my new clients: Brand New had just won the Lazarus jeans brand, which was famous for covering the arses of a range of Clebs. 'Well done, you,' Lars said and raised his bottle of Becks at me.

'Bridget's really, really bossy to the new people,' I told him. I'd promoted her to account manager and recruited two new account execs. Marti had also presented me with the keys to a new office next door to Goldwyn's and we'd moved out of our little basement. 'It's fantastic.'

The pizzas arrived. We listened to Tessa recite her version of 'grace' with what seemed to be an American accent and then started to eat. Then Lars told the children about a trip to Sweden he and Ulrika were taking them on at the start of the Christmas holidays. 'It's going to be really, really cold,' he said. 'With everything covered in snow.'

'Will we see a moose?' Tessa asked.

'Or a reindeer?' Finn said.

'They eat reindeer in Sweden,' Tessa said. 'Grandie told

me.'

'That's enough, Tess,' I said as her brother's face curled up in horror about the idea of a slice of Rudolph on his plate.

*

Later, we said goodbye outside by the roundabout. Lars gave both the kids a massive hug and said he would see them on Wednesday. He hugged me too and said in my ear, 'Great that we can do this,' and what he meant was spend a simple Saturday lunchtime together – on a table for four – with our children. As we walked back down the hill through the park at Alexandra Palace, there was a small bounce in my step. There was that odd feeling I got now when I saw Lars – that the tough times were over and we could approach the future with hope.

40

Rome, Liv-style, involved exactly five minutes at the Coliseum, a quick gasp at the round shard of light that fell onto the Pantheon floor, two entire minutes looking in wonder at the Trevi Fountain and the rest of the time claiming freebies from Rome's up-and-coming designers. Not only was her trip paid for by Brand New, she was now the proud beneficiary of a free new autumn wardrobe.

It was quite awe-inspiring, as was her in-depth knowledge of Roman nightlife – the bars one should be seen at, the restaurants that one simply had to have been spotted in and, most excitingly for me, the LaidBack Club, where apparently you lay down to eat your dinner.

'We do *what*?' I asked when Liv explained what we would be doing with our Saturday evening. 'We lie on beds and beautiful men feed us?'

The waiters were not all beautiful but the crowd, lounging on the white banquettes, propped on plump pillows, certainly was – or maybe, as I lay down and thought how life could be fun again, it was the vast grins on their faces, reflected in the champagne buckets, or the animation of their excited chatter, that made them seem like a very gorgeous in-crowd. When the doors opened at the end of dinner and a tall, thin jazz singer with blonde hair, dressed entirely in white faux fur, came in and, starting with some slow numbers, took the crowd to the state where we were ready for the DJ, with his soaring, never-ending mix of deep South vocals and dance tempo, I found myself shoes off, arms in the air, dancing on the beds along with everyone else.

'God, what fun,' I slurred to Liv as we finally made it home to the discreet spaces of the hotel.

'It's nearly 4 a.m.,' Liv told me.

I wobbled past the night concierge and into the mirrored lift. Liv pressed the button. It shot down and the doors opened at a dark corridor.

'My God, we're in hell,' said Liv.

'Press five, not basement,' I said and she fumbled about for a while and we started to move upwards. 'Are you missing Peter?'

'He sent me a text this morning that said: "Down with mornings without you,"' said Liv as we got to our floor and wobbled along the corridor. 'I mean, how sweet is that?'

'Pretty sweet.' I struggled to wave the card key in front of the door. 'You can blag your way through life together.' I fell into the room followed by Liv. 'That's my bed, damn you. Get off it. And you'd better at least try to take your clothes off before you go to sleep.'

*

I'd chosen a bright red column dress from Prada for the Lux

awards; on first sight, it looked like the sort of dress in which you couldn't either sit down or eat, but it was made of fantastic Spanxy stuff that thrust out the right bits and pulled in everywhere else.

'That's gorgeous,' said Liv, coming out of the bathroom. 'Marti's going to come over all faint.'

'You look pretty bloody fantastic yourself.' Liv was encased in a silver sheath dress – one of her recent freebies – that clung to her body as she moved.

'It's all part of my plan to progress your career,' Liv said. 'If I've got to sit next to Lord Haydon then I'm going to show him a lot of leg all night and encourage him to eat really fatty foods.' She held out her arm. 'You ready, gorgeous girl? Shall we go to the ball?'

*

If the princess castle at Disneyland was based on a real place, it should've been the palazzo where the Lux ceremony was being held. Our taxi circled up a road like a helter-skelter; my stomach churned with nerves. At the open gates, we joined a queue of snaking jet-black limos, poised in first gear as their drivers tried hard to hang onto the road.

'There's Marti,' Liv said as our car swung in front of the double doors. Women in couture and feathers drifted towards the entrance on a breeze of wealth. On the marble steps, a crowd in evening clothes shook hands eagerly with their competitors and pretended that they wouldn't like to see each other rot in commercial hell. Among them was Marti, resplendent in a white dinner jacket and tie, cigar in hand as he boom-boomed greetings.

'Here you are!' We exchanged our first really close moment for several months as he came to kiss my cheek. Then he went towards Liv: 'Now, you're not to show anyone your knickers.'

'Killjoy.' She kissed him hello. 'Are we going to win?'

'Should bloody well hope so but the competition is stiff,' said Marti. 'We're up against the Valentino campaign and the Jimmy Choo one.' He held out his arms and Liv and I tucked our hands in snugly. We progressed through the chattering crowd into the centre of a glittering ballroom strung with thousands of white lights like snowdrops suspended in mid-flight on the wind. Marti introduced Liv and me to a circle comprised of Bridget, looking lovely in a blue velvet dress from TopShop Boutique that I'd helped choose and actually fitted, City investors, high-profile customers and a man from Rigby & Peller that Marti was trying his damnedest to turn into one. Lord Haydon was there and blushed the colour of Chianti as Liv approached.

'Champagne?' Marti passed out glasses and made introductions. Liv flirted around her while I tried very hard to look professional.

'What are our chances?' Haydon turned to me.

'We should be honoured to be nominated.'

'Absolutely,' Haydon said, 'but winning would do wonders for the share price, you know.'

Bridget and I swapped travel stories and then I asked her, 'Did you find out who's coming in Ben's place?'

'Luca Berloni,' she said efficiently. 'Campury's Italian operation. I've put him next to you. That's if he turns up. Strange being so late.'

Marti shepherded us down the circular staircase towards an ocean of white tablecloths decorated with antique silver.

'Do I really have to sit next to the old goat?' Liv hissed in my ear.

'They're all old goats. I have to sit next to an empty chair. Ben's colleague hasn't turned up yet.'

Haydon pulled out Liv's chair with a flourish and she sat down opposite me. We were sixteen in all, counting the vacant seat beside me. Everyone tucked into champagne and I tried to earwig on Liv telling Haydon what was a very naughty story, from the subversive look on her face.

'Good God,' he kept saying. *'Really?'*

'Just tell her to behave herself,' Marti said before turning back to the prospective Rigby & Peller client he was chatting up on his left.

I concentrated on buttering bread. At least Ben had been kind enough to spare me the embarrassment of sitting next to him for the evening, making polite, disjointed small talk. I'll make polite, disjointed small talk with his colleague instead, if he ever bothers to turn up.

The trouble with eating alone, without conversation, is that you always finish before everyone else who is gabbling away. I looked around me and wished I felt part of it.

I felt part of the children and me; this was the resolve that had steered me through the last month. How self-sufficient we were now, in our ferret-infested road.

I saw Liv say to Haydon, 'Listen, are you going to leave the rest of your salmon? If you are, I'll have it.' I didn't know whether to giggle or die of mortification as I watched her shovel his leftovers into her mouth.

As we were served coffee I made patterns with petits fours on my side plate and willed the night to finish.

'Where's Ben's colleague?' Liv asked in the loo as we waited for the ceremony to start.

'He can't possibly be coming,' I said, renewing my lipstick half-heartedly. 'We're nearly at the awards. The first bit will be all glassware to the director's second cousin's best boy's runner.'

As we neared our table, I noticed that a bit of table-hopping had been going on. We were missing two of the clients – probably flirting with other agency bosses to bolster their Christmas stockings – and we'd gained a blonde called Camilla, who'd long wanted to work at Goldwyn and was talking to Bridget. There also a person sitting in my chair – I couldn't see who. Probably someone else who wanted my job, I thought.

'Campury person still not turned up, then?' I blithely asked the table in general, sinking down into the empty chair beside mine. 'Let's hope we don't bloody win, then.'

There was a silence and then the body next to me swung round to face me.

'Seeing as I've rushed all the way from New York to be here, let's hope we bloody *do*, Ami Fitch.'

*

'Hello, you.' He smiled into the silence that followed.

My stomach did a full-on jive number but all I managed to say was, 'But, but, but…'

'I hope you're going to be more articulate than that if you have to make a speech,' said Ben. He looked tired but tanned and happy, his mouth teasing while the lines around his eyes crinkled.

I tried to fix a social smile on my face rather than let on just how amazing it was to see him. 'What are you doing here?'

'Fan-bloody-tastic that you could make it,' said Marti. 'You've missed dinner but we've got to be able to get you some.' He started waving around in an effort to find some service.

'A drink will be fine.' Ben turned and spoke to me. 'You look gorgeous.'

'Thank you,' I said. 'It's a shock to see you. We were expecting someone you worked with from Italy.'

'Supposed to be. The deal in New York was simpler than I thought so I realised I could get here. I binned the guy who was coming – he wasn't happy, already in a DJ apparently.' His mouth twisted into a very happy grin. I couldn't help but smile back. 'Only just had time to jump into a penguin suit myself.'

The knot of his black tie was slightly askew but he looked great. 'You look pretty good, actually.'

'And I got a promotion,' he said. 'Don't want to boast or anything.'

'Seriously grown up,' I said. 'What's the gig?'

'You're only looking at Campury's new European Brand Director. It's on the back of the brilliant work you did.'

I coloured and stopped myself throwing my arms around him. 'Massive congratulations. *So* glad for you. That's fantastic.' I paused, then said, 'You probably don't get much time for hanging out now, then?'

'God, I've missed you,' Ben whispered and my stomach turned its jive into rock and roll.

The MC took to the stage again and addressed us in Italian and then melodious English. Eventually the furious torrent of networking dribbled to a small babble and then silence. A waiter placed new glasses of champagne in front of everyone at the table. Ben turned to Marti and Liv raised her eyebrows in wonder at me. I tried to communicate using facial expressions that it was confusing, but good confusing.

Numerous gongs were presented and, each time, there was a hushed moment of suspense as the nominees waited for the results. There were shrieks in many European tongues from tables of winners; cameras popped again and again as the recipients of Luxes gushed their gratitude to their colleagues in speeches that seemed to last forever.

All the time I was aware, with every sense, that Ben sat a

413

few inches away.

Marti and several of the guests were looking slightly worse for wear by now. Liv was hiccupping and, as she did so, her boobs rose and fell in the silver dress. Haydon was clearly enjoying the sight. Then the MC said that there was going to be a break in the proceedings before the second half: the really important awards.

It was then that I felt Ben's big hand on mine and heard the whisper in my ear. 'Let's go outside and talk,' he said. 'That's if you want to.'

41

I stumbled as Ben took my arm and steered me towards a purple sofa in the plush bar outside. Crowds started to gather around us, closing us off in a private corner.

The sheer pointlessness of the conversation we were about to have hit me. 'I don't know what there is to say,' I said. 'Apart from it's nice to see you.' The intense happiness of seeing him would soon turn into the horrible feeling of missing him all over again.

'You've got to let me do the talking.' His voice was direct and quick.

I raised my eyebrows. 'I do?'

'Yes, you do,' he said, sitting down and holding both my hands. He was very warm.

There was a silence, then he said, 'I think I might seriously like you, Ami. I'm not very good without you.'

I looked at him and tears welled in my eyes. We were still divided by the needs of two sets of children. 'It'll never work with you in one country and me in another one and…' The best we would ever have was stolen weekends and midnight conversations on Skype.

'But it will. We *can* give it a go – *that's* what I need to tell you. Sshhhh. Just for a bit. Really. You've got to let me talk.'

'You stalked me again – this time to Rome.' I smiled a big grin that was sad and happy at the same time.

'I got bored with not stalking you,' he said.

'Seriously?'

'I just haven't been able to think since I left you that night. Maybe I should have begged you not to go back to your husband. And then there you were... back with him. Going on holiday with him.' He spat this last sentence out.

'How did you know that?'

'Bridget told me.'

'You tortured Bridget until she told you where I was?'

'She was singing like a canary the moment I asked. But that's not it—'

'What I don't understand is why you told me to go back to him if you didn't mean it?' I interrupted him.

'You weren't quite over your marriage. I met you and you were...'

'Deranged?'

'You were a bit, actually. But that didn't stop me just adoring you. I couldn't even get drunk near you because I would have...'

'Jumped me?'

'You know, you forget about sophisticated phrases like that when you—'

'Hang out with stuck-up Italian birds?'

'Exactly. Anyway, so I kept on grilling Bridget and she kept on saying you were back with your husband until one day a couple of months back. She said you'd come back from holiday and were spending all day talking to a divorce lawyer rather than working.'

'That's her promotion down the drain, then,' I said. 'So?'

'But mostly there were the kids. I *do* need to be near them, Ami.' There it was. We could be together, but it was always going to be an every-other-weekend relationship and that would be when I could afford it.

'Of course you do,' I said very quietly.

'But then two amazing things happened. And it was somehow as if they were… well, just a little bit meant to be – look, I know I sound like Liv—'

'Just get on with it.'

'Firstly, I got this new job – European-wide remit, could base myself anywhere that suited me; got to be in the UK quite a lot anyway.'

'Well done again, by the way,' I said.

'But that wasn't enough. My children were still in Milan, so I wasn't going to move anywhere. But then…'

'Then *what*?'

'Patrizia's husband got posted to London for a three-year sabbatical at UCL. The kids are moving to London with them and I'm coming back as well.'

'What?' Was Ben coming to London to live? His kids were moving here, so he could too? 'Did you really say you're going to live in London for quite a while?'

'Whether you want me to or not,' he said.

I leant forward for a soft kiss of souls coming together; of

417

potential, of resolution, and it went on and on.

'Oh, God, I can't believe this. I've missed you so much. When did this happen?' I whispered eventually.

'Last week. But then I had to go to New York and I wanted to phone you and say that I was sorry I couldn't be at the awards, but I thought by then you'd have forgotten all about me. Even though it was going to be possible to be together I didn't think you would want to… but I've been a bloody wreck since I left you.'

'Really a wreck?' My grin stretched right across my face.

'A shipwreck. Covered in barnacles at the bottom of the ocean.'

'Really?'

'And then, then it seemed as if everything was falling into place. The New York deal finished early and then, then, all I could think about was whether I could get back and see you at the Luxes and… find out if…'

'You know how I feel,' I whispered. And we kissed and kissed again.

*

'Our award now,' said Ben into the darkness as we finally slid back into our seats. He smiled at me.

The award seemed completely irrelevant. Was it really possible that I was going to be able to hang out with this ridiculous, handsome, laughing man and even, maybe, sleep with him? All I could think about was getting out of this

418

castle on a hill and getting on with it.

Liv was shooting questioning glances across the table at me. All the City people and board members seemed to wake up as the Master of Ceremonies read out the nominations for 'Best Print Campaign for a European Brand'.

'What the hell is that actually?' Liv could be heard asking Haydon under her breath.

'No idea, no idea at all.' He was red in the face from strong whisky with only outrageous desire as a mixer.

Versions of the various advertising campaigns appeared on the large screens on both sides of the stage as the nominations were announced, first in Italian and then in English.

'Wooo, hooo, hooo,' shouted Liv and Bridget when it came to 'Brand New for the Campury, "Who Needs a Man?" campaign'.

I slunk back in my chair. It was bound to have been won by Jimmy Choo.

The winner was read out in Italian first. *'E il vincitore è Brand New per la campagna di Campury 'chi ha bisogno di un uomo?'* said the Master of Ceremonies. Ben was on his feet, stamping and clapping.

'Does that mean we've won?' Marti said.

'We've won. We've bloody won,' Ben cried. He grabbed me and hugged the air out of me but I still didn't quite know what was happening.

The compère repeated, 'And the winner is Brand New for their campaign for Campury "Who Needs a Man?"'

Liv jumped up and rushed towards me. 'This is your fifteen minutes,' she hissed. We'd actually won. All those late nights panicking until we got the right idea. So many hours since we'd got the account, falling asleep over analysing the results. And now we'd actually won.

The crowd clapped and cheered, and all the City people got to their feet and came round to thump Marti on the back. He hugged me hard.

I gave Bridget a huge kiss. 'This is our award. Ours and Jake and Luis'.' She was crying with pride.

'Come on.' Ben pushed everyone out of the way. 'You've got to make a speech.' He edged me gently towards the stage. 'God, I'm so proud of you.'

I snaked through the tables towards the stage in a daze, the cheers continuing as loud pulsating music beat in time to my steps. Then I climbed the few steps onto the stage. The glamorous crowd seemed to shrink as if I were in a plane that was climbing higher and higher. I blinked in the brightness but found I couldn't fall. I was dimly aware that I could still hear Liv's cheering even as the rest of the crowd subdued and I could make out Ben standing on his chair and clapping hard. I airkissed the Master of Ceremonies, accepted the glass bowl inscribed in flourishing Italian and took my place behind the podium.

The audience went silent. From the stage they were a jumble of expectant faces, waiting for me to speak.

I knew what I wanted to say, although I hadn't prepared a speech. 'Campury handbags had always been bought by men for women.' My voice began uncertainly but then became stronger. 'But of course, today, women buy their own bags, make their own futures, decide on the shape of their own families. In putting this campaign together, all we did was reflect that: women with or without a man who are choosing their own futures.' The female elements of the crowd cheered first but then the men joined in, so it was extra loud. I remembered to thank the team at Goldwyn, especially Bridget, and Campury for being 'the client who gave my agency and our ideas a chance'. Then to more frenzied clapping, I climbed down.

At the bottom of the steps, Ben was waiting. He pulled me in for a huge hug.

'I'm so proud of you,' he said again into my ear as the MC started to announce the next award. I smiled up at him as he grinned. 'I know you don't bloody need me, Ami Fitch, but is there any chance you might want me anyway?'

Acknowledgements

Thank you to everyone who has read this book. I love all of you.

Special thanks to lovely Diana Beaumont, a fantastic cheerleader of an agent. And to Lucy Gilmour, editor at Aria, who made me jump around the room when she described *The Story After Us* as a 'feminist text'. And everyone who is a feminist, actually, just for being one.

And the rest of the team at Aria for all your help bringing my baby to life.

A few years back I was lucky enough to be able to attend the Curtis Brown Creative Writing course – thanks to Chris Wakling and Anna Davis for fantastic, inspiring teaching. But more than that, I met the people who formed our spin-off writing group and turned up every other Monday for years. Maria Realf, Lisa Williamson, James Hall, Christina Pishiris, Sara-Mae Tuson and Paul Golden; I loved every heated debate about commas and why there isn't more sex in chapter six.

Also, my old reading group at the Bull pub run by my great friend Louisa Notley. I'm going to give it a miss when you debate mine, but please be kind – And save me some food. And Lou, thanks for reading it too and saving up jokes for the next one and to Mandie for all your amazing help.

Thank you to Fanny Johnstone, who has read it several times and joined in the despair and hope of trying to become a writer: poor country girls, we take our time but get there in the end.

Natalie Emanuel, thank you for believing in me, listening to me and encouraging me – as well as being made to read drafts. The champagne really helped you know – it was medicinal.

Rachel Lichtenstein, for all your encouragement, reading, love and wisdom.

To Diane Johnstone, the kindest and earliest reader, who spurred me to keep going. Also, to Famke Vanluffelen who read an early version because my Mum was excited about it – your feedback was invaluable.

Mum herself, (Jan Hallam) who faithfully read it about a hundred times (always within 24 hours) and gave me feedback and support. She raises loads of money for the local food bank every week through her book stall in Porthleven, Cornwall; I apologise in advance if she bullied you into buying this when you stopped by to browse.

Everyone called Perrin, or married to a Perrin, or associated in some way with a Perrin, offspring of a Perrin etc – thank you for being my family. And in memory of Dad, Robert Perrin, who knew this book was on its way.

And thanks to David Emanuel, who turned out to be a pretty good ex-husband and a very good friend (but no, it's not about you). And all my other friends – you are all spectacular.

Then the kids: Elyse and Sienna, my greatest supporters and the Original Fam. Tom and Laura, lovely step-children. And the pets – Soppy Wagster and Ducky von Fluffy – cheers for sitting everywhere I wanted to type and seeing me as a feeding machine. You've all made the last few years while writing this quite mad but also so much fun. Love to you all and thank you.

And Alan, for being the person I want to sit on a bench with when I'm old, holding hands and laughing at a silly joke. You've cheered me all the way. Thank you.

HELLO FROM ARIA

We hope you enjoyed this book! Let us know, we'd love to hear from you.

We are Aria, a dynamic digital-first fiction imprint from award-winning independent publishers Head of Zeus. At heart, we're avid readers committed to publishing exactly the kind of books we love to read — from romance and sagas to crime, thrillers and historical adventures. Visit us online and discover a community of like-minded fiction fans!

We're also on the look out for tomorrow's superstar authors. So, if you're a budding writer looking for a publisher, we'd love to hear from you. You can submit your book online at ariafiction.com/we-want-read-your-book

You can find us at:
Email: aria@headofzeus.com
Website: www.ariafiction.com
Submissions: www.ariafiction.com/we-want-read-your-book
Facebook: @ariafiction
Twitter: @Aria_Fiction
Instagram: @ariafiction

32833601R00236

Printed in Great Britain
by Amazon